PERFUME OF DESIRE

The perfume of redwood and grapes floated on the warm summer air. The place was deserted except for her and Adam. She heard the hissing of a high-pressure hose bouncing off the walls in one of the room-sized wine vats. Suddenly, she was no longer certain of what to say.

Adam had his back to her, concentrating on his work. Soaked through from the spray, his jeans clung to his long, hard legs. Droplets of water danced in blue-black iridescence on his hair and dripped onto the flexing muscles of his shoulders and back, tracing satiny paths down his tawny skin to vanish below his waistband. Then he turned to face her, clutching the hose as water poured onto the floor in a rainbow of misty colors.

Slowly, Marti began to walk toward him. He reached down and shut off the hose, standing poised as she caressed the mat of hair on his chest. Marti took a deep, unsteady breath, trying to decide what she should do. But he already knew. . . .

She melted against him as he drew her to him for a soft kiss. Two hearts beat fiercely and two bodies moved with deliberation, searching, learning. His caresses grew stronger, hungrier. Then he searched her silver eyes and found the answer he sought. . . .

BOUQUET

SIGNET
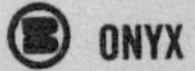
ONYX

by

Shirl Henke

ONYX
Published by the Penguin Group
Penguin Books USA Inc., 375 Hudson Street,
New York, New York 10014, U.S.A.
Penguin Books Ltd, 27 Wrights Lane,
London W8 5TZ, England
Penguin Books Australia Ltd, Ringwood,
Victoria, Australia
Penguin Books Canada Ltd, 10 Alcorn Avenue,
Toronto, Ontario, Canada M4V 3B2
Penguin Books (N.Z.) Ltd, 182–190 Wairau Road,
Auckland 10, New Zealand

Penguin Books Ltd, Registered Offices:
Harmondsworth, Middlesex, England

Published by Onyx, an imprint of Dutton Signet,
a division of Penguin Books USA Inc. Previously published
in Great Britain and the United States by Severn House Publishers Ltd.
under the title *Summer Has No Name*.

First Onyx Printing, July, 1994
10 9 8 7 6 5 4 3 2 1

Printed in the United States of America

PUBLISHER'S NOTE
This is a work of fiction. Names, characters, places, and incidents either are the product of the author's imagination or are used fictitiously, and any resemblance to actual persons, living or dead, events, or locales is entirely coincidental.

For Jim,

whose past life as a judo instructor, cab driver and sailor, in addition to his present vocation as an English professor and avocation as an enophile, made this book possible. A most extraordinary combination of skills . . . a most extraordinary man.

Acknowledgment

In writing our first contemporary novel my associate, Carol Reynard, and I had to do a completely different kind of research than that required for our historicals. We made several trips to California, visiting the wine country and the San Francisco area. I put my partner through a great deal of stress, for which I owe her a special note of thanks. It was Carol who drove our stick shift rental car on the perpendicular hills of San Francisco, holding down the brakes and clutch while I hopped out to talk with condominium doormen on Nob Hill and to photograph the Embarcadero Center. In the Mayacamas Mountains separating the Napa and Sonoma valleys, there is a gravel trail called the Oakville Grade: about twenty miles of hairpin turns and perilously steep drop-offs. To check the accuracy of the truck crash scene, Carol drove that road in our subcompact. Several times we narrowly missed reenacting the crash with wildly careening pickup trucks! Carol says I still owe her for that ride. I'm just grateful we lived through it to finish the story!

Many people assisted us with the research for *Bouquet*. The residents of the Napa Valley were patient, friendly, and informative: the wine growers and their tour guides, the personnel at the Napa County Airport and the Lake Berryessa Marina, the staff at Meadowood Country Club, the restaurateurs, merchants and shopkeepers—all of whom helped us capture the unique flavor of life in their beautiful valley.

We are especially indebted to Joseph Novitski, who wrote *A Vineyard Year* (Chronicle Books, 1983). His poetically beautiful narrative and pictorial work provided me with the insight to create the men and women of this story who loved the vines.

We received additional invaluable information from the chambers of commerce of Napa, Sonoma, Calistoga and St. Helena, as well as from the Visitor's Information Center of San Francisco and the Wine Institute.

Again we are greatly indebted to Hildegard Schnuttgen, head of the reference department at Youngstown State University, for lending us books on the California wine industry from her personal library and for securing additional works on enology through the interlibrary loan system.

Researching airplanes and luxury boats required people with practical expertise. Neil J. Adler was so very kind as to phone me from his home in Suisun, California, to explain the intricacies of flying a crop dusting plane and the rules and regulations governing the pilots who operate them. Donald R. Kollar drew on his years of experience as a commercial pilot to create the sabotage of our hero's plane and to walk me step by step through the crash landing. Robert J. McGowan also worked on the plane crash sequence and secured all the information I needed to describe Peter Kane's marvelous Avanti Sunbridge pleasure craft.

We never write a book without villains, and they always come armed, no matter in what century the story takes place. Once more, our friend and weapons expert, Dr. Carmine V. DelliQuadri, Jr., D.O., has supplied us with the best in modern firearms, guns for hired killers and policewomen alike.

Prologue

San Francisco, 1977

"I'll give you exactly thirty seconds to get those clothes off," the blonde whispered seductively. Casually she peeled down a silk designer dress, tossing it in a glittering heap by the side of the bed. A tall, dark young man was closing the bedroom door against noise from a boisterous party. After flicking the lock, he strode across the beige carpet and stopped just in front of her.

Jolie devoured his graceful body with her eyes. The soft V-neck sweater accentuated the lean, corded muscles of his chest and shoulders. At twenty, Adam was a remarkable specimen, full of promise for the man he would one day be, strong and dark, compellingly handsome in the harsh angular way of the Moreland men. Thick black brows slashed over midnight blue eyes. She reached up and stroked his jawline, then tousled the straight blue-black hair that fell across his high forehead.

"You need a haircut," she teased as she rubbed her generous breasts lightly across his chest. Her lacy bra revealed more than it concealed. He reached up and took a rounded globe in each hand, but she quickly backed away.

"Not until you shed that sweater, baby," she cooed wickedly, turning her back. Reaching down to the bedside table for her drink, she afforded him a full view of lavender silk bikini briefs stretched tautly over lusciously rounded buttocks.

"For an old broad, you do have a great ass," he whispered as he slid his cashmere sweater off and began to unzip his fly.

"Clean living," she replied flippantly as she finished off the drink. "Anyway, I get lots of . . . exercise."

"Just so you get it all with me," he replied darkly, reaching for her. "What do you do all week while I'm at school?"

"Adam, love, don't be jealous. You know Jake hasn't touched me in years. He—"

He smothered her words with a fierce kiss, then murmured against her neck. "Let's don't talk about him, Jolie. Not now, not ever." Like a man consumed, he rained devouring, fiery kisses over the pale golden silk of her body, splaying his long, tapered fingers across her back, caressing the delicate column of her spine. She responded by insinuating her lower body tightly against his, reaching up on tiptoe to trap his hardened phallus between the juncture of her legs. She squeezed her thighs. He groaned and pulled her with him, tumbling them onto the bed.

They rolled across the quilted silk coverlet in a welter of arms and legs, panting and laughing in sheer animal abandon. "Jesus, you're horny," he breathed as she writhed against him impatiently. "All the books say a woman wants it slow and gentle."

"I thought you were studying agriculture, not sex," she teased, grabbing his shaft and stroking it deftly.

"Enology, not agriculture," he gasped as he rolled her on her back and plunged between her eagerly spread legs.

Her voice was harsh with passion as she wrapped her legs tightly around his slim hips and moved with him. "First fast and hard, then slow and easy—that is, if you think you can handle it a second time."

Without missing a stroke, he threw back his head and laughed with youthful bravado. "After a week of midterms, I can handle it!" He leaned forward and fiercely nipped her lips. "In fact, if it weren't for you, I'd *have* to handle it."

Adam could feel her nails digging into his shoulders,

feel the quick shuddering waves of her hungry release as he joined her in a sudden burst of white hot pleasure. He rolled away from her and then reached over to take her delicate face in one hand, observing her sated look with the predatory satisfaction of a young male animal.

"Why are you always in such a hurry, Jolie?" he mused to himself as much as to her.

Already her small hands with their long, lacquered nails were following the patterns of his body hair, across his pectoral muscles, down his abdomen. "Life's short, Adam. Get it while you can," she whispered as her hands sought and found him. She let out a slow, silvery chuckle. Already he was rock hard again. "You are some stud, doll."

"Just so I'm your *only* stud, Jolie. You see I can handle the job," he whispered as he began to suckle her breasts.

Jolie arched against the fierce assault, reveling in her power over him. Her hands worked deftly on his phallus until she felt him tremble in desperation. "Now who's handling who?"

The only trace remaining of the large party was some soft music floating up the stairs. Its haunting, insistent melody awakened Adam, who glanced over at the clock. Past one A.M. He groaned and rolled off the bed, disentangling himself from Jolie.

"Damn. I need a shower," he muttered to himself. How long had they been in the bedroom? They'd arrived around eight, had quite a few drinks and then slipped upstairs unnoticed after the party began to get noisy and crowded. Peter Kane's parents were out of the country on vacation and he had the place to himself.

The sound of the shower awakened the blond woman. While her young lover was occupied, she arose and haphazardly retouched her makeup, brushed her hair, then slipped into her clothes. "Jesus, I need a drink," she muttered, reaching for the empty glass by the bedside table.

When Adam emerged from the bathroom with a towel draped negligently around his hips, Jolie had returned. Seated provocatively on the edge of the bed, she observed his straight black hair glistening with droplets of water. One of her legs swung impudently across the other knee. She held a large martini glass in her hand.

"Pete's passed out on the sofa. A few diehards out on the patio are discussing Reagan's chances for the Republican nomination. Everyone else went home. I made us drinks." She reached over to the nightstand and offered him a glass, all the while admiring his sleek, dark body as he slid into his clothes.

"Christ, I hope Janie and Howard don't give Pete too much hell for this bash," Adam replied as he took the proffered drink and sipped it. "We have a long drive, Jolie. It's nearly two."

"Don't worry, darling. Time for a couple of drinks." With that she stood up and walked silently across the creamy carpet to the door. "Coming?" she asked in an insinuating voice.

"Watch the road, Jolie, for Christ's sake!" With a shuddering grimace, Adam grabbed the wheel of Jake's Continental, straightening it as they sped along the coastal highway south of San Francisco. Her drunken laughter overlaid the soft music from the radio much like the fog from the Bay blurred the road.

"Now, darling, don't be cross. I've driven this stretch a million times just picking you up from school. Think of all the practice I've had . . . every weekend." She added the last in a breathless, suggestive voice, slurred by the effects of the last three martinis that Adam had watched her consume before they left Pete's place.

God only knows how many she had earlier at the party, he thought darkly, watching her squint her face in concentration as she suddenly decided to attend to driving. He studied her profile, illuminated by the dim flashes of passing headlights. *A real stunner,* that's what Pete had called her. His fraternity brother, Peter

Kane, always had impeccable taste in women, especially older women. At thirty-two Jolie looked no older than twenty-five.

Her ash blonde hair was cut to fall in artless perfection framing her equally perfect features. Wide green eyes thickly fringed by dark lashes and elegantly arched brows gave her the appearance of a chic sorority girl. *A very expensive sorority, but that's all right. Jake can afford it. Too bad he can't keep her satisfied sexually as easily as he keeps her in Bill Blass dresses.* Adam's eyes traveled the length of her lush curves, noticing the way the sheer lavender silk seemed to slide and blend with the feline grace of her movements.

"Even drunk you're gorgeous," he muttered, half exasperated, half infatuated.

Jolie turned to him and smiled blindingly. "Just wait until we get to the beach house."

Once more he reached over and straightened the wheel. "Sure you don't want me to drive?"

"You're underage, darling, and I know you had at least two of Pete's wicked Manhattans." She shook her head reprovingly and her silvery hair bounced in the dim light.

He snorted in derision. "Two drinks to your half dozen. SAE men know how to hold their liquor, Jolie."

"And their women," she said with a wink. They both laughed.

Just then she let the wheel slip and the Lincoln veered onto the shoulder again. With a muttered curse, she straightened it and accelerated.

"Slow down. We have all day tomorrow," he remonstrated, suddenly aware of how tired she looked, ravaged from the effects of a night of drinking and sex. The shower he'd taken had refreshed him considerably. "Why don't you pull over and let me drive, Jolie?"

"I'm fine," she replied doggedly, once more speeding up as if to prove her point. Suddenly, the road seemed to evaporate in front of them as she took the big Continental around a curve and into a skid. The car left the road at blurring speed, its momentum keeping it from gaining purchase on the loosely packed earth. Several low lying shrubs flashed past them.

"You've locked the brakes, ease off," Adam commanded harshly as he grabbed for the wheel. When they hit the sand, it flurried around them like wind driven sleet. Suddenly everything seemed to explode. There was a scream of metal as the car crashed against an outcropping of rocks near the water's edge. Then there was only the soft whir of settling sand and the lap of ocean waves on the beach.

"Are you all right?" Adam looked over at Jolie, who sat with her head thrown back against the velour seat. Her fingers were still clamped in a death grip on the steering wheel.

She slowly peeled one small hand from the wheel and stroked her temple. "Yes, I think so. Bumped my head, but no blood. Hurts, though. Damn." She shook her head, trying to clear it. "Will the car start?" Without awaiting his answer, she turned the ignition and pumped the gas. Nothing.

"I could've told you that," he replied drily, looking through the windshield at the mangled hood.

Just then the distant sound of a siren caught Adam's attention and a flashing red light came into view, moving with steady assurance around the treacherous curve that had proved Jolie's undoing.

She let out several expletives and her beautiful face turned hard, then pleading as she looked from the rearview mirror to Adam. "I'll lose my license if they give me another ticket. Quick, change places with me!"

Shrugging, he slid beneath her, lifting her across his lap as they shifted seats. By the time the highway patrolman came striding over to the Lincoln, Adam had the driver's door open, preparing to step out.

"I was heading north when I saw you take that curve a lot faster than you should've. You folks all right?" The stocky uniformed officer looked at the jagged edges of the hood, which now more nearly resembled a lunar landscape than a luxury car.

"Yeah, I think so. Jolie—Jolie, honey!" Just as Adam turned to his blond companion, she let out a small sighing moan and crumpled against him, unconscious.

Adam held her in his arms, trying in vain to revive her while the patrolman radioed for an ambulance. When it arrived, the attendants placed her still, chalky body onto the stretcher as Adam climbed into the van to ride alongside her. Blessedly the small hospital in Pacifica was only a short distance.

It seemed an eternity to Adam, waiting at the hospital, answering questions, signing forms. He'd had to give identification for them both. *What the hell are we going to tell Jake?* he thought distractedly as he paced in the sterile blue waiting area. Just then the doctor who had taken Jolie into the emergency room came through the door, his mouth a tight gray slash.

"I'm sorry, Mr. Moreland. It was a brain hemorrhage caused by a concussion. Your stepmother is dead."

Chapter 1

Napa Valley, 1983

The fog lay like a gray velvet blanket across the valley floor. But the sun was beginning to dissipate its protective shield and caress the red earth with golden light. *It'll be a warm day for April in Napa,* the tall, lean man thought. Thanking the trucker for the lift, he pulled his battered duffel bag from the cab floor and jumped to the ground with graceful ease.

"Good luck finding a job. I don't envy you working them vines," the driver said good naturedly as he shifted his big rig, preparing to continue south on Highway 29.

The hitchhiker nodded and grinned. "I'll manage. There's always work in the vineyards if a man knows the difference between pruning and suckering." He stood in the soft dusty earth by the roadside, his faded jeans and blue cotton workshirt blending naturally with the fields beyond him. The season was well past budbreak and delicate green leaves shot out on the vines like prisoners freed from the gnarled confines of their wooden, winter prison. He recognized the shape and configuration of the vines, a large block of Zinfandel.

His calloused fingers shoved impatiently at the long black hair falling across his forehead while he surveyed the land. The roadside was shaded by Eucalyptus trees that added a lushness to the austerely cultivated valley floor. His keen dark blue eyes took in the strong clean pattern of the trellises and vines.

Whoever did the winter pruning on this land worked by hand, with a master's touch. But the owner needed laborers for the endless toil of summer. Wild mustard and quackgrass still grew between the leafed out vines. *The vintner's behind with his spring ground work.*

Sprinklers, those ever present guardians against frost, stood like sentinels, watching him. After swinging his bag effortlessly across one broad shoulder, he began walking up the long, winding road towards Chateau Beaumont.

As he neared the main grounds, his steps slowed. He looked across the field at several weathered frame barns, obviously used for storing cultivation equipment. Beyond the barns, several hundred feet from the road, stood an imposing three-storey white stucco structure, the crushing and fermentation plant. Nearer, on the opposite side of the road, sat a smaller, low-slung building of the same design. A neatly carved wooden sign by the parking lot proclaimed, "Tasting Room, Hours 10–4 Tues.–Sun." Judging from the size of the newly surfaced parking lot, retail business must be good.

Seeing nothing that looked like an office and knowing that this was a family-owned operation, he shrugged and headed to the plant. When he entered the immaculate interior, several men looked up.

A technician dressed in a white lab coat walked briskly towards the intruder, noting with ill-hidden disdain his shabby boots and faded clothes, the uniform of an itinerant laborer. A second look at the hard planes of the stranger's sun darkened face gave him pause. The drifter was Anglo, with piercing blue eyes that glowed with cynical intelligence. "If you're looking for field work, you'll have to wait for Les Reams, our foreman. He's up at the big house with Mr. Beaumont."

"And just where might the big house be?" The inquiry, made in a low musical voice, ignored the tacit command to cool his heels and wait for Reams. "I want to see Joe Beaumont."

Lab Coat smiled thinly. "You know Mr. Beaumont." It was not a question, but a dismissal. The presumption of this field hand!

Once more ignoring Lab Coat's tone, the drifter said, "Just direct me to the big house." It was not a request.

The technician's voice betrayed an odd mixture of condescension and nervousness. "Follow the road up the rise, past that stand of blue gums behind the tasting rooms."

"Obliged." The stranger moved noiselessly out the door in swift, sure strides as if he knew precisely where he was going. As the idea flashed in his mind, he scoffed. After seven years of drifting, working the vines and the crush, he had led a singularly aimless existence. *Maybe it's time. Maybe this is the place, here in Napa, with old Joe Beaumont.*

While the drifter had been hitchhiking south on Highway 29, two young women were riding north from the San Francisco Airport in a sleek beige Cadillac. The driver turned to her companion and asked, "What fable are you going to tell Papa?"

"I'll think of something, Marti. Anyway, he'll be so glad to see me, he won't care," she answered blithely.

"Won't care that you're failing three courses! Johling was the easiest finishing school we could find. It's a country club masquerading as a college, Riba! If you can't get a degree there, the only alternative is the Jolly Elves' Day Care Center." Marti's clear gray eyes blazed silver while she stared straight ahead at the highway, her slim fingers clenching and unclenching in agitation around the steering wheel. *It's always the same. Every time she comes home! She doesn't care about college. She doesn't care about Papa!*

Riba's laughter filled the plush interior of the car as she waved her hand dismissively. "I don't have to get a degree to get a man. And that, my darling sister, is what it's all about—not your Phi Beta Kappa key from Davis or chairing the latest hospital fund raiser in the valley."

Marti was used to her sister's caustic comments

about her lifestyle. Swallowing her anger, she replied drily, "I take it your remark about getting a man means you plan an engagement. Will Papa approve of him? He did so want you to finish college first."

Riba's green eyes gleamed in anticipation. "Oh, Papa will approve of Larry, all right." She chewed her little finger for a moment, a childhood habit she had never been able to break. "Of course, Larry wants me to finish school, too."

"Chalk one up for Larry," Marti interjected skeptically.

"His family is Philadelphia Mainline. Lawrence Smythe Cameron, very proper and very rich, Marti! He's a junior partner in his father's law firm, but it won't be long until he launches a brilliant political career."

"And you intend to be there by his side—the senator's wife—or do you plan to skip the preliminaries and go straight to the White House?"

A burble of girlish laughter reminded Marti of a simpler time when they were children. *But was it ever simple, honestly?*

"Oh, Marti, Larry's planning to run for lieutenant governor for openers. Even *I* can be patient—especially if I'm back east living in Philly and DC, even in New York—anywhere but dusty old Napa."

"In case he didn't mention it, Riba, your lieutenant governor will have to spend a good deal of time in Harrisburg, not exactly the swingingest metropolis in the east," Marti replied in a voice laced with irony. "How did you meet a man from Philadelphia while going to school in South Carolina anyway?"

"His family has a beach house at Nags Head. We met over the Christmas break—"

"And a lot of other times, I bet, judging from your grades." Marti knew a scolding tone had crept into her voice and tried doggedly to stifle it. Best to treat Riba with dry good humor—that or wring her neck!

"Grades!" Riba grimaced. "I know what I'll do! I'll promise Papa to make better grades during my fall semester—if he buys me that Porsche convertible this summer!"

Looking at the smug gleam in Riba's jade eyes, Marti knew it was useless to remonstrate. *Papa will reward her year of rotten schoolwork with a new sportscar—all she has to do is pout and look pretty.* In bitter silence she ignored Riba's continued bubbly chatter about Larry.

As the highway stretched like a silver ribbon in the midmorning sunlight, Marti drove homeward, remembering the past, the way her father always favored his younger child.

Their mother had been a beauty and the love of Joseph Beaumont's life. When she was killed in a tragic plane crash, the girls were pre-schoolers. Although less than two years apart, no siblings could have been less alike. Martha, with her drab coloring and strong features, took after their father while Rebecca's exquisite loveliness made her the image of their mother, a woman for whom Joseph Beaumont grieved with inconsolable anguish. He never remarried. As Riba grew up to look more and more like Bertrice, Joe transferred all the love and adoration he had held for his wife to his younger child. There never seemed to be much left for Marti.

It doesn't matter what she does, he'll always forgive her. He always has. Of course, Marti realized there were some things about his darling Riba that even their Papa would find difficult to forgive. If he knew, his heart would break, something Marti would never—*could* never allow, she vowed fiercely once more.

Forcing down the clawing pain of old memories, she turned to Riba. "Tell me, when will the Beaumonts be privileged to meet this paragon Larry?"

When the beige Cadillac rounded the bend in the road by the eucalyptus trees, Riba busily scanned the familiar sights of Chateau Beaumont, especially taking note of the workers. Marti watched her sister wave gaily to an assortment of young men working in various fields.

Every male on Beaumont land was delighted with Riba's visit at spring break.

"There's Jules Steiger and Jose Ruiz, oh, and the Mendoza brothers are back, too." Riba's eyes were avidly alight with an excited gleam that always put Marti on edge. "Anyone new hired on lately?"

"No one under fifty," Marti replied acerbically. "How are you going to break the news about your engagement to Boris?"

Riba's raised brow and feigned look of confusion didn't fool her sister for a moment. "I know you were never serious, about him, but Boris is a humorless Russian—you know, Chekov, Gorky and all that?"

Riba laughed languidly. "Oh, poor Boris is stuffy and serious all right—and so damned dull. All he ever wants to talk about is wine."

"I can't imagine why," Marti said innocently. "He's only been our winemaster for the past three years."

"Oh, I'll think of something to cushion his fall." Riba snapped her fingers. "I have it! He lives for this dreary old winery and so do you—"

"Don't even think it!" Marti interrupted with stung pride. "I don't believe in mixing my professional life with my personal one," she added more softly.

"Don't shit too close to your own tepee, huh?" Riba said with a wicked laugh.

"And where did you pick up that piece of wisdom—in anthropology or folklore? Funny," snapped Marti, "as I recall you flunked both classes."

In her version of a Carolina drawl, Riba retorted, "I learned that in Health 109. You know—personal hygiene."

Marti fixed her sister with a frown. "Too bad you cut class the day they were dealing with *oral hygiene.* If you treat Papa to some of that mouth, you'll get a garbage truck instead of a Porsche."

"Always protecting Papa, aren't you, Marti?" Riba shot back, sudden anger in her voice.

For a moment the two women drove on in silence, but Marti still seethed at her sister's suggestion about Boris. *I don't want her leavings!* she thought angrily.

Unable to let the matter rest, she snapped at Riba with uncharacteristic crudeness, "Do you have to drop your drawers for every man you see?" She turned her head to glance at her younger sister.

Suddenly, the blonde's face twisted with rage. "I'm not you, Marti. I'm alive! I like men. You slop around dressed in burlap with a Yale lock on your pussy, but don't expect me to! And, sister dear, my drawers are my own business! If I want to crank them up and down like a goddamned elevator, I will and I don't need your permission!"

Marti shot back in shock, "As I recall, sister dear, there was a time when your elevator got stuck between floors and you had to ask me to get you the repairman!" Seeing the stricken look on her sister's face, Marti felt a sudden surge of self-contempt. *"Oh, my god,"* she thought, *"that was rotten."*

Once more the women were silent. Looking at the road, Marti could think of nothing to say, but she desperately wanted to obliterate her last angry remark. "So, how are you going to handle Boris?" she forced herself to ask.

Shrugging, Riba said dismissively, "I'll handle Boris some which way. After all, I never gave him any promises. I always made it clear I was looking for a man who was going places—and that doesn't mean into a wine cellar—unless it's to bring me a bottle of Dom Perignon."

"Bite your tongue, talking of French champagne with half a dozen California competitors right here on the North Coast," Marti scolded in resignation. *What's the use being angry with Riba? She'll never change.*

As if to verify that fact, Riba gasped and exclaimed in a breathy voice, "I thought you said you hadn't hired any new men under fifty. What do you call *him*?" She pointed unabashedly at the tall, dark man in faded denim who was strolling toward the machinery shed from the bunkhouse.

"I'd call him a seasonal worker," Marti replied in exasperation. "Les or Papa must have just hired him this morning."

"He's gorgeous! Those jeans look like they're spray painted on those long legs," Riba said avidly.

"They're just worn thin with age."

The object of their discussion turned in mid-stride, his blue eyes taking in the slow-moving, expensive car with the two women inside. The blonde on the passenger side was eyeing him like a hungry mountain lion about to pounce on a wounded mule deer. The driver was obscured by shadows inside the car. All he could see was dark hair and glasses. Both women had looked at him, but the brunette had quickly turned her attention back to the road. The blonde continued to stare in blatant interest. He boldly stared back, then gave a brief salute with one hand and walked negligently inside the big shed full of tractors and brush grinders.

"He's scarcely your dream prince," Marti said scornfully. "He looks hard and dirty and dangerous. When will you ever learn to leave these drifters alone?"

"Spare me the lecture," Riba shot back defiantly, her gaze riveted on the stranger disappearing into the shed.

"And here I thought you only had eyes for your lieutenant governor—what's his name again?" Marti asked innocently.

Riba replied with a succinct one syllable expletive.

Just then the car pulled up in front of the big house. The magnificent white frame structure with its double-tiered gallery looked like a re-creation from antebellum Louisiana. The wide French doors and iron grillwork across the front of the place would have fit perfectly on Chartre Street in the New Orleans French Quarter.

Riba flew up the front porch steps into the welcoming embrace of Joseph Beaumont. "Papa, Papa, oh, I've missed you so!"

His sun lined face was creased in a broad grin. "Oh, princess! I'm sorry I couldn't be at the airport, but I had to spend the morning on the phone to our agent in France ordering replacements for those defective Limousin barrels."

The sharply wizened features of the old man's face were softened by love as he picked up his daughter in a welcoming bear hug that belied his thin, five-foot-eight frame. He whirled her around, then set her down for a mock inspection at arm's length. "Well, you don't look any smarter—or more beautiful, but then that's not possible in any case. Doesn't she look a little pale though, Marti?" he said, sparing his other daughter a quick glance before returning his attention to Riba.

"A few days of California sunshine will cure Riba's pallor, Papa," Marti replied gently, ushering them inside. "I wonder what Hilda is going to prepare for dinner tonight?"

"I told her we wanted her world famous tournedos to go with a fine bottle of Chateau Beaumont Merlot," Joe said as he held the door open for his daughters.

The full moon hung suspended beneath a long silvery wisp of cloud that partially obscured its top half in a misty glow. There was a chill in the air and Riba knew her father would probably be out with several of the hands checking the sprinklers in case of a possible frost.

Shivering, she pulled the soft, green wool shawl around her bare shoulders and slipped into the beckoning shadows of the back yard. Behind the dense stand of eucalyptus was a small gazebo and flower garden, her usual place for clandestine meetings with men. The gazebo was near a dusty offshoot of the main road, but so far beyond the house that a cautious driver could ease down it and park without anyone hearing.

She paced nervously and swore, shivering again in the cold. Once the sun dropped into the Pacific, the North Coast valleys were decidedly chilly, even in summer.

"Riba, darling," a low voice called out of the darkness.

Turning sharply on her heel, she looked at the intense, almost pained expression of longing etched on

Boris Staritz's face. *Jesus, this is going to be harder than I thought.*

When he embraced her, Riba returned the hug but stopped him short when he bent to kiss her, pressing her long lacquered nails across his wide mouth. "We have to talk, Boris," she said, twisting adroitly away from the winemaster. His brawny, muscular body had held an appeal last summer, but now . . .

Boris watched her swish away, her spike-heeled sandals clicking as she stepped deftly behind a stone bench, putting a physical barrier between them. He could sense at once there was more. "So, no letters since February—only a post card since Thanksgiving. I should have known you'd find some college boy, Riba."

"It's not like that, Boris. I'm not interested in boys."

"Yes, and you're not interested in a man who makes the finest wines on the North Coast either, are you?" he lashed out.

"The North Coast," she mimicked contemptuously. "Have any of your relatives ever traveled east of the Rocky Mountains since they landed in California a hundred years ago? Do you have any idea there's a whole world out there? A world where people's only interest in wine is to drink it from crystal glasses in five star restaurants? Lots of people discuss other things besides the cork crop in Portugal or the shade of toast on French barrel staves!"

"Who is he?" Boris asked, his voice shaking with rage and jealousy. To have come so close—so close to his dream. He should have known she'd find someone in that fancy eastern school!

"His name is Lawrence Cameron and he's from Philadelphia. He's an attorney," Riba said, trying to suppress the triumph in her voice.

"Someone you met this past winter, some stranger, a rich boy who'll buy you diamonds and take you to the Riviera," he sneered.

"Don't be dense, Boris. I never promised you a permanent relationship. Besides, I know your game. Don't be so goddam holy. You want to marry the boss's daughter so you can get your hands on Chateau Beaumont," she lashed back in high temper.

"Yes, I want to run the winery, but not for money—I want to make fine wine, Riba, using modern technology, experiment with new vines and equipment—"

"Please, spare me. You'd better have this conversation with Marti, not me." She stopped and laughed, her pique forgotten as the irony struck her. "In fact, I told her the very same thing this morning. She cares about this godforsaken valley and your precious vines, your new technology. She wants to bury herself here, but I don't. Ply my sister, Boris. You speak the same language."

He moved toward her with menacing steps and grabbed her by the shoulders before she could dart away from him. Shaking her, he said, "Tell me, last summer and in December when you were home, when I made love to you—didn't we speak the same language then? Didn't we!"

"That was sex, Boris, not love. We both had a good time, but now it's over." She spoke in a quick, soft rush of words, perversely excited by his possessive fury. "I'm engaged to a man who shares other things with me."

"He shares his money and some fancy east coast social connections," he ground out. He paused and looked at the sheen of sexual excitement glowing in her eyes. *The bitch! Bloody little gold digging bitch!* "I could fuck you right here and now and you'd let me, wouldn't you? Then get up, straighten your silk skirt and slip back into your safe warm bed in Joe's big house, no one the wiser." As he released her, he continued bitterly, "You're beautiful, Riba, so enchantingly, wickedly beautiful, but you're a slut."

"You knew that when we met, Boris," she said, her voice now as cold as his spent ardor.

"Yes, I knew it. So do half the men at the chateau . . . everyone but your father, I think," he replied measuringly.

For the first time a genuine hint of fear flashed into

her jade eyes. "If you tell him about us, Boris, I'll deny everything and Marti will back me. You'll lose your job, I swear it!"

His laugh was ugly as he said, "Maybe you're right about trying my luck with Marti." He turned sharply and walked toward the whispering blackness of the trees, pausing to call over his shoulder, "At least with her I wouldn't have to worry about catching a dose of clap!"

Chapter 2

Sweat rolled off his body, causing the fine prickly spray of sawdust to stick in itchy misery to his arms and chest, even to his face below the shield of his safety goggles. Adam hated brush work, but the dead wood pruned from the vines over the winter had to be ground up and mulched through the wide set rows of the vineyard.

Grinning, he realized that he hated the noise of machinery; nothing was more deafening than working a chopper. A man needed to listen to the vines, feel them move. From the first budbreak in sunny March until the last black cluster was picked beneath uncertain October skies, there was a rhythm, a sharing between the men and the land. Machinery interfered with that.

"Heresy," he laughed to himself, as he thought of his professors at Davis, always experimenting with new equipment as well as new ideas. And, he reluctantly agreed, that very willingness to break European rules was what had put California vintners in direct competition with the finest wines of France and Germany.

"Time for lunch, *mano,*" Jose Ruiz yelled over the din. As Adam shut down the roaring chopper, his young coworker offered him a beer from the styrofoam chest at the side of the road. "Napa first aid kit?"

"Thanks," Adam replied, taking the icy can in one hand as he pulled the goggles free from his face and wiped rivulets of sweat from his eyes. Then he held the cold beer against his forehead for a minute. "Damn, sure is warm for April."

Several of the other men agreed and a desultory conversation followed about what that meant for the fall harvest. While they talked, the workers wolfed down sandwiches.

"There goes Old Joe, out for a confab with his children," Ferris Beecher said with a fond grin. Several of the long-time employees chuckled at the private joke about the eccentric vintner's love affair with his vines.

"He told me when he hired me that his vines were like children and that he worked the land himself," Adam said with honest admiration.

Bob Vasquez, a bright young Chicano whose family had been migrant workers for generations, smiled. Although finishing a business degree at San Francisco State, he still worked off and on for Chateau Beaumont. "Yeah, the old man has a real feel for the land. But don't ever let his love for his vines throw you. He's a hard man whose father survived Prohibition. Joe Beaumont brought this chateau up from near bankruptcy to become one of the largest independently owned operations in the valley."

"And he's kept union organizers out," Jose added with rancor.

Adam shrugged as an argument between the loyal old time hands and some of the younger, more militant workers began. Catching sight of a woman walking toward the hillside, he interrupted, wanting to shift the topic before it turned ugly. "Who's the girl with Beaumont?"

Bob Vasquez replied, "Oh, that's Marti—Martha Beaumont, Joe's older daughter. Surprised you haven't met her. She handles payroll and all the paperwork."

Adam watched an animated exchange between father and daughter taking place several hundred yards away on the steep hillside. "I'll meet her tomorrow, I imagine. Supposed to go up to the office and sign some stuff, Les Reams told me earlier," he said absently, draining his can of beer to wash down the last glutinous hunk of bread and salami. As he swallowed, he watched the woman. She was coltishly slim, dressed in loose slacks and a baggy T-shirt. Her hair was long, knotted behind her head in some sort of frowzy, unfashionable bun.

"Nothing like the blonde I saw her with in the Cadillac yesterday," he said, half to himself.

Juan Moreno snickered and Ferris Beecher cast him a quelling look, but Jules Steiger, another long-time hand, seemed more willing to talk. "Might's well tell him, Ferris. He'll find out soon enough 'bout Riba, if he ain't already." His shrewd brown eyes locked with Adam's intent blue ones.

"Riba?"

"Yep. Mr. Beaumont has two daughters. Miz Riba's the younger one. Just back for a weekend 'er so, from some fancypants eastern college."

"It's taking her a while to graduate," Bob Vasquez put in with a wry grin.

Several of the younger men laughed and then one said, "She's got more on her mind than school books. Like you said, she 'n her sister ain't nothin' alike. Miz Marti's all business 'n no foolin'."

"A real lady, even if she ain't a fancy looker like Riba," Ferris said in a tone of voice that indicated the conversation about the boss's daughters was closed.

By mid-afternoon, Adam had most of the brush in the field fed through the chopper. At break time he took a beer from the ever present ice chest and wandered off towards the shade of a eucalyptus at the road's edge where three of the younger men were sitting. Untying his shirt from around his waist, he used it to wipe the sawdust covered perspiration from his face and chest. Just then a small red Mazda pulled around the curve of the road from the big house. The blonde was behind the wheel.

Several of the men waved to her, yelling welcome home greetings. Adam watched in detachment as the car stopped and Riba called out, "Hi, Juan, Bob. Say, who's the new recruit? You fellows sure gave him the rottenest job," she added, her green eyes seeming to count every particle of sawdust ensnared in the curly black hair on Adam's chest.

"Low man always takes the drag jobs, Miss Beaumont," Adam said with a nod and slight smile. Leaning indifferently against the tree, he made no move to introduce himself.

"This is Adam Wade," Bob volunteered for him with a look of devilry in his black eyes.

"So, Adam, are you really the lowest man?" Riba asked in a seductively teasing voice. She seemed intrigued by his indifference, rather than put off by it.

"Just the last hired, so I drew the chopper. Fair turn's okay with me," he replied levelly.

Riba observed his striking facial features and the hard, guarded look in those beautiful blue eyes. A mystery. With one last raking glance from head to foot and back over his bare, sweat-soaked torso, she said, "A man with a sense of fair play. Or do you just love grinding?" When Adam failed to respond, she revved up the engine. "Maybe you'll get a fair turn and maybe you won't, Adam Wade." With that she was off in a plume of dust, driving much too fast down the gravel road.

A chorus of ribald laughter greeted Adam after she was gone. "Shit, I haven't seen Riba eat a man up like that since that pretty college boy from Denver worked here—musta been three summers ago. You remember, Bob, the blond kid that lifted weights?" Juan said with a chuckle.

Bob grinned, then nodded and turned to the tall man still leaning against the tree, staring out across the fields as if a world away. "Watch out for her, Adam. She's foxy looking and fun to kid around with, but if you get involved, well, it's nothing but trouble."

"Hell, trouble's the story of my life, *mano.*" Uncoiling from the tree, Adam retied his shirt around his narrow waist and shrugged. "But I lost my taste for blondes a long time ago . . ."

* * *

The evening meal around the oval table in the Beaumont family's dining room was a formal affair. It had been ever since Joseph Sr., the patriarch of the family and founder of Chateau Beaumont, had presided. When he died and his son married Bertrice, the tradition continued. The snowy linen tablecloth was graced with gleaming flatware, fine china and thin crystal wine glasses every night.

In the nineteen years since Bertrice had died, the frilly schoolgirl frocks of her daughters had given way to expensive silk gowns. Joseph still wore the same conservative cut of suits and his thinning grey hair was always neatly slicked back.

That evening Riba wore a royal blue dress with a rounded neckline, simple enough for propriety yet bright and flattering enough to win her father's admiration. Marti, in a tan shirtwaist dress looked like a mud hen in comparison.

"But Papa, you know how much I've been wanting a Porsche. That dreary ancient Mazda isn't safe to drive," Riba cajoled.

Marti chuckled. "The way you tear around, an armored car wouldn't be safe enough!"

Joe shot her a look of surprised annoyance, then turned back to Riba. "Martha is right, honey. You do drive too fast on these gravel roads sometimes. You're going back to school in two days. Plenty of time when the semester's over for us to discuss a new car. Speaking of semesters, your grades, I understand, haven't been the best."

Riba put down her fork with a sigh and sipped from the gleaming ruby liquid in the crystal wine glass. "Marti's given you a complete report on my academic shortcomings, I suppose. Papa, I'm sorry I'm not a scholar like my brilliant sister, but—"

"Nonsense, Princess," Joe waved aside her tearful plea. "I'm not comparing you to your sister. Few women—or men either—have her brains." He glanced at his older daughter with a genuinely proud smile. Both he and Marti missed the flash of jealousy that Riba quickly suppressed. As the old man returned his attention to the pretty blonde, he sobered. "I suppose your bad performance might have been influenced by this young man, Lawrence Cameron. I intend to check on his family and learn a good deal more about him before you announce an engagement, Riba," he finished sternly.

Her eyes lit up. "He'll stand the test, Papa. Even the Beaumont test. And as for school, well, he wants me to finish, too. I only need one more semester. I'll make you a deal," she said with the same engaging grin she'd used to charm her father since she was seven.

"What deal?" Joe questioned with narrowed gray eyes. The faintest hint of a smile tugged at the corner of his thin mouth.

"You buy me that Porsche and I'll buckle down and really study next fall. Word of honor." She raised a slim hand, her palm outward as if in a scout's pledge.

As Marti watched the scene, she shoved a tender morsel of lamb around on her plate. *He'll buy her that expensive car and she'll flunk again in the fall.* She forced herself to take a drink of the '76 Cabernet as she changed the subject. "This is a particularly fine Cabernet, Papa. Good color, well defined legs, a really sturdy wine with backbone."

Joe snorted. "All right, all right, I know. It's the first year we experimented with American white oak aging."

"No perfumey finish like your Limousin," Marti said with a twinkle.

Disliking the turn of the conversation which bored her to tears, Riba interjected, "Speaking of wine, I noticed Les has expanded the summer work crews. I met a dark-haired, sullen fellow named Adam Wade yesterday afternoon. What do you know about these drifters who sign on?" she asked innocently of her father.

Marti's eyes flashed between the two and then settled on Riba in warning, but Joe only laughed indulgently. "Les didn't hire Wade, I did. Seems he's a Davis boy," he said with a wink at his elder daughter.

"Of course he never graduated like Martha, here, but he has good references from several growers. Say, he didn't say anything fresh to you, did he?" Joe asked suddenly, remembering the casual arrogance of the young drifter when he had interviewed him the previous day.

Riba laughed dismissively, "Heavens, no. The other men would flatten anyone who ever said a rude word to me or Marti, wouldn't they, sis?" She didn't even wait for Marti to reply, nor did Joe turn for her reaction. He did not see the speculative, worried look in Marti's eyes either.

The next morning, shortly after daybreak, Adam headed for a quick breakfast in the cook shed adjacent to the bunkhouse, then ambled down the road toward the tasting room, where the foreman, Les Reams, had instructed him the office was located.

"Let's see if the boss's older daughter is an early riser," he muttered beneath his breath. He was certain the younger one was not. The front doors to the tasting room were still locked but the side door was ajar. Wondering if he should knock, Adam approached the entrance and peered inside. The office was neat and cheerful with an old fashioned roll-top desk in one corner. A large table with sturdy wooden chairs around it stood near the far wall.

His eyes scanned the precise stacks of papers on the desk and noted the contrast of a delicate ceramic jar filled with spring wildflowers sitting on top of it. A decidedly feminine touch, as was the water color hung on the wall over the rough, masculine-looking pine table. The painting was a misty soft rendering of the Beaumont house with its massive stands of eucalyptus and willow trees.

Just then a door from the inside opened and a slim young woman entered with a stack of mail in her hand. Obviously not seeing him leaning against the far wall, she stepped over to the desk and sat down. Early morning sunlight filtered in and did lovely things to her hair. What he had perceived yesterday as dull brown was now highlighted a changeable russet hue. The simple fat braid hanging down the slim column of her spine gleamed softly, inviting a man's hands to unplait it. He studied her profile, strong and straight with high cheekbones and a determined jaw. Completely devoid of make-up, her face was not conventionally beautiful like Riba's, but there was something engaging about the soft pliancy of the lips and arch of the brows. She wore a simple cotton T shirt again, but now had on a rather businesslike A-line khaki skirt.

"Exquisite," he said softly, causing her to gasp and whirl to face him, dropping her pencil on top of the pile of letters.

"The water color on the wall is exquisite. I noticed the signature. Beaumont."

"I painted it," Marti said, gathering her composure and standing up to face the intruder. Her black-rimmed reading glasses had slipped down her nose and she pushed them up in irritation.

"Somehow I didn't think your sister would have the patience for something so delicate," he remarked drily.

"You're Adam Wade, the man Papa hired while I was in San Francisco," she said with an accusatory tone to her voice.

"And you're Miss Martha Beaumont," he countered, wondering why she hid such lovely silver-gray eyes behind those ugly glasses. "I was told to report her for some . . . processing," he added with a slow smile whitening a slash across his dark face. He watched her reaction, controlled and businesslike, but oddly unsophisticated for a university educated woman in her mid-twenties. She turned back to the roll-top desk and began to pull an assortment of forms from the neat cubbyholes in it.

"I'll need your social security number, age, place of birth, the usual," she said briskly, then looked up into those disturbing dark blue eyes. "I don't suppose you're an alien," she added waspishly, wishing she could reasonably demand that he produce a green card and shoo him out if he failed to do so. There was something about him. When she and Riba had first seen him the other day, he'd been dusty and disheveled from a long hitch on the road. Now, freshly showered and shaven with his inky hair brushed off his forehead, he looked arrestingly handsome in a hard, almost foreign way. For once she and Riba agreed about a man's attractiveness, but she didn't like the feeling, not one bit!

Grinning at her sally about his citizenship, he took the forms and pen from her and sat down at the table to complete them. He wrote with bold clean strokes, filling in the blanks with practiced assurance. After years of watching functional illiterates and non-English speakers struggle laboriously with the task, Marti knew he didn't belong with them; he didn't belong here. He was too old to be a college student and too well educated to settle for this kind of job. Still, Papa had said he worked for some of the best names in the business. Perhaps he hoped to prove himself and move up to a permanent position, even Boris's job. She smiled wryly, not believing it at all likely.

When he finished the papers, he looked up to see her frown of concentration. Silently he handed her the forms and the pen.

"Paydays are on first and third Fridays. Be sure to report any injuries to Les Reams if they occur on the premises. I assume you're settled in at the single men's bunkhouse and mess hall?" she inquired perfunctorily, feeling a peculiar need to have the interview terminated.

"All business, aren't you?" he said with one black brow arched wickedly.

"My job is to run this office—do the payroll and keep the books. Yours is to do whatever the foreman tells you to," she replied coolly, wanting to look away from the long bare strip of bronzed neck and chest exposed where his shirt lay open. Still, she was reluctant to meet those piercing blue eyes again.

"Why so tense and hostile, lady? I'm no threat, just

a hired hand . . . and an art lover," he added as an irresistible afterthought.

She stiffened. "Just so you confine your loving to your own time, *away* from Chateau Beaumont," she replied over sweetly.

"That supposed to warn me off your sister—or you?" The minute he uttered the taunting question, Adam could have bitten his tongue. What the hell possessed him to say that?

"Both, Mr. Wade, *if* we needed protection from your charms," she replied icily.

"Somehow I doubt Miss Riba needs protection from anyone. As for you . . ." he let his words trail away when his eyes caught her fingers nervously twisting the end of her braid.

She dropped the guilty hand as if scalded and turned back to her desk. "Good day, Mr. Wade."

The unseasonably warm days of April turned abruptly cool in May after causing a sudden burst of growth in the springy green canes. The delicate leaves, always susceptible to frost, had to be protected from budbreak in March through to the blossoming in June. Every morning and evening old Joe and his foreman watched the sun and the sky, relying as much on their lifetime of experience as on meteorologist's reports. The sprinklers hummed and hissed through many nights in May, coating the infant fruit buds with protective water that crystallized into an icy shield, dissolving and refreezing continuously, protecting the infant crop from the worst of the frost damage.

Marti walked between the rows of leafed-out canes one night, wet and cold, her jeans plastered miserably to her legs. She had spent exhausting hours in the fields, working with her father and the men. "God, I stink of smudge pots and fertilizer," she muttered ruefully, brushing a stray lock of hair from her forehead.

Adam watched her trudging dispiritedly toward the end of the row. He was not surprised at Joe's hours in the cold and damp; many of the tough, old vintners he had worked for did the same. But he was frankly amazed to see the prim, ladylike Marti climbing up to fiddle with jammed sprinkler mechanisms, soaking her hair and clothes, slogging through the mud from place to place late at night as well as before dawn. He could never imagine Riba, now warmly ensconced back in her South Carolina college, doing what her older sister did.

In fact, in the past six weeks, Adam's estimation of the quiet, efficient Martha Beaumont had risen steadily. "A real lady" Ferris had called her and that she was. Of course, she scarcely looked the part at the moment, but her wet clothes, mud-stained and worn as they were, outlined a startlingly well proportioned body. Just then his perusal was interrupted. Marti slipped in a patch of mud on the steep ground at the base of the row and slid down to land abruptly near his feet.

Struggling to sit up, she blurted out a very unladylike, "Son-of-a-bitch," then looked straight ahead at a pair of age-softened leather boots, well caked with mud. Her gaze followed the long legs upward toward the sound of soft masculine laughter.

"Such language from the prim boss lady."

"Go to hell!" she croaked out furiously just as Adam reached down to take her by the elbows and pull her from her squishy, cold seat.

He chuckled, ignoring her attempt to pull away from his touch. "You sure look a lot prettier without those stupid glasses."

"I'll just bet, with mud for mascara," she snapped back, jerking free and almost slipping once more. He steadied her as she spat out, "If you did the harrowing right, I wouldn't have fallen." She felt petty and testy, humiliated to have him see her this way.

Adam noticed the agitated rise and fall of her breasts, starkly revealed through the clingy wet shirt. Her loose jacket had come unzipped as she fell and was pulled off one shoulder. Bemused, he reached up and tugged gently at the knot of braids in back of her head, freeing the waist-length plait of dark hair. "When you wash it, wear it loose."

She suddenly felt a bizarre warmth infuse her shivering body. Angry at his bold gesture and words, she ignored the heady sensation and jerked up the zipper on her jacket, only to have it lodge half way, so caked with grime that it jammed.

"Here, let me." Again those warm deft hands were on her, freeing the caught pull tab and gently finishing the job, careful to lift the fabric away from the swell of her breasts as he did so. She prayed silently that he couldn't see the way her nipples had contracted into hard points. She could certainly feel them!

"Marti, you over there?" Her father's voice called across the trellises. He only called her Marti when they were co-workers in the fields, never at the house, and never in front of Riba.

"Yes, Papa, I'm coming." Forcing herself to look Adam in the eye again, she said coolly, "Please excuse me, Mr. Wade."

"Misters don't slog around muddy vineyards. Call me Adam." That smile again.

Suddenly, she felt bitchy, rude and decidedly confused by her conflicting emotions. Managing a wobbly smile, she said, "All right, Adam. I have to go now. Papa's waiting."

"Let's hope he didn't hear what you said when you hit the bottom of that mud hole," he returned with a devilish wink.

As quickly as the cold snap arrived, it was gone and the end of May came in dry, warm and golden, perfect preparation for June's blossom time in the vineyards. Miraculously, through everyone's combined efforts, the crop had escaped all but a touch of frost damage. To celebrate, Les Reams arranged a party one Saturday night down at the bunkhouse. Married workers who lived in the small migrant cabins came with their families. A number of the cellarmen, even the young plant technicians and the imperious winemaster, Boris Staritz, put in an appearance. Staritz seemed to be squiring Marti, although her father was walking with them so it was difficult to tell.

Adam watched as she greeted the long-time workers and their families. Aloud he murmured to Bob Vasquez, "She treats them all like old friends. Even the college kids and hardcase drifters respect her."

Vasquez smiled fondly, recalling how long his family had worked for Joe and his daughter. "Why not? She works alongside them. Has ever since she was a girl. Nothing she or Joe could ask us to do they haven't done themselves."

Several of the men had musical instruments, and soon guitars strummed out haunting melodies and fierce rhythms on the cool evening air.

Marti was dressed in a dark rose-colored print skirt and blouse that hung loosely over her lithe body. Adam wondered why she chose such unattractive clothing. Once more her hair was knotted behind her head and her glasses were in place. *She's hiding!* The sudden revelation washed over him. But why?

Just then Juan Moreno handed him his guitar, saying, "I've heard you play, *mano.* Take a turn?" Looking across the flickering bonfire at Marti's slender figure, Adam took the instrument and sat down. After randomly strumming a few chords, he began to play an old familiar melody, a Neil Diamond tune.

". . . for she was a lady and I was a dreamer, with only words to trade . . ."

Marti listened to the warm low resonance of Adam's voice, hypnotized as she stared into the dancing orange flames. Without looking she could see the long tapered fingers that caressed the guitar strings. She remembered those warm, sure hands zipping her jacket.

Ever since he'd come to work at the winery, Marti had felt antagonistic towards him. But after that startling encounter in the mud, she had become acutely aware of his presence. That night when he had touched her mud spattered body everything had changed.

Marti knew she would never forget the feel of his hands. Shivering, she hugged herself and looked at the straight black hair falling across Adam's face as he bent his head in concentration, lost in the music he was making. Then as she stared unabashed, he suddenly looked up and their eyes met over the leaping flames.

He knows, a small voice inside her cried, and she answered desperately, *no, he can't!*

Chapter 3

"May in the Napa Valley must be when the artists come out of winter hibernation," Adam said as he stood watching Marti sketch. "I wondered when you ever found time."

"I make time," Marti replied evenly as she put down her pencil and looked up. She was perched on a big rock, partially shaded by a small stand of pines that grew on the steep hillside.

"You look like the type who'd be in church on Sunday morning," he chided. Dressed casually in jeans and a cotton shirt, he walked over to stand behind her.

"How do you know I didn't go to church?" she asked crossly, then followed his eyes as they surveyed her disheveled hair and dusty old clothes. Defensively she replied, "So, I'm a lapsed Episcopalian who'd rather sketch than pray." Looking out across the clear sunny valley, she added almost to herself, "You know, on days like this I think being out here on my hill, smelling the pine trees, it is a form of worship."

Adam replied softly, "I know what you mean." He gestured broadly around the magnificent valley floor spread before them. Turning back to her, he asked, "Let me see your drawings?"

With reluctance, she made herself hand him the pad, then watched nervously as he flipped slowly through the half-dozen sketches.

Several were of the hillside view of the valley, but one caught his particular interest. "This one is perfect for your water color technique," he said, handing the book back to her. "The others are good, but panoramic, more suited to oils."

Startled, she blurted out in amazement, "I've already done a water color of it. I call it 'Budbreak' and it's entered in the county art fair next weekend."

"Where can I see it?" he asked with one black brow arched curiously.

"You really want to see my work?—I mean, no one but Alice ever . . ." her words trailed off uncertainly.

Adam could well imagine how much interest her father or sister would ever show in something so fanciful as water colors. "Yes, I really do. Who is Alice?" he asked softly.

"Alice Marchanti. She runs a small shop in Napa—a gallery. She's encouraged me to paint, even sells my water colors and charcoals on consignment." Her glasses slid down her nose. Unconsciously, she reached up to push them back.

"Don't," he said with quiet intensity, taking them gently from her face. "You have lovely eyes." He watched her blush and was suddenly enchanted, unable to remember the last time he'd seen a woman blush.

"They're gray, like pewter. I take after my father," she said flatly.

Sensing her discomfort, he whispered, "Green-eyed blondes like Riba are plentiful in California. But a silver-eyed woman with russet hair—that's not conventional. Not conventional at all." His fingertips lightly caressed one high cheekbone, dusted with fine freckles that he was certain she detested.

Marti knew she should be affronted by this bold overture from a drifter, a man with no past and no future. Coolly she pulled away from the hypnotism of his fingertips and reached for the glasses.

He laughed lightly, a rich warm sound as he held her glasses up for inspection, well out of her grasp. "You don't need glasses at all, except for reading—and they don't have to have these ugly black frames either. You're hiding, Marti."

She yanked the glasses from his hand and stood up, clutching her sketch pad protectively to her breast. "I do *not* hide Adam Wade, not from you, not from anyone!" With that she stalked down the brushy hillside in stiff angry strides.

"Not from anyone but yourself, lady," he whispered softly after her retreating figure.

As he walked slowly down the hillside, Adam pondered the twisted relationships in the Beaumont family. Listening to the men talk, watching the flamboyance of Riba and hearing about old Joe's treatment of both daughters, Adam could imagine why Marti retreated behind drab clothes, ugly glasses and unflattering hairdos. "Joe should've stuck to making wines, not children," he muttered darkly.

Bitterly, another thought occurred to him. *Jake should have, too.* He hadn't thought of Jake in years. In fact, he'd climbed up the mountainside that morning just for some simple peace and quiet, never imagining he'd run into Marti. He'd been increasingly disturbed by watching her, even dreaming of her. He shook his head and laughed in disbelief. A Phi Beta Kappa plain Jane who shrank from his touch.

"Shit, she makes Bette Midler look like Miss America. Hardly the type you've ever favored, my man," he muttered ironically.

Marti kicked up pebbles and dodged scrub pines, descending the steep, rocky hillside in a fraction of the time it had taken her to climb it. She was almost to the back patio of the house when she heard voices—her father, Les Reams, and Boris Staritz, having one of their frequent Sunday morning business brunches, no doubt. The owner, general foreman, and winemaster often gathered to discuss plans for seasonal work assignments. Listening to them argue, Marti realized she felt peculiarly detached.

Normally, she shared in these discussions, sometimes siding with her father's conservative intuitions, sometimes with their talented and innovative young winemaster. But a reticence of spirit had plagued her all spring. Perhaps that was why she had fled this morning so early to hide on her private hillside and sketch. Her art was an expression of her innermost self, something no one but a few friends had ever appreciated or understood. *No one until Adam.* The traitorous thought arose unbidden. She squelched it.

Hearing chairs scraping and gruff farewells, Marti realized the men had adjourned. Les headed down the road, toward his nearby house while her father went indoors. But Boris was walking her way, the only one of the trio to notice her hanging back in the shadows.

"Good morning. Missed you at our meeting. Hilda was grousing about your leaving the house so early you skipped breakfast." Boris's face was surprisingly pleasant, almost handsome when he smiled, covering what she had always laughingly called his "Russian dourness."

Smiling in return, she inquired, "Did I miss something important, or was it the usual?"

He sighed and walked up to her, guiding her steps in a circuitous path down the road and around the house, as if for a private stroll. "The usual, I'm afraid. Marti, you know as well as I that if we T-grafted those blocks of Gamay we could produce some light white wines that would sell like crazy, not to mention using the Zinfandels for blush wines."

"In terms of the market demands for pop wines, I know you're right," she began carefully, "but Papa wants to produce fine reds with real backbone. Wine to lay down for years to come."

"And how many customers with money to buy wines to lay down in a cellar for ten years are going to know or care about Chateau Beaumont? They buy French and German wines! We'll go under if things keep on like Joe wants," he said with an angry gesture.

Marti smiled. "I keep our books and go over profit-and-loss statements with our accountants, Boris. We're not making what we could with all the new growing and marketing techniques you want, but we're in no danger of losing the winery."

"I'm sorry to be complaining about the same old things. It's a beautiful day and we should enjoy it. Drawing pictures again?" he asked with a grin, showing no interest in looking at her work, just glancing at the sketchpad on her arm.

"Yes, I went up the hill to watch the sunrise and do a few pencil sketches for possible water color work later on," she replied uneasily. Boris had never asked her about her hobbies. His next question really threw her.

"I'm driving over to Healdsburg this evening for dinner at the Dry Creek Inn. Would you like to go?" His black eyes glowed with anticipation and some other alien expression she could not read.

Flustered after fleeing Adam Wade's unnerving touch, the last thing she expected was a dinner invitation from Boris Staritz. "It's a long ride, Boris. I have some things I have to do first." She hesitated at his eager nod indicating that he perceived her reply as an acceptance. "Boris, if you want to discuss Riba—"

"No. That's over and done with," he interrupted, his black eyes turning wintry. He stopped walking, but smiled at her again. "Forgive me, Marti. I know everyone around here thought I was madly in love with Riba. But you and I both know she never returned my affections. The news of her pending engagement really opened my eyes . . . to a great many things." He paused now, looking at her assessingly. "I was only infatuated with her, I didn't love her. Hell, I couldn't even talk to her—not about the things I really want to talk about."

"Wine," she said with a wry smile.

"I'm afraid so," he nodded.

Marti was uncertain of what to say. "I'm flattered, Boris," she replied carefully.

"I don't intend to sweep you off your feet, Marti, and I don't mean you're my second choice. In fact, in a way I'm glad you brought Riba up so we can clear the air about her. It would never have worked between her and me."

"That doesn't automatically mean I fall to you by default, either, Boris," she reprimanded, somewhat put off by his high-handed assumption that her sole passion in life was winemaking.

"I'm bungling this badly, aren't I?" he asked earnestly. "Let's just try to be friends, Marti. Give me a chance to show you how much we have in common."

"Let me have a few days to think things over, Boris." *Maybe once Riba's home you'll change your mind.* At his look of utter dejection, she softened and added, "Maybe next weekend we could go to the dance at Meadowood. It's *de riguer,* you know, for all the wine people in the valley."

"I'll see you tomorrow at the plant then," Boris said with a resigned sigh. "But if you change your mind about tonight, call me."

Well, he isn't gilding the lily and telling me I'm beautiful or even that he appreciates my "great personality" and sense of humor, she thought as she watched him drive away.

Yet there remained a deep, persistent ache inside her, a longing to be something more than a bookkeeper and a vineyard worker. "But I'm not an enchantress, probably not even a very good artist. I can scarcely expect a grand passion. I belong here." Sighing, she turned and walked slowly into the house.

She had made it only half way up the big winding staircase when her father called her. "Oh, Martha. I have something to discuss with you."

He stood at the bottom of the steps, some papers clutched in his hands. When she descended, he thrust them at her with a big smile. "Riba will be home next Tuesday. She just called and gave me her flight number. Her new fiancé's arriving next Friday for an inspection visit. This can be a sort of welcome home and pre-engagement gift for her."

Quickly scanning the pages she saw they were a bill of sale and the registration papers for a new Porsche 911 Turbo convertible. "Quite a handsome gift," she said nonchalantly. "But do you honestly think it'll improve her grades next fall?"

Joe grinned, oblivious of Marti's quiet disapproval. He had bought her the Cadillac two years ago and she expressed no interest in even having the men wash and wax it. "I guess if I like this young lawyer and approve of his family, she can marry him. The degree isn't that big a deal."

"No, Papa, I guess it isn't," she echoed woodenly, remembering all her nights of studying to make straight A's. *Of course, I needed to get a degree. Who'd marry a brown wren like me? I have to run the winery.* "If you'll excuse me, Papa, I have to make a quick phone call."

As her father watched her run up the steps, a frown of puzzlement creased his face. Then remembering Riba's imminent homecoming, he headed to the kitchen. Hilda must plan some special meals.

As she dialed the phone, Marti sat stiffly on the edge of her bed, praying, *Please, Boris, be home.*

Riba debarked from the plane with her usual flourish, dressed in a designer suit of turquoise and lavender butcher linen. The flight stewards and male passenger's eyes followed her as she waved gaily and dashed to hug her father and sister.

All the way home she chattered about Larry and his weekend with the family. "Just wait until everyone at the country club meets him. All the women will be green," she said with a laugh. "You are coming to the dinner dance with Papa, aren't you, Marti?" she asked as an afterthought, twisting to look back at her sister, who sat in the rear seat of the big car.

"As a matter of fact, I'm going with Boris Staritz," Marti said casually. She had to smile inwardly as she caught the startled, vaguely disquieted look on her sister's face.

"Boris. How nice. Of course, you two would have so much in common."

"Of course," echoed Marti. *She has the same idea Papa had when I told him Boris asked me out.*

Joe's surprise for Riba was waiting on the front drive when they pulled up. White with black pin striping, the Porsche convertible fairly glowed, dripping with every accessory. Riba let out a squeal of adolescent delight and reached over to give her grinning father a fierce hug, then slithered out of the car to inspect her prize.

She eyed the stick shift lever on the floor in dismay. "It's not automatic," she said with a start.

Marti hid her smile behind one hand. When she had picked up the car yesterday at the dealership, she had immediately recognized what Joe had blithely overlooked. Riba had never learned to operate a standard transmission. "That's pretty much expected, little sister. If you want a high performance sports car, you have to be able to take it through the gears."

"Marti or Boris can teach you, Princess. It's not hard to learn. I never thought when I ordered it . . ." Joe began.

"Don't worry, Papa," Riba interrupted him with a big squeeze and kiss on the cheek. "Like you said, there are lots of people to teach me."

"Let's get you unpacked and settled and then you can try it out," Joe said with a smile.

They adjourned indoors and Joe instructed the elderly butler, Perkins, to call down to the bunkhouse and have a couple of the men come up and unload Miss Riba's considerable number of trunks and suitcases.

Adam and Bob Vasquez walked at a leisurely pace toward the big house. Although only midmorning, the sun was scorching in its June brilliance. They had been running the tractor, making a second pass between the vines to turn under plantain, quack grass and other weeds. It was hot, dusty work.

"So now we get to play bell boys for the glamour girl on our break time," Adam said with an aggravated sigh.

Bob looked at his tall companion. "Most of the men would love the chance to play anything with Riba. You should've left your shirt off," he added with a ribald laugh.

Adam only shrugged in indifference. Then, seeing the Porsche parked in front of the Cadillac, he gave a low whistle. "Some fancy new toy."

"Somehow I don't feature old Joe bought it for himself," Bob said wryly.

"I'd damn well bet he didn't buy anything that flashy for Marti either," Adam added. When Bob looked at him questioningly, he turned sharply toward the Cadillac where the butler was standing with the keys.

Opening the spacious trunk, Adam said, "I can see why you asked for *two* men." The whole compartment was packed like a Chinese puzzle with expensive luggage, and even more was mounded in the back seat of the car.

It took them their break time and then some to get all the gear unloaded. Both men made repeated trips up to the second floor to Riba's spacious room where Jesse the maid waited patiently to unpack. Adam admired the downstairs of the big house with its wide entry hall, high ceilings, and elegantly curving staircase. From the muted pastel greens and beiges to the soft glow from the crystal chandelier, it was tasteful and conservative, the kind of place that quietly whispered "old money."

But Riba's room, although expensively decorated, gave him a totally different feeling. The ice blues and lavenders seemed formal and cold, the ornate French Provincial furniture busy and cloying.

Absently, he wondered how Marti's room would look. Simple and rustic with rich wood grains and soft earth tones, he'd bet on it. Ruefully, he realized how his daydreaming in Riba's bedroom door must look to the frowning maid. Suddenly, on a roguish impulse, he licked his lips, winked at the startled Jesse, and sauntered out of the room.

When he left the house he could hear women's voices. Marti and Riba were standing by the white convertible. Bob had obviously walked back to the field. Adam strode down the front steps and began to turn in the same direction when Riba called to him.

"Oh, Adam. Please come here." Riba was sitting in the driver's seat with the door open.

"Want to show off your new toy?" he asked as he walked slowly toward the car.

"Not exactly." She cocked her head. A lazy, seductive smile spread over her glossed lips as she watched the way his clothes clung to his sweat dampened body and the black hair curled over the open collar of his half-buttoned shirt. "Papa bought me this beautiful car, but he forgot that I've never learned to handle a stick," she said with a wicked low laugh.

"I expect you'll do all right. I've heard you've had lots of practice," he replied with an unsmiling expression on his face.

"Not true! I've never done four-on-the-floor. I've never done anything on the floor, but you could teach me," she challenged, intent on matching his coarseness with her own. "It would be ever so much nicer than diddling around on an old . . . tractor," she flung back, daring him to pick up the cue.

"But your father hired me to diddle around on the tractor, Riba," he said with a grin in spite of himself, "not to diddle in a Porsche."

Marti observed their exchange silently, feeling for all the world like a homely high school freshman at her first dance, watching the prettiest cheerleader and the captain of the football team necking in the cloak room. She was caught off guard when Adam suddenly mentioned her name. Despite his scowling rejection of Riba's blatant invitation, he had seemed wrapped up in the beautiful woman's presence. "I . . . I beg your pardon. I wasn't listening," she responded, her cool gray eyes meeting his intent blue ones.

"I said, I bet Marti can teach you. You do know how to shift a standard transmission, don't you?" he asked with a teasing smile.

"I learned to drive the harvest trucks when I was fourteen," she replied levelly.

Riba rolled her eyes in exasperation. Adam laughed. "I always knew you were a woman of many talents, Marti."

Their eyes dueled briefly once more, then he won

a reluctant smile from her. Ignoring Riba, he winked at her and turned to walk casually down the road.

"He's certainly a hunk," Riba said as she watched his retreating figure.

"You mean he's certainly a challenge." Marti couldn't keep the tiniest hint of glee from the acerbic tone she usually employed against her sister.

Riba turned and looked at Marti as if her sister had just stepped off a shuttle from Mars. "He actually seems attracted to you. My, my, our proper little business woman now has two beaus. Whatever will you do with them?"

"If I have any questions, I'm sure you can coach me," Marti said drily. "Anyway, Adam's not—"

"He's not the type of man either of you should be bantering with," Boris interrupted pompously. He had come around the side of the house from the rear patio and had obviously been eavesdropping on the conversation.

Both women bristled at his arrogance. "You're tiresome, Boris. I'll talk to any man I please," Riba said with a scathing look at him as she slammed the car door shut and turned on the ignition. "I think I'll wing it. All I can do is strip the gears." She took off with a screeching lurch, but managed to keep the engine from dying as she struggled to shift into second.

Marti ignored her as the Porsche careened in jerks and starts down the drive. Turning furiously on Boris, she said, "You have no right to tell me who I can talk with or to eavesdrop on my conversations." Her eyes flashed silver in fury. She assured herself that she was merely angry at his presumption, not at her own reaction to Adam Wade.

The winemaster looked contrite. "I'm sorry, Marti, I didn't mean to sound stuffy. I didn't eavesdrop either. I cut across the field from the plant on my way to the house. Then I heard the three of you out here," he finished with a dark scowl.

Marti shrugged in acceptance of his poor excuse for an apology, not wanting to discuss her feelings about his proprietary airs any further.

"Wade's a drifter and a troublemaker. I can always tell the type. Maybe even a union organizer," he said.

Marti laughed at that. "Considering how my father watches for them, you can bet that's the last thing he is! As to being a troublemaker, he seems quiet and hard working. He's obviously had a formal education and knows about growing grapes. Papa said he went to Davis for a while."

Boris scowled again. "Surely your father wouldn't approve of him associating with you socially?" He thought he had played a trump card, but Marti surprised him.

"Since I'm twenty-four-years old, I think that decision is up to me, not my father—or you!" she snapped, once more annoyed with him and perversely, with Adam Wade, too. She turned toward the house and did not see Boris's narrowed eyes as he watched her angrily retreating figure.

Chapter 4

Adam bounced along in an ancient Ford pickup, headed over the picturesque beauty of the Oakville Grade that linked Napa and Sonoma Counties. Given the narrow, head-on treachery of the road and the rickety condition of the rusted-out truck, he concentrated on driving, but idly wondered why that sour-faced winemaster Staritz had chosen him for this chore. When he had gone to the fields that morning, Les Reams had sent him over to the plant. The fancy lab coats had some new white oak barrels made at a small cooperage in Healdsburg. They were due to be picked up immediately by special order of the winemaster.

"First I'm a bell hop and would-be driving instructor for Riba, now a delivery boy for Staritz. Shit!" he muttered to himself, pumping the low brake pedal carefully as he rounded a curve on a steep hillside. The Mayacamas were really foothills, not mountains, but in the morning fog, as he met farm trucks and carloads of tourists who paid more attention to the scenery than their driving, Adam wished he had a more roadworthy vehicle. Les employed a mechanic, supposedly to keep all the heavy machinery and trucks in working order, but Adam felt certain this old rust bucket was low on the man's list of priorities.

It took him the better part of two hours to coax the truck to the small cooperage firm on the outskirts of Healdsburg. He and a strapping youth from Kentucky loaded the sixty-gallon barrels onto the truck bed and tied them carefully with new rope.

"Yore rope's in a tetch better shape 'n yore truck,"

the boy volunteered with a grin as his big hamlike hands finished the lashing job.

"No lie there," Adam replied easily. Having already signed for the delivery, he swung up in the cab with a word of thanks to the boy and took off. He made good time on Highway 101 south of Healdsburg, but when he turned off Highway 12 north of Sonoma onto the Oakville Grade again, his pace once more slowed to a crawl. Now loaded down with the weight of the barrels, he trusted the brakes even less on steep inclines and sharp turns. At several stop signs in Santa Rosa he had really had to struggle to keep from rolling into the intersections.

As he crested a steep hill, Adam was suddenly confronted by a large gray sedan coming straight at him—on his side of the narrow road! He hit the horn, tapped the brakes and turned the wheel all at once, acting in lightening reflex, but even as he did so, the sedan continued to come at him head on. The road took a sickening curve to the left with a sharp rocky drop off on the right-hand side, which had instantaneously become his only option to a head on collision.

He made a split second judgment to clear the oncoming sedan on its passenger side. The wheel fought him as he used every ounce of strength he possessed to steer the wildly careening truck into the opposite lane without kissing the rocky wall of the hill at the left side of the narrow shelf of the road. Sweat popped out on his face, his breathing came in leaden gasps and split seconds felt like hours. The whole scenario played in seeming slow motion as he avoided the sedan by the width of a coat of paint. It vanished around the curve while he tried in vain to right the truck as it ran full tilt down the wickedly curving hill.

Luckily, there were no other cars in sight. It took him several wild S-curve turns to maneuver back onto the right side of the road. But that solved only one problem. By the time he had the truck under control he had rolled through the steep ravine and up another hill. Now as he tromped and pumped on the brakes he was cresting the rise—and it was distressingly evident that whatever braking power the truck once possessed had now evaporated. The momentum of the heavily laden pickup sent him down the hill like a runaway stagecoach in a B western.

Jesus, this is the place where the hero jumps clear and rolls into the grass, then gets up and brushes himself off. Sharp rocks and steep, hard packed earth studded with clumps of mesquite and scrub pine flashed by. *Even Clint Eastwood would go splat if he jumped out of this goddamn thing now!*

Adam swore every oath he could think of with startling rapidity and inventiveness as he looked ahead, trying to remember if the hellish road had any level, grassy places where he could pull the truck off and bank it to a gradual stop. Cresting the next hill he finally got what looked like his best and only shot—a shallow creek bed at the end of a low, bumpy meadow. By this time he had flown past three oncoming cars. "Thank God not everybody in Sonoma County drives like a fucking Englishman!" he muttered.

Still, no more pushing his luck, waiting for a better place. If he lost control on a curve, he could hit a carload of innocent people. He knew he could never handle that—if he were lucky enough to live through it! Gritting his teeth, he took the truck over the shoulder toward the stream, praying it wouldn't flip over. It didn't. But the ride was rough enough to delight an avaricious orthodontist. Every tooth in his mouth must have been loosened as the Ford bounced over the uneven ground.

As he neared the shallow stream, the grade leveled off and the truck began to lose momentum. Aiming the grill for what he hoped was a springy copse of willows by the bank, he braced himself for the crash.

Suddenly it was over. A whooshing impact, the hiss of a broken radiator, but no screaming twist of smashed metal. Miraculously, the windshield wasn't even broken! The young green shoots growing at the edge of the stream were indeed his salvation. They and the soft ground had cushioned the impact. If he'd gone into one of those jagged shale outcroppings . . . he could well envision the difference.

He took inventory of his body. Every inch of him ached as if he'd been beaten with a crow-bar, but nothing was broken, cut or bleeding.

Adam climbed from the cab slowly and felt his boots sink into the cool soft mud. Never in his life had he so appreciated mud. Looking back at his cargo, he had to grin. That kid was right about the rope. It had held. Not a single white oak barrel appeared to be damaged. Unfortunately, the truck might even be salvageable, but that was up to Beaumont's mechanic.

"Look, Mr. Reams, I never got time to check the brakes on that truck," Nate Benteen said with a surly glance at Adam. "I only hired on here last week. Lots of them old trucks and tractors need fixing," he added defensively. The small mechanic stood in a greasy jumpsuit that had once been striped denim but was so filthy it was unidentifiable.

Looking around the cluttered room with benches full of tools dumped out in random array, Adam wondered how Benteen could even find a wrench, much less repair anything. "I was almost killed because of faulty equipment, Nate. I'd take it as a personal favor if you'd check that truck as soon as it's towed back here."

Les reached up and put a fatherly arm around Adam's shoulders. "Lucky thing you're alive, son. That gray car had a little to do with the accident, too. Sure you can't identify it?"

Adam shrugged. "No, just a late model light gray four-door. Considering everything, I didn't have much chance to jot down the license number. I couldn't even see the driver inside."

"Probably some fool kid out on a joy ride with his daddy's good car," Nate put in with a low laugh that grated on Adam's frayed nerves.

Feeling Adam stiffen, Les said, "You had a hell of a day, Wade. Lucky to hitch a ride back here with that farmer. We got plenty boys to unload Boris's precious barrels when they tow the Ford back. Why don't you take the rest of the afternoon off—with pay?"

"Sounds good," Adam replied with a nod of thanks. Then turning to Benteen, he added, "Don't work overtime to salvage that rust bucket."

Les chuckled and waved Adam off. "Don't let Joe hear you say that. He's still got trucks running that his daddy bought!"

After taking a hot shower and shaving in the concrete block building that served as the hired men's washroom, Adam felt much better. Feeling reasonably calm after his narrow brush with death, he mulled over how to spend the rare afternoon of freedom it had earned him.

Marti's austere face flashed into his mind as it often had over the weeks past. What was it about her? Some illusive quality beneath her dowdy façade drew him to her. He shrugged ruefully as he put on a clean shirt and tucked it into his jeans. Maybe Alice Marchanti, Marti's art gallery friend, could give him some clues. On impulse, Adam decided to borrow Bob Vasquez's car and take a ride into Napa.

The gallery was easy enough to find, located on a small side street just off Jefferson in a neat row of newly refurbished store fronts. A charming boutique was on one side of it and a brilliantly arrayed flower shop on the other. *I wonder if anyone ever bought Marti flowers,* he thought idly as he parked Bob's old Chevy.

He could well imagine her sister being deluged with long-stemmed, blood-red roses from a horde of admiring suitors like the pedigreed eastern attorney who was arriving tomorrow for Joe's inspection. "They probably deserve each other," he muttered sourly as he opened the glass door to the gallery.

The interior was surprisingly spacious. Skylights and large picture windows at the rear provided the illusion of California sunshine brought indoors. Shiny scheffleras and lacy ferns, no doubt from the adjacent florist, added to the feeling of airy openness. But the art work was the real key to the atmosphere. Every selection on the muted white walls was delicate, light and natural. The gallery owner obviously favored water colors as a medium and landscapes as a subject.

Adam was deep in concentration, staring at a lovely rendering of a coastal sunset, when a gravelly female voice from behind him interrupted cheerfully, "Some of my critics would say it's pure California, all light and no substance."

He turned to stare at a small plump woman with curly yellow hair and a Joan Blondell face. Her Jersey accent seemed to fit with the loose, paint-smeared smock, tight white chinos and high heeled wedgies she wore. "You must be Alice, Marti's friend," he said, stretching out his hand.

She shook it with a frankly curious expression on her face. "Funny, you don't look like her type. Not exactly country club. You a grower?"

He smiled at her forthright assessment. "Let's just say I toil in the vineyards. And you're right, I'm not her type."

She shrugged in good-natured defeat and grinned. "All right, neither am I. But I do know real talent when I see it."

"Marti has that. I've watched her sketch. She mentioned one water color that she entered in the art fair. I believe you're displaying it—"

"Budbreak," Alice interrupted. "Yeah, it's one of her best. I call it the marriage between her two passions, art and viniculture."

"There are those who consider viniculture an art, too," he said in a teasing tone as he followed her across the room to view the watercolor.

"Spoken like one of Joe Beaumont's loyal employees. You do work for him, don't you?" She asked although she already suspected the answer.

"I work for him," he said noncommittally as he stopped in front of the large picture. He stood transfixed by its delicate beauty. "I've never seen so many shades of green in any treatment but an oil of the Northwest rain forests. This is so much more light and alive . . . exquisite." Almost as an afterthought, he added in a low voice, as if speaking to himself, "Spring, the rebirth of life, a chance to begin again."

Alice suddenly felt like an intruder, a rare emotion for a brassy kid from Hoboken. She studied his profile. *Definitely not the type to be interested in Marti. Any man with his looks would naturally head for the sister.* But then she considered his genuine appreciation of art and obvious involvement with the vineyard. "Look, Mr.—say I didn't ask your name."

"Wade—Adam Wade. I hired on over a month ago as a field laborer." There was no hint of apology in his voice.

"Well, I'll be blunt, Adam. Marti is a special friend. When I first moved out here and started this gallery, business wasn't exactly booming. In fact, I almost lost my shirt. Then this high-society type walks in here and takes a look around. Says she's Joe Beaumont's daughter. Next thing I know she's bringing in half the art colony from around the valley to exhibit their best work and half the country club set from Meadowood to buy it. It must've been three months before she got up the nerve to show me some of her own work—just sketches and chalk pastels then."

Before she could continue, he interrupted gently, "And you wonder how a down-at-the-heels drifter like me has the nerve to eye-up the boss's daughter?"

She let out a hearty laugh. "Well, you're as direct as me. That's a good sign." She studied his face as if trying to read what lay beyond it. "Who are you, Adam Wade?"

"Like you said, just a drifter."

"No, *you* said it. I think there's more to you than that. Every good looking young stud who works for Beaumont makes a play for Riba, not Marti."

"And Riba usually plays back," he supplied as he turned once more to stare at the painting. Dismissing Riba, and any discussion of himself, he changed the subject. "Do you have any other of Marti's water colors?"

"Two right now, and a few pastels. Her work really sells. She makes a fortune for the art fair every year—

it all goes to charity, you know, same as the wine auction."

He turned to her and smiled. "See, just like I said, wine and painting go together."

"You and Marti may have more in common than I thought," Alice replied as they walked over to another display screen.

"Tell me about her. Why does someone with her artistic talent donate her work to charity and then slave in the vineyards like one of her father's hired men?"

"Why does a man with your looks and obvious education drift from job to job, slaving for men like Joe Beaumont?" she countered shrewdly. "At least she'll inherit the family business."

"Touché," he replied with a fleeting trace of pain quickly veiled in his dark blue eyes.

"Okay. That wasn't fair. I'm just protective of my friends," she replied in apology.

"And Marti needs protection?"

"You've met Riba," she said in explanation.

"I work for Joe and I wear pants—how could I miss? She gets all the attention and Marti does all the work. But Marti doesn't have to stay. She could leave," he replied reasonably.

"She could, but she figures the old man needs her. Anyway, Riba's getting married and going back east to live, permanently from what I hear," Alice said with obvious contempt in her voice.

"Marti doesn't need to worry about competition from Riba," he replied obliquely. "It's been a pleasure, Alice. I have to run. I suddenly remembered an appointment I have down the street."

Alice Marchanti watched him drive off in a battered old Chevy, wondering what his interest was in Marti. For the past two years she had hoped Marti would meet someone interesting, and if Adam Wade wasn't interesting, she wasn't from Jersey! *Closed-mouthed as hell about his past, though,* she thought with a worried frown.

While Alice stewed, Adam made a quick trip to the

bank where he withdrew over a month's pay. Then he headed to Craig Williamsons, the best men's shop in Napa.

The feel of a dress shirt and dinner jacket brought back memories and a sharp twist to his guts. *Still a perfect 41 long,* he thought wryly as the tailor fussed with the lapels. By the time he finished making his selections, a combination of impeccable taste and a wad of money had changed the dubious look on the clerk's face to one of decided respect.

Meadowood was as impressive as a travel agent's five-star dream, a chalet-type structure of pastel gray and white, with gingerbread trim. Shaded by magnificent towering evergreens and kissed by weeping willows, it seemed to stretch in every direction, like a beautiful three dimensional patchwork quilt with decks, stairs and French doors at every angle. The grounds were as manicured and verdant as a fine block of lovingly cultivated Cabernet fields. Home of the prestigious Valley Wine Auction, it was a conference center for businessmen from Tokyo to Wall Street.

Marti looked around the Vintner Room, its understated elegance such an integral part of her life that she was unaware of the ornate sterling table settings, monogrammed peach and gold china, or even the magnificent floral sprays that graced each table. The gathering was an annual affair with only the oldest and most distinguished of North Coast society invited.

Joe Beaumont also found it an excellent place to put Riba's new fiancé on display for all the right people. The gala party with a small band and seven-course dinner delighted Riba. She had always favored the posh country club where an old monied name such as the Beaumont's commanded meticulous respect.

Marti served on the committee that had made all the arrangements. *What a great social secretary I'll make for Riba when she becomes first lady,* she thought wryly as she watched Larry dance with her sister.

Lawrence Smythe Cameron was of medium height,

clean cut to the point of Ivy League O.D., with a close-cropped hundred dollar haircut and an impeccably tailored Oleg Cassini suit. Blond and athletic with symmetrical if unexciting features, he looked bright, ambitious and earnest. Just the right balance for a politician, she considered judiciously, except for the pronounced absence of a sense of humor.

Riba acted her part to perfection. Dressed in a simple lilac chiffon gown that looked both chic and youthful, she danced and chattered with artless grace and complete decorum. Having seen her sister in frequent performances that would have put the most enthusiastic exotic dancers in San Francisco to shame, Marti had to admire the role Riba was playing tonight.

"Maybe, Larry Cameron, you'll finally help her straighten herself out," she said in a voice so low no one around her could hear. *Am I glad she's finally going to be out of my life? Out of Papa's?* It was a disloyal thought and Marti quashed it, turning to watch her father in animated conversation with several other vintners.

"So pensive, Marti. Here I've brought you some sparkling wine—Kornell, of course." Boris handed her a tulip glass half filled with the palest golden bubbles.

She was grateful that he was her escort tonight. She disliked his pomposity and possessiveness, but at least with Boris she was comfortable. They had gone to a concert at the Mondavi Winery and planned to attend the wine auction together next week.

As they exchanged small talk, Marti's eyes scanned the room, festive and filled with glittering, beautiful women and expensively dressed men. Suddenly, she sensed a tension in Boris as a scowl darkened his face. Following the course of his angry stare, she was stunned. Strolling confidently into the room was Adam Wade!

"What the hell is he doing here?" Boris ground out with surprising venom.

Marti, too, was taken aback at the man's nerve, but Boris's vehemence startled her almost as much as Adam's appearance. The drifter was dressed in a white dinner jacket that fitted with the unmistakable stamp of custom tailoring. He wore the elegant evening clothes as effortlessly as Larry Cameron. "All he needs is a Cartier watch," she murmured.

Her voice must have betrayed the amazement and admiration she felt, for Boris turned his black-eyed glare from the uninvited guest to her. "I'm shocked any sensible merchant would give him credit for a suit, let alone accessorize it," he snapped.

"Maybe he didn't buy it. He might've rolled the maître d'." Why couldn't she resist teasing? She knew Boris's sense of humor was on a par with that of her college room-mate's Afghan hound. So was his disposition when he was crossed. And he definitely had that air about him now. Marti placed a restraining hand on his arm as he began to rise from their table. "Boris, please, don't make a scene and embarrass Papa," she said earnestly.

"Wade's a common field laborer," Boris reiterated through clenched teeth, but mercifully he sat down again.

Dressed as he was, Adam looked anything but common to Marti. She forced her attention away from his swarthy elegance to concentrate on the seething man at her side. "Perhaps he was having dinner in the Starmont with some friends and just stopped in out of curiosity," she said placatingly.

Just then Jim Ames and Sam Brian, winemasters from two other large wineries, came toward their table and the conversation quickly turned to a technical discussion of new fermentation techniques for Chardonnay. Surreptitiously, Marti watched Adam sip a drink and mingle with the crowd. *He fits perfectly,* she realized at once. When Lori Morris, the beautiful daughter of the valley's largest horse breeder, took his arm and headed to the dance floor, Marti wondered how he must be passing himself off to gain such easy acceptance, a stranger in this closed society.

Riba and Larry came over to the table with Joe. As her father introduced her fiancé, Riba whispered to Marti, "I need your help in the powder room. My skirt caught on my heel when I was sitting outside. I'm afraid I ripped the hem."

Making their excuses, the two sisters headed toward the ladies room. Adam watched their progress from across the floor. *The preening peacock and the ugly duckling,* he mused to himself. Riba's lilac vibrance made Marti's taupe paisley look like jungle fatigues by comparison. He had noticed Riba's eyes on him earlier, but had expected that. It was her sister's reaction that interested him, however. A strange stirring of predatory satisfaction came over him when he first caught sight of her astonished face. But she sat with that damned Russian and he knew it would be worth his job to approach her until she was free of him. *What asinine game am I playing anyway? If I had an ounce of sense, I'd get in Bob's car and head back to the bunkhouse.*

But he knew he would do nothing of the kind. Something about Marti Beaumont, her hidden beauty, her ladylike grace, her acerbic wit and paradoxical shyness all fascinated him. She drew him inevitably towards a world he had walked away from seven years ago. For a moment he stared at the door through which the sisters had vanished. Excusing himself from the group of growers with whom he'd been talking, he headed out to the deck for a breath of air.

"Did you feast your eyes on our mystery guest?" Riba whispered as soon as the men at the table were out of earshot. "From sweaty brasero to GQ model."

"I can't imagine why he's here," Marti said darkly, not liking the glow in her sister's jade eyes.

"Who cares? He is and he looks good enough to eat! And this *is* a banquet, after all," Riba added with a wicked, silky laugh.

"You're here with the man you plan to marry, Riba, for God's sake! What will Larry say if you start slathering over Adam Wade?"

"That's why I made up the story about my dress—to get away from Larry." Riba looked at the warning flash of censure in Marti's eyes. "Now don't panic. I'm not going to drag him off in the bushes and rape him."

She considered for a moment. "At least not now. I'm just curious. I want to talk to him without having to make awkward introductions. I'll find a way."

"Yes, you always do," Marti replied bleakly, *or you find someone else to get your way for you.*

They exited by one door and Riba headed to another on the opposite side of the crowded room after instructing her sister. "Wait on the patio for a few minutes and then rejoin the men. Tell them I won't be long." She was gone before Marti could do more than open her mouth in protest.

Shrugging in defeat, Marti realized how useless it was to argue. Riba would only create a scene and then go crying to Papa, who would doubtless blame *her.* "I hope he fires you, Adam Wade," she gritted as she opened a French door and walked onto one of the many decks that graced the immense clubhouse. The night air was cool and crisp, pleasant after the press of the crowd.

"Here I was wondering how to run down my quarry and voila, she appears as if we had arranged the tryst," an all-too-familiar voice interrupted.

Marti whirled and gasped like a pinched schoolgirl. Adam was lounging against the wall behind the door, grinning as he eased away from the rough shingles and reached out to take her hand before she had the presence of mind to jerk it away.

"The music's playing. Dance with me." Before she could react, she was in his arms on the deserted deck.

Chapter 5

Marti was alternately numb, then keenly aware of his body pressed intimately against her own. She shivered and she tingled, but she could not for the life of her break away. When he reached up, took off her glasses and slipped them into his pocket, she didn't even protest.

"Such exquisite eyes, as silver as the moonlight," he murmured in perfect cadence with the music.

Imagining Boris saying anything so romantic, she chuckled, breaking the terrible tension that had held her captive.

"I don't usually evoke laughter from a lady when I get her in my arms in the moonlight," he said half-aggravated, half-curious in spite of his slightly wounded male vanity.

"I was just thinking of what Boris would say about my eyes. Perhaps that they had the gray sheen of powdery mildew on Chenin Blanc grapes!"

Adam threw back his head and laughed, then sobered and took her chin in one hand. "I hope you're not taking his 'courtship' seriously. All he wants is your father's winery, Marti."

"Why, of course," she said stiffly, trying to pull free of his embrace. "A plain old maid has to use any dowry she can to land a man."

"Only if she's plain and only if she wants to settle for a man like Staritz," he said in a velvety voice. "You're not plain, Marti." As he spoke, his fingertips traced a delicate pattern on her brow, cheek, jawline, throat. Then as she closed her eyes and once more relaxed in his arms, he reached back and began to unfasten the tightly coiled chignon. Thick, silky ripples of dark hair fell down her back when he had finished the job with gentle thoroughness. Tossing the pins and wire doughnut over the veranda, he ran his fingers like a comb through her hair, loosening it and pulling coils of it over her shoulders to frame her face.

Marti felt her heart stop beating for a moment as she opened her eyes and looked up at him. Then her blood began to thrum furiously as she watched him slowly lower his mouth to kiss her. He did so with utmost, exquisite gentleness, as if she might break. His lips were firm and warm, persuasive as they worked havoc on her senses, softly nibbling at the corners of her mouth, brushing her eyelashes, trailing down her cheekbones to her throat.

One hand pressed into her spine, holding her tightly against him. Adam could feel her heartbeat accelerate. With his other hand he tipped her jaw back slowly and let his mouth roam over her bared throat to the fluttering pulse just above her collarbone.

"You smell like orange blossoms," he whispered against her skin as his mouth traveled upward again to meet hers. This time he centered his lips over hers and pressed, then teased, letting his tongue glide around the edges of her mouth until she opened for him and he savoringly entered, slowly, waiting to be invited.

Marti held tightly to Adam, feeling like an awkward schoolgirl, but at the same time, like the most desirable woman in the world. It was marvelous; it was shocking. She felt the warm, insinuating insistence of his tongue gliding around hers, drawing her to emulate his actions as he deepened the kiss. When she responded, arching against him, kissing him back, she could hear the ragged, low moan that vibrated deep in his throat. Gradually, he slowed and softened their passion. The deep, probing kiss ended with soft nips and love bites, but still he held her trembling against him as he buried his face in the cloud of her hair.

She could feel the hardening of her breasts as they ached and swelled, pressed tightly to his chest. Her whole body felt drugged, weak and yet possessed of a strange, fierce need that had been awakened from a lifetime of dormant sleep.

As if reading her thoughts, he tilted back her head, looked into her eyes and whispered, "Budbreak. You've discovered some new feelings, haven't you, Marti?"

"I . . . I don't know what I feel, Adam. I'm confused . . . and a little frightened," she said very softly.

He smiled. "Only a little frightened? I've been around considerably more than you, and I'm scared to death. What mysterious quality do you possess?"

Marti disengaged herself shakily and walked over to the railing. Holding onto it she raised her head and took a deep breath. Riba's words about a practical liaison with Boris came back to haunt her. *Does Adam want me for the winery, too?* "Whatever quality you speak of, it obviously isn't my drop-dead good looks."

"Only because you won't let yourself *be* yourself," he said in exasperation. He stepped up behind her, not touching her but standing so close he knew she could feel his body heat in the cool night air. "Turn around," he commanded, his voice steel clothed with velvet.

Against her will she obeyed, angry with his presumption yet daring him by facing those mesmerizing blue eyes. His gaze moved from her face down her body as he stepped back a pace for a thorough, silent inspection. "Anyone under the age of sixty, moving in your social circles who would dress like this is deliberately masquerading." He reached his right hand up and took the limp lapel of her paisley dress in one hand, then dropped it in disgust. "I've seen you in jeans and T shirts. I know how you're put together." He paused a beat to enjoy her blush. "This is the sort of stuff they cover visiting room furniture with at nursing homes."

"What do you expect me to do? Go around in skin-tight leotards and spike heels?" Marti knew that the sarcasm was lame. She was blushing and hated herself for it.

"Buy some new clothes, create your own style. You don't have to copy Riba. You have a lot more class. You're a Phi Beta Kappa. You figure it out. Soft things that cling to your body." He illustrated by running his hand down her shoulder, brushing her breast lightly, curving into her waist and down the flair of one slender hip. "Clear warm earth colors—gold and orange like the vineyards at autumn frost, to bring out the russet tones in your hair, rich greens to complement the beauty of your complexion. And, please," he bent down and kissed the tip of her nose lightly, "some high heels to show off those long legs."

She felt oddly drawn to confess to him, beginning hesitantly, "When we were children . . . I was always tall for my age—all gangly with long arms and legs, hands and feet too big for the rest of me." She gave him a rueful smile, her composure once more in place. "And Riba . . . Riba was dainty and perfect."

"Forget Riba, just concentrate on Marti. You're all grown up now and some kind of lady—business woman, artist. I met your friend Alice the other day and saw your work on display."

Her eyes widened in surprise. "What's the verdict? Does 'Budbreak' live up to the promise of the sketch?"

"More than. Alice thinks you should win first prize at the art fair. So do I." He moved closer again and took a lock of hair, pulling her into his arms.

She put her hands up against his chest, running her fingers along the lapels of his jacket. "You wear these clothes as if you were born to them. How did you get in to a grower's private party?"

He grinned. "Just walked in, after a discreet inquiry in the Fairway as to where the Vintner Room was located. Told your father's friends I'm an attorney for a big New York negotiant with offices in Sausalito."

She looked at him warily. "You *could* pull it off, especially dressed like this. But why? Why spend all that money for clothes just to come here? I suspect you already know how the other half lives."

At that sally his face became shuttered, but he did

not let her go. "Maybe I do, but that's not important now. I came because I knew you'd be here." He looked past her shoulder at the swaying willow trees ringing the lush, manicured grounds, his eyes dark and fathomless. "Hell, Marti, don't ask me to explain it. I just wanted to."

Suddenly she remembered Riba and her ploy to look for Adam. Boris and her father were probably looking for *her* by now! "I have to go in."

"Afraid to be seen with the hired help? Boris wouldn't approve. I know you came with him," he said with a hint of anger in his voice.

"Boris is a friend, nothing more, but I did come with him—"

"And it's rude for a lady to leave her escort," he interrupted, his good humor abruptly restored. He reached in his pocket to return her glasses.

Just then the door on the opposite side of the deck opened and Boris stormed out as if conjured up by their conversation. "Marti—everyone's been looking for you," he said with a menacing tone as he took in her long hair, glowing like a cape around her shoulders. She stood far too close to Adam Wade. Wade looked far too possessive and arrogant for Staritz's taste.

"You aren't a guest here, Wade. If you want to keep your job, I suggest you leave at once."

Adam didn't move. "This deck is a public place. A man can have dinner in the Starmont if he can afford the price—and the fees of Acme Rent-a-Suit." He smiled caustically, running his thumbs under the length of his jacket lapels.

Turning to Marti, who was struggling to suppress a laugh, he said quietly, "Sorry for stepping in on your private bash." Ignoring Boris he handed her the glasses but closed her fingers around them and whispered, "Put them in your handbag." With that he gave her a wink and walked past the stiff, angry figure of the winemaster as if he were invisible.

"I'm going to speak to Joe about him. He's a troublemaker," Boris said as he walked over to Marti.

"No! That is, he did nothing so terrible, just walked in on the party for a few minutes. Papa thinks he's a good worker. So do I," she added defiantly.

"What did he do to you?" he asked harshly, taking her hair in his blunt fingers and splaying it outward like a fan.

She shook it free from his touch, instantly realizing how much she would dislike his hands on her, traveling the paths Adam's hands had. "He did nothing I didn't *allow* him to do," she said boldly, walking past him with her head held high. "Please make my excuses, Boris. I have to go to the Ladies Room to do something with this hair."

He stood brooding on the deck, watching her move with surprising grace as the long silken curtain of dark hair swayed with every step. *Wade unpinned her hair, touched her and took liberties I could never dare! The bastard,* he thought in helpless, furious frustration.

His immediate impulse was to go to Joe and tell him what he'd seen, but although it would likely guarantee Wade's discharge, it would also assure Marti's enmity. And Boris did not want that, not at all. Riba had been right about him and Marti. They were a natural pair. Unlike her cheating slut of a sister, Marti loved the winery and was devoted to Joe. If only he could turn that loyalty and energy in his direction, he would have everything he ever dreamed of possessing. Of course, there was the matter of that pretty boy Wade to deal with, but a harsh smile etched itself across Staritz's coarse, angular features. He had watched dozens of drifters like Wade come and go over his years in the wine business. He would handle Wade when the time came.

But Marti, now she was a far more prickly problem, the total opposite of Riba in every way. He needed an entirely new game plan for handling Marti. She was a strong-willed woman for all her lack of sophistication. Odd, he'd always thought her plain, but somehow, tonight . . . Dismissing that as an illusion of the moonlight, he retraced his steps to the party. Her looks were immaterial—as insignificant as the drifter.

He would deal with both Marti and the field hand, but first he had to make a few critical reassessments.

"I'm going down to the pool for a dip. Want to join me or do you have too much work to do?" Riba inquired.

Standing in the back of the long hallway near the rear door of the house, she looked over at Marti who was clad in jeans and T shirt, as usual, with her braided hair hanging down her back in a fat plait.

"Thanks for the invite, but I do have some letters to get out before I meet Papa. We're going to walk the new block of Zinfandel we put in last year," Marti replied with a smile.

"Lord, I'd forgotten how boring this place can be. Now that Larry's left, all I have to do is work on my tan. Bridal white with a golden complexion," she said in martyred resignation and turned toward the back door. Her pink terry beach robe barely came to mid thigh. Marti watched the gleaming curvy legs move with feline grace. Riba's toenails were painted the exact shade of the robe. *Everything about her is coordinated,* Marti thought with a flash of irritation.

Sitting at the big desk in the library with the window open, Marti took off her glasses and rubbed her eyes. She had been doing books for over an hour, listening to the thunk and whoosh of the spring board as Riba made repeated dives into their backyard pool. The splashes sounded inviting. It was hot, nearly noon and she had been up late last night. Still, the prospect of donning her dingy old one piece suit and knotting her hair up to keep it from tangling in the water did not appeal to her.

No, be honest. You don't want to challenge your sister to a swim suit competition, she admitted. Marti's ambivalent feelings about Riba had blossomed into a full-fledged preoccupation ever since Adam Wade had arrived.

She closed her eyes and once more envisioned the look on Riba's face last night. When she had returned to the Vintner Room with her face flushed and her hair in a haphazard twist atop her head, Marti knew her sister was aware of how she had become so tousled. Even with a rich, attractive fiancé in tow, Riba wanted Adam as a diversion.

Everything's a game to her. She plays with people's lives. Was it Adam for whom she feared, or Riba, who could lose Larry if discovered—or did she fear for herself, fear that Riba would take Adam away from her?

Shaking her head, she plopped the bookkeeping ledger closed and stood up. "I'll just get my sketch pad and some pencils and head for my hill," she muttered aloud in the empty room.

Just then she heard Max directing someone towards the office. A familiar masculine voice thanked the butler. Idiotically, she smoothed her wrinkled shirt and started to pull her glasses off, then caught herself and pushed them back on her nose defiantly. *I'm acting like a high school kid with a crush,* she chided herself. Taking a deep breath she strode to the door and stepped into the hall.

"What can I do for you, Adam?" The look he gave her, innocent enough to any casual observer, still made her blush. *Damn! Everything I say to him turns on me!*

"Unfortunately, right now you can't do anything for me," he replied with a lazy grin. "Your dad ran across me near the new Zinfandel block and asked me to come remind you you're late for an appointment." Watching her defensive air of bravado, he thought, *Damned, if I don't shake her up.* If only he could elicit a more positive response.

Marti glanced at her watch. It was nearly two! "Oh, God, I promised Papa I'd meet him almost an hour ago, but I got bogged down with accounting ledgers."

"You work too hard," he said, "and you don't take advice, even when it's for your own good." The blue eyes fastened accusingly on the glasses. "Does Boris think they flatter you?"

"That's none of your business," she replied in affront. *As if Boris would ever notice.* "I was totaling up columns of figures. You wouldn't want me to get eye strain, now would you?" She forced herself to sound casual, the way Riba would.

"But you're finished with books now," he countered reasonably, taking a step closer to her. What was it about her that made his hands itch to caress her face.

As he reached up and removed her glasses, she found her eyes staring at the open collar of his soft cotton work shirt. A thick tuft of curly black hair was visible above it. She could see the sweat droplets beading on his throat and running down until they caught in his chest hair. She fought the urge to reach up and touch the damp shirt front.

"You'll have to excuse my appearance, but I was stapling trellis wires in the hot sun when I was told to fetch you."

"That kind of work does make a man sweat," Riba interrupted from the back doorway. Her green eyes swept Adam's tall lean body, traveling from his thatch of straight black hair to the wear-thinned shirt that spread tightly across his broad shoulders, then down past his narrow waist. Her glance lingered on his hips and long legs. The sweat dampened, soft clothes clung to his body. Licking her lips with a tongue as pink as the robe that carelessly trailed from her hand, she purred, "Why, you're almost as wet as I am."

Now it was his turn to stare at Riba. Her golden curves were barely contained in an almost translucent French bikini with a white and fuchsia splashed pattern that highlighted her magnificent tan. Shaking her wet curly hair back from her face, she smiled at his frank assessment.

"You look hot, Adam. The water in our pool would be soothing. Want to go for a plunge?" The tip of that tongue darted out again as she glanced from Adam to the frozen Marti.

"I don't think your father would want the hired help polluting his fancy swimming pool, especially when I'm being paid to work," he replied, looking from Riba to Marti. "What do you think, Boss Lady?"

"You're right about taking off work. As to contaminating our pool, I doubt Papa'd be concerned about that," she said smoothly. A sudden surge of fury at Riba's crude invitation had brought her out of her trance.

He shrugged good naturedly at the dripping blonde. "You'd better dry off and get dressed. Although I doubt you'll ever be cold, you are staining the carpet." He looked over at Marti's angry, flushed face. Her eyes glowed with an unholy silver light. "I'll walk you down to the field where your papa's waiting," he dared her.

"Why not," she shrugged and walked stiffly down the hall without a word to Riba.

"Does she embarrass you like that often, or do I seem to bring out the worst in her?" he asked Marti as they strolled down the road.

The walk allowed her to work off some of her furious anger. She looked up at him, realizing he had done nothing to initiate that confrontation. "Don't feel special. She acts that way with every attractive man she meets."

"I take it good old Larry hasn't cramped her style any?"

"I don't think she'll ever—why on earth am I discussing my sister with a virtual stranger?" she interrupted herself in sudden consternation.

"Forget Riba. You said your father wouldn't care if a field hand swam in his pool—on his own time, that is. Are you as democratic, Marti? Would you go to dinner with me? Say, Friday night at the Old Adobe in Napa. Not much on atmosphere, but the food's sensational." His smile was hypnotic. "Unless you and Boris—"

"No, Boris has no claim on me, despite what he may think." She paused to consider her answer. Every instinct told her this attraction between them was crazy and she would be mad to encourage him. But, walking down the road with the warm sun on their backs, feeling the tingle of disquiet his presence always engendered, she knew what her answer would be.

"I guess I'm more democratic than I thought. The

Old Adobe sounds like fun," she said with a dazzling smile lighting up her face.

"Alice, I'm going shopping. And I want you to help me choose a new wardrobe."

Alice Marchanti looked up at her friend in frank amazement. "Not that it isn't long overdue, but what's brought about this sudden change of heart?" Her hazel eyes had a decidedly knowing twinkle as she stepped from behind the counter and shrugged off her smock. "It wouldn't have something to do with that gorgeous stud who came here to admire your work last week, would it?"

Marti's eyes, too, had a gleam in them. "What if I said it was because of that surprising speech by Boris I told you about?"

"Bullshit," Alice shot back cheerfully. "Boris wouldn't notice if you wore one of those burlap bags they ship wine corks in."

Both women laughed, but then Marti sighed. "I'm afraid you're right. Boris just doesn't make me feel . . ." Her voice trailed off for lack of words.

"You mean he isn't Adam Wade?" Alice supplied.

"That's just it. Why would a man like Adam want me—unless it's because of my father's winery," Marti said, her teeth worrying her lower lip nervously.

Alice snorted. "I'd sooner accuse that pompous winemaster of wanting your winery. No, I'm a fair judge of people and I'd say Adam Wade sees the real Marti Beaumont. Your sister never turned his head, did she?"

"Not that she hasn't tried," Marti agreed darkly. "But I'm still not sure. After all, Riba's engaged now and I'm the 'heiress' spinster left on the shelf."

"Only if you value yourself so little you believe that. Marti, you're looking at a gal who's been knocked through the ropes of romance a time or two. Speaking from experience, kiddo, don't let this kind of a gift from the gods slip away. Grab the gusto." She let out a hearty laugh, reached for her handbag and hung the "Shop Closed" sign on the front door.

As they drove into San Francisco for a day of shopping, Marti was strangely pensive, staring out across the Golden Gate Bridge like an awestruck tourist. Alice knew the silence had nothing to do with the magnificent view. "Still brooding about your sudden deluge of suitors?" she inquired.

"No, just remembering a drive into the city on a Monday morning much like this one. The fog had cleared off early, like today. It was a long time ago . . ."

"You and Riba," Alice said knowingly. Marti sighed and shivered despite the warm sun pouring in the window of Alice's Volvo, which they had decided to take for ease of parking.

"Want me to turn off the air, honey?"

Marti forced herself to look away from the hypnotic expanses below her, back to the concerned face of her friend, the only living soul she had ever told about that day. "No, I'm fine, really. After all these years, you'd think I could forget. Anyway, it's past and done."

Wanting to change the subject and cheer her friend, Alice said, "Tell me about the party at Meadowood."

"How did you—he *told* you he was going to be there, didn't he?" Her gray eyes flashed in surprise.

"Not exactly, but after he left my place I decided to close up early and go to the plaza to do some shopping. Now, who do you think I saw coming out of Craig Williamson's carrying a suit bag and an armload of boxes? With that big shindig coming up, I just sorta put two and two together," Alice said offhandedly, eagerly awaiting the details of the night.

Marti gave a highly edited version of their encounter on the deck, describing his elegant attire and how naturally he carried off the charade that gained him entry to the private party. She finished by saying incredulously, "He told me to take off my glasses—let my hair down, and to get some clothes that fit—even told me what colors!"

Looking back, she was still puzzled about her own acquiescent behavior. She couldn't bring herself to describe the way he had touched her and kissed her—or her own response to his advances.

Alice chuckled. "Imagine his nerve! Just because you dress like a society dowager from the 1920's!"

Marti made a grimace of mock disgust and stuck out her tongue. "You're impossible."

"I'm only glad you finally decided to get smart when a man comes along who can see your potential. Just let me get you outfitted and that hair worked on, then to a really good cosmetic studio I know."

Laughing, Marti protested, "If I have so much potential, why do I need so much help?"

"Without a good haircut, some mascara and a designer dress, Liz Taylor would look like a bag lady. Your sister spends plenty on make up and clothes—right?"

"Yes, too much money. It seems a waste to me."

Alice sighed. "Just wait until Adam sees the new you. Then you won't think it's such a waste of money. Your growth's been stunted, girl!"

"You mean because of Riba," Marti said defensively.

"Let's just say I'll be happy to see her go east and marry her fancyassed lawyer. He's probably one of those shyster Ivy League shits, a perfect match for her," Alice said sourly.

Marti laughed in spite of herself. "As a matter of fact, he's really very nice."

"Poor slob. Still, I'm glad he's marrying her. When's the date?"

"They haven't set one yet. Sometime next winter, probably around the first of the year. Riba is supposed to finish her degree fall semester." Marti's tone of voice indicated what she thought of the possibility.

Alice only snorted. "So, she'll be hanging around this summer. With or without lover boy Larry?"

"He has a law practice in Philadelphia. I imagine Riba will fly back and forth a few times," Marti replied.

Chapter 6

As they drove down Soscal Boulevard in Bob Vasquez's old Chevy, Adam kept stealing glances at the stunning woman seated next to him. Unbidden the vision of her in an elegant vintage Mercedes flashed into his mind. Yes, definitely an old Mercedes, not a new Porsche.

Marti had chosen vibrant cerulean blue slacks that fell in soft flattering lines, tapering narrowly to her slim ankles, which were accented by bone colored high-heeled sandles. A sweater of the same color, cut in a gentle scoop across her collarbone, clung to her breasts. The matching blue and bone butcher linen jacket added the perfect touch of casual elegance.

"I like the outfit, but what on earth did you do to make your hair fall like that? It's beautiful," he whispered appreciatively as he opened the car door for her after pulling into the restaurant parking lot.

"Let's just say Alice knows a good hairdresser," she replied with a serene smile.

As they walked across the gravel lot toward the Old Adobe Restaurant, Adam watched her nervous gesture as she ran her fingers through the layered curly hair that cascaded below her shoulders.

"Up tight about a date with a day laborer?" he asked. "Your father won't be back from the airport until Riba's safely on her plane for Philly. With the usual flight delays you can be safely tucked in bed before he returns."

She looked at his shuttered face, wondering if he was really concerned about the difference in their social positions or merely teasing her. "But a good girl might ask, safely tucked in *whose* bed, Adam?"

"That sounds like Riba talking," he replied with a frown.

"Maybe we're really sisters under the skin," she answered sweetly.

He scowled darkly as he reached for her slender wrist and suddenly pulled her against him. "Not bloody likely. Just because you'll turn heads looking like you do now doesn't mean you're anything like her." He continued holding her close to him. "You're beautiful, Marti, but not in Riba's way. And I don't think you really want to be. You're avoiding the real issue—being seen with me."

She inspected his immaculate white open-collared sports shirt and perfectly fitted chinos. Simple clothes for a casual evening, but on Adam Wade anything looked good—better than good and he damn well knew it! "You'll pass inspection as my escort of the evening, Adam. What do you want me to say—that I'll storm into Papa's study and announce I'm going to have a mad fling with you?"

He grinned at her defiant answer and raised his hands in mock surrender. "Okay, I guess I'm just a mite touchy, a poor coolie taking out the Boss Lady."

She looked at him oddly for a moment, then said, "Hilda made the strangest comment the other day . . ."

"That one Chinese can always tell another?" he interrupted. "Your cook is right. Mrs. Lee and I had a chat last week. She spotted me the first time she saw me. My maternal grandmother's people were from Canton—generations ago. Came to work the railroads originally."

She nodded as they walked toward the front door of the big squat adobe building. "You said something about a Hispanic ancestor, too. Quite a fascinating lot of California history in your geneology."

He shrugged carelessly. "My great—I forget how many times removed—grandfather, David Kane, ran off from the Alvarez landgrant and married an Irish saloon girl he'd won in a poker game. Real classy stuff—if you go for high melodrama."

Her eyes flashed with curiosity, but he forestalled any more questions as they entered the restaurant. It was dimly lit with strings of multi-colored Christmas tree lights tacked along the edges of the low ceilings. The walls were three feet thick. To utilize the luxury of electricity, the owners had simply run stainless steel conduit pipes into each of the adjoining small rooms. Built a hundred and fifty years ago, it was the oldest structure in Napa. Adam looked at her and shrugged at the decor. "Jose Ruiz brought me here last month. Not exactly elegant, but they make the best margaritas and homemade gazpacho you ever tasted."

Marti's smile was radiant as she followed a genial older waitress from room to room until they were seated in a quiet out-of-the-way booth. "I think it has real atmosphere. Elegant is boring if you grew up the way I did. Best gazpacho, huh? I'll tell Hilda on you."

"I've never tasted Hilda's gazpacho, so I can't be held responsible for my ignorance. Just wait until you try it here and compare for yourself." He ordered two large margaritas and a platter of homemade nachos while they perused the menu.

As they pulled the crisp chips apart, long strings of melted cheese trailed after. They laughed as they gobbled the hot, sticky mess, getting it on their fingers and faces.

"For a Creole lady, you know your way around a mess of nachos," he said as he dipped a chip and its oozy cheese and guacamole topping into the red sauce. "You haven't even complained that the salsa's too hot."

Taking a sip of her drink, Marti wiped a wisp of cheese from her lips, "It's not. Remember, I'm third generation California, no matter if my grandfather was a Frenchman from New Orleans." Then she looked quizzically at him. "You knew about my family already, didn't you?"

He shrugged, "Just the usual talk about where the old wine families came from."

"And beside Canton and Spain, where did the more recent Wade family come from?" she countered.

"Everywhere," he replied rather too carelessly, inwardly cursing himself for giving her another opening to discuss his past. A past he wanted to forget, not recount, not even for Marti. Reaching across the table he took a loose curl in his fingers, then let it bounce free. "The new hairdo brings out the russet color in your hair. Just don't let Alice's hairdresser friend cut it too short. I like long hair on a woman. It's a sign of independence."

Marti looked puzzled for a second, then reconsidered. "I'd always thought of it as a sign of tradition and submissiveness to male ego, but in this day of unisex hair salons, I guess it may be a sign of defiance to let it grow—I always felt it was me, somehow."

Adam raised his glass in a toast. "Here's to you, Marti. The real you."

They laughed, they stuffed themselves with wonderful and abundant Mexican food, and they talked, late into the evening. They argued about politics and the Sierra Club, music and art, and they discussed wine. But unlike the obsessive, single-minded drive of Boris, who could talk of nothing else, Adam spoke with eloquence and near reverence. He could relate wine making to art and nature in ways that would mystify the pragmatic, scientific Russian.

"You know, there's a kind of symbiosis in farming—grapes or anything else, I guess. Sometimes when I run a tractor, turning mustard and other wild grasses under, I can watch a hawk circle, waiting until my machine drives the mice and jackrabbits from their cover between the trellises, out into the open. I plow. He swoops. Growth, death." His look was pensive and sad.

Marti instinctively reached out her hand and touched his arm. "Maybe not just death, but the natural cycle of life—life for the hawk, of course, but life, too, for the new vines wrested from the wilderness of weeds that only fed mice before."

They were drinking a rich young Zinfandel with

their main course of spicy beef. He raised his glass. "To wine. To life. To us."

The night was cool and crisp with a million stars blazing across the sky when they left the Old Adobe. "Good brisk night after a warm dry day. Ideal combination for those new blocks of Zinfandel and Merlot," Adam said as he looked up at the sky.

Marti nodded in contentment saying, "Papa's been very happy with the weather this year." She wanted, oddly, to lean her head against his shoulder as they walked. *It must be the margarita going to my head.*

As if responding to her thoughts, he put his arm around her waist and drew her to him. She leaned into him and matched her steps to his long, slow stride. When her head lightly touched his shoulder, he smiled.

The door lock on the Chevy jammed and he had to play with the key several times before he could open the passenger side for her. *Shit, I'm sick of borrowed junkers,* he thought in aggravation as the vision of Marti sliding across the rich leather of a Mercedes' bucket seat once more flashed in his mind. *Marti doesn't fit in this cheap, shabby car.*

Looking at him as he babied the ignition to turn over the engine, Marti was struck by the same intuition. *He doesn't fit here—not in Bob's car, not in a bunkhouse. But he does fit in the fields, working the land, tending the grapes, just like Papa, like me.* She'd learned enough tonight not to press him for the reasons he had chosen this path.

He interrupted her reverie, looking at her with a question in his glowing eyes. "It's early yet. That is if you don't have to beat your father home . . . or explain where you've been."

She sensed the dare, also something more, something intense, almost desperate behind the casual words. "Are we back to that 'safely tucked in *whose* bed' scenario again?" She cocked her head and waited, silvery eyes meeting his blue ones with more calmness than she felt.

A grin quirked the corners of his mouth. "Something like that."

"It's a nice night for a ride," she replied in a steady voice, while the quaking one inside her asked in amazement, *What are you doing Martha Marie Beaumont?* Neither one was exactly certain.

They road in silence for a few minutes as Adam drove north up the Silverado Trail. The countryside was serenely quiet, with neatly plowed, trellised rows of vines stretching for miles like black lace in the moonlight. The famous names of Stags Leap, Caymus and Beaulieu appeared before them on sign posts, along with countless other smaller wineries sprinkled across the "winiest valley in North America." Marti rolled down the window and inhaled the perfume of new growth aloft on the night air.

"Watch out, someone's sure to be dusting sulphur on a night as cool and still as this," he cautioned.

Shortly, the unmistakable smell drifted into the car. Wrinkling her nose, she rolled up the window. "You'd think after growing up with it, I'd get used to the stench."

He shrugged. "I had a friend who grew up in Tacoma. He said the pulp mills smelled just as bad to him as they did to the tourists."

"I bet that smell doesn't eat the rubber covers off their swimming pools like the sulphur dust does here," she replied with a grimace.

Adam laughed. "Hard to say. They don't do much swimming in the Pacific Northwest." As he spoke he turned off the main road onto a small gravel trail that twisted laboriously toward a stand of pines in a wild uncultivated area near a small lake.

"I have a friend, an old fishing buddy who works the harvests. That's his cabin. He's not home this summer," he said as he pulled into a lovely clearing overlooking the water. "Let's walk." He issued the invitation, waiting for her to respond.

When she nodded and reached for her door, he quickly slid out and came around to help her out of the car. They walked toward the edge of the moonsheened water, still and silvery in the silence of the night. The cabin stood close by, like a question as yet unasked, a sentinel, small and shabby, yet homey and inviting.

She dug her hands into her pockets and walked a bit ahead of him, uncertain of what to, or of what he would do. When they reached the water's edge, he stood beside her, feeling the tension radiating from her. When she shivered in the cool night air, he put his arms around her and she leaned willingly against the warmth he offered. "I could build a fire inside. The cabin's not fancy, but Bill keeps it clean."

The place was clean and obviously masculine with simple pine furniture and a rack of trophy antlers on one log wall. The fireplace was big, made of basalt rocks, with a neatly arranged pile of logs with newspapers for starter, ready for a match. She was certain both of them were aware of the symbolism as he knelt and set the room alight with leaping orange flames. While his back was turned, she looked across the cabin to where the big bed stood. Made up with a white chenille spread and puffy high pillows, it seemed the focal point of the room.

Adam stood up and immediately followed her eyes to the bed. "As to *whose* bed it is, his name is Bill Dougherty and I've known him for five years." Slowly, he walked over to her and took her in his arms, then began to caress her softly with his lips, running them along her temple, around the curve of her cheek, across her lashes, down her jawline to her throat. He buried his face in her hair and held it with both hands, letting it fall softly between his splayed fingers.

"When Boris did that I hated it," she managed to whisper between labored breaths.

"I take it you don't feel that way when I do it," he responded, centering his mouth over hers for a deep, tantalizing kiss. The way she opened to him and let their tongues entwine gave him his answer. Adam groaned as he ran his palms up and down her back, cupping her small, rounded buttocks and pressing her pelvis intimately against his.

Marti felt her body spiraling upward in a dizzying trip toward some distant, unknown destination. The room was warm and her clothes seemed suddenly restricting. She mindlessly helped him when he peeled off her jacket.

Her sweater was soft and loose, easy for him to slide his hands underneath. Warm, calloused fingers traced patterns up her backbone and then around to cup an aching breast. Marti sucked in her breath in surprise. Adam let out a strangled sound of pleasure as he touched the taunt nipple. "Oh, lady, yes, yes," he murmured as he reached back and unsnapped her bra with a deft, practiced move. When his fingers returned to take a hardened nipple in each hand, hefting, circling, teasing, he could feel her arch into the caresses. He slid the sweater up, over her head. The bra quickly followed it to the clothes pile on the chair.

Before her dazed, mesmerized eyes he fairly tore the buttons from his shirt and yanked it off. His hard, hairy chest glowed like molten bronze in the firelight. It seemed the most natural thing in the world to press the soft pale globes of her breasts against him until they were crushed, even as his mouth ground down on hers and devoured it fiercely.

Marti responded, clinging to him, crying out his name, suspended somewhere in time and space as their lips and bodies brushed, rubbed, promised each other. Then he picked her up in his arms and carried her to the bed, never breaking the blending warmth of the kiss until he had laid her down on the wide, soft mattress. When the heat of his body left hers, she felt a sudden anguish, followed by an abrupt rush of awareness as she watched him reach down toward her spike-heeled sandles. Taking one delicate ankle in his hands he began to unstrap the shoe.

From a distance, the realization of what he was doing—of what she was doing—dawned on her. It was so effortless on his part, as if often practiced, this getting a woman undressed and in bed with him. Held frozen in thrall, she watched him unfasten her shoes and toss them onto the floor.

Sensing a withdrawal, a stiffening in her, Adam put her leg down and sat beside her, once more trailing his knowing, questing fingers to her breasts as he bent to kiss her. He slid onto the bed, loafers kicked carelessly onto the floor, and lay alongside her. Marti felt the length of his hard body pressing head to toe with her own, rolling her slowly toward the center of the bed as their arms and legs entwined. *Isn't this what you wanted? What you knew would happen if you came here with him?* a voice inside her taunted. Yes, yes, *damn you*! But still a suffocating feeling began to extinguish her earlier passion, paralyzing her with dread and stiffness. When his hand moved to the waistband of her slacks, she found her own closing over it, pushing it away.

Adam became immediately very still but for his labored breathing. He raised up on one elbow and looked into her stricken face. "Marti, what's wrong?" His voice held genuine confusion. She had been all warmth and compliance until he put her on the bed and began to remove her shoes. Her face was turned from him. When he reached one hand over and tugged gently at her chin, forcing her to meet his eyes, the tears ran in soft, silent rivulets across her cheeks.

"I . . . I can't. I'm sorry, I can't, Adam," she choked out.

Baffled and more than a little frustrated, he forced his emotions under control. Getting his body to obey would take a little longer. "Okay, babe, it's all right. I guess I've gone a little too fast." He eased away from her and then wiped her tears away with his fingertips.

She could feel his weight leave the bed, but even then found it difficult to open her eyes. His half-naked body gleamed with corded muscle as he reached over to retrieve her clothes from the chair by the fire.

He's magnificent, bright, warm, gentle, everything I could ever ask for in a lover. Why, oh, why? But she knew the answer even before her mind tormented her with the question.

When he had placed the sweater, bra and jacket in

her hands, he turned away and shrugged on his shirt in swift, angry motions, leaving it half unbuttoned, tucking it roughly into his chinos. "I'll wait for you outside," he said in a hoarse, low voice as he reached for his shoes by the bed.

She did not move until the cabin door closed with a soft click. Then like a dream walker she sat up, realizing her linen jacket was clenched so tightly in her hands that it was irreparably wrinkled. Wiping the tears once more from her eyes she began to dress with clumsy, stiff fingers.

Adam paced in the cool darkness outside. For the first time in the five years since he had quit smoking, he wished for a cigarette. The night embraced him with the soothing balm of softly lapping water and the hum of insects. Yet he felt raw and aching, both physically and mentally. Why the abrupt and painful turning from him? She was no practiced tease like her sister. *It isn't a game with her, but what in hell is it?* Never had he felt this vulnerable. *Guilty,* he amended. But why guilty—just because he had made her no promises about "happily ever after"?

"Hell, she's twenty-four years old. She knew exactly what to expect when I asked her to drive to a deserted cabin late at night," he muttered under his breath. A frog croaked a sarcastic sounding "ribbit" at him and he skimmed a rock across the water in the general direction of the peace disturber.

Marti stood poised in the front door, watching him pace in the bright moonlight. She could see by the agitated way his usually graceful body moved that he was angry. And she could not blame him. How to explain? If only she *could* explain?

Sensing her presence he turned and looked at her, slim and shivering, her arms wrapped protectively around herself as if to ward off a blow. Something inside him softened and the anger dissipated. "I'll take you home," he said simply, reaching out a hand, palm up as a peace offering.

Swallowing nervously, she forced herself to meet his eyes, no longer angry and accusing, but filled now with confusion and some other more tender emotion. *Don't pity me, Adam. I couldn't bear your pity.*

Adam spent the next several days avoiding Marti. It was not difficult with the myriad summer chores that had to be done to get the winery equipment in shape for the crush. Fall was "the crush," winter "the pruning," spring "the frost" and "the bloom." But summer had no name. Summer was hosing down redwood tanks and painting crushers and gondolas, oiling mechanical harvesting equipment and dusting ripening fruit with sulphur to keep powdery mildew at bay. There was work to do, hard and dirty, and plenty of it. Adam found he had an excess of nervous energy to burn off.

The following weekend he saw Marti for the first time since their disastrous date. She and her father had just returned from the airport with Riba. Marti was getting out of the Cadillac, dressed in a bright apricot sundress that complimented her skin as it hugged her slim, supple waist and flared just below the knees of her long elegant legs. No more the drab wallflower who faded by comparison, she was every bit as noticeable as her curvaceous blonde sister.

He wondered how Riba felt about the competition, then dismissed the idea as absurd. Marti had no interest in flirting with the hired men. She still projected the same aloof but friendly demeanor with the employees. When Staritz walked up to the car and greeted her admiringly, Adam was glad to see she treated him coolly.

"If I had the sense of half a brick, I'd stay the hell away from her," he muttered darkly and continued on his way to the field with the heavy tool chest he'd fetched from the equipment shed. A tractor was down and Nate Benteen was supposedly repairing it. Adam had never seen a worse mechanic. No, he reconsidered, Benteen was not maladapt so much as lazy and indifferent. "I'll end up fixing the damn thing." He swore. Adam was no stranger to back breaking labor, but he hated engine grease embedded stubbornly beneath his fingernails. *Give me the natural clean feel of the earth and the living, growing things that spring from it.*

As he walked away hefting a large metal box on one broad shoulder, Riba watched his retreating figure. She knew he must have been staring at Marti. Lord, her sister had undergone a radical transformation in the weeks she'd been gone. If he had been interested in her when she looked like a titmouse, how must her new image affect him? Then the thought struck her that perhaps Adam Wade was the reason for the change. Eyes narrowed, she decided to find out.

It was easy for Riba to obtain the schedule of work assignments. Adam had drawn a clean-up detail at the winery the next morning, scrubbing several of the older wooden presses. Dressed in a pair of tight designer jeans and a halter top, she headed toward the north side of the big plant.

He was stripped to the waist in the noon heat. Sweat trickled down his temples and arms as he applied a brush with sudsy vigor to steel and redwood. His jeans were sopping, clinging to his legs as he knelt in the mud, oblivious to her approach.

"Do you always bust your buns even when the boss isn't around?" she asked by way of greeting, her predatory eyes taking in the calm way he turned and lay down the brush.

One long-fingered hand combed straight black hair back from his forehead as he looked up at her. He made no attempt to stand. "I do what I'm told by the boss," he said, his arm now resting casually across one knee.

"Is my sister the boss?" she asked as she circled him and the press, careful to keep her Italian sandles away from the mud puddles.

Adam grinned broadly. "Les Reams gave me this assignment. Miss Marti only signs my paychecks."

"*Miss* Marti, now, is it? From what I heard last night, you two are on more personal terms than that," she said cryptically.

His eyes changed from clear blue to midnight, but

otherwise he gave nothing away. Hand still draped in a relaxed fashion across his knee he asked, "And just what kind of bunkhouse scuttlebutt are you privy to, *Miss* Riba?" He was damn sure Marti had told no one about their date.

Her lips curved in a wintry little smile. "Don't act so self-righteous, darling. It was Boris Staritz who told me that you and my sister have been an item. Since that little incident at Meadowood, as a matter of fact," she fished.

That remark was rewarded with a full-fledged scowl. "I hardly think a chance encounter in a public place qualifies us as 'an item.' "

Remembering the circumstances under which her quarry had eluded her that night, Riba once more felt her temper simmering. She kept a tight control on it. "Boris was rather upset when he found you and Marti together. Now suddenly, she goes and buys out every boutique in San Francisco. I doubt she did it to impress him. Did she do it for you?" She fairly purred the question.

Adam shrugged in dismissal. "She's a classy lady. Maybe it's time she made everyone notice that fact with a few new clothes and a haircut."

"And, of course, you noticed," she said cattily.

"I have better eyesight than Boris," he replied with a cheeky grin, enjoying her jealousy of Marti in spite of his annoyance with her.

"Just don't get your hopes up, Adam. My sister may be a late-blooming rose, but she's still a Beaumont—society all the way. Like you said, a classy lady. She'll marry someone in the business—and it *won't* be a hired hand, I promise you."

"Somehow I doubt it'll be Boris Staritz either," he replied with more calm than he felt.

"She'll choose someone she can handle," Riba said scornfully. "Someone proper and dull, someone Papa approves of. He's her real hero, you know. She's just a frigid, snobby do-gooder with a Phi Beta Kappa Key and a king-sized Electra complex."

Her taunt about Marti's social position rankled, but

her attack on her sister set his temper ablaze. "Marti behaves like a lady. Intelligence isn't snobbery and helping with her father's business scarcely qualifies her as a neurotic."

"I've seen her turn men off for years. New window dressing won't change what's underneath." Riba's voice was deceptively sweet, as if she were teasing a half-bright child. "She's a frigid, castrating bitch, Adam."

Finally he stood up and faced her. "I've heard enough around the bunkhouse to know that you sure as shit aren't frigid, Riba. Now, a castrating bitch . . ." His laugh was harsh and deliberately insulting.

When her hand came up to slap his face, Adam made no attempt to stop her. He merely stood there, icy blue eyes watching her stomp away. She was too furious to speak. She stiffened and broke stride for an instant when he called after her, "Poor Larry. It's going to be hell going through life wearing chain mail jockey shorts."

Chapter 7

Briefly, Adam speculated about whether Riba would run to daddy and have Joe fire him, but nothing happened. He was on the work roster the next day, assigned to wash down the redwood tanks in a far wing of the plant. The solitary work suited his mood. He brooded about what Riba had said. Was there any kernel of truth in her jealous spite? Did Marti's affection and loyalty to old Joe border on such an obsession that she could have no normal relationship with a man?

But he remembered how she had reacted to that first kiss at Meadowood. Closing his eyes he once more envisioned how she had looked at the Old Adobe. She had certainly wanted to please him with her appearance then. Her first responses that night at the cabin had been ardent, but something had made her pull away. Just thinking about that encounter made him ache with frustration. He yanked angrily on the heavy length of hose, glad for the physical release afforded by plain, hard work.

Adam was not the only one frustrated and restive. Marti had lain on her bed night after night, staring at the ceiling, afraid to close her eyes and be transported back to the drowning pool of sensations Adam Wade had awakened in her that night at the lake-side cabin.

I'm a fool, a frightened child in a woman's body, she berated herself, once more seeing his angry scowl and then the softening of his features when he looked at her trembling, crestfallen face. She had been avoiding him while vainly attempting to decide on a course of action. Perversely, the longer the days stretched without seeing him, the more she missed him. The haunting blue eyes, the blinding white smile, the gentleness of his calloused fingertips as he touched her arm in a casual gesture. Above all, she missed his teasing wit and the earnest discussions they had shared.

He's the first man beside Papa I've really been able to talk with, she realized one warm morning in July. She sat on the patio, idly stirring cream in her coffee. *In fact, if I was honest,* Marti admitted, *I told Adam things I could never tell Papa. All we ever do is discuss business.*

That disloyal idea triggered thoughts of Boris, who also talked of nothing but viniculture. His behavior had been increasingly annoying of late. Having lost Riba, he was fixated on courting her plain, dutiful sister, now ironically metamorphosed into a tolerably attractive woman. She laughed wryly to herself. If it hadn't been for Adam, she would have remained a wallflower. But Boris still would have turned his attention her way. He wanted control of Chateau Beaumont.

What did Adam Wade want? A casual summer fling? Or did he, too, covet her father's winery? Once more Marti pondered the enigma of the drifter. He was an educated man with obvious polish, well exhibited that night at Meadowood. He came from money, or at least somewhere in his past he had become accustomed to it. Why did he work here for seasonal wages if not to seduce a lonely woman like Joe Beaumont's elder daughter?

Still, he had seen an inner beauty in her, had coaxed and taunted until she had responded by blossoming into a woman whom other men did look at. Not only Boris and the hired men, but male friends in town extravagantly complimented her on the transformation and asked her out. She had gone on two pleasant dates in the past week, one with an attorney and one with a wine negotiant. They were wealthy and successful, hardly the types to covet her father's property. *I could lead a normal existence, choose a man who would gen-*

uinely appreciate me. I could build a life. But no one possessed the magic of Adam.

"Damn him, he's in my blood and bones," she muttered, tossing the spoon with a clinking splash into her cup. "And I'm a coward hiding here at the house, playing at being a social butterfly instead of finding out if I can ever be an independent adult in control of my own life." Abruptly, she stood up and pushed back the wicker patio chair.

Whether her future lay with Adam Wade was dubious, but that was not the issue, Marti realized. He might yet prove a shallow fortune hunter, but he was the only man she wanted to make love with and until she overcame that obsession, she could never get on with her life. All the new hairdos and wardrobes from Napa to Rodeo Drive were meaningless.

In measured, resolute steps, she headed down the road toward the plant before she lost her nerve. Les told her she could find Adam in an isolated area that held the largest of their redwood storage tanks. He had been assigned to scrub it down that morning.

As she neared the thirty-thousand gallon vats, she could hear her footsteps echoing on the cool stone floors. The place was deserted but for her and Adam. Then she heard the hissing of a high pressure hose in the distance, bouncing off the walls of one of the room-sized tanks. The perfume of redwood and grape must lay redolent on the warm summer air. Marti spied a pair of boots and a soft cotton shirt discarded in a careless heap beside the far wall. Suddenly, she was no longer certain of what to do or say. Her steps slowed and her heart beat accelerated. When she stopped in front of the small opening into the tank, the hose jumped. She could hear Adam swear as he tugged on the heavy line. It slithered like a big tan anaconda past her ankles, further inside the vat.

She felt compelled to follow it. Squatting in front of the circular opening, she held onto the top and slid both long legs inside in one smooth, practiced motion. Adam had his back to her, concentrating on his work, unable to hear her because of the noise of the water.

Soaked through from the spray, his jeans clung to those long hard legs. Droplets of water danced in blueblack iridescence on his hair and dripped sensuously onto the flexing muscles of his shoulders and back, tracing satiny paths down his tawny skin to vanish below his waistband.

Adam suddenly sensed that he was not alone. Inexplicably, he knew before he turned that Marti was there, standing just inside the opening, watching him. He turned to face her, and looked into her wide gray eyes, trying to read their message. The hose was clenched in his hand. Water poured onto the floor in a rainbow of misty colors.

Slowly, Marti began to walk toward him. Methodically, he reached down with his other hand and shut off the noisy cascade. The sound of the nozzle hitting the aged redwood planking echoed mutedly around the walls of the tank. He stood poised. She reached out and caressed the thick, crisp mat of hair on his chest, releasing clusters of beaded water trapped in it. His skin was warm, his muscles hard. She could feel the pounding of his heart even though his stillness belied the tension sizzling inside him.

Marti took a deep, unsteady breath, trying to decide what she should say. But he already knew. His hand came up to lay over hers, pressing it even more securely across his pounding heart.

She melted against the slick, hard length of his body as his other hand looped behind her neck and drew her gently to him for a soft kiss. Two hearts thrummed fiercely yet two bodies moved with deliberation, searching, learning, knowing.

His tongue teased entrance to her mouth. She opened to receive it eagerly, twining her own with it in an embrace as warm and soft as the one their bodies shared. She arched and rubbed in rhythm with the artful coaching of his hands. He slid them down to cup her buttocks and lift her against him, then released his hold to run deft fingertips up and down her spine, insinuating his hands beneath her shirt.

Marti let her hands trace patterns on the flexing

satiny muscles of his shoulders and back, then reached up to comb his thick unruly hair with her fingers.

Gradually, the caresses grew stronger, hungrier, fiercer. Yet he was slow and careful, waiting for any resistance when he reached between them again and began to unfasten her slacks. His lips nipped gently at hers, breaking the seal of the kiss. Then he searched her silver eyes and found the answer he sought. Marti helped him with a lithe swish of her hips that let the soft, loose cotton slacks drop to the wet floor. He unbuttoned her blouse as she kicked off her sandals and discarded the slacks from around her ankles.

Boldly, she unsnapped his jeans and began to unzip his fly. He reached behind her and unhooked her lacy bra. Her busy hands froze against his belly when he finally gained access to her breasts, suckling one, then the other, sending frissions of ecstasy down to her toes.

She clenched the open waistband of his jeans and arched against him as he lowered her gently to the wet floor, which was imbued with the fragrance of old wines. She inhaled the unique blend of redwood and male musk, mingled with her own scent, a thing unfamiliar until now, until Adam awakened her. She was lost in newly born sensuality, smelling the pungent wood, tasting her lover's salty skin, feeling the knotting and flexing muscles of his hard body on hers, hearing the sound of their ragged breathing breaking the silence.

Adam looked into her eyes, glazed with passion. Her lips were parted breathlessly; her breasts were upthrust proudly. She tossed her head from side to side and her hair fanned out across the floor, gleaming against the age-darkened color of the wet wood. It all seemed oddly right. *She belongs here. So do I,* he thought as he ran one hand over the hard budding point of a nipple, then caressed lower, over her silky belly, down to the dampened tangle of curls at her mound. No stiffening or shrinking away this time.

She reached up to him in supplication and he lowered himself to kiss her once more, their mouths opened and demanding. He trailed kisses from her lips to her throat while his hands continued to work tingling magic over her thighs and up the curve of her waist. With an anguished groan he pulled away from her and struggled to peel off his wet jeans.

Marti watched the rapid, desperate movements, unable to tear her eyes from his dark hard male beauty. Instinctively, she reached up and touched the center of him, enclosing his aching shaft with her hand, feeling the velvet-coated, steely length with wonder.

Adam shuddered and struggled to control the overwhelming impulse to spill himself in desperation. All the weeks of watching, wanting, waiting were over. He knelt and looked into her eyes, molten silver with desire. Reaching down he guided her hand and its willing prisoner toward the tangle of reddish brown curls. She opened to him, welcoming him as he lowered himself on top of her and entered.

At his first thrust and withdrawal, she embraced him fiercely with legs clenched tightly around his hips. Her lips searched out his mouth for another kiss and her hands knotted in his hair, lowering his head to hers. She was incredibly tight, yet wet and yielding, arching up to envelope all of him.

They bucked and writhed in the frantic, fast rhythm of hungry wanting for a moment. Then, fearing to lose the last of his control and end the ecstasy far too soon, Adam slowed the pace, his hands guiding her hips to a lazy, drugging pace. After several minutes of the delicate mutual torture, he raised his head from feasting on her mouth and studied her flushed face. She was obviously breathless with pleasure now. He continued his relentless rhythm, waiting for the unconscious signals she must give him.

It mustn't be too fast—easy, gentle, oh, let it last, his brain hammered out as he kept up the steady stroking, alternating between watching her incredibly lovely face and kissing it. He could feel her hands rubbing against his back, then suddenly clenching his shoulders as she let out a tiny cry of wonder and stiffened beneath him. Her face and neck were stained with a crimson flush that spread down across her breasts as she shuddered in release.

As he witnessed her pleasure, a subtle warmth infused him, quite separate from the driving need for his own sexual gratification. Lowering his mouth to hers he renewed their kiss and then, blessedly, found the release his body had sought for so long.

Marti could feel him swell and pour himself deep inside her. Eyes squeezed tightly closed with tears thick beneath her lashes, she held him fast, feeling free and weightless despite his hard embrace and the pressure of his body atop her own.

Slowly, they both returned to reality. Adam carefully moved off her and rolled into a sitting position, looking down at her with troubled eyes. His hand gently traced the delicate outline of her jaw and caressed the pulse at the base of her ear. She looked up at him uncertainly and read in his expression clear knowledge of the truth.

Oh, don't ask me questions, Adam, please don't. She sat up and instinctively reached for his embrace. He held her in his arms and ran one hand through the damp curly hair hanging down her back as she burrowed her face against his chest. She felt protected and at peace.

Then he shattered it with a few soft words. "You've never done this before, have you, Marti?"

Her voice felt clogged in her throat as she whispered, "Was I so awkward you could tell?"

Her reply was muffled against his chest and she was trembling. He raised her face with one hand, taking her chin in his fingers like a priceless piece of porcelain. "You were wonderful, warm and natural. But there were a few things you tried rather hard to conceal. You were so anxious to get that first penetration over with before I could feel what you obviously felt. I never . . . well, I've never been with a virgin before, but you're very tight and small. I'm not complaining, Marti," he said softly with a glint of humor sparkling in his eyes. "But I didn't want to hurt you."

"You didn't. I wasn't sure what I'd feel, but it really

didn't hurt at all." Her voice was losing some of its hoarseness, but it was still difficult to talk. The hypnotic spell he wove with his gentle caresses soothed her, but his words had the opposite effect.

"Now I understand about the time at the cabin. Why didn't you tell me?" He waited a beat. "Or couldn't you tell me?"

She gave a sad nervous laugh. "Just how does one interject it into the conversation?—Oh, by the way, I just happen to be the oldest living virgin in North America!"

"It isn't conventional these days, that's for sure, but like I said, I'm not complaining, just baffled." His eyes were darkened with some unnamed emotion.

"In case you never considered it, before I met you I wasn't exactly the Belle of Napa Valley. Men are still blinded by the reflection of Riba's glitter when they look at me—if they notice me at all," she added acidly.

"Forget Riba," he commanded sternly. "You camouflaged yourself, Marti. You wanted to turn men away from you. It had nothing to do with your sister."

"It had everything to do with my sister!" she shouted back in a voice both beseeching and angry.

He held her tightly now, kissing her brow and eyelids as tears trickled down her cheeks. Somehow Adam knew that no one had seen Marti Beaumont cry since she was very, very young. "Let it out, babe. You can't keep it bottled inside you forever," he murmured.

"I've only told one other person . . . about my sister and what happened," she replied in a whisper.

"Alice." He was certain Alice Marchanti was Marti's only real friend despite all her social connections and activities.

"Yes, Alice," she said with a wobbly smile. Taking a deep breath she plunged in. "It was eight years ago. I'd just gotten my driver's license for my sixteenth birthday. A good thing, too. I had to drive Riba to San Francisco. Al arranged everything, even paid for it, but he wouldn't take her. I guess he wanted to eliminate any chance of being charged with statutory rape if Papa ever found out. He was twenty-two. Riba wasn't quite fifteen."

Adam sucked in his breath. "She was pregnant."

"Yes. She was always wild. I've never really understood why. We started dating about the same time—she was thirteen, I was fifteen. My dates consisted of hand holding and a goodnight peck with neighborhood boys. But she met Al Rollis. His father was a big negotiant in San Francisco and he came to the house that summer to see if he could get Papa to sign with their firm. I guess he saw her vulnerability . . . or whatever it is that draws men to Riba. I realized later on that it was more than just her beauty. She's always been self destructive. Men seem to sense it—to take advantage of it."

"Sometimes it's the woman who takes advantage, Marti," he said quietly.

"Oh, I'll admit she knows her way around now. But then—oh, Adam, she was fourteen, pregnant and scared to death. She came to me and told me Al had arranged this appointment with an abortionist—a 'real physician' he'd told her. He turned out to be a backstreet butcher! On the way home, driving across the bridge she started to hemorrhage. There was so much blood. It's bizarre now, but I can remember thinking afterward how lucky we were that the upholstery was vinyl. It all washed off.

"She cried and told me about Al and her first time with him, how he seduced her. Even then my sister was incredibly graphic." She shuddered. "I saw the results . . . blood and death. Death for that nameless baby, almost death for Riba. I drove her to a friend of our family, a nurse. She understood about Papa and what it would do to him if he ever found out. By the time we got there, the bleeding had stopped. She kept Riba at her house for two days to make certain she was all right—even took her to the doctor she worked for. I had to go home and tell Papa a pack of lies about Riba staying with a girlfriend in Sonoma. I even called Sally Walthers and got her to lie for us."

Adam could feel her quaking, feel the icy cold sweat breaking out on her skin. "And you equated that ugly mess with making love and never formed a relationship with a man since."

"I tried . . . in college. I dated several guys that I felt attracted to—or at least I did until. . . . But always I'd see the blood, hear Riba cry. I just couldn't." She paused and took a deep breath. "Then I began my disguise, as you call it. It wasn't a conscious thing at first. I'd always taken a back seat to Riba, but by the time I was nineteen I had buried myself in books and knotted my hair up in a braid. When I read late at night I got eyestrain; the glasses were another phase of the camouflage, I guess." She shrugged helplessly. "No man ever noticed me until you, Adam."

The silvery glow of her eyes warmed him, but the horror of her confession and the scars in her young life tore at him. "Only a blind man or a fool could miss you, Marti—the real you, warm, loving and lovely."

"And scared, Adam. I'm frightened," she whispered, wanting desperately to hear some avowal from him, something about his past to match what she had painfully shared with him.

He kissed her lips softly once more and then reached for their damp, discarded clothing, handing her things to her and then beginning to slide into his stiff jeans. "You'll do fine, babe, just fine. Now that you've faced up to those memories of Riba, you can begin over. In fact, you just did—with a bang." Adam looked at her and his smile faded, replaced by a look of tenderness. "Okay, Marti, it was a lousy joke, but you aren't afraid of me, of making love anymore, are you?"

She paused in the midst of buttoning her shirt and looked at the splendid male beauty of him. *My lover. A man I can talk to, confide in.* "No, Adam, I'm not afraid of making love." *But I am afraid of your power over me.*

They walked slowly back to the house, both wet and rumpled. The warm late afternoon sun curled her hair as it dried. Her clothes, too, dried in stiffened wrinkles. His jeans were still darkened with moisture.

Adam's arm rested casually around her shoulders as they strolled. It seemed natural to walk this way and they met no one as they cut across the fields between the trellises. When they neared the side of the big house, he halted and drew her into his arms.

"What happened today could get to be habit-forming, you know," he said with a slow smile. "Don't you have to display your paintings at the art festival this weekend?"

"At Alice's booth, yes," she replied uncertainly.

"Can I take you? I want to see you win the blue ribbon for 'Budbreak.' "

His hands holding hers were warm and steady, reassuring her. If ever she were going to break free of the past, this was her one, best chance. A dazzling smile lit her face.

"So, you're sure I'll win, huh? So's Alice. How can I not agree with you both? Yes, I'll go with you on Sunday—if you're positive you have the day off from scrubbing tanks."

He laughed and kissed her, then gently turned her toward the big house. He watched her retreating figure for a moment and then headed back to the mess hall for supper.

Joe Beaumont and Boris Staritz had been talking on the porch, discussing the fall crush. When the old man walked inside, the winemaster headed for his car, parked out front. Then he heard the blended laughter of Adam and Marti coming from the east field. Curious, he walked towards a stand of ornamental poplars at the edge of the hillside and concealed himself. Marti was walking directly up the hill to the house and Adam Wade was ambling in the opposite direction. Boris' eyes narrowed as he noted her damp, rumpled appearance. Then he recalled Wade's work assignment for the day—scrubbing tanks. An ugly suspicion began to take shape in his mind.

So, she was just like her sister, a tramp with no more morals than an alley cat. And all this time he'd been fooled like all the other men at the winery. Everyone thought Marti was a lady. After she passed by him unawares and entered the house, his low ugly laugh rent the warm air.

Chapter 8

Adam walked slowly to the bunkhouse. The laughter and bantering of the men discussing their weekend plans held little interest for him. Always quiet and aloof, he felt even more isolated that evening.

"Hey, *mano,* you awake or asleep?" Bob Vasquez asked Adam.

Looking down the table to where his young friend sat, Adam forced his mind to focus on the conversation going on around him. "Oh, the car . . . nope, I don't need to borrow it Saturday."

Jose Ruiz laughed. "You mean you ain't takin' the boss's daughter to the Adobe again?"

"She has fancier taste than that—more like the Old Grist Mill in Glen Ellen," Luke Tiller said with a grin and a wink.

It took all Adam's willpower not to reach across the table and knock Tiller's yellowed teeth down his throat. He settled for one succinct expletive and continued methodically eating in brooding silence. *I should've figured the hands would know.* He swore to himself as his eyes scanned the grizzled faces, old and young, up and down the long trestle table.

Wanting to diffuse a tense situation, Bob and Ferris shifted the conversation to a discussion about the fall crush.

Adam quickly finished his food, picked up his utensils and walked over to the washtub, tossing them in the soapy water. As he left the mess hall he could still feel the speculative glances of the other hands follow him. *Damn!* Remembering all the rough talk that circulated about Riba and other growers' wives and daughters, he winced, realizing that he could not tolerate having Marti's name dragged through the muck that way.

She's so vulnerable. He considered the beautiful idyll of the afternoon. She had come to him, trusting him. Was she asking for love? Commitment? Or was it just simple therapy with someone sympathetic who had glimpsed the real woman hidden behind all the masks? "I'm the one who's afraid to find out," he muttered darkly, knowing he lived with old wounds, raw and unhealed, simply more skillfully hidden. When a man drifts rootlessly, no one can get close enough to examine him. No one until Marti.

But like a fool, I pursued her. If I'd let it alone and not gone after her, we'd both be better off. He eased himself down on his bunk and lay staring at the rafters, hands folded behind his head, deep in tortured thought.

That's how Bob Vasquez found him a few minutes later. "I'm going to town for a couple of beers. Wouldn't mind some company. I have some thinking to do about family trouble. I imagine you have some personal things to sort out, too. No true confessions, Adam, just company and a good therapeutic drunk." His dark eyes were warm and his smile engaging.

"Hell, why not?" Adam replied, unwinding his long body from the narrow bunk.

Bob was as good as his word, making few conversational demands on his companion as they rode into Napa and pulled up in front of a large, popular tavern where the drinks were cheap and the lighting dim. They left the old Chevy in the back parking lot and headed in the rear door.

Once inside the smoke-filled room, they paused to let their eyes adjust to the darkness. Just as Adam was feeding change into a cigarette machine, he heard Bob let out a low whistle.

"La de dah. Look who's a player, tonight."

Adam followed his gaze over to a pool table near the bar where Riba Beaumont was draped over a large, burly man in a gaudy cowboy shirt. Adam noted her tight silk pants and off the shoulder blouse. "Slumming," he said sourly.

When the big man's turn to shoot came, she exchanged a few whispered words and insinuating movements with him as he handed her the pool cue. She made a clean rail shot, sinking the seven ball in the far corner pocket.

As she squealed in delight, all of her adoring male companions whooped and downed drinks to her health. Adam turned in disgust. "Great choice of bars, Vasquez," he muttered, lighting up a cigarette.

"Since when'd you start on the cancer sticks, *mano*?" Bob rejoined as they strolled over to a table in a far corner, away from the raucous pool game and Willie Nelson wailing on the jukebox.

"Since I met Joe Beaumont's daughters," he muttered, exhaling smoke into the already polluted air. "Who's the lady's escort?" he asked Vasquez without much interest. Bob, born and raised in the valley, knew everyone.

"Lon Chambers. Small grower from Sonoma. Quite a lady's man since his divorce last year, if the lady's inclined towards beer and Waylon Jennings, that is."

"And pool," Adam added drily. "Looks like she's had practice."

"Maybe she's got the hots for old Lon, *quien sabe*?"

Adam shrugged. "I doubt it. She's got bigger ideas—back east, old money ideas. More along the lines of Dom Perignon and Pavarotti. Chambers is just a night's diversion. She'll marry her Mainline lawyer . . . or someone like him."

It was on the tip of Bob's tongue to ask Adam if he knew as much about the other sister, but some sixth sense warned him it was best left alone. Obviously his friend felt quite differently about the two women. If Adam wanted to talk about Marti, he would, but somehow, Bob doubted it.

He was right. They discussed Bob's parents and their dreams of law school for him—a dream he didn't share. He wanted to finish his business degree and go into a wine negotiant's firm in San Francisco. The evening wore on and both men steadily consumed pitchers of beer. Their waitress was attentive to the two attractive, unattached men and made frequent stops by their secluded table.

"Nice ass," Bob said after she walked off, hips swaying, tray balanced artfully above one shoulder.

Adam swallowed his beer and looked across the crowded room absently, deep in brooding thoughts he could not reveal to the earnest young man. "You've had to earn everything the hard way, Bob. And you'll succeed—practice law or ship wine, doesn't matter. You'll make it. Now, speaking of making it, go do what you've wanted to for the past two hours. I can always hitch a ride back."

"What if I ask her if she has a friend?" Bob asked with a grin.

"No thanks. Got me some serious thinking to do," Adam replied ponderously, his speech faintly slurred. "On your way out, ask your friend to send one more pitcher over here before she departs for Chevy heaven with you."

Laughing as he tossed several bills onto the table for his share of the beer, Bob did as Adam requested.

Adam sat and drank, mulling over what to do about Marti. Hell, he knew what he *wanted* to do. Every baser impulse in his body cried out for him to spend the summer making love to her. But what about after that? His own plans when he came to Beaumont's were uncertain, even before he met her. Would he stay? *Should* he stay?

"You have a lot of sorting out to do," he muttered thickly into his beer. *And a lot of issues unsettled from your past,* a voice nagged inside him. Until he faced the past, he could not build a future. Everything he'd done since his arrival at Beaumont's, culminating in his extravagant gate crash at Meadowood, had centered around Marti. *And you didn't want a simple roll in the hay either,* he admitted painfully. Still, he had never imagined he would discover such an innocent, vulnerable woman with a hidden past.

Or, did I? Was that the intuition that drew us together

from the start? His head was beginning to spin from a combination of too much beer and too much introspection. Deciding to walk it off, he stood up unsteadily, testing his legs. Good. They worked.

Adding to Bob's pile of bills, he headed to the exit, only to have a sleek hand with long red nails catch his arm as he reached for the door.

"Well, where have you been hiding?" Riba purred, running her fingertips up and down his biceps.

"Minding my own business, Riba. Look, it's late, I'm drunk and work begins at sun-up, so if you don't mind . . ."

"You going to walk back to the bunkhouse?" She eyed him speculatively.

"It'll sober me up," he replied gravely.

"Give you a lift? My Porsche is parked in front," she offered, taking his arm and ushering him through the door before his beer-sodden brain could frame a reply. Sober, Riba possessed a distinct advantage.

"What happened to your buckaroo?" he asked with no particular interest as she stopped in front of her sleek white car.

Riba laughed dismissively. "We just met for a friendly game. Lon's hardly the type Papa'd let drive up to the house to call for me."

He opened the car door and plopped down into the bucket seat with the careless ease of one well-lubricated by drink. "Tell me, Riba, just who is the type your Papa'd let call on a Beaumont belle?"

She turned the key in the ignition and inspected him from the corner of her eye slyly. "Dressed like you were that night at Meadowood, you could call on me."

He threw back his head and snorted in derision. "That evening cost me over a month's wages. Anyway, I thought you were already spoken for—or has dear Larry escaped?" He half-hoped she'd get so furious with him that she'd evict him from the car.

Instead, Riba pulled away from the curb with a sudden lurch and took off far too fast, heading toward the highway. "Larry is working in Philadelphia and

I'll be flying there in late August to begin wedding arrangements. The date is October 26," she said serenely.

"Why not make it the thirty-first and you could walk down the aisle in a black satin gown to the strains of Swan Lake?" he asked, cocking one brow in a drunken attempt at humor. "I can picture Larry in an open-collared shirt, baring his throat for you in front of the altar—with a drape over the chancel cross, of course. Too bad he's not smart enough to carry a pointed oak stake."

"My, my, aren't you a fanciful bastard when you're drunk," she said lightly. "Maybe that's your charm for me. I do so love a challenge." Tilting her head back to catch the cool night wind, she accelerated.

Adam took a few deep bracing breaths of air, letting it fill his lungs, hoping it might sober him up. Useless. Still, even though drunk, he could feel the vibrations of the small car hurtling north on Highway 29, now narrowed to a two-lane road. "Slow down, Riba."

"Are you afraid of fast women, Adam?" Her green eyes glittered in the moonlight.

Knowing that he would only goad her into more dangerous antics if he replied, he leaned back and closed his eyes as if to sleep. It was easier to do than he'd thought. He passed out.

When she turned onto the gravel road at the edge of Beaumont property he awakened abruptly as his body was walloped against the side of the car door. "Ouch, dammit!" He rubbed his shoulder in aggravation, grateful the seat belt had kept him from more serious injury.

"Well, it speaks. Have a good nap?" She slowed the car and reached one hand over to rest lightly on his long leg, which was cramped in the small car. When he made no move to dislodge it, she chuckled and headed the car quietly up the road, taking the cutoff toward the rear of the big house. She'd traveled it so often she could have driven it without headlights, an unnecessary precaution. The cover afforded by the eucalyptus trees was ample.

Adam sat up and began to rub his temples. When he raised his right arm, his shoulder ached almost as abominably as the pounding in his head. "Shit! Where the hell are we, Transylvania?" He looked around at the trees shrouding them like some scene from an old Hammer movie. "Christ, I was only kidding about the vampire wedding."

She let out a low laugh as she turned off the ignition and doused the lights. "Now, are you all rested up? I promise to let you take shameless advantage of me." Her hand slid across his thigh, gripping it from the inside as she scooted closer.

He was sobering up fast by the time she pulled his head down and opened her lips, meeting his in an inviting kiss. Adam could feel the enticing curves of her breasts when she wriggled against him. For a fleeting moment he considered letting her continue the practiced seduction. But only for a fleeting moment. Then he felt an aching catch in his shoulder when he reached for her. His head added a sudden timpani of dull throbs. Enough was enough.

He pulled away. "Sorry, Riba. I'm in no shape for this. Too much beer and not enough sleep." *Or judgment.* He reached for the door handle, half surprised not to hear abusive recriminations from her.

She slid silently back behind the steering wheel and turned on the ignition. "Wade, you bastard, you'll wish to hell your oak stake had been pointed tonight," she hissed.

For a moment he thought foggily that she might be planning to run him down. But before he could do more than jump clear and slam the door, she hit reverse and was backing the car rapidly down the curving drive, heading it toward the big garage on the west side of the house.

He shrugged and began to walk, at last getting his bearings. He looked up at the hill behind him, remembering the day he had found Marti sketching there. "What the hell was I trying to do, make a comparison between sisters?" he muttered savagely to himself as he skirted well clear of the house and cut across the vineyards toward the bunkhouse.

Riba entered the house quietly. Checking to make sure Joe's door was closed and his light out, she headed quickly to Marti's room. It was past midnight, but she knocked softly, then slipped inside without waiting for an answer. The moon was bright enough to see all the way down the hill on the east side of the house, the path Adam must surely travel to the bunkhouse.

"What are you doing here, Riba?" Marti said, swinging her legs over the side of her bed.

Adam walked slowly in the cool air, letting the rich fecund smells of the soil and the vines soothe his troubled soul. Relief flooded his senses as he realized how narrow his escape had been from Riba. Of course, if he made it with her a few times, she'd quickly tire of him and turn her attention elsewhere. That solution to his dilemma did not appeal.

He forgot Riba as he walked, concentrating on his real problem—Marti. He would have to be very careful how he handled things with her, for they were both at risk in the relationship. "If there *is* a relationship," he muttered to himself as he headed past one of the larger storage sheds.

As he walked under the shadow of the shed roof, he slid on a small rock and lurched clumsily, grabbing the rough plank wall to right himself. In that split second a crash resounded inches away. Something very solid and heavy hit the ground with sickening impact. Then he heard the object roll several feet and come to rest against a tractor. A sixty gallon white oak barrel gleamed in the moonlight.

Dazedly, he looked up at the gaping hole of the storage barn's loading bay. This was where the new shipment of barrels had been placed until room was made for it in the plant. Nothing but silence and darkness greeted him as he peered upward. He moved cautiously away from the wall and glanced at the barrel. Quite intact, which was far more than could have been said of him if it had dropped full force on his head. *Or been thrown full force.*

Some primordial survival instinct left over from his two year Navy stint gave him a surge of sobering adrenaline. He felt transported back to the Philippines again, to the stench and the danger of the Manila waterfront. Was someone in the shed? A prickling around his collar told him yes. The pounding throb of his temples told him he was in no condition to investigate.

He scanned the area around the tractor for some sort of weapon. A very rusty socket wrench presented the only possibility. Hefting it dubiously in one hand, he began to edge carefully toward the side of the big shed. The door was locked. Odd. None of the work sheds at the vineyard had ever been locked. He circled the building and found nothing, then once more returned to the front and looked up into the open bay. Faintly now, he could see stacked barrels. It was possible one of them had been toppled out by a raccoon who had been trapped in the building. The curious beasts were always raising hell around the outbuildings. Kicking the heavy barrel with one booted foot, he somehow doubted that he had almost been brained by a coon.

"Well, my man, you can sit here and wait out some phantom assassin or you can get what's left of a night's sleep." The wicked throb of his hangover made the decision for him.

Marti lay in bed staring at the soft golden patterns of light playing across the ceiling. So much had happened so quickly, and so devastatingly. After her idyllic interlude with Adam that afternoon she had spent the evening like a fanciful schoolgirl, imagining all sorts of beautiful, wonderful, *impossible* things. He was a drifter, a man with no past, no future and no morals! *A man who had seduced a frightened emotional cripple!* How naive she had been.

When Riba's car pulled in she had awakened, knowing the familiar sounds of her sister's nocturnal habits.

Even before the preening blonde had come to her room to announce her triumph, Marti suspected. She had been awake, confused and restless, pacing and looking out her window. That was when she had seen Adam strolling slowly across the same field that he had walked that afternoon with her. It took no genius to put together her sister's late arrival home and the direction of Adam's route to the bunkhouse.

At least he did me one favor. I know I'm not some sort of frigid freak. I can respond—but to the right man, never again to that Lothario with his monumental case of machismo.

With a defiance born of heartache, Marti showered, curled her hair and applied light makeup. She dressed with great care in a stunning mint-green linen suit with a matching cream and green striped silk shirt. Slipping into a pair of bone Papagalo sling pumps, she inspected herself and decided she'd pass muster. Last week she had made an appointment to lunch with the director of the Symphony Society to discuss the fall programs. She would keep to her schedule of activities and Adam Wade be damned!

Swearing silently at her sister and the man who had caused her sleepless night, Marti descended the curving fan of the front stairs. Her father stood below watching her with penetrating gray eyes.

"Morning Papa. I must've overslept and I have an appointment in town."

"Some admirer I haven't met?" he questioned unsubtly.

"If you'd call Mr. Pfeiffer an admirer, you're really trying to marry off your spinster daughter," she said brightly.

Joe laughed. Hans Pfeiffer was sixty-five, a retired music professor from Berkeley, balding and overweight, not to mention married.

"You've changed so, honey. That's all I meant. With your new hairdo and clothes, well, you look glamorous. I expect some young blood around here will snap you up in no time. You got a few minutes to look at some lab reports before you go?"

At her affirmative nod, they proceeded down the hall to Joe's cluttered office. "With Riba going so far away to marry her lawyer, we're going to be all alone, honey. I'd always hoped you'd both settle down in the wine country."

"Somehow I don't think spending her life in Napa was ever in Riba's plans," she replied more caustically than she intended.

Joe Beaumont seemed to shrink into himself, shoulders slumped, head lowered as he shuffled papers awkwardly on the desk, looking for the reports amid the clutter. "Look, Marti, honey, I know you and your sister were always different. She's so like Bertrice. Your mother loved parties. Big city lights and elegant living. But she loved me enough to take a dirt farmer and teach him the right utensils to eat with at a fancy set table."

"And Riba's beautiful and fun-loving just like Mother," Marti said, amazed her voice carried past the lump in her throat.

Joe looked at her then, as if seeing her for the first time since she was a child. "You're beautiful, too, honey, like your mother. I have two wonderful girls—so much of Bertrice. I've been a lucky man in spite of losing her."

Marti had never understood the obsessive love her father had for her mother . . . until that moment. She took the papers he held unaware in his hands and laid them gently on the desk. "You don't want me to check lab reports, do you, Papa?"

He sighed. "You can always see through the old man. You and me, Martha, we love the land, the grapes, making something that lives for years after the harvest. Neither your mother nor Riba could ever share that with us. And now . . ." he spread his gnarled, sun stained hands in a helpless gesture. "I see you changing so much, so quick." He paused again and faced Marti, gray eyes meeting gray eyes levelly. "You gonna go off and leave me, too?"

"A few new clothes and a haircut hardly mean an elopement's in the wind, Papa," Marti replied as smoothly as she could. "I just got tired of looking like a frump. My friend Alice talked me into a new look. That's all."

"You been going out with some fellows from town. Anyone in particular?"

"No. I've had a few dates the past weeks. You know the men, Papa. I'm not likely to elope with an east coast socialite." *Do you want me to leave Chateau Beaumont at all?*

Her father's next words were an answer to her silent query. "What about Boris? I know he's asked you out. You got a lot in common, Martha. He'd be a good man for you."

For me or for you, Papa? Anguished, she turned away. "I don't have any plans to marry, Papa. Boris and I work together. That's all. I'm just testing my new wings with a few dates, nothing more."

"Just see you let me check your callers out. I like Riba's Larry even if I do wish he lived in California, not Philadelphia. He's from good stock. Blood will tell. I want the best for my girls, Martha, only the best."

"Yes, Papa, I know you do," she replied gently.

Chapter 9

"Damn Ansel McGee!" Joe Beaumont paced around the packed earth in front of the mechanics barn, looking at the sky—a brilliant azure dome dotted with a few fleecy puffs of cloud and a rainbow array of hot air balloons. But the drone of a crop plane did not disturb the silence of the early morning. "That old son-of-a-bitch is drunk again in some gutter."

Joe swore some more as Les Reams tried to placate him. "Ansel's been doing real good. Dusted Wilkens and Selms last week. He's been on the wagon all summer. I called the director at the Davis Airport before I even went over to his place this spring."

Joe angrily gestured northward to the small air strip they used for the crop plane. "You see him coming up to hit us or are my eyes failing me?"

"No. I'll go and see what's happened, Joe. Maybe we could get Barths to do it if Ansel can't," Les supplied worriedly.

Joe snorted in derision and swore again. "I just checked with Barth and every other small contractor in flying distance this morning. It's the busy season and they're all booked. Been such a damn good year the vines are already too big and thick for running machinery between the rows."

As they talked, Joe and Les's loud voices carried across the field to Marti. "Ansel still hasn't shown or called?" she asked, as she approached the two men. She read the answer on their faces.

"I'm going over to his place—"

"I'll go, Les," Marti interrupted. She had known Ansel McGee since her childhood and felt a special affinity for the old flying ace. "You have enough to do here."

"He's probably drunk. Won't answer his phone," Joe declared, turning on his heel to stomp inside the tool barn. "Hell with him! Les, see how many tractors Benteen can get operating to dust again from the ground."

"Joe, that'll break the vines . . ." Les's words faded as Marti walked with long strides up the hill to the garage. She decided to take the Jeep since Ansel's place was a small shanty on a back county road in the foothills.

As she drove, she recalled the kind old man who had been a decorated pilot in the Second World War. When she visited his cluttered old shack as an awe filled child, Ansel had let her examine his Distinguished Flying Cross and the other medals he'd won in two theaters of the war.

That was before he began to drink. Perhaps the war was why. Once he'd mentioned bombing runs over Dresden and Cologne. When she was in college and read about the phosphorous bombing of civilians, Marti began to understand Ansel McGee's reasons for drinking. Mostly he went on benders in the winter season when he couldn't fly. During the summer he had been reliable, if a trifle red eyed and rumpled when he came to collect his pay. Now he was a lonely old man, living a virtual hermit's existence except for his forays into the cheap bars in town. But he had never missed a dusting job for Joe Beaumont. It took her over half an hour to reach his house northeast of town in the rough foothills.

When she pulled up in front of the dilapidated old building, Marti was appalled at its condition. Always shabby, it now looked positively neglected, soaked by rain and baked by sun until the cheap tar paper shingles had peeled off the weathered boards beneath, exposing them like obscene sores. The yard was thick with waist high weeds and only a twisting path of sorts indicated a safe route from the road to the door. Glad of her jeans and boots, she jumped from the Jeep and headed along the tortuous path, pushing aside clumps of wild mustard and dock. When she reached the door, her first rap sent it swinging inward.

"Ansel? Hello. It's Marti Beaumont." Slowly, she stepped inside and let her eyes adjust to the gloom. Dishes encrusted with burned food and green mold were piled across the sink and table. A carry out pizza box was balanced precariously on a McDonald's milk shake cup. The contents of both had been partially consumed. The smell of curdled milk, rancid meat and sour whiskey blended together, smelling like scrapings from the San Francisco drunk tank late on a Saturday night.

She scanned an alarming series of empty pint bottles, leading like a trail toward the closed bedroom door. When she opened it, she saw Ansel sprawled across the bed, fully dressed, face down. Quickly she dropped to one knee by the bedside and checked for a pulse. He was breathing, but his pulse was erratic and his skin burning up. After several futile attempts to rouse him, she picked up the phone and dialed for an ambulance.

Hilda answered the phone at the big house nearly an hour later and took a frantic message from Marti to her father. Ansel was gravely ill, apparently the after-effects of an all night drinking binge, but the doctors at Queen of the Valley Hospital weren't sure yet. She was staying until he regained consciousness.

When Joe heard the news, he pounded the side of a big John Deere hood, nearly breaking his hand in a fit of temper. "Goddamn drunk! I bet he hasn't even got his plane in shape to fly or the sulphur loaded."

"What difference if he has? We can't fly it without him," Les said sourly.

Several of the hands had gathered in the shed, working on tractors with Nate Benteen, the mechanic. Adam, who had been bending over a big grease-coated engine, straightened up and put his tools down. "If it's in running order, I can fly the plane and dust."

Les's jaw dropped. "You got a pilot's license?"

"For small aircraft, yes," Adam answered. Anticipating the next question, he added, "My California agricultural applicator's license is updated, too. If the owner of this plane agrees and the airport will clear me, I can handle the sulphur. I've done it up north."

Juan snorted. "Spraying from a plane sure beats hell out of doing it from the ground." Several other men chimed agreement, especially since it meant they didn't have to do it.

"It's easier on the vines, that's for sure," Joe said and the matter was settled. "Dig out that license and head for the airstrip. I'll phone the Napa Airport and see if they'll let you land for refueling if you need to."

"That's okay, Mr. Beaumont. Let me handle the director myself. I'll need to get McGee's signature on some papers before I can use his plane anyway. I'll call you if and when I can get his crate airborne. I've heard stories about Ansel up and down the coast for years. If that old Boeing Stearman is flyable, I'll do it."

"Anything to keep the grease from beneath your fingernails," Bob called good naturedly after Adam.

Nate Benteen spat on the dirt floor contemptuously and said, "Pretty dude better be ready for hell in a hand basket if he goes up in that old drunk's wreck. Me, I'll take the grease."

Adam drove first to the Napa County Airport and explained the problem with Ansel, whom they knew well. He could pick up McGee's old Stearman at the small private airstrip, but the Napa Airport no longer let crop dusting planes land at their facility except to pick up extra fuel. Adam settled that matter with the aviation director's office before he left the airport. Next he headed across town to the Queen of the Valley Hospital to see if McGee was able to sign release papers for him. Of course, he'd have to be careful so Marti didn't see them, or his license with his real name on it. Adam Moreland.

He hadn't seen her in two days. But tomorrow was Saturday and the next day he was taking her to the art show. Before then he had to get some things sorted out. He could not tell her about himself yet, but at least he felt more certain that their relationship could continue. After his night of drunken reflection and the following day of hungover penance, he knew he was in pretty deep.

"Shit, here I am mooning over a date at an art show," he muttered as he drove the old truck across Trancas Street and pulled into the hospital parking lot. He grinned. Already he couldn't wait to see her, talk to her, touch her. "Marti, woman, what have you done to me?" He went whistling into the hospital.

When he finally located Ansel McGee's room, Marti was engaged in earnest conversation with the grizzled old man. Just watching the sun gild her hair with amber highlights made his heart race. He knocked on the open door and she raised her face to look at him. Instead of the welcoming smile he expected, she gave him a frosty look of inspection as if he had just taken a Wassermann and flunked.

"What are you doing here, Adam?" she asked in cool perplexity.

Adam felt like a third grader sent to the principal's office. "Seems your daddy wants me to fly a plane for him," he replied, equally cool.

Now the facade broke as her eyes widened. "You? Fly Ansel's plane? But, how . . ."

"I've had a license for years," he replied, wanting to dismiss the discussion until a more private time. He turned his attention to the haggard man with thinning gray hair sticking out at Dagwood angles. "Mr. Beaumont wants to know if your Stearman's fit to fly, and if you have the sulphur on board. I can pick up any extra fuel at the county airport."

Ansel McGee turned his very bloodshot eyes toward Adam. "Tank's filled with enough gas for today. Engine's all checked out and sulphur's ready to let 'er rip, son. I expect Mr. B's madder 'n Bejesus cause I let him down," he added sourly. "I was just telling Marti, I never done no drinking the night before a job . . . until last night. This here dude in the Wrangler Bar was buying and took a real personal liking to me . . ." his words trailed off aimlessly as his big thick hands began to fidget with the bedsheet.

"You're lucky to be alive, Ansel," Marti said gently. "Who was this dubious benefactor of yours?"

"Dunno. Never seen him before. From somewhere south of here. Heard him mention the Big Valley, I think," Ansel replied wearily.

"I have some papers for you to sign, McGee. That is, if you'll trust me with your plane. I've been cleared by the Napa Airport and I have an agricultural applicator's license." He looked at the old man questioningly, deliberately avoiding Marti's recriminating stare.

Ansel shrugged, then winced and gripped his stomach. "Sure, son. I owe Mr. B and this here little girl and I let them down. If you can fly it, you got yourself a plane."

Quickly, Adam slipped a sheath of papers from his back pocket and neared the bed. He laid them on the bedside table. When he reached out to roll the table across the bed so Ansel could reach it, Marti stepped back, careful not to brush against him. He could feel the stiffening in her body without even facing her.

"You have a pen we could use?" he asked her.

She rooted in a small leather bag for a moment and came up with one. When he reached for it he deliberately touched her fingers and felt her pull away. *Damn woman! What's wrong with you?* He watched her help the old man lean forward to sign the papers, plumping pillows behind his back like a regular Florence Nightingale.

Ansel signed where indicated without reading the releases. His hand shook from a combination of guilt, exhaustion and illness, Adam surmised as he thanked the old man and offered a handshake. "I should be done tomorrow by the latest if I can't finish today."

"No problem," Ansel replied with another wince of pain. "I ain't going to use it for a good while if them doctors are right."

"Do what they say and you'll be at the throttle soon enough," Adam said as he folded the papers and replaced them in his pocket. "Can I talk to you outside for a minute, Marti?" Without giving her a chance to reply he snatched her hand deftly, leaving her with the choice of making a scene or complying.

"I'll be right back, Ansel," she said with a hostile glare at her captor. Once out in the hall, he ushered her into a deserted sitting room. She fairly yanked her elbow from his grasp and whirled furiously on him. "Keep your hands to yourself, Adam Wade!"

His puzzled look quickly darkened into a scowl as he stared at the silver-eyed fury facing him. "Don't play games with me, Marti. You came looking for me in that wine tank. Having second thoughts about how your father will react if he finds out you're acting like Riba?"

Emitting a wounded gasp, she reached up to slap him, but his hand shot out and grabbed her wrist. He shook his head in mock reproof, then dropped the slim arm roughly. "If you really want to copy your sister, you'll need a lot more practice." With that he turned and stalked out.

Marti stood and stared after his retreating figure as tears blurred her vision. Furiously, she dashed them away. How could he just waltz in that room so casually after what he'd done to her? And then to have the nerve to mention Riba? Surely he knew Riba would tell her about her triumph.

She hugged herself like a child with an unbearable ache, unable to tell anyone where it hurt. *I hurt all over, I guess,* she thought forlornly, comparing herself to the desperately ill old man down the hall. *We both need a friend, don't we, Ansel?* She felt uncertain if she could even tell Alice about Adam's betrayal. Forcing it from her mind, she stiffened her spine and returned to McGee's room.

A nurse was there, giving Ansel a shot. He grinned at her, a bit green around the gills, but trying to put on a game front. "This here lady says it's sleepytime for me. I want to thank you, Marti. If you hadn't come out to my place, I'd be a goner by now."

She gave him an affectionate peck on the cheek. "Just don't let friends buy you drinks all night long—

ever again, Ansel McGee. You hear? We need you to dust our grapes."

"Looks like that young fellow could handle the job all right. Real take charge kind, that one. Nice looking, too. You and him seem to know one another pretty good . . ." His voice trailed off as he began to doze.

The nurse winked at Marti and said, "He needs some rest, Miss Beaumont. Dr. Buche will call you if there's any change."

"All right. I'll be at home for the rest of the day. Tell Ansel I'll come back tomorrow when he'll feel more like company."

On the way home, Marti deliberately kept her mind blank, concentrating on the drive, trying desperately not to replay the vivid images Riba had described of Adam making love to her. Oddly, for the past two nights they had become intermingled with dreams of herself and Adam. She could still smell the perfume of wine must and male musk, a heady sensual blend that made her heart ache more with every mile.

With the wind beating against his body, Adam felt the old familiar vibrations as the bright yellow Stearman took off. The respirator and goggles offered some protection, but it was a hot, dirty job and he hated it. This plane was older than the last ones he had flown but the operation was basically the same. God, he loathed the stink of sulphur. But it was a job to be done.

As he circled and headed down for his first pass at the southernmost block of grapes, he thought of the aloof, beautiful woman who had complicated his life. Why was she suddenly so cold? Then angry? He hadn't meant to taunt her with that cruel comparison to Riba, but her withdrawal had hurt him more than he had believed possible. Then suddenly it hit him. Riba! That night in the bar—the ride home and her clumsy seduction attempt. He had staggered down to the bunkhouse while she parked her new toy in the garage. "I'll bet she broke a leg getting up to Marti's room to make up one hell of a story, that vicious, lying, little bitch," he ground out as he pushed the gate handle forward, releasing a spume of sulphur over the long straight rows of trellised vines below.

Just then the plane made a sudden lurch as he swooped low. The Stearman was bucking like the meanest brahma bull at the Pendleton Roundup. Then the engine began stalling. Despite its age and the dubious reputation of its owner, the plane had flown perfectly since takeoff. It wasn't now. From the ground Joe, Les and a number of the hands had been watching Adam's descent.

"Shit! He's flopping like a headless chicken," Bob said, watching the erratic sideways motions of the biplane.

"Damn McGee! When's the last time he worked on that crate?" Les rasped furiously.

"Mebbe Wade just don't know how to fly an old Stearman. Seems right hard on the equipment 'round here if you ask me," Nate Benteen said, scratching his greasy shirt with complete indifference.

"No one asked you, *mano,*" Bob replied with a steely tone in his voice. He stepped menacingly toward the small mechanic, but just then sounds coming from the plane caught his attention once again.

Marti had left the hospital and driven straight home. When she heard the familiar drone of Ansel's plane she had driven her Jeep down to the field. In spite of herself, she was curious to see Adam fly. If she went to the house she'd doubtless encounter her late rising sister, a particularly distasteful idea at the moment. Then she, too, saw the plane in distress and watched with eyes glued to the sky as Adam circled unsteadily and headed south in the direction of the Napa Airport's larger and safer landing surface.

She found herself praying he would make it as she jammed the Jeep in reverse and backed around to follow him. The dust kicked up by her four wheel drive was nearly as thick as a spume of sulphur. *Please, Adam, please land safely. Oh, God don't let anything happen to him!*

Adam was doing a little praying himself about then. The right elevator wasn't working at all and the left one barely. The vibrations that jarred the careening small plane would tear it apart in midair if he didn't put it down immediately. The problem was how to do that without the elevators. He'd seen old World War II films where the flying ace "side slipped for the runway" and made a hairbreadth dramatic landing. It suddenly struck him that he'd seen too many B movies. Still, if he could use the aileron and rudder to compensate for the malfunctioning elevators, maybe he could make it—if he could keep the crate from ripping apart first!

Considering that the old biplane was nothing more than a metal frame with painted linen stretched over it from nose to tail, that was a big "if." He looked at the ground and realized trying such a desperate landing in the trellised vineyards, interspersed with their windmills and irrigation equipment, would be suicide in the cloth plane. If only he could make it to the open strip at Napa, there might be a chance.

"Damn," Adam muttered as his feet worked the rudders, trying to compensate for the collapsed elevator, which seemed to be blocking the right rudder. The Stearman bucked and lurched crazily, but somehow held together as he neared the runway at the county airport.

To get the plane down he had to use the throttle to control descent, opening it up full power, then cutting back to idle. As he dropped precariously by this erratic method, the engine surged, then choked, then surged again. He was soaked with sweat and found breathing nearly impossible, but had not a free second or free hand to rip off the respirator. In fact, a pair of extra hands and feet would have been welcome about then as his right hand moved the stick while the left worked the throttle. Both feet pumped on the rudder pedals like a madcap cyclist in the circus. As the runway came up to kiss him in his lurching, surging approach, he wondered if the plane would hold together on impact. Given how much practice he'd had at stunt flying, the chances were about as good as a *National Enquirer* reporter winning a Pulitzer Prize. "I'll probably fry with this crate," he muttered as he felt the wheels make jarring contact with the ground. Miraculously, despite the absence of any semblance of control, the plane stopped bucking and zigzagged crazily to a standstill. It was even on the runway . . . well, almost.

"Either Ansel McGee works on his plane while he's dead drunk or he lied in front of Marti about checking this fucking hunk of junk," Adam muttered furiously. He was soaking wet and trembling as he angrily yanked the respirator and goggles off. "First a truck without brakes, then a plane that stalls out." Of course the truck had some help from that damn joy rider who took the British side of the road. Something niggled at the back of his consciousness as he climbed shakily out of the plane. "A truck accident, a plane accident and don't forget nearly being brained by a sixty gallon white oak barrel the other night."

By this time several men had run across the field towards him. "Some touchdown, son, considering," the field manager said. "What in hell happened? Looked like you couldn't have made it a dozen feet further. Ain't like McGee to send a man up if his plane wasn't tip top."

"He was in a bar getting swacked yesterday afternoon," Adam said uncharitably. Then it hit him—*This here dude in the Wrangler Bar was buying and took a real personal liking to me.* The field manager's comment caused Ansel's words to flash into his mind.

He unzipped the suffocating jumpsuit and peeled it off, then walked to the rear of the plane. Quickly, two of the other men, a mechanic and another pilot, followed to help him. The search took only a couple of minutes.

It was an easy job, but devilishly clever. Hardened by several layers of paint, the linen covering on the elevators had been soaked through on their underside with some sort of solvent. The cloth was soft and eaten away, rendering the elevators virtually useless. Fortunately the left one had not been as completely damaged as the right. He rubbed his fingers across the bottom of the remaining cloth on the left elevator and smelled. "Turpentine," he muttered. Easy enough to detect now, but invisible when he took off. If he'd crashed and been incinerated in a fiery explosion, no one would ever have found it!

When Marti drove onto the field her heart was hammering. She'd heard no crash. Surely there would have been the sound of a crash—an explosion. No! He had to be on the ground by now, safe, alive. When she saw Ansel's plane at the end of the runway, she gunned the Jeep blindly down it and skidded to a halt a few yards from them, her eyes frantically scanning the small group of men for Adam.

He heard the approaching vehicle and turned in time to see Marti leap from the Jeep. Adam could feel the breathless rush of air being expelled from her lungs as she catapulted into his arms. Unaware of his grimy hands and shirt, he embraced her and began to kiss the tears from her cheeks and eyes.

"I'm all right, babe. It's all over. Everything's okay," he crooned.

"Oh, Adam, I thought you—" she shuddered in his arms and then brought his head down to meet hers once more, giving him a fulsome, life affirming kiss, totally oblivious of the gaping audience.

Slowly, as she calmed, Marti became aware of the eyes fastened on them. Without releasing her, Adam began to walk them around the plane, away from prying curiosity.

"Look, babe, I know why you were so cold at the hospital."

She looked down at the ground, realizing how her wildly reckless display must have appeared to the men. *I must be crazy!* "I found out about—"

"You listened to Riba," he interrupted. "How about giving me a chance to explain? After I left you in the afternoon, I went to town with Bob Vasquez for a few drinks . . . I needed to think things out. He picked the place—a bar and pool hall in a rundown neighborhood. Riba was there, with some grower she knew from Sonoma." He could sense her stiffening. "Bob and I drank for a while and then he took off with a waitress. I needed to clear my head, so I planned to walk back. Riba caught me at the door and offered me a ride. Hell, it was a long walk and I'd gotten drunker than I realized. I took her up on the ride."

Her eyes questioned him, daring for the first time to meet his.

"When we got to the big house, she—"

"She pulled into her back yard lover's lane behind the pool," Marti interrupted, her voice weary and sad. *How many times has she done this by now?*

He shrugged with a bitter smile. "I imagine she could drive that stretch blindfolded. But that's the end of my story, babe. She parked just as I was coming to. I, er, dozed a bit on the return trip. *Nothing* happened. Shit, even if I'd wanted to, I was too damned drunk. I told her good night and headed to the bunkhouse. I can just imagine how fast she ran to your room. Tell me, did I succumb to her charms—or did I try to rape her?" He waited with his heart caught in his throat.

When she searched his face silently, he was goaded to ask, "Who do you believe, Marti? Your sister or me. It's that simple."

"No, no, it isn't simple at all, damn you! I know what Riba is, but you're the cypher, Adam. I don't know you . . . who you are, where you come from, why you came to Beaumonts. Why you ignored my beautiful sister and noticed me in the first place! After we made love why did you have to go to town and get drunk?" *He's telling the truth about Riba, but it doesn't solve anything.*

Adam could read her thoughts, so transparently did her face and body language reveal them. Softly, he stroked her cheek, then smiled and reached for a handkerchief to wipe the smudge of sticky yellowish paint his hand had left. "I've marked you, I'm afraid," he said.

"More than you know, Adam," she replied, her silver gray eyes meeting his dark blue ones levelly, waiting for him to say . . . what?

"There's so much I need to tell you, babe, to explain, but it's not easy."

"Like how a seasonal worker happens to have a pilot's license?" She skirted the underlying issues, suddenly afraid of what he'd reveal.

"Maybe I learned in the Navy," he said, trying to defuse a ticklish situation.

"And your flight instructor taught you how to dust grape vines with Agent Orange," she shot back with rancor, moving angrily away from his touch.

He came up behind her and put his hands on her shoulders. "Marti, all I can say for now is that there are some things I have to clear up. Things I've been running from for a long time."

"And what then, Adam? What am I supposed to do? Wait by the fire like a damned housecat?"

He turned her in his arms and forced her to look at him. "Can you trust me for a few weeks?"

The worry behind that level blue gaze reached out to her and she wrapped her arms around his waist with a sob. "What is it, Adam? Why can't *you* trust me?" *Don't you love me?*

He stroked her hair, murmuring low, "We both have specters from our past to face. You haven't told your father about us, have you?"

Her breath caught in her throat and she knew he felt her reaction. "After today, I imagine the gossip will beat me to it," she replied weakly.

"Like all the stories about Riba? When it comes to old Joe's daughters, they're royalty. No one but you will tell him."

"All right. Checkmate. I can't tell a vulnerable old man about becoming involved with a stranger—a man with no past and no future. Riba's escapades would kill him if he ever found out. She takes that chance. I won't. When I tell Papa about Adam Wade, I want to be able to answer every question he can ask."

"When you tell him, Marti, I'll be there with you

and I'll answer anything he can throw at me," he replied levelly. "But for now, let's clean a little of the evidence off you. Nothing as damning as fingerprints." Lightness once more pervaded his voice as he kissed her nose and then began to daub at the yellow prints on her face, neck and arms.

"You're covered with paint from the Stearman. Why were you checking Ansel's plane? Had he neglected something so it malfunctioned?" She was busily engaged in rubbing a large streak from her upper arm and didn't notice the shadowing of his expression.

"Ansel didn't neglect anything. Just one of those routine foul ups in old planes," he lied with soothing skill. "Now, I have to see about getting this crate repaired so I can finish the job. You head back to the vineyard and tell your father not to worry."

Before she could argue or question him any more, he gave her an affectionate kiss and turned her back toward her Jeep.

When she had driven away he walked back to the group of men at the plane. "I need a favor. No one here say anything about this plane being sabotaged. Okay?"

Chapter 10

After supper that evening, Adam walked outside with Bob Vasquez. Bending forward to light a cigarette, he looked casually around to see if they were alone. "You know everyone from here to Mendocino."

Bob grinned. "If I don't my Uncle Hector does. Why?"

"A man was in the Wrangler Bar last night, buying drinks all around, especially for Ansel McGee. I'd like to know who he was. Ansel said he wasn't local. Also, anything you can find out about Benteen—especially if he ever worked on crop dusting planes."

Vasquez let out a long low whistle. "You saying that trouble today wasn't an accident?"

Adam gave his friend a capsulized version of the incidents with the truck, the oak barrel and the tampering on Ansel's plane. "Everyone knew Ansel had a drinking problem. Mighty strange that he's provided with a free larder the night before he's slated to dust Beaumont grapes," he concluded darkly.

"But if Nate or someone did tamper with the plane they thought Ansel would be flying it, not you," Bob said in confusion. "How—"

"I told Joe and a big crowd of men, including Benteen, that I'd do the dusting. Don't forget, after getting rid of Ansel, someone had plenty of time to set me up. I drove to the airport, to the hospital for Ansel to sign a release, then over to get the plane. Benteen would have had plenty of time," Adam said, flipping his cigarette across the dusty ground. It arched like a firefly in the darkness, then sputtered out when it hit the earth.

"You have any idea who has a real abnormal urge to see you dead, *mano*? I don't figure a guy like Benteen would do anything without being paid."

"Just find out who the dude buying the drinks was and if he's connected to Nate Benteen. I'll work on the rest," Adam replied.

"I thought you were at the fairgrounds setting up with Alice." Adam greeted Marti with a smile, pausing in the midst of cleaning a winepress.

"Nope. Now it's only one entry per contestant. Alice told me she has my 'Budbreak' and four other entries to deliver. I decided she could handle that. Since the judging's not until tomorrow and the awards are on Sunday, I thought I could be more useful around here today." Marti was dressed in her usual T-shirt and jeans with comfortable sandals on her feet. But her hair was piled atop her head in a casual tumble of curls secured with a bright blue cotton scarf. She wore a light touch of makeup and looked wonderfully wholesome.

"You look delectable, lady—too pretty to scrub rusty old machinery," he said with a dare shining in his eyes.

Planting her legs firmly apart with hands on hips, she grinned cheekily back at him. "I'll have you know these jeans have been exposed to more rusty water and spider webs than yours."

"Prove it," he replied, tossing her a wet rag.

She caught it in both hands with a resounding plop and set to work. They spent the rest of the morning scrubbing, then hosing down presses and gondolas. If the other men noticed the bantering informality between Marti and Adam, no one acknowledged its significance. When the hot summer sun signaled lunch time, Marti was as sweaty and soaked with soapy water as any of the workers. Cheerfully ignoring her dishabillé, she swiped at a piece of sudsy foam itching her nose, then adjusted her slipping bandana to keep her hair from falling.

Adam watched her, marveling still at how naturally

she worked alongside the men. *Alongside me.* "Want some lunch? It's not elegant, but the beer's cold and the sandwiches are filling."

They strolled companionably toward the mess tent, laughing at a story Bob Vasquez was telling about his cousin Jorge. Noticing Boris Staritz striding past in the distance, Adam commented to Marti in a low voice. "Any special reason he's hanging around?"

"If you mean is he spying on us, I doubt anything so melodramatic. Papa probably mentioned you did such a good job with the spraying that he had to check it for himself," she teased.

"To see if I missed a grape," he replied drily.

"Are you going to do any more flying? Ansel's being discharged this weekend," she added with a worried frown.

"He can have the spraying, respirator, body suit, goggles and all. God, I hate the stink of sulphur."

"Rather smell like rotten wood, huh?" she said with a mock sniff.

"Or a wet dog," he shot back, giving a yank on her damp, stained T-shirt.

"I'll fix you, Adam Wade, see if I don't," she promised. The devil danced in her eyes with an unholy silver light. "We'll see who's a wet dog before the afternoon's done."

They returned to the scrubbing within half an hour, this time working in an open area in front of the winery where a long line of grape-hauling gondolas had been placed in a row. The big steel bins, designed to tip their loads of ripe grapes into the crushers, had been sitting empty since the last harvest. Home for industrious spiders and a thick accumulation of grime, they required a thorough cleaning before the fall crush once more got under way.

Marti grabbed one of the big high pressure hoses before any of the men beat her to it and set to work. First they used a special soap preparation on the gondolas and then pulled them one by one over to where she sprayed them until all remnants of dirt and cleaner were removed. Adam, directed by Ferris Beecher, had worked on one particularly dirty, older model. It was the last in line to be rinsed. When he rolled it up to Marti for hosing down, it seemed as if all the other hands scattered on a prearranged signal. It was near quitting time and Adam was hot, tired and eager to finish up. Preoccupied by the past week's events, he did not notice Marti as she readied the hose. Just as he tripped the lever to turn the gondola on its side, she struck. Instead of spraying the bin, she soaked him. Bent over, his jean clad rear end provided an irresistible target. Her aim was perfect.

Adam straightened up with a yelp of surprise as the needle spray stung him. "Sonofa—you!" He whirled on the grinning woman with a scowl. "Give me that hose!" His advance was rewarded with a blast squarely on his chest that nearly peeled his open shirt from his body. Laughing and swearing, he dodged and rolled over to where another hose lay innocently coiled against the wall. He hit the spigot and turned the nozzle just as Marti's third shot soaked him, plastering his hair in an inky splotch over his eyes. Standing up, he shook his head like the "wet dog" she had taken umbrage at and then aimed his weapon.

The first icy blast caught her on the hip as she turned quickly to provide a smaller target. Then the stream of water arced higher, soaking her T-shirt and knocking the bandana from her head. Her hair spilled in dark cascading waves down her back as she shrieked and backed off, protesting, "Adam! You weren't supposed to be armed, dammit!"

"This is a fair fight—women's lib and all that rot, right?" He advanced with his hose.

Suddenly she pulled a sneaky maneuver, dropping to her knees and then rolling to the side of one of the gondolas for cover. From there she aimed her weapon squarely at his navel—then lowered it.

His return spray went wild, hitting the flat metal side of the bin and bouncing off with a fine mist of rainbow colors that matched his vocabulary perfectly.

By this time both duelists were howling with laughter and the onlookers were cheering boisterously and making bets about who would emerge the winner.

Adam had recovered his breath and was once more in control of his weapon, aiming for his scrambling antagonist who had retreated beneath the gondola. Her spray came out at ankle height, soaking a good pair of boots. "Coward! Stand and deliver," he roared out in his best Lawrence Olivier voice. The spray danced around her derriere as she scooted further beneath the machinery with a whoop.

Then, in an abrupt reversal, she leaped to her feet on the far side of the gondola, nozzle in hand, hitting him square in the face. But her haste was her undoing. The length of her hose, pulled from beneath the bin, entangled her legs and down she went in an ignominious heap, dropping her weapon and rolling out onto the exposed dirt road. Adam was on her at once, holding the shut-off nozzle of his hose to her throat.

"Now I've got you where I want you," he breathed, looking down at her heaving breasts as she lay stretched across the ground.

With a water logged whoosh she flailed against him, knocking the hose from his grasp and rolling on top of him as he fell back. Both were convulsed with laughter, shaking, coughing and gasping for air. His hands, warm and caressing, roamed across her back, molding her soaked clothing to her body as she straddled his hips. Suddenly they were both acutely aware of where they were and what they were doing. Her soft bra did little to conceal her breasts and her thin shirt was all but transparent. Adam could feel her hardened nipples pressed against his bare chest. Marti could feel the flexing of his thigh muscles as he struggled to control a very primal instinct. As they rolled apart and began to rise an angry voice cut through the noise of the laughing onlookers.

"Marti! Are you hurt? What the hell has he done to you? Wade, you're fired!" Boris Staritz's black eyes blazed and his jaw was clenched with fury as he reached down and yanked Marti up.

All his precipitous action did was reveal more of

her anatomy to the men. Furiously she turned, wrapping her arms about her breasts and gritting out over her shoulder, "Try not to make a bigger ass out of yourself than you already have of me, Boris!"

Before he could reply, Adam had yanked off his shirt and was draping it around her. "Go back to the house. I'll handle Staritz," he commanded.

"You won't do shit! You're fired!" the winemaster rasped.

"Joe Beaumont hired me. He can fire me," Adam replied levelly, squaring off against the menacing Russian.

"Both of you, shut up!" Marti hissed, juxtaposing herself between the two men. "No one—neither of you will say a word of this to my father. Is that clear? Or, by god almighty, *I'll* fire you both!"

"Nobody'll talk to Joe, Marti," Adam replied with leashed anger, giving her a forceful nudge from between them. "Now go to the house before he comes looking for you and doesn't like what he finds. Let the winemaster and me settle this for ourselves. I think he's been waiting for a long time. Right, Staritz?"

"You fucking gigolo," Boris grated in a voice so low it did not carry to the men on the other side of the road, who were watching with even more interest since the winemaster had intervened in the horseplay. Ignoring them, he turned to Marti and said stridently, "Wade's right. Look at you—virtually naked, rolling around on the ground like—"

"Like my sister? You're far better acquainted with her than you are with me, Boris, so save your lectures!" She turned on Adam then, clutching his shirt protectively around her shoulders. "Beat one another senseless for all I care and be damned!" With that she stalked up the road toward the house in long steady strides, never looking back.

"Now, Staritz, it seems you have something to settle with me," Adam said with a sharkish grin. He stood, bare chested with water glistening on his body, waiting for Boris to make his move.

The thicker, slightly shorter man obliged with a

lightening fast jab toward that insolent grin, but Wade moved quickly, too, dancing backward to avoid the neatly executed blow. "You boxed in college, eh, Boris?"

"And I'm going to give you a lesson," Staritz said, once more jabbing with his left, then following through with a strong right to the midsection. This time Adam was unable to avoid the second punch and staggered, but remained on his feet, once more circling and watching as he regained the breath forcibly expelled from his lungs.

"Not bad for a college boy," he said as he grabbed the Russian's wrist, pivoting under the man's outstretched arm.

Thrown off balance by the maneuver, Boris suddenly found his arm, extended for a jab, being levered across Adam's shoulder. Adam bent forward and twisted, sending the Russian's body arcing over his shoulder and crashing to the muddy gravel.

"You need to learn how to fall, Boris," Adam said evenly.

"And you need to learn how to duck," the infuriated winemaster replied as he quickly shook his head and rolled up in one motion, fists raised. He snapped a series of surprisingly fast punches at Wade's midsection and jaw, connecting several times before Adam pivoted and knocked Staritz's elbow to the right so the jab missed his face. Instantly, Adam came in once more, driving the heel of his hand under Boris's chin. Once more the Russian went down with sickening impact. This time he rose a fraction slower, but nonetheless doggedly raised his hands again. He was winded but his infuriatingly unruffled opponent stood back and waited with casual disinterest.

"I guess I need to finish what you started, don't I?" Adam said with a resigned sigh. This time he didn't wait for the heavier man to move in and punch but took the offensive with one lightening kick to the Russian's left kneecap. When Boris's leg buckled and he pitched forward, Adam's knee came up with wicked impact and caught him under his jaw. This sent the winemaster reeling and left him open for Adam's elbow blow directly into his solar plexus. Staritz collapsed backward and doubled over. He hit the ground on the seat of his pants, gave one loud gurgling choke and keeled onto his side, out cold. Adam's maneuver was executed with blurring speed and machine like efficiency.

Ferris Beecher was the first man to reach Adam, who was now somewhat visibly out of breath and rubbing his midsection gingerly. "No one ever beat that Russian," he said in amazement, his dislike of the arrogant winemaster evident in his voice. "He was a college boxing champ."

Adam grinned past his split lip. "I was on a team, too . . . sort of. Shore Patrol on the Manila waterfront. Navy taught us a smattering of martial arts." He turned toward the bunkhouse saying simply, "I need a dry shirt," and strode quickly away as the men crowded around the winemaster who was groaning and beginning to regain consciousness.

As Adam changed clothes, he brooded. It had felt good to take out his frustration on Staritz, but it solved nothing. In fact, it only complicated his relationship with Marti. Damn, she was the cause of it all. No one had bothered him, much less tried to kill him, until he became involved with her—or until he came to work for Joe Beaumont, he considered uneasily. *I hope Bob gets a line on the big spender in the Wrangler Bar.*

Before he could tell Marti who he was he had to uncover the dangerous man or men who pursued him. But, he thought bitterly, the lady was scarcely in a mood to listen at the moment. She was still terrified that her father would object to her relationship with him. Would it matter whether or not he was a penniless drifter? Or was the real problem *any* man who would take the old man's crutch away from him? *Someday you'll have to choose, Marti.*

Tomorrow he was supposed to take her to the art fair. Somehow he suspected she might have changed her mind about their date. She was afraid of the physical bond that seemed to draw them irresistibly together. He recalled the way her wet, pliant body felt as they wrestled on the ground after the water fight, and he realized that he was as afraid of that attraction as Marti.

Affirming his surmize, Old Jules Steiger delivered a note to Adam at the bunkhouse just before supper. Marti's neat flowing script conveyed a succinct message—it would be better if Adam did not accompany her to the art fair. Her father had decided to take the day off to go see his daughter's daubing. Angrily, he crumpled the paper and tossed it in the trash, muttering to himself, "Any of her father's attention she can wrest from Riba, Marti'll grab. Damn it to hell!"

He had more pressing things to do, anyway. Adam ambled down to the concrete bath house. It was filled to capacity with men getting ready for big Saturday night dates. Bob Vasquez was busily slapping aftershave on his face in front of a steamy wall mirror.

"Any more of that shit and your date will need Ansel's respirator to breathe," he said with a grimace.

"Rose loves 'this shit' as you so uncouthly call it," Bob replied good naturedly as he applied a comb to his unruly black hair.

"Find out anything about Benteen yet?"

Vasquez looked around the noisy, crowded room. Over the din of showers and raucous yelling, they had privacy. "Funny thing. I asked Les if he had any references when he hired him. Told him my cousin Jorge was a better mechanic—he is."

"That wouldn't be hard," Adam said darkly, then waited.

"Well, Les said he'd hired Nate because a couple of the lab coats vouched for him."

"One of them wouldn't happen to be Staritz, by any chance?"

Bob's eyes took on a hard gleam. "As a matter of fact, bingo." Then he considered for a moment. "Hell, Adam, I admit I don't like the bastard either, but hiring someone for murder doesn't seem our winemaster's style." He laughed. "Hell, he doesn't even know how to fight dirty."

"But I do, Bob. Don't sell Staritz short, either," Adam replied softly.

"I'm still checking on the Wrangler Bar mystery man. Tomorrow's dinner at Aunt Josefina's place. Everyone'll be there. I can start my Chicano grapevine working on it. Wonder if it might just lead back to Staritz," he said consideringly.

"Or, somewhere else," Adam replied, deep in thought.

The beige Cadillac wended its way toward Chateau Beaumont at a steady pace as its three occupants discussed the day's events. Stifling a yawn, Riba said, "Another day of artsy glitz in La-La Land. Well, at least you won a ribbon for your painting, Marti."

"It's a water color, Riba," Marti corrected waspishly.

"And first prize," Joe added with a proud glance at his elder daughter. "Budbreak. What better subject for a Beaumont, huh?"

Marti smiled in spite of her unsettled mood. She wanted to be with Adam, not her family. *Damn you, Adam Wade. Once I'd have given anything for this kind of interest from Papa!* "A wise man once said wine and art are linked inextricably."

"Who was that, Toulouse-Lautrec?" Riba interjected.

"Maybe Vincent VanGogh," Marti replied cryptically.

"Drunk *and* crazy. Not bad." Riba regarded her sister with an over-bright gaze. "Did your suitor perhaps cut off an ear or some other token? I wondered why you lacked an escort for your day of glory."

"I just chose to go with my favorite date," Marti replied with a wink at her father.

"Who have you been seeing, honey? That nice young lawyer from the city hasn't been around. How about Boris? You two went to dinner a few times," Joe said wistfully.

"I wonder who's nursing his wounds? Boris hasn't got any lopped off appendages," Riba said speculatively.

Recalling the fight between Boris and Adam the day before, Marti responded darkly, "I wouldn't bet on it, little sister."

Marti was so bone weary that it sapped every bit of the pleasure her triumph at the art fair should have brought her. Alice was right about her work. First prize. Best of show. And her father was there to see it and meet her artist friends. A few weeks ago that would have thrilled her. Before Adam Wade. Restlessly she paced around the study, still clad in her stylish silk slacks and bright African print shirt. Joe had retired, planning an early morning's work. Then Riba had left with her new toy, the Porsche. Marti had gone to the office, kicked off her shoes and made a nightcap, knowing she'd be unable to sleep.

Rubbing her eyes, she wondered for the hundredth time if she had made a mistake sending the note to Adam breaking their date. She *was* angry with him and his high handed threats to Boris about going to her father. The thought surfaced again about whether her sister knew she was involved with a hired hand. Riba had made several sly remarks that afternoon that could be interpreted that way. *If she knew I'd made love with him, I wonder how she'd react?* With scorn? Jealousy? More likely mercilessly condescending taunts, Marti decided. *Her holier than thou sister's finally fallen from grace with a man every bit as unsuitable as her worst!* She took a long sip of her bourbon and soda.

Just then a knock sounded softly, interrupting her jumbled thoughts. Hilda Lee stood at the door with a worried look on her usually calm Oriental face. "Adam Wade wants to see you. He's waiting by the trees behind the patio," she added uncertainly.

That was Riba's usual trysting place. *Wouldn't it be a howl if we collided there?* Marti thought. Dismissing that unlikely possibility since her sister had just left for town, she nodded to the cook. "I'll take care of it, Hilda, thanks."

Adam lounged casually on the stone patio bench. The cool bright moonlight reflected on the harsh, handsome planes of his face as he scowled, wondering if she'd respond to his summons. He'd seen the light in the office window after Riba took off and was sure it was not Joe who sat up late, but his troubled older daughter. Just then he heard footsteps on the patio and turned to watch Marti materialize out of the shadows.

"You must be familiar with this spot," she said with an acid undertone to her voice.

"No more than you. Or, on second thought maybe so. I did nearly get run over here last week."

An unwilling smile twitched at the corners of her mouth. "Our reckless driver is off for the night."

"Let's be off, too, before she gets back. I have Bob's car." He waited, his blue eyes gleaming with a dare.

"Just where would we go? To your friend's lake house?"

"If you want to. It's private and we need to talk, Marti."

"Like we did the last time we were there?" she shot back.

"Don't you think things have changed a little since then?" he countered. "Of course, if you're afraid Joe might find out . . ."

"If my father finds out anything, it will be about that ridiculous brawl you and Boris had yesterday!"

"And about what precipitated the brawl? Marti, we're involved in a way that's becoming evident to everyone else, even if it isn't to you."

"If it isn't to me!" she echoed in whispered disbelief. "I always stay up pacing the floor and drinking at midnight."

He uncoiled from the bench and stepped over to where she stood. When he took her in his arms, she didn't resist. Looking up, she touched her fingers lightly to his cracked lip. "Lose any teeth?"

He grinned. "No, but I suspect your winemaster has a very sore ass, not to mention throat and stomach."

"He always had a reputation as a fighter. Riba said he beat a man unconscious in a bar once when she was with him."

"And you didn't warn me," he reproved.

"Let's just say my intuition told me you knew a trick or two of your own," she said angrily. "Anyway, you were bent on a fight and so was he." She shrugged.

"You owe me a shirt," he interrupted irrelevantly. "An impoverished worker needs every one he owns."

"Wear the silk one you had on at Meadowood," she replied.

"Only if you let me kiss you like I did at Meadowood." Without waiting for her response, he tightened his embrace and bent down to rain soft caresses across her neck and throat with his mouth as his hands slid up and down her back. "I felt this when you were soaking wet."

Marti was warm and breathless in spite of the cool night air. She struggled to breathe and pulled away from him. "No, not here." *Not in Riba's place.*

Chapter 11

Riba had driven to several of her favorite haunts but found no one of interest to her. Then she decided to return home and seek out Adam Wade. This wouldn't be the first time she had a man rousted out of his bunk with a message delivered by whatever hapless worker got up for a late night trip to the washroom, she thought with a wry laugh.

But when she pulled in the garage, she saw headlights through the trees on the back road. Some instinct made her follow the old car to the main road and then onto a cutoff to a small private lake northeast of the winery.

When Adam and Marti reached the cabin, he stopped the car but did not get out. They had talked little on the ride, both wound up tightly and turned inward on painful private thoughts.

He looked across at her. "You still mad about yesterday—my fight with Boris?"

"You were damned high-handed, Adam Wade, shoving me out of your way like some Neanderthal who just sighted a Woolly Mastodon."

He grinned. "Sorta fits Staritz, doesn't it?"

Her lips twitched. "That's beside the point. I'll make my own decisions, not have them settled on a field of 'honor' by two conceited males."

"But you're willing to let your father make your decisions for you. He'll choose Staritz, Marti. That way he can't lose—he keeps a good winemaster and you to run the business in the bargain."

That hit too close to home. "Don't be cruel, Adam.

I know Papa's never appreciated me like he does Riba, even though he needs me more."

"Aw, babe, I didn't mean to hurt you," he whispered low, taking her into his arms. "I'm sorry. I apologize for being an overbearing ass yesterday, too—but not for what I did in the water fight," he added with a wicked chuckle. He was rewarded when he felt her shake with repressed laughter.

As her eyes met his, the laughter died. They moved toward the kiss, each desperate, hungry for the taste, the touch of the other. She opened her mouth for his plundering tongue, surprising him with her ardent response as she quested back, exploring his mouth, tracing the contours of his lips. As he returned the exquisite caresses he groaned and felt her quivering response. "The cabin," was all he could gasp as he opened the car door and slid out with Marti still clinging to him. He pulled her across the seat and lifted her into his arms.

"I can walk," she whispered, but didn't quite believe it herself. Her body felt like a thin wax taper set on a blazing hearth. He consumed her.

And she consumed him. Adam walked quickly to Bill's secluded cabin and shoved the door open. Marti's arms were wrapped around his shoulders, her face burrowed into his neck, nibbling kisses while her breasts pressed against his chest. He slammed the door closed with one foot and without breaking their embrace let her slide down the length of him till her feet touched the floor. As they kissed fiercely, they tore at each other's clothes, baring flesh that their feverish hands caressed.

They moved instinctively toward the bed in the far corner of the room. But the cabin was dark and Adam's bare shin collided with the edge of a chair, eliciting a sharp oath.

Marti held onto him in the darkness. "Are you hurt?"

"Only my pride. It's a good thing it was a knee high chair, not a table that got in my way." As she stifled a giggle, he walked carefully to the hearth and groped for a moment, till he found the matches and struck a light. She reached for a fat candle sitting on the table and offered it to him. Lighting it, Adam carried it over to the bedside and set it down. Then he looked up at her with a question in his eyes.

Marti knew he was recalling the last time they'd lain on this bed, and her fearful reaction. *We can read each others' minds at times like this,* she thought in wonder. Still, he was a stranger who hid his past from her. But as she looked at his splendid body, beckoning her so beguilingly, Marti lost all reason and walked hypnotically into his arms, her eyes never leaving his. "Yes, Adam," was all she said.

It was enough. Gently, he scooped her up and laid her on the bed. She watched him finish undressing, taking off his shoes and socks and sliding off his jeans. When he turned and rolled on his side next to her, he noticed how the soft light from the candle gave her skin a warm glow and cast burnished bronze highlights in her hair.

Adam reached behind her to unsnap her lacy bra. He discarded it and began to caress her breasts with his hands. His lips and teeth did maddening things to the aching, hardened nipples. Marti ran her hands experimentally up and down his arms and across his shoulders to his back. Feeling the muscles bunch and quiver as he braced himself over her, she ran her palms in rough circles over his warm, slick skin, running splayed fingers through the thick, crisp hair of his chest and abdomen, then boldly, lower.

Adam's sharp gasp of surprised pleasure when she stroked his hardened sex and held it firmly in her hand was Marti's reward. His fingers quickly insinuated their way inside her sheer briefs to the wet pulsing bud that ached for his touch. They caressed softly, breathlessly. He tugged at her bikinis; she gave a lithe swish of her hips, freeing them. As he tossed them to the floor, he reclined back on the bed pulling her on top of him.

At her puzzled, uncertain expression, he smiled cryptically and placed his hands on her hips, guiding her to envelope him. She quickly caught the rhythm, feeling wantonly exhilarated as she arched her body and threw her head back, meeting his hard thrusts boldly like a pagan goddess. His hands held her, guiding her. His fingers dug into the soft flesh of her buttocks, the sharp pressure of his grip heightening the pleasure that spiraled upward, ever upward.

Adam's eyes devoured her bouncing breasts, the satiny skin of her belly, her hair flying back like a wild gypsy mane. As he observed the telltale rosy splotches move across her breasts and upward, he commanded, "Look at me, Marti, look at me, love. Let me see it happen."

She bent her head downward and her eyes opened slowly as she stiffened in that final surge of ecstasy. She could feel his swelling, pulsing release as their eyes locked for that moment suspended in time. Their passion spent, he slid his hands up to embrace her as she collapsed onto his chest.

"You are positively pagan," she breathed into his neck with a warm, low chuckle, surprised at her feeling of utter abandon.

"You did the riding, Brunnhilda—I think I heard a chorus of 'Ride of the Valkyries' in the background toward the end." She pummeled him in the kidney with her fist. "Ouch, you witch! You'll pay for that," he growled, rolling her under him and tickling her thrashing, laughter-convulsed body until they had wrestled themselves half off the bed.

"I don't know about you, but I've worked up a thirst," he said devilishly, giving her bare rump an affectionate smack as he pulled her back onto the bed. "Let's see what Bill left in his frig."

"Maybe a Napa first aid kit," she said with a wrinkled nose. "I hate beer."

"Not likely to find any cooled Chenin blanc or Chardonnay. Sorry babe," he said with a wink as he knelt before the small refrigerator and opened it.

Marti watched his splendid body, muscles rippling in the harsh light thrown out by the refrigerator. He was totally unconcerned by his nakedness. Every movement was natural and graceful as he stood up and gave her a cheeky grin. A large jug of cheap table wine dangled by its handle from his index finger. "Red and cold, but . . ." he shrugged. "This or beer, babe."

"Is there a glass or do I have to hold it over my shoulder like a Kentucky moonshiner?" She watched him search the small metal cabinet in the corner. "How does a slightly chipped cup sound?"

"Gimme," she replied, sliding to the foot of the bed with hand outstretched. He poured the inky contents of the jug into two old coffee mugs and handed her one. After taking a sip, she said, "Our best Cabernet never tasted as good as this!"

"It's the company," he replied arrogantly. "Remember when I told you art and wine go together . . . so do love and wine." He hefted his mug in a toast.

They sat on the bed, naked in the flickering candlelight, as they sipped and then kissed, tasting the strong red wine on each others lips and tongue. After a few minutes he took their cups, placing them on the bedside table. "Now . . . thirst taken care of, it's time for hunger . . ." He rolled them back onto the bed and began to rain winey kisses all over her body.

The landscape blurred by as Riba pressed the gas pedal to the floor despite the narrow, twisting road and the darkness. The Porsche's headlights knifed through the fog illuminating the dotted line of the deserted highway.

"Damn them! Damn them! That hypocritical fucking slut and that fucking bastard." She pounded the wheel and swore more inventively, dredging up every filthy shred of obscenity she'd heard in bars and poolrooms from Napa to the Atlantic seaboard. The scene she'd watched through the window of that cabin replayed before her, over and over. She could see her sister like a wild thing with Adam's dark hands all over her body, caressing her in their frenzied ride. Riba squeezed her eyes shut against the vision and almost missed a curve. She slowed, righting the car and forcing her temper under control.

Her first impulse when she had discovered the lovers at the cabin was to burst in on their love nest and shriek at them. She wanted to castrate that perverse drifter who had insulted and ignored her while he lavished his charms on her prim, prissy sister. She itched to claw Marti's eyes out. But a lifetime of calculating to achieve her ends held her in check.

If she stormed in and confronted them, Marti might be humiliated, but Adam would certainly turn that cutting wit of his on her and dismiss her—even pack her off forcibly if she threw a tantrum. Putting a lid on her temper, she had quietly walked back to her car. She considered going to her father and telling him that his perfect elder daughter was screwing a cheap drifter. But Marti had far more damning evidence against her, and even if her sister chose not to use it, she might well defy their father and go off with Wade. Joe would soon be begging his irreplaceable business manager to return. "God, I hate her!" she hissed.

After venting her spleen for a couple of hours in furious reckless driving, she came up with the perfect solution. It was so very simple and the irony of it appealed to her twisted sense of humor. She would watch and wait until the two lovers had their next tryst. Then, once Marti was home, she would act . . .

As he rubbed his sleepy eyes the next morning, dreading the long day ahead, Adam considered his plans. *Hard to think with a dozen men yammering and laughing around you when you only had three hours of sleep.* He grinned ruefully, recalling the long wonderful night at the cabin. They planned to meet again tomorrow night. Marti had a dinner engagement with Alice in town to discuss an upcoming art show and he would meet her at the cabin afterward.

I can't stay away from her, he thought in resignation. But the secrecy of their relationship bothered him. Adam disliked sneaking around behind Joe Beaumont's back. Even more, he hated keeping the truth about himself from the woman he loved. *Christ, I never thought I'd think that, much less ever say it.* And he hadn't said it, not in so many words. But he knew he must reveal his past and confess his love to Marti soon.

How will she feel when she finds out who I am? he wondered for the thousandth time. He'd face that problem when he could tell her—when the deadly tangle of his brushes with death had been cleared away. First he needed to find out what Vasquez had learned about the man who had set up Ansel. Of course, he could always try beating the truth out of Nate Benteen. That idea did hold a certain appeal. He was positive the nasty little mechanic had tampered with that truck and the plane, probably even rigged the "accident" with the barrel.

He shrugged. First he would see if a lead on the guy from the Wrangler Bar turned up, then he would deal with Benteen. That might quickly unravel the whole mess. Of course, it meant he would have to face a deadly enemy, either here, if it was Staritz, or there, if it was—.

"Time to hit it old buddy." Bob interrupted Adam's ruminations, giving him a nudge that slopped hot coffee onto the rough trestle table.

"You didn't get much sleep last night. Hope she was worth it," Luke said with a wink.

Adam grunted noncommittally and got up, following Bob outside. Once they were alone he questioned his friend and learned that Vasquez's cousin had just taken a job tending bar at the Wrangler. "Give Alonzo a few days and he'll find your big time spender," Bob answered with hearty assurance.

Adam wasn't the only one who found it difficult to wake up on Monday morning. Marti slept so late that she arrived at breakfast long after their father was out in the fields, just in time to share it with Riba.

"You look a little bleary-eyed," Riba said over the rim of her cup. "Have trouble sleeping last night?" Her smile was vacuously innocent.

"As a matter of fact, I scarcely slept at all," Marti replied, sure her sister could not know how she had spent last night.

"Must've been all the excitement of winning a ribbon at the art fair. I imagine that kept you tossing and turning till dawn." Riba's eyes glittered like green glass and her voice was brittle with sarcasm.

Marti sighed. "I know Napa isn't New York—or Philadelphia, Riba. Speaking of excitement and big cities, why don't you break your boredom and visit Larry. I'm sure we could handle the work around here without you," she added acidly.

"Maybe I will . . . in a few days," was the cryptic reply.

Marti spent Monday and Tuesday working on payroll and general bookkeeping, all the while feeling caged. She wanted to go into the fields and seek out Adam, but realized the folly. There was enough gossip already after that disastrous water fight and the awful brawl between Adam and Boris.

After their long night of rapturous loving at the cabin, she had willed him to tell her he loved her, that he wanted to build a life with her. But he had been his usual taciturn self, teasing her and drawing her to talk about her life, revealing nothing about his own.

They had agreed to meet at the cabin on Tuesday evening after Marti had an early dinner in town with Alice. Ostensibly, she and Alice were planning an exhibition at the gallery. In reality, Alice was giving Marti an alibi for being out late. She hated deceiving her father.

I'm becoming as devious as Riba, she thought Tuesday afternoon as she dressed to go to town. But she knew she could not stay away.

When she walked into the Old Adobe, Alice waved to her from a corner table. "You're right. This is the best damn margarita I've ever tasted. Funny, I've lived here for years and never tried this place. Nachos are great, too. We owe your Adam a favor for showing us this place."

As Marti pulled up a chair, Alice continued to stuff herself with the crisp tortillas dripping with soft stringy cheese, sour cream and hot salsa. She waved expansively at the waitress. "A margarita for my friend and another for me while you're at it, hon. Thanks."

Marti nibbled at the chips and twisted the glass stem of her drink until Alice stopped talking in mid sentence. Looking up in confusion, she asked Alice, "What? I'm sorry, you were describing the new exhibition."

"And you were a million miles away. Or maybe I should say, about thirteen—at a certain cabin on a small picturesque lake?" Her eyes gleamed as she ran her long artificial fingernails through her permed yellow ringlets. "For a lady with a hot date with the sexiest stud in northern California, you sure don't look happy. What gives?"

Marti twisted the stem of her glass again, then took a long steadying gulp of her drink. " 'Sexiest stud in northern California,' huh? Well, you know as much about him as I do, then."

Alice threw back her head and laughed. "Don't I wish! But if you want to describe . . ."

"Alice, you're incorrigible!" In spite of herself, Marti laughed.

"See. It's always easier to talk if you lighten up first. Now tell me what's wrong. If he won't tell you about the past, concentrate on the present and plan for the future."

"How can we have a future if we have to keep meeting in secret? Oh, Alice, when it all began I told myself it was just a temporary sort of thing—therapy for my messed up psyche. I'd expect nothing more to come of it. But then . . ."

"You fell for the guy. Hardly a big surprise. He's gorgeous, sensitive, intelligent, and, I'm sure, incredible in bed. I've got a sixth sense about that. Why do you think I encouraged you? If he couldn't get you over your hang up, no man alive could!"

"Oh, he did that, all right. In fact he succeeded too well. It's all I can think about." The minute she said the words, Marti reddened in mortification, but Alice only patted her hand.

"Seems perfectly natural to me."

"But it isn't fair. Alice, I've bared my soul to a man and I don't even know his middle name, if he has a family, where he grew up, nothing. I can't wait to fall in bed tonight with a virtual stranger." She paused and looked nervously around them, but no one sat near enough to overhear her.

"And most of all you hate not marching up to your dad and presenting Adam as your fiancé, all gift-wrapped in a pedigree like Riba's lawyer." Her shrewd hazel eyes were warm.

"Sounds so old fashioned when you put it that way, but yes, I guess I do hate the subterfuge and the uncertainty. I love him, Alice and I'm afraid to lose him."

"Quickest way to lose a fish is to yank on the line too soon."

"Is that a bit of your country wisdom?" Marti asked with a quirked brow.

"Even a kid from Hoboken got to go fishing with her dad down at the river now and then. I know a thing or two about hooking them." She chuckled ruefully. "Hell, come to think of it, I haven't had as much luck with men as carp, but the principle's the same."

"Just ease off and wait," Marti said consideringly. "He's asked me that. Something about handling some problems that he can't discuss." She shrugged helplessly. "What can I do?"

"You're both hooked. Just hang in there." Alice said with a grin.

"Some advice from a fisherman," Marti returned sourly.

When she arrived at the cabin, Adam was waiting. It was dusk but she could see Bob Vasquez's old Chevy parked in front. Eagerly she leaped from the Cadillac as he came out the front door to sweep her up in a fierce embrace of welcome.

"What time do you have to be back?" he questioned hoarsely between kisses.

"Earlier than Sunday night. I was lucky not to wake the whole household at four a.m.," she answered breathlessly.

"Well, I'll just have to work faster," he said with a devilish glint in his eye.

"Not *too* fast," she countered as they walked toward the cabin.

About a hundred yards away in a thicket, Riba stood watching. Clad in jeans and boots, she'd planned her hike from up the road so as not to chance being discovered. Of course, considering how "busy" they were the last time, it was unlikely they'd notice if the Blue Angels flew down in tight formation and strafed the cabin!

When Marti told Joe she was having dinner with Alice and planned to spend the evening in Napa working on an upcoming exhibit, Riba's antenna had begun to hum. *She's meeting him tonight. Separate cars. He'll come back here later, after she's home. Perfect.*

And it was. After several hours of playing tapes in her Porsche, hidden just off the main road, Riba observed her sister driving home. She waited in the car another half hour. When Adam did not appear, she slipped out of the Porsche and once more approached the cabin. The Chevy was there and the cabin was dark. *So, you're spending the night in a comfortable bed, darling. Sleep tight,* she thought darkly as a cold smile shaped her sensuous lips.

Riba pulled in the garage and noted with satisfaction that Marti's Cadillac was parked in its usual spot. She tousled her hair, smeared her lipstick and ripped several buttons from her blouse. Then forcing tears, a trick perfected in early childhood, she began to run up the long driveway toward the house. By the time she arrived at the back door, she was out of breath and sobbing wildly. It was nearly midnight. Surely Joe would be asleep and so would Marti. Luckily their rooms were at opposite ends of the long upstairs hallway.

Joe awakened at the low insistent tapping. "Who in hell's up at this hour?" he muttered as he threw on a robe and walked to the door. One look at his hysterical daughter made him blanch. Before he could say a word, Riba was inside the room and in his arms, having shoved the door closed swiftly behind her.

"Riba, princess, what's happened?" he asked as he held her, his heart squeezed with dread. He walked her over to the small sofa against the window and sat down with her slowly, as if she were still a six-year-old with a skinned knee.

"Oh, Papa, I've been so stupid. I've done something awful. Please don't hate me," she sobbed in a low, muffled voice.

Joe took in her disheveled clothes and smeared makeup. "Who did this to you, Rebecca?" His voice was ice cold.

"Adam Wade," came the whispered reply.

"He's just a hired hand," Joe said incredulously.

"It's all my fault. He seemed decent, never acted fresh. So when he asked me to go for a drive I never dreamed—oh, I guess I missed Larry and I was bored. I'm sorry—but he . . . he seduced me. I never did that before—not even with Larry. Before I knew it, he . . . he . . ." She subsided in low weeping.

Joe could see shame and humiliation written all over her young, innocent face. When he started to get up, Riba held on to his arm and pleaded, "Papa, please don't tell anyone—not even Marti! I don't ever want to see him again!" She looked up at Joe's cold gray eyes, fearfully, expectantly.

"Don't worry, Rebecca, no one will know. You won't ever see Adam Wade again." His words were low, clipped and deadly.

Chapter 12

The small alarm on the bedside table jangled its five a.m. wake up call. Adam rolled over and swatted at it, then sat up, orienting himself to the blessed quiet. "Sure beats hearing twenty men swearing," he muttered sleepily as he swung his long legs over the side of the bed. In spite of being glad to escape the crowded chaos of the bunkhouse, he felt lonely in Bill's deserted cabin. *Marti.* As he dressed swiftly in the cool morning air, he wondered how it would feel to awaken every day with her sleeping by his side.

Insidious, how a woman can get inside a man's head. He loved her, but he had never told her so. The knowledge had slipped up on him like a slow tide washing ashore, gently caressing the sand with its warmth and life. Marti was that—warmth, life, all things good. In the clear light of morning, he regretted not admitting the truth last night. He knew after they made love that she wanted him to reassure her, wanted some sign of commitment.

He had held his peace because he was still uncertain of how to tell her about his identity, and concerned about the threats on his life. But his silence had hurt her. Suddenly, Adam knew that was more painful for her than telling her the truth. *Take the plunge, my man. In for a dime, in for a dollar.* His mood lightened with that abrupt resolution and he began to whistle as he walked from the cabin into the soft light of sunrise.

He was about half-way across the yard when he heard the truck pull down the rutted old road. It was a beat up old Ford, like several Joe Beaumont owned. The truck screeched to a halt rather hastily, for all the seeming nonchalance of the burly driver who ambled toward him. Two other men slid from the opposite side of the cab and fanned out, backing the leader.

A prickle of apprehension rippled down Adam's spine as he watched the swift, silent maneuver. He looked them over quickly noting their dirty denim clothes and grizzled unshaven faces. The worst water-front bar in Manila had a better looking clientele.

"You Wade?" the leader asked, returning Adam's scrutiny.

"You the census taker?" he shot back, observing the way the other two fanned out in a semi-circle, now tightening like a noose around him.

"Smart ass bastard. Let's get it done," the smaller fellow on the left muttered.

Suddenly Adam recalled the gravel voice of old Ry-gelski, his martial arts instructor from Shore Patrol school: When you're up against a crew of punks after your ass, make the first move. Cripple one of the fuck-ers fast and maybe the rest'll back off. At least it'll cut down the odds.

As the three moved within arm's length, Adam seemed to focus on the leader facing him, then sud-denly lunged at the man on the left, thrusting his arm forward, palm open, stopping a couple of inches in front of the thug's nose as if signaling for traffic to stop. All three men were taken by surprise, none more so than the one staring at the open hand. That was a costly split-second mistake, for Adam simultaneously snapped a wicked kick at the man's genitals. The blow, delivered without any warning eye contact, landed slightly off target on the inside of his thigh. Cursing, the thug stumbled backward, doubled over.

Before Adam could fully pivot toward the leader, a hamlike fist caught him above the right eye, opening a wicked slash over the brow. He shook his head to fight off the pain. Blood began to seep into his eye and he blinked to clear his vision. The "Census Taker" wanted a quick kill and carelessly took an-other roundhouse swing at his dazed victim.

Although groggy, Adam's reflexes seemed to be on

autopilot as he blocked the punch. He grabbed the big arm and pivoted to lever its owner in an arc over his shoulder. The ground almost shook when the burly leader landed, but before Adam could savor that small victory, the third man was on him from behind, clamping a chokehold on him with a forearm across his throat.

Adam snapped his head back, hoping to rearrange the mugger's nose. He was rewarded with a grunt of pain but he missed his target, catching the strangler on the cheekbone. The suffocating pressure increased. Through the ringing in his ears he could hear a string of oaths that would have done old Chief Rygelski proud. The smallest fellow, who he'd dropped with the groin kick, was limping toward him.

"Okay, lover boy. It's payback time."

The punch to his exposed midsection tore him in two—or at least he thought so. Sheer terror drove him to thrash his head sideways in a desperate attempt to reclaim some of the air forcibly expelled from his body. He got one gulp before the arm tightened again, but it was enough to give him strength for another wicked kick. His boot connected solidly with his tormentor's shin.

"Fuck! Eddie, can't you hold the son-of-a-bitch still. It's like fightin' a shittin' kangaroo!"

The man holding Adam relaxed his grip for an instant as his companion backed off. Another breath of air rushed into Adam's pleading lungs. At the same time he reached back with his left hand and grabbed between the strangler's legs. On target this time, he squeezed and was rewarded with a sharp gasp and freedom from the chokehold.

Adam had no time for a third breath, however. A tackle from the right that would have done the best linebacker in the NFL proud sent him crashing to the ground. The "Census Taker" was back in the fray. He and Adam were locked in a bearhug as they rolled across the clearing. Adam finally came up on top, his fist swinging down at the leader's face. He felt his knuckles connect with an eye socket the same instant the world exploded behind his head.

The explosion created a chain reaction as bursts of agonizing pain ricocheted up and down his body, wracking his face, chest, stomach and kidneys. He felt a splintering in his right arm and knew it was broken. So was his nose. All at once the kicks and punches stopped. Or maybe they didn't and he just couldn't feel them anymore. Then he heard a voice. Or maybe he didn't and it was just the ringing in his ears.

"Knock it off, goddammit! We can't stomp the bastard to death. Old Beaumont said he wants the fucker sorry, not dead."

"Okay. Pretty boy ain't so pretty now anyways. He won't be screwin' Beaumont puss again."

"Eddie, help Alf load him in the truck. I'll drive this car back to Beaumont's and clean out his gear when the other men leave for the fields. Wait for me on the back road where we agreed."

The voices faded away, along with the pain, along with consciousness.

Riba watched with a slow smile playing across her lips as Joe paid the big ugly looking thug. The two men stood on the back patio, but even from where she was hidden in the shadow of the trees, she could see the darkening bruises on the scarred veteran's face. *God, Adam must have put up a fight. I hope they beat him so his own mother couldn't recognize him!*

Humming softly, she headed back to the house, hungry for a big breakfast. Friday was payday and Riba knew Marti would be in for a surprise when her favorite field worker wasn't there to collect his wages.

Marti worked on payroll down at the business office that day, but she kept catching her thoughts waywardly drifting back to the previous evening. Over and over she relived their wild, abandoned loving. *Oh, Adam, whatever it is you have to work out, let it be soon, please, let it be soon.*

A soft rapping on the office door pulled her from one such reverie. Dropping her pencil in a flush of embarrassment, she looked up as Bob Vasquez walked in the open door. His expression sent a prickle of unease down her spine, for the youth's usually smiling, open face was downcast and worried.

"Yes, Bob? What seems to be the problem?"

He hesitated and looked around uncertainly, then cleared his throat. "Adam borrowed my car last night," he began slowly.

Color suffused her face, but she remained silent, frozen at his next words.

"The car's back, keys in the ignition, but Adam's gone."

"What do you mean, gone?" Her voice surprised her with its steadiness.

"He wasn't there when Les gave the work assignments this morning. I checked the bunkhouse on my break and all his gear's gone. I . . . I didn't know who else to ask." He hesitated again. "Did he collect his pay?"

Feeling her knees turn liquid, Marti was grateful she was sitting down. She struggled desperately to hide her shaking as she replied cooly, "No, he didn't Bob, but that's scarcely unusual. Seasonal workers often drift without notice. What's one week's pay to a man like Adam Wade?" Her flippant reply was tossed out like a dare. She prayed the youth would have the good grace not to pursue the mutually embarrassing situation further.

Vasquez seemed to consider something for a moment. Then he looked into Marti Beaumont's stricken silver eyes. *Whatever happened, she doesn't know anything. I wonder if he did just slope off?* Deciding it could serve no purpose to frighten her by mentioning the attempts on Adam's life, he said, "I suppose you're right, Miss Marti. He's been on the road a long time now," he added gently as he nodded his farewell and walked out the office door.

Marti finished the day like a sleepwalker. When Les came to the office that afternoon to report Wade's absence, she told him what Bob Vasquez had said.

His seamed face creased in a frown. "Funny. Bright

guy. Real worker, too, like he was ambitious. Never would've thought he'd drift like some college kid or a Chicano with a forged green card."

"I guess you never can figure a man like Adam Wade, Les," Marti said quietly. "Educated men who work the crush are crazy to begin with, aren't they?"

That evening, after dinner, Marti excused herself from the table early. With nerves already raw, she could not stand her father's fawning solicitude to Riba, as if his younger daughter had just suffered some grievous injury. *I'm bleeding to death inside and no one even notices!*

She wandered out to the yard, then found herself looking down toward the single men's quarters. Knowing she was only prolonging the inevitable, she walked firmly back to the house for her bag and car keys.

As she pulled the Cadillac up in front of the cabin, she wondered idly about Adam's mysterious friend, Bill Dougherty. Would he reclaim it this fall?

What damn self punishing instinct brought me back here? Even as she asked herself, she knew it had been the faint, feeble hope that he'd still be here, be waiting to welcome her, to take her to the bed and. . . .

She opened the door and looked inside the empty room. Silence and desertion clawed at her. Slowly, with wistful sadness, she walked over to the chair that Adam had bumped his shin on the other night. She ran her fingertips over the rough wood, then moved to the refrigerator. The half empty jug of red wine sat on the top shelf like a piece of evidence in a murder trial. *And it is a murder,* she thought, *a murder of your dreams, your love. Adam Wade killed your love.* Then she looked over at the bed and knew that she was lying to herself.

Over the summer the vines grew toward a bumper harvest with clear warm days and cool dry nights. Ansel McGee, fully recovered and startlingly sober, again took to the skies with his Stearman humming smoothly, spreading plumes of sulphur across the acreage of Chateau Beaumont. Joe and Marti walked the fields, examining the rich, healthy clusters of ripening grapes. If her father noticed Marti's reticence, he did not comment on it. After all, it had only been that spring that she had blossomed into a head-turning beauty. After one radical personality shift, her recent somber mien and moodiness were marked off as feminine whim. Perhaps she was more like her sister than anyone had heretofore imagined. Riba had always been subject to a mercurial temperament.

Marti didn't have tantrums, wheedling and coaxing, then screaming and crying, to get her way. She simply withdrew into a more aloof shell, talking less to the men, spending less time in the fields, even going so far as to hire a clerk for the office to handle payroll and paperwork. She continued to date a few men from Napa, a vintner and a physician as well as the wine negotiant from San Francisco.

For outward purposes she was still a prim, if far more alluring, society lady. Everyone expected her to announce an engagement and marry within the year, especially her father. If the men who had known Adam Wade wondered about her relationship with the handsome drifter who had left so precipitously, they kept quiet about it out of respect for Marti's feelings.

Boris, too, watched Marti's brooding behavior after Wade's disappearance. When she accepted invitations from other men for dinner and social events in the valley, he decided once more to press his suit.

After one of their usual Sunday morning breakfast meetings, he waited until Joe and Les walked onto the back acreage and then casually inquired of Hilda where Marti was that morning.

The stolid Chinese looked at him measuringly as she replied, "She's gone to church. Should be back any time now."

"I'll walk down to the garage and see if she's returned."

As he strolled outside, Hilda's eye followed the big Russian. She had never liked him, nor trusted his motives with Miss Marti. Too bad his fling with the younger one didn't work out. Boris and Riba *deserved* one another!

Boris arrived at the fork in the road leading to the big garage just as Marti's Cadillac pulled in. She stepped out of the car and gazed down the road at his deliberate approach.

"Shit, blow a spiritually uplifting morning by starting the afternoon with him," she muttered under her breath. The tension between them had never really eased since his preemptory possessiveness toward her after they had a few casual dates in the spring. When he had tried to interfere in her relationship with Adam she had resented it. After the spectacle of their fisticuffs that day in July, Marti had been wary of his uncertain temper. Her own had been on a decidedly short fuse for the past weeks.

Boris watched her walk down the road to meet him with that cool, faintly superior smile in place. She wore a buttercup yellow linen dress, belted carelessly around her slim hips with a gold concho chain. Her hair was caught up in soft curls and twisted cunningly into a French roll at the back of her head. Her wide brimmed apricot hat and matching pumps set off the California casual look of breezy comfort. Her transformation into such a striking woman had not pleased him. When she was a plain little wren, the field had been open for him—except for that obnoxious drifter Wade. Staritz rejoiced at his departure. Yet now Marti was besieged by eligible men and he had foolishly antagonized her.

Hopefully, he could remedy that situation now. After all, he knew he had Joe's blessing. The old man had been upset when Marti hired Dorine to do the office work. Bit by bit Marti had been divorcing herself from the winery. Joe would love nothing better than for her to marry his winemaster. Boris and his employer were in complete agreement. Now, if only he could convince Marti.

"We missed you this morning at breakfast, Marti," he said by way of greeting.

"I felt a need for some spiritual uplift, Boris—you know, choirs and candles, all that."

He looked at her amused gray eyes. "You used to think walking the fields was communing with God," he replied with a reproving smile.

"I can do that six days a week. Today I felt . . . Episcopalian," she said quirking one brow at him.

He frowned, then gave her a look of genuine concern. "Well and good, but you're rarely in the fields anymore. In fact, you seem more taken with charity fund raisers and art shows than with your own business. That's not like the Marti I've always known." He waited for her to respond as they walked slowly through the lazy noon sunshine.

Finally she said, "Maybe you never really knew me, Boris." *Maybe I really never knew myself.*

"You've been listening to that artist, Alice Marchanti, too much," he shot back, stung by her seemingly careless indifference.

She stopped and faced him directly. "What you mean, Boris, is that I listened to Adam Wade too much. I decided that I have the right to a life outside Chateau Beaumont—and I do. Neither you, nor my father, will chain me to this business."

"But if your lover Wade hadn't run off you'd still be working in the mud alongside the common laborers, wouldn't you? You didn't mind this business then, did you?" His black eyes glowed ferally as he fought to control his temper.

Marti subdued the impulse to slap his hateful face. "You are an insufferable snob and a tactless boor, Boris," she ground out in a low, steady voice. "A most disagreeable combination. If you'll excuse me."

As she pivoted to brush past him, he reached out and grabbed her. Instantly, feeling the stiffening recoil radiating from her body, he realized his mistake and released her. Still, his temper was too far out of control to stop him from saying, "When Wade put his hands on you, you never pulled away, did you?"

Ignoring his taunts about Adam, Marti said scathingly, "My sister found your nasty Slavic temperament an aphrodisiac. I merely find it childishly unpleasant." Once more she moved past him and started up the road.

"I apologize, Marti." There was a note of abject pleading in his voice, even startlingly genuine contrition. "I know I have a lousy temper and I was out of line about Wade. I'm sorry. I . . . I'm afraid I'm jealous. I want us to be friends but all I seem to do is antagonize you."

Marti took a deep breath and looked back at the burly man facing her. His posture reminded her of a shuffling adolescent. She smiled in spite of herself. Gently she said, "Boris, you don't want to be friends. You want something more binding. Marriage. And control of the winery."

"It isn't that mercenary, you know. I really do care for you," he replied quietly.

"I'm certain you do and I appreciate that, but it would never work. You live for this place, the same as Papa. I don't anymore. I want to travel, to paint, to experience all sorts of things I never gave myself permission to try before. But Papa needs you and if you just learn to curb that fierce Russian temper and cajole him, you'll win the day with your new ideas. I'll lend my support, but that's all I can do. I don't love you, Boris," she finished simply, watching his shoulders droop.

"It's Wade," he said. No question or accusation was left in his voice now.

"We don't choose who to love, Boris. Adam and I weren't meant to be either. I have to make other plans now."

"And they don't include me. Okay. I'll have to accept that at present, Marti. But I want you to know I'll always be here and if you ever change your mind . . . well, you'll know where to find me." He gave her a lingering farewell look, noting the convulsive way she swallowed back tears and nodded to him.

They walked their separate ways to the fork in the road, Boris down to the winery and Marti up to the house.

* * *

"You're the first appointment of the day, Miss Beaumont," the nurse said brightly, marking her clipboard and motioning Marti to take a seat in the empty waiting room of the expensive San Francisco gynecologist's office. She had barely picked up the latest issue of *Cosmo* and begun to thumb through it when the efficient nurse was at the door asking her to please come this way.

I already know what he's going to say, Marti thought, willing herself to appear calm.

Dr. Rush was a middle-aged man with sparse gray hair and a quiet, solid manner that probably reassured most of his female patients. Marti had chose him for other reasons—impeccable credentials and a practice sixty miles from Napa. He smiled warmly at her and offered her a low slung white oak chair with thick gray velvet upholstery. Marti sank gratefully into its comfortable depth and awaited the verdict.

"As you already surmised from the E.P.T., you are pregnant, Miss Beaumont. Judging from the results of the physical you took last week, I'd say your due date is March 15, give or take a few days. First babies are a trifle unpredictable." He paused and looked at her calmly, knowing she was unmarried but financially independent. The decision about whether to terminate the pregnancy was hers alone. A self-possessed young woman, Martha Beaumont had already told him on her initial visit that if he confirmed her pregnancy, she planned to have the child.

"I'll need a referral for a good physician, Dr. Rush. Someone in New Orleans," Marti said quietly.

"New Orleans. That's quite a long ways, but you're fortunate. It's also quite a medical center and I know several fine obstricians who practice there." As he wrote the names on a script pad, he wondered idly if she had family in the south or if she was merely choosing an exotic, far away city as a good place to escape from her family in California. He didn't ask.

That night at dinner, Marti debated about when to tell her father that she was moving to New Orleans.

It would be over a month before Riba returned to Philadelphia to finalize wedding arrangements with Larry. Marti could not wait that long to tell Joe she, too, was leaving. But did it have to be tonight? *I'm just a coward, putting off the inevitable. But he'll be so upset.*

Riba chattered about her wedding plans and how eager she was to see Larry. By the time the dessert course was served, Marti had pretty well tuned her out, her thoughts far away. Then her sister's remarks riveted her attention.

"Of course, Marti will handle all the arrangements, Papa. I want the Vintner's Room and terrace at Meadowood and that orchestra—you know, the one that played at the Kenley's wedding reception."

Joe was beaming at Riba's vivaciousness. "Yes, Princess. I know Marti will do a splendid job, won't you, honey?"

Marti looked from Joe to Riba. "Job?" she echoed blankly. "I'm sorry. I was daydreaming I guess. Back this up a bit for me."

"Larry is flying out here the end of this month and I want to give the kids a real engagement party—officially this time. Riba's working on the guest list, around three hundred, I think, right Princess?"

"Yes, Larry's parents are coming. Isn't it going to be grand, Marti?" Riba's eyes glittered in the candlelight. She had always loved big parties, especially when she was the guest of honor.

She and Joe continued to discuss the lavish gala, both assuming Marti would do all the work.

Joe even echoed that sentiment. "Now that you have so much free time since you don't do the books, you can really take charge of this party, can't you, honey?"

"I hired Dorine so I'd have more time to paint, Papa, not to become Riba's social secretary."

Joe's face turned incredulous, then harsh. "I think helping your only sister with her engagement party is more important than your hobby, Martha."

Marti looked at the unnatural luster in Riba's eyes.

She's enjoying this, she thought in rising fury. Slowly Marti stood up and tossed her napkin across her barely tasted fresh peach pie.

"My 'hobby,' as you call it, Papa, has earned me enough money to live on. In fact, I plan to do precisely that. Aunt Lese has written me there's a wonderful art colony in New Orleans. I plan to go there and sell my work to support myself while I study."

Joe's face blanched. He sat speechless.

Not so Riba. "So, the fledgling is going to test her wings. Rotten timing, sis. You'll just have to wait until after my party though, won't you?" She looked from Joe to Marti with an engaging plea in her voice.

Marti had watched this scene one time too often. "No one consulted me about this little fiesta. A party for three hundred people should be planned a bit more than three weeks in advance. It's a tall order even with my formidable skills—were I to devote full time to the project. I simply can't do it."

Joe regained his voice at last. "Can't or won't?" He, too, stood up now, but the anger evaporated, replaced by confused hurt.

"Both, Papa. I've felt a need to move away for a long time now. Lese invited me to come to New Orleans and live with her last year. Now . . . well, now I'm ready. This is something I have to do. Please try to understand."

"But your whole life has been here, working in the vineyards. I thought you loved the valley and wanted to stay here, to marry and settle down here. These visits to Aunt Lese, I know she's encouraged your drawing, but—"

"My drawing," she echoed quietly. "That's all it will ever be to you. I love Napa and the winery, but I'll always live in your shadow here. You don't need me, Papa. You have Les and Boris to help you. I'm entitled to my own life just the same as Riba." She was still angry despite her father's obvious show of hurt. *Damn you, Joe Beaumont, for being so blind all these years! Damn me for the same stupid thing!*

"I don't understand you, Martha," he said tiredly, sitting down again in baffled defeat.

"But what about my engagement?" Riba asked with a hysterical edge to her voice, realizing that her father had actually given in to her sister.

"I suppose you'll just have to make the arrangements yourself. You said it—all you had to do this summer was work on your tan. Now you won't be so bored." Marti gave her a frosty smile and excused herself from the table.

As the plane took off, Marti sat back in her seat, her eyes closed, her fingers kneading tight little circles on her aching temples. *I handled the whole thing badly,* she thought morosely, the image of her father's gaunt, harshly lined face reappearing in her mind's eye. He had driven her to the airport and hugged her goodbye with fierce gruffness. Riba, furious over her upset plans, was at the country club that morning. The sisters had scarcely spoken in the week since Marti announced she was leaving. The icy rift between them also upset Joe, who appealed to Marti to meet him in Philadelphia for the wedding.

By late October she'd be visibly pregnant. What a hit that would make at the society wedding of the year! An unmarried, pregnant bridesmaid. Picturing herself marching down the aisle in one of the sleek raspberry satin attendant's gowns, belly protruding, she was torn between laughter and tears. Marti could never tell her father the truth about her pregnancy any more than she could have told him about Riba's. He was a stern old fashioned man with unbending values.

But she should have been kinder, not thrown a jealous temper tantrum because of Joe's plans for Riba. One spoiled darling in a family was enough. Since she had to leave within the month, Marti should have softened the blow with a private explanation to her father, not thrown down the gauntlet. As it was, she had to plan a way to give her child a legitimate identity before she could tell Joe Beaumont that he was a grandfather. Aunt Lese would know what to do. She remained the brilliant, resilient family matriarch, even as she neared her eightieth birthday.

Regrets, she had so many of them, for her sister, her father, for Adam, who had failed her most of all. Marti shuddered and forced back the tears.

Chapter 13

He squeezed his eyes shut tightly and tried to turn away from the blinding light. Pain lanced through every nerve in his body. He was being held down. The pressure on his arms and legs pulled them as if he were being drawn and quartered. A hiss of breath involuntarily sucked through his clenched teeth, causing him to realize there was something wedged in his mouth, down his throat. His gag reflex went crazy as he tried to wretch but was unable to turn over. *I'll choke in my own puke,* he thought frantically, now desperate enough to open his eyes against the searing brightness.

A tall dark-haired woman dressed in white rushed toward him, but his frantic struggling and blurry vision kept him from focusing on her. He could feel her hands, however, firm yet soft, capable hands, like Marti's.

"Well, you finally decided to wake up. Mr. Yung'll be relieved," she said she she pulled the offensive apparatus from his mouth. He sucked air into his lungs in a great gulp, then once more hissed in agony.

"Those ribs are broken. I wouldn't try any deep breathing exercises for a few days if I were you," she said cheerfully.

By now Adam could focus his eyes, after a fashion. "Why's everything so fuzzy?" he asked inanely, ignoring the thrums of agony emanating from each separate molecule of his body.

"Pain medication, a first rate concussion, sedatives, take your pick. You've been napping for over a month, Mr. Moreland."

"You know who I am?" His throat was beginning to burn. Sensing his problem, the nurse poured a small amount of chipped ice into a cup and propped his head up with the admonition, "Just let these dissolve on your tongue, slowly. You haven't had oral nourishment or fluids since you arrived. As to who you are, that was pretty tricky. You were brought in beaten half to death, without a shred of identification. A hobo found you at the freight yards and flagged down the cops. Probably saved your life. The police ran some sort of check. Fingerprints, I guess, and found you were Jake Moreland's missing heir. His attorney, a Mr. Yung, has been phoning a dozen times a day waiting for you to regain consciousness."

"Mort always was persistent," Adam said around the ice chips in his mouth.

"Don't swallow too much of that at once," she admonished. "Yeah, that lawyer's almost driven my girls at the desk nutty. His office calls at all hours."

Adam gingerly moved his head to gaze around the antiseptic hospital room. Private. It figured, once they found out he was a Moreland. He looked down at his body and understood why he had the sensation of being trussed up like a victim for the Inquisition. He had more tubes sticking out of him than a laboratory experiment in a Vincent Price movie. He moved his left arm and two IV bottles clinked in unison.

His right arm was in a cast up over the shoulder, both legs were in traction, and his chest was tightly laced into a torture jacket that protected his broken ribs. He could feel the bandages around his head. Beaumont's boys had been thorough.

"Is there anything on me that's not broken?" he asked glumly, once more sinking toward the blessed oblivion of unconsciousness.

"Not much," the nurse replied cheerfully, "but I'll let Dr. Soames discuss that with you later this afternoon. Right now I think it's happy time again."

"Before I trip off to dream land, where the hell am I?"

"Fresno," she replied with a grin.

"Where the *hell* was right," he muttered as he felt his eyelids droop. The vision of Marti's luminous silver eyes flashed before him, superimposed over those of the dark haired woman in the starched white uniform.

Adam awakened to stare into the owlish face of his father's attorney, Morton Yung. Fiftyish, tall and gauntly thin, he exuded an aura of self discipline in a world of corporate cutthroats who were usually as self indulgent as they were ruthless.

"Dr. Soames assures me you'll recover fully, Adam," Yung said with a slight smile.

"How inconvenient for most of the known world," Adam replied caustically, looking at his second cousin. Mort was full-blooded Chinese, unlike Adam's mother.

"It would seem you've added materially to your already significant list of enemies during the seven years of your . . . absence," Yung replied in precise English. He cultivated the elaborate diction patterns of a British barrister, probably his only conceit.

"Speaking of my enemies, how's Jake doing?"

"Your father is gravely ill, Adam," the older man said with concern in his black eyes. "In fact, his physicians don't expect him to live a great deal longer. He's been searching tirelessly for you ever since—"

"Let me guess. Since he was diagnosed as seriously ill," Adam interrupted.

Yung nodded, the Oriental facade once more in place. "Yes. It's cancer, slow moving at his age, but lethal. He wishes to reconcile with you, Adam."

"I bet Booth was thrilled by that news," Adam said drily.

Ignoring the reference to Jake's brother-in-law, Yung said smoothly, "Your father's been bedfast for several months, Adam. When we received word of your unusual arrival here in Fresno, he asked me to notify him as soon as you were lucid. I shall do so immediately, although I much doubt either of you will take up your bed and walk to the other in the near future."

Adam grunted disgustedly. "You and that nurse

seem to have all the scoop from the medics. When can I talk to this Dr. Soames?"

"About three to four months, I should guess before we can discharge you, Mr. Moreland," Dr. Soames replied with the breezy nonchalance of a man used to dispensing catastrophic news. "Of course, you'll be transferred out of ICU as soon as your ribs and head injuries are significantly improved. The broken arm and collarbone and the dislocated shoulder should all heal cleanly. There is torn cartilage in the left knee. That may require some corrective surgery at a future date."

"You mean I'll miss my draft chance with the Forty-Niners," Adam said sarcastically. Damn, he hated having his anatomical parts discussed like disembodied entities!

After the doctor left, Mavis came back, this time bearing a steaming tray, his first solid food. At least he was finally off the IV's. One look at the "soft diet" Soames had prescribed made him wish for more glucose. "You sure this is food?" he asked darkly, poking his spoon at a dish of obscenely bouncing jello cubes. Their green and orange brilliance would've looked more appropriate on a pinball machine than a sickroom tray. Biliously, he moved the spoon toward a grayish gruel he assumed was some form of soup.

"Cream of mushroom," came Mavis's reply to the unspoken question. "Everyone wonders," she added with a puckish grin.

Since he'd first regained consciousness, the charge nurse, Mavis Preston, had become the bright spot in his confinement. He waited eagerly for her to come on duty each day.

Adam knew that Mavis took more than a professional interest in him despite her calm, low key manner. He had learned through their conversations that she had listened to his garbled cries when he had nightmares, reliving the beating. Since he also dreamed frequently about Marti, he assumed the nurse knew about her, too, although Mavis had never mentioned it.

After a week on semi-solid foods with numerous examinations and x-rays of his fractures and concussion, Adam was finally allowed to walk around the room—with assistance. Carefully swinging his legs over the side of the bed, he fought down a renewed surge of dizziness.

"You sure you don't want to wait until tomorrow?" Mavis asked dubiously. "Dr. Soames said only when you felt strong enough."

"I'm strong enough—or would be if I could get some real food. Tell you what. If I 'earn my spurs' by cantering around the room, will you get me a steak—rare, *without* mushrooms." He arched one black brow and winked.

"Let's just see about one slow walk around the room first," Mavis replied noncommittally. "I'm not sure your loosened teeth are up to a hospital steak. A shame to have the orthodontist save all those pearly whites and then lose them gnawing on gristle."

He sighed and stood up, an exercise he'd been allowed for several days now. His left knee was tightly wrapped and hurt like a bastard, but it held his weight. Flexing it experimentally, he grinned. "I may make the draft after all."

He took a couple of halting steps and Mavis quickly slipped his good arm around her shoulder for support. "I wouldn't try out for quarterback just yet, hon," she said with a grin, holding up a good portion of his hundred and seventy-five pounds.

"Jesus, that knee hurts," he gritted out, but doggedly continued to walk clear across to the door, trying to ease some of his weight off Mavis's shoulders.

"Doc thinks you might not need surgery on the cartilage."

"Best news since I found my plumbing worked without a catheter," he said with a cheeky grin and they both laughed.

As they turned and headed back toward the bed,

the door opened and a tall, well dressed man with close cropped blond hair stepped inside.

"Amazing resilience, Adam. At death's gates last month, now laughing with a pretty nurse," he said with a sharkish smile directed at Mavis.

Adam pivoted more quickly than he should have, and had to fight back the dizziness by focusing on the ice blue eyes locked on him. "I wondered when you'd pay a call, Booth." As he mentioned the name, Adam could feel Mavis stiffen. *I talked a lot when I was delirious. Shit!*

"I intended to get to Fresno sooner, but," he gestured to the briefcase in his hands, "business, you understand."

"Mort's been filling me in," Adam replied as he eased onto the side of the bed. Mavis sensed his need to appear strong while facing Booth. She raised the bed so he could remain sitting yet lean back for support.

"Ah, yes, Morton, Jake's ever efficient legal advisor. And now, yours, too. But then you are blood kin, even if your eyes aren't slanted," he added with seeming guilelessness.

"Pity you were born too late, Booth. You would have done just dandy in the SS," Adam returned with a nonchalance that belied the frisson of animosity between the two men.

"If you have business to discuss, I'll leave," Mavis said. She flashed a hard-eyed stare at the blond man. "Ten minutes. Mr. Moreland is under doctor's orders not to exert himself."

"She'd make a good referee for a hockey match," Booth said as she swished briskly from the room without a backward glance.

"Don't cross her. She'll make you sorry, Booth," was all Adam volunteered about Mavis. Waiting for the other man to speak, he shifted positions on the bed to ease his throbbing knee.

"You know, of course, that Jake's dying? And that he wants to see you again. Despite your irresponsible behavior seven years ago, you are his only son and he wants you to inherit."

"I bet you turned handsprings when I surfaced, didn't you, Allard?"

Booth Allard shrugged. His ice blue eyes and perfectly sculpted features could be as expressionless as Morton Yung at his most inscrutable. "I'm merely Jake's associate. We've worked well together for ten years. I see no reason you and I can't do the same."

Adam smiled darkly. "Even if we hate each other's guts?"

"Business is business, Adam. Personal animosities are an indulgence your father and I have never allowed ourselves. I hope you've matured enough now to agree."

Adam studied the man in front of him. Immaculately barbered and manicured, cold as Antarctica. "I always did have a short fuse—and a long memory, Booth. How about your memory? As I recall, the reason I left made your lose your business detachment." Adam was rewarded with Allard's first betrayal of emotion.

Knuckles whitening as he clenched his briefcase, he ground out slowly, "Jake's a fool to trust you. You're still the same petty boy you were seven years ago."

"If I come back, we can't ignore Jolie, Booth."

"My sister is dead," Allard said in an icy voice. Recovering, he continued in a detached tone. "I've had seven years to put the past behind me. Jolie was wild and self-destructive. Marrying a man Jake's age was as ill-advised as her affair with his son. And don't delude yourself," he added with a nasty smile, "that you were her only conquest."

"But I'm the only one who'll inherit." *I wonder if you'll try to stop me, Booth.*

"I no longer blame you, Adam . . . at least not for killing her. It seems a witness turned up after you'd vanished. A college friend from that party at the Kanes. Jolie was driving the car, not you."

"How convenient," Adam said as expressionlessly

as Allard. "I'm absolved. But like you said, Booth, business is business after all."

"I don't expect we'll have to like each other to work together," was all Allard replied in acknowledgment. "But, Adam, if you plan to fill Jake's shoes, I hope you've learned a lot more than the bedroom tricks Jolie taught you seven years ago."

Adams eyes darkened, but his facial expression didn't change. "I've learned one or two other kinds of tricks, Booth." With a terse, icy nod of understanding Allard quit the room.

"Gestapo," Mavis said with a grimace of distaste, closing the door after him.

Adam let out a mirthless laugh, recalling his words about the SS. "My deceased stepmother's dearly beloved brother, Booth Allard by name."

"I've read about him. Doesn't he work for your father?" she asked guardedly.

"If Morton Yung hasn't exaggerated—and that is not one of his faults—I expect Booth is running Moreland Enterprises by now," Adam replied grimly.

"And you expect to fight him for control?" A frown marred her smooth forehead and her light, golden eyes darkened with worry.

"He won't fight me openly. Booth's too clever for that. He came today to feel me out—see if he could make peace. I have a feeling there's a lot I have to learn before I can get on with my life . . ." his voice trailed off as a pair of clear silvery eyes flashed before him.

"Before you can go back to Napa for Marti?" She voiced his thoughts aloud.

Tension hung in the air for a moment. Then Adam smiled wearily at Mavis. "I guess I really raved when I was sedated, huh?" She nodded and smiled. "I have to talk to Marti, explain why I disappeared. Been mulling that one over since my head's quit fuzzing. How do you tell the woman you love that her father had you beaten half to death and thrown on a passing freight train?"

"Better she should know the truth about her father

than think you skipped out on her," Mavis countered reasonably.

"But it's not that simple. I lied to her about *my* father. To her and Joe Beaumont, I was Adam Wade. Hell, I've been Adam Wade ever since I left the Navy and started drifting through the vineyards."

"And now you're Adam Moreland again, heir to one of the largest wine cartels in the country. Pretty wicked competition for one north coast grower," she said sympathetically.

"I don't give a damn about that old bastard, only what he's done to his daughter's life . . . and what I've done," he added darkly.

"Maybe the first thing to do is get back on your feet and out of here. Next week you get a promotion—kicked upstairs to the ambulatory floor for rehab. In a month or two, you ought to walk out of here with only a few minor scars."

"My first stop will be Livermore, I guess."

"A reunion with your dad?"

"Before I go back for Marti, I have to settle who I am. Joe Beaumont will find it a little harder to make Adam Moreland disappear than he did Adam Wade."

"You're getting that kick-ass cocky look again. A good sign," Mavis said with an affectionate grin.

"Just watch the papers for the Forty-Niners starting line up next fall," he replied. "I'll make quarterback yet!" Then he considered for a moment. "Mavis, get me a pen and some paper. I have to write a lady a love note."

After agonizing over it for half the morning, Adam finally framed a cogent message to Marti, telling her only that he had been hospitalized after a bad accident and that he would be back to explain it all as soon as he was discharged. *"I love you and I'll never leave you again,"* he wrote in conclusion and signed *"Adam."* By the time he addressed the envelope, he was dizzy again.

"No return address?" Mavis asked as Adam handed her the missive.

"I don't want her to find me here. First I have to

face Jake and know where I stand. Then I'll go back for her," he said with a stubborn flex of his jaw.

Mavis knew the discussion was ended. With a shrug she took the envelope to the hospital mail room.

The hot dusty weather did nothing to soothe Riba's irritation. "God, what a bitch this late summer heatwave is," she fumed as she pulled her Porsche up in front of the big house and hopped out. She scratched at the fine gritty powder that blew from the fields and seemed to embed itself in her hair and clothing. "I did have to get a damned convertible," she muttered as she headed up the walk.

Perkins opened the door for her with his usual officiousness. He had never approved of her, the humorless prig! Another of Marti's darlings. Every servant in the house was devoted to her. With a smug grin Riba winked at his poker face and thought of the young studs who worked in the fields. Now, *they* were devoted to her—at least most of them were. Her thoughts shifted to Adam Wade, then back to her absent sister and her blood boiled.

"Running off to New Orleans and leaving me stuck with all these elaborate wedding plans to make long distance," she gritted out beneath her breath as she stomped down the hall toward the office. Midway, she stopped, swore and kicked off her shoes, adding them to the trail of clothing she had already left for the longsuffering Max to pick up. Her handbag lay collapsed on the table just inside the doorway and the smart linen bolero that matched her sundress was tossed over a chair in the foyer.

Named by a literati mother who loved Thomas Wolfe, Maxwell Perkins did possess a sense of humor. It had been that or kill the old girl. He really had been rather fond of her, but when it came to Riba Beaumont, his humor wore decidedly thin. Ever since Marti had left and Riba had to arrange her own fancy engagement party, she had been even more mercurial than before, screaming at caterers on the telephone and crying on poor Joe's shoulder. Her father finally hired a professional from San Francisco to finalize the Meadowood party. Mrs. Schaft was supposed to coordinate the Philadelphia wedding with Mrs. Cameron's social secretary as well, but quit after a screaming match with Riba two days ago.

Max sighed as he picked up the discarded sandals and added them to the pile of Riba's belongings. There were days he wanted to quit, too. If it weren't for Joe Beaumont needing him so much now, he would do it, by damn! He trudged to the foot of the stairs and called for Jesse to come collect Riba's things.

Riba entered the office at the end of the hall. She needed to talk to Papa about replacing Mrs. Schaft immediately, but he was not there. She swore, rubbing her temples, feeling another headache coming on. Just one glance at the ton of mail heaped on the desk made the pounding worsen. Dorine, the new bookkeeper, took care of the winery business down at the tasting room office, but Joe was supposed to handle the rest here.

Since Marti left he just moped around and daydreamed, she thought resentfully. "As if my sister's life isn't going great while I'm stuck with Larry's hag mother who wants to dictate every last fucking detail of *my* wedding!"

Making a snap decision to fly to Philadelphia tomorrow and face the old battle ax, she reached for the phone. The pile of mail on the desk slid as the phone cord caught in it and several pieces fell to the floor. Riba ignored them. Probably bills anyway. Just as she began to dial her travel agent, one letter left on top of the stack caught her eye. It was addressed to Marti—and written in a bold scrawling hand. No return address but the postmark was Fresno.

Intuition humming, Riba put down the phone and reached for the letter. After glancing at the open door and hearing no footfalls in the hall, she ripped the envelope open and read the contents . . .

Riding was still a bitch, especially the last seventy-five miles. Royales, the Moreland family chauffeur, had arrived at the hospital at ten that morning to drive him home. He shifted his aching knee and swore beneath his breath as he gazed out the car's tinted glass window at the countryside. The low, gold hills were hazy in the distance as neat rows of vines stretched across the earth, their leaves now turning to flame with the coming of fall. The silver Lincoln sped north to the western edge of the Big Valley, toward Livermore. He was going home. Odd how empty the word sounded. Home was a lavish mausoleum of a house set on twenty wooded acres, like a superbly mounted and polished diamond, just as cold and lifeless as one, too. In Livermore a man waited, the father he had adored with the unwavering faith of childhood. Jake Moreland now lay dying.

Where did it all go wrong? When Elizabeth died? It was then Jake had moved out of the realm of simply being a vintner to being a mass marketing magnate in the jug wine boom. Or had it been when he remarried? *Everything keeps coming back to Jolie.* Resignedly, he vowed to lay her memory to rest once and for all.

Adam rubbed his temples and again shifted positions on the seat. Mort had tried to talk him into using an ambulance, but he'd refused. "One bedfast Moreland is enough," he'd stated flatly.

"You having pain, Mr. Moreland? Shall I stop so you can get out and take a stretch?" Royales offered.

"Thanks, Sean, but I'm all right. Let's just get the hell back to Livermore," he replied distractedly. The chauffeur had been hired shortly before he'd left, so he barely knew the fellow. Sean Royales seemed congenial enough. If he knew about the family skeletons, he was discreet. Considering the mud storm the media had stirred up when Jolie was killed, Adam doubted if anyone owning a television set didn't know that he'd had an affair with his stepmother.

Pushing that thought aside, he once more contemplated the dismal prospect of facing Jake. The last time they'd spoken, he had been heartsick with remorse, his father icy with wrath. He'd never told Jake he was leaving, just packed a few changes of clothes in a suitcase and walked out the door late one night. *The night before Jolie's funeral,* he reminded himself guiltily. *You were a scared, spoiled boy then, Adam Moreland. What are you now?*

When Royales pulled inside the big wrought iron gates, Adam could almost hear them clang shut behind him, like a prison. *If it doesn't work out, you can always leave.* The thought hammered at him as he watched the enormous Victorian house loom up through a stand of eucalyptus trees, like some monstrosity from a Bulwer-Lytton novel.

"I hear a car in the driveway, Randolph," Jake Moreland said impatiently. "Is it my son?"

The white haired servant moved gracefully to the window of the large tower room and peered out. Below him a dark man slowly unfolded his tall frame from the silver Lincoln. He walked with a slight limp, but without assistance from Royales. "Yes sir, it's Adam."

"I want to see him immediately, before that goddamn nurse comes in with her pill tray," he commanded in a surprisingly strong voice.

"He's been injured, sir. Perhaps . . ." Looking at the fierce blue eyes in that wasted face, Randolph let the thought fade and turned to leave the room with his summons.

Adam walked carefully up the smooth stone steps and entered the front foyer. The polished walnut floor still gleamed. The Dresden vases had not been moved a centimeter on the oak library tables lining the walls. But his mother's softening touch of fresh flowers was missing. She'd made the place warm, somehow. Jolie had never bothered with flowers or any other feminine touches. She had hated the house. As he negotiated the slick cold floors, Adam was struck by the irony of the situation. Soulless and opulent, the house and his stepmother had a great deal in common.

The winding staircase leading to the second floor stretched endlessly in front of him, as if a gambler were daring him by fanning his cards in a smoothly curving wheel on a gaming board. There were fifty-four steps. He'd counted them as a boy. Two more than a deck of cards, but then his imaginary gambler would doubtless have a couple of aces on the bottom of the deck. *Christ, the place must be haunted. What weird thoughts!*

Just then the dignified form of the old family butler, Randolph, materialized from across the hall. His usually reserved face was wreathed in an uncharacteristic smile. "Welcome home, sir."

"Thank you, Randolph. I assume I'm expected upstairs immediately."

"Just so, sir, but if I might suggest in view of your injury . . ." He gestured behind him to the open door of an elevator. "We had it installed last year when your father had his first surgery and found the stairs difficult."

Adam turned from the stairs like a criminal reprieved at the foot of the gallows. Grinning at the servant, he said, "Lately I find stairs difficult, too."

The butler opened the door to the big tower room at the end of the hall. Jake had chosen its immense circular confines for his master suite when he bought the house. When Adam was a child, he had overheard one of the maids dub Jake "king of the castle."

Jake Moreland no longer looked like a king. The minute Adam walked inside the heavy walnut doors, the stench of death filled his nostrils. Only Jake's eyes hadn't changed. They were still that same dark unnerving blue that skewered people like butterflies on pins. But the lined face that had possessed such harsh, angular strength had deteriorated. Its brittle yellow skin was like parchment stretched painfully over a death's head. Although Jake sat up in bed, Adam knew what the effort must be costing the old man.

And I was afraid to climb those damn stairs. "Hello, Jake," he said simply, waiting for his father to react.

"I know I look like hell, but I've earned it. What's your excuse?" Jake rasped out, giving a hollow sounding laugh.

"Would you believe there were three of them, all bigger than me? I know Mort gave you a detailed dossier on how the cops found me, right down to the hairline fracture on the right side of my skull." He walked closer to the bed, eyeing a big maroon leather chair nearby. "Mind if I get the weight off this leg? It's throbbing like a bitch."

"That's what you get for drifting around like a cheap day laborer," the old man snapped.

"There are no high paid day laborers, Jake. They've got lousy unions. You ought to know. You broke enough of them," Adam said wearily, sinking into the soft cushions.

"Still the same stupid arguments, Adam. Unions, workers. Am I going to die and leave all I slaved for to a bleeding heart who'll give it away?"

"You could always leave it to Booth."

"Booth's had a damn free hand running the whole operation this past year. But he's not my son. You are." He paused, but Adam didn't speak. With a shaky breath, the old man continued, "I've been a fool, Adam, for a man who outsmarted every vintner in the state. My brain must've turned to mashed potatoes when I met Jolie Allard."

At the mention of Jolie's name, Adam's eyes narrowed. Still he sat quietly, content to let his father speak.

"I know now what she was. Hell, I know some things about her you couldn't even imagine. The point is, she married a rich old idiot and then seduced his teenage son."

"I was twenty years old, Jake, hardly a virgin when the whole mess started," Adam confessed.

"And she was twelve years older—shit, more like a hundred in experience. I blamed you for her sins. She had lots of lovers before you and she always drank too much. You see, in trying to locate you, my investigators were pretty . . . thorough." He paused and reached for a glass of water on the bedside table.

Adam stood up and handed it to him noticing the way the veiny hands shook ever so slightly and how the old man tried to hide it. Looking away, Adam returned to his seat.

"My snoops found out you weren't driving the car that night. Damn fool thing, taking her place behind the wheel."

"She would've lost her license," Adam replied. "If that had happened earlier, she might still be alive," he added consideringly.

"I doubt it. Her kind don't die of old age, even if they do die in bed more often than not. Forget Jolie. She's not on your conscience, or mine."

"You never had a conscience, Jake," Adam said, his voice oddly without accusation. All this was past history, the old man was right there. "Why did you want to see me now? To absolve me before you die? Somehow I doubt it's that simple."

Jake's penetrating gaze studied his son. "You've gotten a few hard knocks and I don't just mean that thumping you took up in Napa. You been learning about making wine."

"I spent two years in the navy before that, in the Philippines. I can cut and shoot with the worst of them, Jake. Think I'm qualified to take on Booth Allard? That is what you're leading up to, isn't it?"

For the first time Adam saw a trace of a grin hover around the old man's mouth. "Learned to use your head for more than a punching bag, I hope. Yes, I want you to run Moreland Enterprises and that means you'll have to start by reclaiming my lost authority from Booth. Not that he can't be valuable to you, Adam. He's shrewd and ruthless and he's used the past years to make contacts and put out due bills. Can you make him work for you?"

"I'll handle Booth, if I take the job. I didn't just leave because of Jolie, you know. I left because I didn't want to be driven like you. My mother spent her life begging for crumbs of affection from you. So did I when I was a kid."

"I cared for Elizabeth," Jake said reminiscently. "I truly did, but you're right, my work came before her—or you. Maybe that was a mistake, maybe not. But like Jolie, it's done with now. I've built an empire and you're my blood. My only heir. It's yours, Adam. If you don't want it for yourself, take it for your mother's sake. I don't think she'd have wanted her son going through life on a seasonal worker's wages." He paused. "There's also the matter of the Beaumont girl. You think Joe'll let her marry a drifter?"

"Your detectives *were* thorough," Adam said levelly. "Do you think she'll want to marry a Moreland?"

Jake shrugged. He was badly in need of his medication, but he would not relent until things were settled to his satisfaction. He observed as Adam considered the options.

"I always knew I had to come back here and face you before I could tell Marti who I was." He looked up at the old man, a tired old man, ready to die after living an empty life—without love, without integrity. Adam knew he wanted more than the wealth Jake had amassed and driven himself relentlessly to keep. He wanted Marti, a family, an identity. But he had to begin with the past.

"You're right. I'm your only heir, Jake. I *can* run the business and I *can* handle Booth, but I'll do it *my* way."

"Just don't go giving everything away to charities and unions," the old man said sourly, but the light of triumph glowed in those fierce blue eyes.

Chapter 14

"I'm sorry, Mr. Moreland is in a meeting right now. Yes, so is Mr. Allard. May I have one of them get back to you?" Pris Watson, Jake Moreland's executive secretary for the past twenty years, jotted down the overseas number of a large negotiant in London. Her name suited her appearance perfectly. She had silver hair styled in a precise French roll and ramrod straight posture. Her makeup was light and meticulous and her shrewd hazel eyes missed nothing. She turned agilely on her desk chair as Booth walked through the door of the president's office. Adam stood in the doorway just behind him. It was the acting president's first day on the job and he had spent the entire time in high level meetings.

Noticing that Adam's limp had become more pronounced, and Booth's expression more tightly set, Pris said, "I have a list of priority calls for you, Mr. Allard." She handed him a neatly typed sheet of paper.

Grabbing it roughly from her hand, Booth quickly scanned it. He turned to Adam and said, "I'll talk to Drummond tonight and we'll get this set up in the morning." With that he strode away from the president's office toward his new one, stopping to give brusque instructions to his new secretary.

Adam's lips betrayed the hint of a grin despite the tired lines around his mouth. "He isn't being overly gracious about vacating Jake's office and giving up the best secretary in the corporation, is he?"

"I rather pity Kate," Pris said with a glance at the harried younger woman in the outer office who had begun to place the return calls for Booth.

"You got him off my back. Thanks for the diversionary tactics, Pris," Adam said with a smile.

Watching the way the white slash turned his taunt face warm and almost boyish, Pris felt herself near to blushing at the simple compliment. Jake had never been big on amenities. "You've had a long day—the first day for anyone around here is rough, especially if he's just been discharged from the hospital. And Mr. Allard can be most . . . difficult."

"To paraphrase my father, Pris, Booth can be a grade A bastard." He paused and ran his hand through his hair, combing it off his face. "You've been with Jake for a long time and I think you know more about what's going on at Moreland Enterprises than anyone. More to the point, I can trust you, Pris. If you're free tonight, I'd like to buy you dinner and talk about Jake and Booth."

She looked up at him. "I can tell you what you need to know, Mr. Moreland. But I'm not sure you're going to like all of it."

He scoffed. "I'm sure I'm not going to like *any* of it!"

It took Adam two weeks of intensive work, uncovering the tangled webs of corruption that Jake and Booth had spent years weaving. He knew it would take years to reverse the course of Moreland Enterprises.

Jake had been a shrewd guesser in the 1950's, when California wines were still regarded as a bare cut above Carolina moonshine. He had foreseen the opening of a whole new industry with a diversified buying public that stretched around the world. Like a number of other wine entrepreneurs, Jake hired college trained professionals to experiment with new grape varieties, to develop new yeast strains and to research new techniques for fermentation. He made wines of consistently higher quality and marketed these new wines more efficiently than anyone in the industry. That was the beginning.

The boom of the seventies brought Jake's dreams to fruition, but created new problems. He needed a larger supply of grapes than those harvested on Moreland land. He began to buy out small vineyards and wineries. But the cost of California real estate escalated, so Jake developed some inventive tactics to get what he wanted at the price he was willing to pay.

Even as a college student who was not interested in the business that had deprived him of a father's love, Adam had been aware of Jake's reputation. Of course by then, Jake had married Jolie Allard and her brother Booth had become Jake's right hand. The maneuvers were trickier and the deals rougher after that. Jake and Booth forced out smaller competitors, broke unions and waged court battles with federal regulating agencies.

As he drove toward Napa, Adam mulled over all he had learned in his recent crash course on Moreland Enterprises. Pris had been right; he didn't like it. But he was not surprised by what Jake and Booth had done. Already he was formulating plans to leash Booth and use him. The business was prosperous and could remain so without power-mad squeeze plays.

I'm going to live a different kind of life than they have. His leg still pained him and he suffered from occasional headaches, but he was otherwise recuperated from his brush with death. He glanced at his reflection in the rear view mirror and smiled. He patted the small box in his jacket pocket. Christmas was only weeks away now and he was going to surprise Marti with a special present.

During the months he had been hospitalized Adam had considered phoning Marti to explain in more detail what had happened to him. But the enormity of his own deception and her father's ruthlessness made that seem an unwise choice. He reasoned that he needed to explain to her face to face.

Once he had arrived at Livermore, Jake's illness and the power struggle with Booth Allard had taken several more weeks of precious time. He still had not obtained evidence about who had tried to kill him in Napa, but that was something to work on later. Now he would see Marti and answer all her questions, admit his past and offer her a secure future. He envisioned the two-karat diamond engagement ring winking at him with a blazing silvery fire to match his love's eyes. It had been in his mother's family for generations. She had worn it as a pendent, but he'd had it remounted as a ring. He hoped the platinum setting would please Marti.

Putting aside all misgivings about his long absence, he turned up the winding drive to Chateau Beaumont. He smiled at the difference in the way he had arrived last spring and how he would arrive today. Dressed in a custom tailored gray wool suit, driving a pale green Mercedes 560 SEL, he presented a starkly different image than the dusty drifter, Adam Wade. If she loved a penniless nobody, surely she would love him now, even though he was Jake Moreland's son. *He may be my father, but I'm not like him anymore than she's like Joe Beaumont.*

He pulled up in front of the house. The weather and the land, too, were in contrast to his previous arrival. An icy drizzle frosted his suit with a pearly sheen as he walked from the car to the house. The ground was brown and bleak, the vines leafless skeletons awaiting winter's pruning. A chill of foreboding clutched at his heart. He rang the doorbell, deciding what he would say if old Joe answered it. There was every chance he would not. If Perkins or Hilda greeted him, he knew he'd receive a warm, if amazed welcome.

Riba's sleekly beautiful face at the opened door was one surprise he had not counted on. Her blonde hair hung provocatively across one cheekbone as she tipped her head to the side and stared. Her cat's eyes traveled up and down his body. She noted the scar along his eyebrow with intense satisfaction. With a feral grin she made an extravagant gesture of welcome, purring, "My, my, do come in, Adam. It *is* Adam Wade, isn't it? Did you go into the rackets—or just hot wire that Mercedes?"

He stepped inside as she ran one long, lacquered nail under his lapel. Ignoring her suggestive inspection he replied, "I'm Adam Moreland, not Wade, Riba." He could feel her fingers tighten on his jacket for an instant as she digested the startling announcement.

"Then why the hell masquerade in the mud in this godforsaken hole?" Her eyes narrowed as she continued to inspect him, all the while her brain raced ahead, trying to solve the puzzle of this man who fascinated and infuriated her as no other ever had.

Adam watched her calculate with a cool smile on his face. "I like vineyard mud, Riba," he replied. Before he could ask to see Marti she interrupted him with a triumphant snap of her fingers.

"Now I remember! I was only a freshman in high school but the scandal hit all the local news, from Frisco to the valley—Moreland heir vanishes after stepmother is killed in lover's tryst," she mimed the six o'clock news reporters. Her chuckle was catty and insinuating. "Was she a brunette or a blonde like me, Adam?"

"You're just like Jolie, Riba, right down to the scum on your soul." God, how he hated dredging up the pain again! Impatiently, he brushed past her, more intent on explaining his life to Marti, not her twisted sister.

He looked past her, down the hall. "I've come to see Marti."

Her chuckle burst into full scale laughter, a low, ugly sound that gave him an acute case of the creeps. "Your bridegroom ought to keep a net on you."

She began to calm then and replied acidly, "My beloved 'bridegroom' is nursing his wounded ego back in Philadelphia with his mama. I'm home for the holidays. Unfortunately for you, my sister isn't." She paused now and the venomous look in her eyes took his breath away.

"What do you mean, she isn't here? Where is Marti?" His voice grew stronger without rising in volume.

"Poor Adam. Even if you aren't that dollar short anymore, you are a day late. And I bet . . . yes," she said as she patted his coat pocket with the practiced ease of a vice cop frisking a pimp, "Yes, it's a ring box. Maybe an engagement ring for my darling sister?"

Adam resisted the urge to shake her until every cap on her teeth came loose. "No more games, Riba."

"I'm not the one playing, Adam. Marti is. She's in France, the Riviera for Christmas, I believe. Oh, by the way, your engagement ring isn't appropriate—she already has one, and a wedding ring to go with it. She and her husband Eves are blissfully happy, so Papa tells me."

Adam stood frozen, digesting what Riba spat out with such spiteful glee. His mind wanted desperately not to believe her, but a coiled knot in his guts told him it was true. "When did all this happen?" *How could it have happened?*

"Oh, let's see, she called from New Orleans the end of August. She was visiting our great aunt Lese and met this gorgeous Frenchman. From what she told Papa, it was quite a whirlwind courtship."

August. He was still lying unconscious in an intensive care ward then! Without a word he turned and yanked the door open.

As he stalked through the misty rain to his car and pulled away from the house in a spray of gravel, Riba watched with a malevolent smile curving her lips. Freezing air poured in the open door, but she felt warm. Smiling, Riba closed the door and went humming contentedly upstairs to dress for dinner. She would have to give Adam's new identity some consideration. When she had destroyed his note, Riba knew he would return one day. What exquisite luck that he chose this particular week.

"So, the drifter is really a millionaire. Poor, poor Marti. She didn't need to go to France looking for a husband after all," she murmured to herself with a giggle.

Adam drove straight to the gallery in Napa and parked his car in a tow away zone. In a moment he was inside the warm spacious room, his eyes quickly searching for Alice Marchanti as he called out her name. She walked around the corner and her round friendly face whitened in shock as she looked at the elegant stranger with the coldly furious blue eyes.

"Well, haven't you come up in the world," she said scathingly. "Amazing what a few months can do for an itinerant field hand." Hands on her hips, she stopped squarely in front of him, unintimidated. "Why'd you come back, Adam? To gloat?"

"I suppose you're going to tell me I broke her heart," he said with soft sarcasm.

"You walked out of her life and never looked back—it nearly killed her," she barked furiously.

He smiled insolently. "Well, for somebody at death's door, she staged a miraculous recovery according to Riba. Marti did marry some damn Frenchman in August, didn't she?"

A trifle less belligerently Alice replied, "They met in August. They were married in September at his family home in France."

"Is it by chance near Lourdes? It must've been some miracle—a woman stricken by her lover's desertion, marrying some Continental gigolo a month later!" The mask slipped and the raw anguish showed on his face in that moment. He forced down his rising bile and turned to leave.

But Alice saw the lapse. "Adam, what happened? Marti was so hurt, so confused when you vanished without a trace. She had to get away from here. She's got a great aunt in New Orleans who asked her to visit and spend some time so she could get her life back together."

"Well, obviously she succeeded beyond her wildest expectations," he said in a clipped voice, pausing at the door. "If she's married, Alice, there really isn't much point in my explaining, is there?"

Alice watched him from the gallery window and noticed for the first time that he was favoring his left leg. There had also been a new scar on his right temple. "What the beejesus is going on?" she murmured in frustration.

When Marti had left for New Orleans, she had

seemed calm and resigned, so joyless despite her protests about starting a new life. Alice had been frightened for her. Then came word of the engagement. Alice was sure it was a foolish decision to marry on the rebound, but from so far away, she could only send her congratulations and hide her misgivings. Seeing Adam Wade again brought them back in an avalanche. *Oh, Marti, if only you'd waited* . . . The rain continued in a steady gray rhythm.

Adam had a lot of time to think as he drove through the gathering darkness toward Livermore. He held the anguish of Marti's betrayal at bay, forcing himself to concentrate on the future. *A future with no conniving women in it!* She was Joe Beaumont's daughter as sure as he was Jake Moreland's son. He damn well should act his part. She was acting hers. If he'd pushed all thoughts of retaliation against Joe aside when the old man was a prospective father-in-law, that reason was invalid now.

Some day, Beaumont, I'll pay you back with interest, you and those goddamned goons you hired. Then his thoughts shifted from that near miss to the others. Could Joe have learned about him and Marti and been trying to kill him all along? He'd suspected Booth and even Beaumont's stupid, jealous winemaster, but now he had a third suspect. Any one of them could have hired the kind of amateur-night help available in Napa for the plane and truck set up, not to mention that clumsy incident with the oak barrel.

He considered contacting a first rate private investigator in San Francisco and putting someone on the trail of his would-be assassin or assassins. The idea of hiring a bodyguard also crossed his mind. As the acting head of Moreland Enterprises he was sure to make more enemies, and he already had a surplus.

When he walked in the front door of the house that evening, Randolph was waiting for him in the foyer. One look at the old man's face and he knew.

"It's your father, sir . . ."

"When?" was all Adam said as he slipped out of his damp suitcoat.

"About an hour ago. His passing was quiet. He just never woke up from his afternoon rest. May I get you a brandy, sir? Perhaps something to eat?"

Adam was grateful the old man offered no false condolences. "Thank you, Randolph. I'd appreciate a brandy brought to my room. I assume Mort has been notified."

"Yes, sir. Mr. Yung is handling the arrangements. He'll arrive later tonight. I wasn't certain how to reach you."

"That's all right. Show my cousin into the study as soon as he arrives and then call me." He turned to go but the butler cleared his throat and Adam stopped.

"Mr. Allard called. He's on his way over, sir."

Fucking vulture! "Of course he would be. I'll be back down as soon as I change, Randolph. Leave the brandy in the study, if you please . . . the whole bottle." *The king is dead, long live the king,* he thought bitterly as he walked deliberately up those fifty-four steps, counting each one.

The blue-green waters of the Mediterranean were serene and the sun golden that afternoon as Marti stretched luxuriously and reached for the suntan lotion.

"Enjoying your honeymoon?" a high pitched voice chirped.

Marti ran her hands over her expanding belly and laughed. "Some honeymoon. I look like a blimp. Poor Eves. What do you imagine he'd think of his fat bride?"

Lese Kidder sank down into a beach chair with the birdlike grace that made people doubt she was eighty years old. She tapped a thin finger against a translucent cheek consideringly. "Well, poor Eves would certainly not let you lay out here alone, day in and day out, fat or not."

"I wish my baby could be born in the United States, Aunt Lese," Marti said wistfully.

"Now, we've talked it over, child. The baby will be an American citizen, but it's better for appearances if you wait for several months after the delivery. A grandfather is never sure what size a baby should be, especially a grandfather as obtuse as my nephew Joseph." Lese ran her tiny hand through the bouncy cap of snow white curls on her head and pulled the beach umbrella nearer to shade her delicate complexion.

Watching her great aunt, Celestine Beaumont Kidder, Marti could see her as she must have looked sixty years ago, an outrageous flapper with bobbed golden hair and that devilishly alluring dimple in her smile. "Aunt Lese, you know I'd never have been able to get through this muddle without your help. Thank you."

Looking at her grave niece, Lese laughed dismissively. "Nonsense! You have a level head on your shoulders and you'll survive splendidly. I just happened to be from the old school of devious southern belles. When would you like poor Eves to meet his tragic demise?"

"You are outrageous!" Marti said, doubling up with laughter. "Well, in all due consideration—and to keep Papa from rushing to my side to console me, I think we'd better let Eves live several months after the baby's born."

"Yes, of course. Something believable and not too macabre. As you said, we don't want Joseph on the next plane to console the grieving widow. I expect I can put him off until we return to New Orleans." She considered a minute, then said, "How about being washed overboard off his yacht?"

"Too melodramatic," Marti rejoined. "I was thinking along the line of your simple, everyday highway crash." She put her wrist to her forehead and said with a flourish, "You know how he loved to race his Ferrari."

"Quite perfect!" Lese clapped her hands. "I must say, when I first concocted this imaginary husband for you, you showed far less enthusiasm. It must be the spring air on the Riviera."

"When I came to you in New Orleans, I was panic stricken about appearing at Riba's wedding in maternity clothes! I'll admit at first I wasn't crazy about the idea of deceiving Papa, but seeing me in that condition would've broken his heart. This scheme of yours saved a scandal in the Beaumont family."

Lese snorted with amazing indelicacy for a petite southern lady. "A woman having a baby without benefit of clergy is the least of our family skeletons. This is 1984—only your father would be shocked by what you did. You do know, my dear, that when I married Francis Kidder in 1922 the noble Beaumonts and Flamencos were shocked into apoplexy—and your Uncle Christopher was born seven months later. A premature baby, of course," she added with a wink.

"The family never questioned Uncle Kit's birth?" Marti looked dubious, having never heard this tidbit before.

"They were still in too much of an uproar that I eloped with a man from Pennsylvania to think about counting on their fingers. Remember, he was a Yankee. Your grandfather moved to California to live down the scandal."

Marti's laughter burbled at the idea of her stolid grandfather fleeing New Orleans at the hint of a social scandal. "I find that hard to believe, Aunt Lese, even in 1922. The Civil War was a long time ago."

"Not to New Orleans Creoles! Of course, you must realize the Beaurivage family had already been tainted by a Yankee strain nearly a hundred years before that. We have Armstrong blood in us, too," Lese whispered as if confessing a venereal infection. At Marti's look of frankly piqued curiosity, she explained, "My great grandmother, Lenore Flamenco eloped with a Yankee banker named Caleb Armstrong. It took two generations for my grandparents to be accepted into southern society."

"Well, I'm just the latest generation in a family of unconventional women, I suppose. Still, all the rest of you did have husbands," Marti said quietly. Her eyes grew pensive as she rubbed her protuberant abdomen.

Lese waited expectantly. Marti had spoken little about her baby's father since her initial explanations last August. "It isn't good to keep the pain bottled up inside you, child," she said gently.

"Aunt Lese, I loved him so much. Dumb, wasn't I? He was a drifter, a man who chose that way of life. I know he came from a wealthy background, but he turned his back on it for some mysterious reasons—he never told me what they were. Yet I trusted him."

"You loved him—trust comes along with love, Marti. Are you certain he won't ever come back? He wrought miraculous changes in you, child. When you visited me two years ago you were a plain little mouse, hiding your beauty, absolutely impervious to my every attempt to glamorize you. Your Adam succeeded where I failed. For that alone, I thank him."

"Someone finally noticed Riba's frigid sister," Marti said bitterly. "At least I should thank him for getting me past that hangup."

"And what do you plan to do with your newly discovered sexuality—after a decent interval of mourning, of course?" Lese inquired, trying to ease Marti's sudden bitterness.

"I don't plan to compete with my sister, that's certain. I talked to Papa last night. Riba and Larry are fighting again Aunt Lese. She's spending some time at a lakefront house she just bought—on the Nevada side of Tahoe."

"How convenient for her. I assume she used her foolish young attorney's money to buy the property?"

Marti shrugged in indifference. "She has a trust fund the same as I do."

"How is Joseph taking all this?"

"Pretty well, all things considered. Of course he blames all their trouble on Larry." She paused and took off her sunglasses. "Aunt Lese, Papa always blamed anyone but Riba for her faults."

The old woman nodded in affirmation. "Before you met Adam Wade, you never would have admitted that."

"Maybe not, but he's gone . . . for good."

"So, what are you going to do for the rest of your life—wither on the vine?"

"I'll have a son or daughter to raise. And I can continue with my watercolors. You've seen my latest efforts. What do you think?"

Lese would not be derailed from her train of thought. "I know you have immense talent. You've already had two highly successful shows in France, for God's sake! If you return to New Orleans, you can earn a handsome living to support your child. *That* is not what I asked you, Martha Marie Beaumont!"

Marti laughed and said, "Tell me the story about how you met Uncle Francis in St. Louis Park again."

At first Joe Beaumont stood rooted to the floor, then sank down onto a big wing chair. He took a long, slow breath and drank a swallow from his glass. The brilliantly subtle and flinty Chardonnay tasted like pond water to him. Setting the glass aside, he watched Riba pace angrily across the living room. She was still wearing the designer jeans and T-shirt she had pulled on in Tahoe before having a private jet fly her back to Napa. Her face was flushed and he could tell she had been drinking.

"So, you barge in here without so much as a phone call and announce you're divorcing Larry. What the hell is going on, Rebecca?" he demanded in bewilderment. "You can't work out a lover's quarrel with him in Philadelphia and you in Nevada—or here."

"Lover's quarrel!" Riba parroted the words back at him with a snort of derision, her usual pleading abandoned in exhaustion and anger. "Why do you think I left Philly in the first place, Papa? That old bat of a mother-in-law hates me. And Larry always sides with her! I told you at Christmas how impossible it all was." She stopped pacing and looked at him, forcing herself to calm down.

Before she could say anything more, Joe began, "When I was back for that visit in February Estelle Cameron didn't act any different than she had at your wedding. Old family proper, I'll admit, but you knew her nearly a year before you married her son." Perplexity knitted his brow as he looked at her, waiting for some explanation to the sudden divorce. More was going on here than Riba was telling him.

She threw up her hands angrily and flopped down across the sofa. *If only I could think straight! What kind of stuff did they give me in that abortion clinic?* Three stiff martinis on the plane from Tahoe had not helped calm her frayed nerves. She struggled to focus on her father's hurt and angry face. He had been so impressed with her marrying into Philadelphia Mainline, even liked all those boring society types. They were all like Marti with her do-gooder fund raisings and symphony society shit. She took a deep breath and replied, "You weren't there when darling Estelle had me alone, Papa."

"Is it the mother or the son who's the problem, Princess?" he asked sadly.

"Well, I said he always agrees with her," she shot back defensively.

"Give me a for instance," Joe coaxed.

"Oh, I don't know, Papa." Her guts ached and her head was swimming. Why had she even tried coming home now? It had been a crazy impulse, but she had been so alone and scared up there on the lake.

"Larry told me he wanted to start a family, but he said you didn't want kids." Joe wanted her to deny it, prayed she would, in fact.

Riba shot out of the chair like it had been hotwired. "So that's it! Having babies again. I'm not some frumpy old brood mare. I'm only twenty-three. I wanted to wait, that's all. He just wants his two point five children so they'll look good in his campaign photos anyway," she added bitterly. "Larry only married me because I was beautiful—the perfect candidate's wife. Step two was the children. He spends all his time at oven fried chicken and instant mashed potato dinners, gladhanding smarmy little ward heelers. I'm supposed to tag along and smile on command, like a trained chimp!"

Joe sighed wearily. "Larry wanted to enter politics when you met him, Princess. I thought you knew a politician's wife would have a hard time of it. I even warned you about how tough it would be, honey. So did Martha."

Riba's face froze with brittle fury. She stood very still for a moment, forcing her voice several octaves lower than the shrill scream she wanted to use. Then she spoke. "We're back to Marti again, aren't we? It always comes back to her. My perfect, brilliant sister with her millionaire Frenchman and her model marriage. Even a baby on the way. How appropriate, Papa, that your more worthy daughter should present you with the first Beaumont grandchild, while I have a failed marriage and come home alone and heartbroken!" She started to run from the room but Joe intercepted her at the doorway where he stood and held her in his arms, awkwardly stroking her back.

"Aw, Princess, you know I didn't mean it that way. I'm sorry. If you don't want children right off, that's not unreasonable. Larry's a good boy, honey. I think if I call him and ask him to come out here we can work—"

"No!" Riba bolted backwards, her eyes dilated in fear. "N-no, that is, don't call him, Papa. Please. I beg you!" She hugged herself and began to cry in earnest now, really frightened. What if Larry told him everything?

Joe again reached out for her and ushered her back toward the big sofa facing the mantle. Bertrice Beaumont's portrait smiled serenely down on her husband and the younger daughter who was her mirror image. Her father attempted to soothe Riba's hysteria and make sense of the story she began to blurt out in fits and starts between bouts of weeping.

"You don't know Larry. He's not what you think. I wanted to . . ." she hiccuped, "to . . . to spare you, Papa. I'm a failure. You see, Lawrence Smythe Cameron told me so himself . . . I did get pregnant even though I didn't want to be. I was so sick, Papa. It was just awful . . . and then . . . then, I lost the baby. I had a miscarriage! Larry said it was all my fault. That I wasn't a g-good w-wife . . . That's when I went to Nevada and bought the house at the l-lake."

As she cried convulsively now, Joe felt his heart constrict with guilt and horror. "Oh, sweetheart, my princess, I'm so sorry. If I ever see that young punk again I'll make him wish he could trade shoes with that damned drifter Wade!"

Riba's torrent gradually subsided as Joe continued to hold her and croon endearments, assuring her all would be well, that he loved her just as much as Marti and that she would find another man, one as fine as Eves Martin.

Riba dried her red puffy eyes and stared across her father's shoulder, looking vacantly up at the beautiful face of her dead mother.

Lese could hear the squeal of the baby even before the hospital doors opened. Anxiously she wrung her hands. *I only pray I did right, staying in the south of France for this delivery.*

The beaming nurse who ushered her in to see Marti set her fears to rest, chattering in French about how beautiful the baby was and how uncomplicated the delivery. Fluent in the language, Lese nodded and eagerly rushed to Marti's bedside.

"Let me see my great, great nephew," she whispered in excitement.

Marti looked tired but blissful as she raised the squalling, red-faced bundle for inspection. "Aunt Lese, meet Heath Joseph Beaumont—er, Heath Joseph Martin," she corrected with a conspiratorial wink and grin. "Won't Papa be thrilled?"

Chapter 15

Adam stood by the sliding glass door looking down at the glitter of San Francisco, diamond bright and pristinely beautiful under the cloak of darkness. He liked the darkness. It hid the seaminess of slums and softened the glare of neon signs. The city promised every variety of enticement: massage parlors on sleazy back streets, exotic dancers in expensive private clubs. But by night, he could see only the clean shine of lights from his Sacramento Street penthouse on Nob Hill. He preferred the distance. So did Linda.

Rubbing the scar across his right eyebrow, an unconscious habit he'd developed over the past four years, he turned from the panorama of the city and walked across the living room to a large mirrored bar against the far wall. He could hear the bathroom door opening and the sounds of Linda vigorously toweling her short black hair into casually unkempt curls. He liked her best that way, swathed in a large terry robe with her hair damp and fragrant after a shower. He poured generous splashes of Chivas over ice in two glasses and waited for her to walk through the hall door.

When she silently padded across the thick dark green carpet, he offered her a glass. They touched drinks lightly together with the easy camaraderie of a man and woman who've been companions for years and then sipped the scotch in silence. Like Linda, Adam was freshly showered and dressed in a comfortable robe.

They'd just returned from a lavish, boring dinner party at the home of one of the city's leading wine negotiants and they were tired. Sliding onto the big comfortable cinnamon colored sofa, he stretched out, pulling her with him. He propped his bare feet on a large ottoman in front of him and she rested her slim ankles across his legs.

"Long day," he exhaled softly, kissing the crown of her head.

She nodded. "The captain had one of his nifty afternoon debriefings on those wharf murders," she replied. "Seeing his smiling face when I clocked in was at the bottom of my list of ways to start the day."

He grunted a half laugh. "I bet Carrington's party tonight wasn't much higher. You know, Lin, you don't have to go with me to these business affairs. You're not my body guard, sergeant. Nobody's tried to kill me in nearly four years."

She looked up and gave a silky laugh. "I have a vested interest in guarding your body, Adam. Besides, how many body guards sleep with their employers?"

Adam laughed.

Her brown eyes clouded with worry. "Don't get over confident, Adam. Someone with a nine-mm Smith and Wesson missed you by inches that day in the parking garage."

"And a very sexy homicide detective with great legs was assigned to my case." He grinned, trying to lighten her mood.

"But I struck out," she replied bleakly.

"Considering the tenor of our relationship over the past three years, I think I resent that," he replied teasingly.

She waved her drink in dismissal. "Be serious, Adam. I never found the shooter. For all we know, he could still be waiting to kill you tomorrow on your way to work."

He took a long drink. "That why you put up with me? To catch your shooter?"

She set her drink on the teak table beside the sofa, then stretched up to kiss his throat. Pulling his robe open, she nuzzled his chest and ran her fingers through the thick black pelt on it. "I live with you for very base, non-professional reasons, Adam Moreland."

He pulled her up into a solid embrace and kissed her lips hungrily. After a night of false smiles and forced postures, this was honest and healing. "Lin, Lin, I'm so glad you're here." His voice was muffled as they rolled over on the wide sectional sofa, entangling in their half-opened bathrobes.

After a few minutes of heated caresses and kisses she rolled off the sofa, shedding her robe to stand splendidly naked in front of him. "Let's go to the bedroom before we ruin this fancy velour couch," she said with a grin, pulling on his robe belt.

Catching her wrist, he grinned as he shrugged the loose garment off, and stood beside her. "You're always worried about details. Who cares about the damnned sofa. I can afford another one."

"On a cop's salary I can't. Anyway my job *is* details. Now," she struck a seductive pose pulling her robe across her flared hips like a Venus de Milo drape. "Just imagine me without arms and ravish me."

"Fat chance you'd ever be so timid, copper," he said as he whisked the robe away and embraced her. As if to prove him right, her arms encircled his waist and she pressed her hips and breasts close against him.

"We're going to get arrested for indecent exposure some day," she murmured as she glanced at their naked full length reflection in the sliding glass door of the balcony.

"No one can see up this high," he said, nuzzling her breasts.

"Anyone on the next hillside with a mail order telescope can see us," she said, pulling him toward the hall that led to their big bedroom.

"Details, again," he groused, following as she led the way.

The alarm went off like a dentist's drill. Adam flung an arm down on it to stop the hideous sound as Linda rolled over and rubbed her eyes. "Why the hell do you have to use this accursed relic? I have a perfectly good clock radio alarm," Adam complained.

"I sleep through news and music," she replied, muffling a yawn. "Anyway, a good old Timex jolt gets a cop's adrenaline pumping in the morning. Go back to sleep if you don't have an early call. You had a late one last night." She rolled off the king sized bed, then bent down on one knee to plant an affectionate kiss on his brow.

"As a matter of fact, I do have an early call. A meeting with Booth." He could feel her troubled gaze on him as he sat up and planted his feet on the opposite side of the bed.

"What's the sultan of sleaze up to now? A new scam to extract the body fluid from migrant workers and peddle it as jug wine?"

Adam shrugged, sharing Linda's aversion to Booth Allard. "Something about moving our operation into the North Coast and buying some good independent chateaus."

Her hands froze on the belt to her robe. Brushing her tousled black hair from her eyes, she asked softly, "Napa wineries?"

Adam sensed the tension in her questions. "Napa and Sonoma," he replied casually.

She walked around the bed to confront him. "Look, I know we have an understanding about business and pleasure, but Napa's where you nearly bought it four years ago. That knee's never completely healed."

He put his hands gently on her shoulders. Barefooted, they were nearly the same height. Detective Sergeant Linda Drake was a very tall woman. As memories of Napa flashed through his mind, Adam could see another woman's face in Lin's place for a fleeting instant. He quashed the image and said, "No one's tried to mug me or shoot me in almost four years. Going back to Napa's hardly going to trigger a rash of assassination attempts. I don't even think the two incidents were related. Relax."

Linda stood stiffly, her eyes hard and professional now. "The last attempt was on my turf and we never caught him. You're not immortal, Moreland, no matter how damn lucky you've been. Anyway, I wouldn't go to church with Booth Allard, much less ride down a deserted stretch of Highway 29 with him."

Adam chuckled but his eyes were hard as sapphires. "I never turn my back on Booth. All I'm doing this morning is listening to his ideas. I'll read the reports he has. Hell, I may not even have to go to the valley to close the deal . . . if we make one."

"If you go," she said sternly, "make damn sure you take someone you trust along with you."

He grinned. "You sound like a wife."

"Shit! I sound like a cop. And cops, as we all know, make lousy wives."

"But they're great in bed. At lease *some* of them are!" He gave her a quick kiss and headed for his bathroom.

Linda, too, headed to her bath at the opposite end of the room, turned on the steaming hot water and stepped into the spray. Raised in a poor neighborhood in Oakland, she'd never get used to the opulence of Adam's lifestyle.

Thirteen years ago she had been a new bride, fresh out of high school with a husband who worked as a garage mechanic. When the marriage went sour, she found a job waiting tables and began to take night classes at San Francisco State. It took her five years to graduate.

Then she entered the police academy and realized her greatest dream. She invested everything in her career, including a second failed marriage to a fellow officer. "Cops should never marry other cops," Dave told her. "Cops should never marry anyone," she replied. So far Linda Drake had held to that resolution.

She made sergeant just before her thirtieth birthday. Being a homicide detective was an around-the-clock job. So was heading a corporate empire like Moreland Enterprises. She and Adam had their obsession with work in common.

In fact, that was exactly how they met. Closing her eyes as she ducked her head under the hot pulsing water, she could still picture the first time she had laid eyes on him. It was not exactly a routine case when one of San Francisco's richest tycoons was nearly shot. Responding to the call, Linda arrived at the parking garage of his luxury condominium on Sacramento Street. There she found the most elegantly handsome man she'd ever seen brushing plaster chips and cinders from an eight hundred dollar suit as calmly as she'd brush danish crumbs off her formica breakfast table.

After her divorce from Dave, Linda had sworn never to mix her personal and professional life again, but once Adam Moreland's blue eyes fastened on her, she knew she'd break that oath no more than the case was closed. The investigation led nowhere. Moreland was reticent about his life and any possible enemies, only giving the police a brief sketch of his exile from the Moreland family. He never mentioned the beating in Napa that had nearly cost him his life. Linda dug into his past and found a trail to the hospital records in Fresno. He then explained about his altercation with some unknown thugs in Napa, but assured her there was no connection between that and the shooting. Every gut instinct honed by her years on the street told her he was concealing something. Four years later she still did not know what it was.

When the case was finally closed, Linda Drake and Adam Moreland became lovers. The next logical step was for her to move into his huge penthouse. It was conveniently located for her work and he offered her the only kind of relationship she would have accepted. Separate careers, no strings. Neither of them had time for commitment and family. After two disastrous attempts, Linda was no longer willing to mix careers and husbands.

Adam was an enigma. Being the last man in the Moreland dynasty, he should have wanted a family. But he had never been married and made it clear he never planned to be. After three years together, she had gleaned bits and pieces of his past life—his relationship with his father, the affair with his stepmother, his rootless wandering after a stint in the navy. All of it added up to create a man who was a natural loner. Or did it? Something had happened to Adam Moreland in Napa—something that changed his life more drastically than Jolie's death. But he never explained and she never asked. The answer lay shrouded in the spring fog of Napa, she'd bet her badge on it. Detective Linda Drake only prayed Adam Moreland was not betting his life on it.

As he drove to work that morning, Adam's thoughts also turned to Napa. At the party the previous evening Booth had alluded to his contacts in Napa. Two small but prestigious wineries were ripe for their picking. Chateau Beaumont lay between them. Larger and under more sound financial management, it was still an old-fashioned operation producing fine red dinner wines that comprised a shrinking share of the market.

Once Adam had admired the old man's integrity for not producing popular whites and blush wines. But that was before Joe Beaumont had hired three bonebreakers to beat him half to death. He had never retaliated. Marti was gone and he had simply closed the door on that part of his life. Now Booth had a scheme to reopen it. Rubbing his jaw in consideration, Adam turned into the underground parking lot at the Embarcadero Center. He'd listen to what Booth had to say.

The late afternoon sunlight was faint as it filtered into the west window of Marti's Chartres Street studio. Chalk dust and the acrid smell of paints hung in the air. The place was in orderly disarray. A huge skylight cast its soft benediction on numerous water colors and oils. Another large counter top banked by overhead lights was covered with pencil and pastel drawings.

Marti replaced the phone in its cradle and slowly walked over to open a window. Already the muggy gulf air promised summer heat, although it was only February. *It's cool and rainy in Napa now. Papa's men have just finished pruning.* Taking a deep breath, she let the smell and noise of the exotic French Quarter fill her senses. "I belong in New Orleans," she said aloud, as if trying to convince herself it was true.

But Joe Beaumont's phone call had cast a disturbing pall on her hard-won peace of mind. Marti heard the front door downstairs open and close as she rubbed her temples in concentration. She could hear the exuberant scuffling as Heath half-crawled, half-bounded up the stairs with Lese trailing behind him at a far more sedate pace. *He'll be three next month* she thought in amazement as her small son burst into the room with a squeal of delight.

"Grandma gave me a guun," the child said, enunciating the vowel in the last word with great relish. He proudly produced a small hand made wooden pistol, obviously from one of the French Market shops.

"Grandma buys you far too many toys," Marti said, but found it hard to disapprove of Lese's spoiling the child, who was so good natured it seemed not to hurt. Lese's own grandchildren were all grown now with the youngest, her daughter Lenore's son, graduating from Tulane this spring. Having Heath live with her brought genuine joy to Lese Kidder, joy Marti was loathe to remove.

The old woman walked quietly into the room and watched Marti and Heath in an animated exchange as he demonstrated his new toy. In spite of the fact it had no moving parts, the little gun was a veritable arsenal in the three year old's vivid imagination. But his mother was preoccupied as she stroked his shiny black hair and hugged him. Marti scooped him into her arms and walked over to the window, letting him look down at the people on the busy street below, while at the same time explaining patiently why he could not pretend to shoot at them with his new treasure.

When their cook, Lylabeth, came up to announce milk and fresh-baked cookies, she had an eager taker in Heath. Lese shooed the chattering child along with the trusted old servant and then turned to Marti. The silence was eloquent as the two women walked over to a large comfortable sofa against the inside wall of the airy studio.

After they were seated, Lese spoke first. "Your father called again, didn't he?"

"Just before you came home. He's not doing what the doctor told him to."

Lese snorted indelicately. "If I did what the doctor told me to, they'd have buried me thirty years ago! Joseph is my brother's son and they don't come any tougher than that. One mild heart seizure won't confine him to a wheelchair, Marti. Best thing for him is to keep busy. His father had a bad heart and lived to be seventy-nine, working every day until he died."

Marti ran her fingers nervously through her curly mane of sun streaked bronze hair. "I guess it's more than his health." She hesitated, then plunged ahead. "Riba's new husband is into drugs . . . cocaine, according to what Riba told me on her last call. She was drunk. Now she's home for a visit while she sulks about Oliver. I don't think this marriage will last as long as the last one. Lord knows a Mainline attorney is a lot more stable than a Hollywood film producer."

"Stability isn't Riba's forte either," Lese said wryly. "Why should she pick a stable husband? I'd rather imagine she likes life in banana land's fast lane."

"I've seen her so seldom these past years, I honestly don't know, but I do know it's killing Papa," Marti said sadly.

"It's about time he realizes what she's really like. You can't protect a sixty-three year old man, Marti. He'll have to take his lumps like everyone else. In fact he's long overdue."

"But so much is happening at once. First Riba's divorce, then my phoney widowhood, then his heart condition. Now Riba's second marriage sounds like it's on the rocks and someone is trying to sabotage the winery," Marti replied in agitation.

Lese's clear blue eyes focused sharply on Marti. "Sabotage the winery? Whatever for?"

"It seems some giant conglomerate, one of those Big Valley outfits, is trying to buy out a string of smaller wineries in Napa. Several of the boutiques have already been sold."

"But Chateau Beaumont is a large operation, hardly a trendy, boutique winery," Lese argued impatiently.

"Well, it won't stay large for long if the machinery is damaged and someone's tampering with thermostats on cooling tanks. If Papa hadn't been watching every detail himself a whole year's harvest of Chardonnay would have been vinegar!"

Now genuine concern filled Lese's voice. "Do those corporate cutthroats really resort to illegal tactics to force an independent vintner to sell?"

"Well in this case, considering the reputation of Moreland Enterprises, I'm not surprised. The old man was a pirate from what Papa always said. Now the whiz kid son who's taken over is apparently even worse. His agents have called on Papa twice already." Marti stood up and began to pace agitatedly.

"You feel you have to go back and stand by your father," Lese said quietly.

Marti turned with a beseeching look on her face. "I . . . I don't want to go back. I've made a life for us here. I have a good career, a wonderful child, you, our friends. Oh, I don't know."

"What will Graham say?" Lese's shrewd blue eyes fixed Marti until a flush stained the younger woman's face.

"Gray and I have no claims on each other," she replied uneasily.

"You know he disagrees, Marti. Not that I'm pushing you to marry him, mind you. But I don't want you rushing back to that winery on the west coast with the misguided notion that you and you alone can save Chateau Beaumont. You did 'the weight of the world syndrome' most of your life and you were never happy until you broke with the past and made your niche here. Consider everything—what's good for you and Heath—not just what's good for Joseph or me. We're two tough old people who can survive on our own." She raised one bony but elegant hand in a pledge. "End of lecture."

Marti knelt in front of the sofa and embraced the

woman who had filled the place of the mother she had never known.

Graham Kley was a handsome man, if a woman fancied the sensitive type, he always told himself with a touch of humor. He was tall and fine boned with curly blond hair and a neatly trimmed beard. His thin, aristocratic face was enhanced by clear amber eyes and a devilish, boyish grin. As one of the most successful commercial artists in the county, his annual income was securely in the six figure bracket and his reputation as a fine oil painter was just as soundly established. With two to three shows a year in New Orleans, he regularly won critical approval.

If only things had worked out as smoothly in his personal life, he mused sadly as he walked the short blocks to pick up Marti that evening. She had called earlier to say she must talk with him. Somehow, he had a feeling that it was not to accept his latest proposal of marriage.

Galatoire's on Bourbon Street was a pleasant ten minute stroll away. As usual, the place was packed and the noise level high as tuxedoed waiters bustled between crowded tables, balancing big trays with effortless ease. Gray and Marti were seated at his usual table in a far corner, away from the kitchen.

Taking a sip of his drink, he looked into her eyes and said baldly, "Enough small talk. What do you want to discuss with me? You sounded serious on the phone and you're as jumpy as a cat tonight."

Marti twisted the stem on her wine glass and looked down into its pale gold contents, summoning up her courage. "Papa called today . . ." She paused.

"So, he calls at least once a week—has ever since I met you two years ago." He waited to hear what he knew she was struggling to say, but damned if he'd help her.

"His calls lately have been real downers, Gray. You know that. But now, well, now someone—a big wine conglomerate—is trying to force him to sell Chateau

Beaumont. Our equipment and stock are being sabotaged."

"You said 'our.' I take it that your four-year absence hasn't changed your proprietary feelings about the winery. Marti, hasn't Lese been able to talk some sense into you? Your life is here in New Orleans. You have a successful career. You're gaining a national reputation as a watercolor artist. You're building a life of your own, without your father."

"But he still *is* my father, Gray. And he may be in danger. Oh, I don't plan to stay in California. But don't you see, I have to go, at least until this thing is over—the threats and destructive acts."

Prying her hands from the wine glass, he raised them to his lips and kissed the fingers softly. A frown creased his brow as he asked, "It really is that serious? I'm sorry, darling. Of course you have to go. If you want, I'd be glad to come with you."

Marti shook her head distractedly, "No, thank you, Gray. I have to face the old memories there on my own." Her clear gray eyes were steady and he knew it was useless to argue the point.

They walked from Galatoires to his loft on Dumaine. The night air was soft and warm and Marti knew she'd miss it. Going through their familiar ritual, he poured two snifters of Henessey X.O. and heated them in his microwave. The pungent aroma of the fine old brandy filled her nostrils as she inhaled, then sipped. They sat on a small loveseat in one corner of his parlor, a quaint Victorian recreation that Marti always felt perfectly suited Graham Kley's personality—proper yet comfortable, handsome without being opulent.

After several moments of companionable silence he took the half emptied snifter from her and set it on the glass topped table. "So, you're off to California for a showdown with a pack of sharks in Ivy league suits. Before you go, I have to show you something that I hope will bring you back."

He stood up and drew her with him, heading for his studio across the hall. Flicking on a light in the vast room, he headed straight for a covered easel. "I've about half finished it now. By the time you return, it'll be done."

When he pulled the drape from the canvas Marti gasped. It was a portrait in acrylic. Clear gray eyes, framed by tumbled bronze curls, stared down at her with a vibrant life of their own. "Gray, it's . . . it's unbelievable. Do I really look like that?" She touched her own face in rapt fascination.

He chuckled softly. "I may have come close, but I'll never be able to capture the real essence, will I, Marti?"

She turned into his gentle, comforting embrace. His soft beard brushed her neck and his warm lips tugged at her earlobe, trailing kisses slowly to her mouth. She responded, kissing him back slowly, savoringly. "Oh, Gray, I'll miss you so. You and Aunt Lese saved my sanity, you know. Heath and I would never have survived without you."

He held her at arm's length. "That sounds like you're saying goodbye, not just 'until I return,' Marti."

Marti melted into his arms again. "I've been thinking this through for a long time, even before Papa's troubles at the winery, Gray," she began hesitantly.

"And," he prompted, his heart constricting.

"If—no, when I come back, we can't see each other any more. I'll only hurt you, Gray. You're too good, too fine a man to be hurt. You've given me so much—my whole sense of self worth as a woman and an artist. But I don't—I *can't* love you. And I won't burden you or hold out false hopes for marriage or any lasting relationship. You deserve that kind of love—a love I can't return."

He dropped his arms in resignation and stepped back from her. "What you can't do is go through life in love with some callow drifter who deserted you and his own child. You've never let go of him, have you?"

Two years ago when she first began to date Graham Kley, Marti had told him about Adam Wade and Heath's paternity. Gray had been her confidant and lover, bringing her to life after Adam's desertion had made her numb and devoid of all sexual feelings.

Tears spilled down her cheeks now and she hated herself for causing him this anguish. "All I've ever done to repay your love and cherished friendship is cause you pain, Gray. I may never be able to love a man again the way I loved him. Maybe I'm an emotional cripple—but whatever I am, I won't do this to you." Her voice was steady now and her eyes were unwavering as they locked with his, pleading for acceptance of what she knew must be.

He smiled sadly and kissed her on the forehead with gentle affection. "I guess I'll have to live with that. Somehow I'm certain once you go home, you won't return to New Orleans."

Chapter 16

The flight into San Francisco International was as uneventful as a trip with a three-year-old child on his first plane ride could be. Heath alternated between chattering and staring in wide-eyed wonder. By the time the familiar old beige Cadillac pulled up in front of the passenger pickup area, Marti felt an odd mixture of apprehension and pleasure.

She was glad to be home, smelling the dry brisk air of the bay after the sultry Gulf Coast stillness she'd left in New Orleans. *You never realize how much you've missed such a simple thing until you rediscover it,* she thought, taking a deep breath. Still, Joe was not there to greet her, only Perkins, the family's oldest retainer.

"Hello, Max," she greeted, giving the reticent old man a quick hug.

He surprised her as a half smile moved across his usually impassive features. The smile broadened when he saw Heath. "So, this is the new master of Chateau Beaumont. He looks every bit as capable as his grandfather," Perkins said to Marti.

"How is my father, Max? I expected him to be with you," she added in disappointment.

The old man turned from her to open the trunk so the waiting skycap could load their bags. Looking at her compassionately he said, "Dr. Kane is with him now. It seems he had a minor setback this morning—nothing serious, but that young doctor is quite adamant, even against a man as formidable as your father, Miss Marti."

She smiled worriedly. "All the better I'm here

then." She forbore to add, *all the better Riba is not.* But the nagging thought that there was a relationship between Joe's relapse and her sister did not leave her on the ride into Napa.

The valley had changed little in the past four years. An aching bittersweet feeling of homecoming filled her senses as she watched graceful clusters of blue lantana flowers sway with the breeze. Within a few weeks the bottlebrush trees would open their fuchsia blooms. She could scarcely wait. When they turned off Highway 101 onto Highway 37 she observed the sunlight and shadows cast by gigantic stands of blue gum that grew like sentinels along the whole route. When the first fields with their orderly rows of pruned vines came into sight, Marti found her eyes straining for signs of budbreak. It would be any day now. *I'm still as much vintner as artist, Papa. Oh, Papa.*

Hilda Lee was at the front door when they pulled up in the driveway. Waiting eagerly for her first glimpse of Marti's child, the elderly cook came charging out to embrace Marti and inspect Heath. Her shrewd dark eyes took in his finely chiseled features and straight black hair as she knelt down and offered him a freshly baked sugar cookie.

One Chinese can always tell another. Adam's words about Hilda Lee suddenly echoed in Marti's mind. She looked worriedly down at her son, then over to the cook.

Hilda stood up with Heath in her arms and waited quietly until Max had walked up the steps, laden with luggage. "No one will ever suspect, Miss Marti. You do have some pictures of your husband?"

"Yes," Marti nodded as she took the boy from the older woman. "Yes, of course." Lese had culled through hundreds of Beaumont and Flamenco family photographs until she found a distant cousin with straight black hair and angular features. Once recopied and superimposed with recent snapshots of Marti, the fabrication of Eves Martin became tangible.

Smiling serenely, Hilda ushered Marti toward the house.

"Your papa's been real anxious to see this young man. Last time he visited you in New Orleans Heath was just starting to talk."

"I talk good now," the child said proudly between large bites of the crumbling cookie.

"He seldom stops," Marti lamented with a laugh as she paused in front of the large curved staircase. "Is it all right to go up now, or should I wait for Peter to finish his examination?" she asked Hilda hesitantly.

"I had strict orders to send you and Heath straight up as soon as you arrived," the cook said with a reassuring smile.

When Marti knocked and then entered the big master suite at the end of the hallway, her heart was thudding with dread. Peter Kane, her father's physician for the past several years, stood beside the bed with a broad smile slashed across his handsome face. Tall and blond, he was a casual acquaintance from college when she had been a freshman and he a senior. The following year he'd entered Berkeley's medical program.

"This man's about to climb the walls waiting for you and that grandson of his, Marti," Peter said as he folded a blood pressure kit into his medical bag.

Marti's eyes locked with her father's as she walked into the room. How could a man change so much in six short months, her mind cried. When he'd visited her last fall he was the same wiry, vigorous man he'd always been, leathery and sun tanned. Now his cheeks were sunken and a yellowish pallor lurked beneath the tan. Always thin, now he was emaciated.

"Hasn't Hilda been feeding you?" she asked crossly, trying desperately to keep the fear from her voice and tease him instead.

Joe looked at her and Heath, his pale gray eyes bright in an otherwise wan face. "Some greeting! Yeah, she cooks and I eat . . . when I feel like it. All those damn pills this quack gives me keep clacking around down there. They don't leave much room for food." He patted the bed for Marti and Heath to sit down and hugged her with surprising strength when she did so.

"Grandpa, I got a Saints football from Grandma Lese," Heath volunteered eagerly.

Marti was relieved the child remembered who the ill old man was, considering it had been so long in a three year old's life since he'd seen his only grandfather. Of course, they talked by phone weekly and she kept showing Heath photographs and talking about Joe regularly. Obviously, her father was delighted with the boy and attentively responded to his chatter.

Planting a quick kiss on Joe's forehead, Marti said, "You two have a quick visit while I see Dr. Kane out. I'll be right back."

"He'll just tell you some hocus pocus in five dollar words out of a medical dictionary," Joe said, waving her off to do what he knew she would.

Once outside the room, Marti looked up and down the long hall, then asked, "How bad, Peter?"

The young doctor shrugged. "We've gotten the blood pressure under control—if he keeps on his medication. The heart isn't damaged badly enough to warrant surgery. In fact, we're not really sure he suffered an attack per se. It was more like a seizure. Admittedly, his blood pressure at the time was dangerously high—and the cigarettes certainly didn't help. Neither does the sulphur dust and other toxic materials he breathes all the time around the fields."

"But he quit smoking and I promise now that I'm here I'll keep him out of the fields when they spray *anything.* I don't understand about the heart—if he isn't in danger of an attack and has no blockages that warrant surgery, then what *is* causing him to look so awful? He's lost weight he can scarcely afford to lose."

Kane's face betrayed some perplexity as he considered how best to proceed. He knew Marti was too sharp to be put off with vague excuses. "First of all, to get his serum cholesterol down, we had to restructure his diet—no eggs for breakfast and no thick beefsteaks for dinner. He's a stubborn man, used to eating what he wants. Since he was never overweight, when he refused to eat the foods on his new diet, he lost weight. I think you and Heath being here may be a tonic for his appetite—just keep him on Hilda's regimen." He hesitated.

"That's not all, though, is it?"

"No," he sighed. "I'd be the last one to lay a guilt trip on you for finally starting a life of your own, Marti; but in your absence, your sister's really put the knife to him and twisted."

"Brutal truth I asked for, brutal truth I get," she mused. "Okay, I've kept abreast of her life, secondhand, from Papa's phone calls. He always adored her and she could do no wrong in his eyes. I guess the last few years have been harder on him than I ever dreamed."

Peter put his hand on her arm and said firmly, "You are not to blame for what she's done or for your father's blindness to her faults, Marti. And you can't spend your life holding his hand. He's got to come to grips with his own life and decide to face reality. Visit a while, help him adjust to taking medication and following the diet, get him to open up about his feelings toward Riba, if possible—but this is my prescription for *you*. Don't bury yourself here again and give up your career or your freedom for him. I've listened to him talk about how the two of you used to run this place. He doesn't need to retire from field work, and you don't have to fill his boots. He has Staritz and Reams and he can get any other competent help he needs. No martyr complex, all right? It won't help either of you."

Marti smiled and raised her hand. "No martyrdom, I promise. But I do know there's more to Papa's business worries than my absence. Someone's been sabotaging equipment and a big San Francisco combine is trying to force him to sell. That would kill him, Peter."

"And exactly what do you plan to do about it?" he asked with a frown creasing his face.

"I'll find out from Boris and Les exactly what's going on, maybe hire an investigator. Certainly I'll fight to keep Chateau Beaumont from being sold off at gunpoint. Once we get on firm footing and this threat's over, Papa may feel more secure. Then I'll decide what my future plans are."

"From what I've read and what Joe's told me, you have quite a career back east as an artist."

"No law says I have to live in New Orleans to paint. I have a good friend right here in Napa who first encouraged my work. Now that I'm home, I find I really missed the valley."

Kane grinned. "Sulphur fumes and all?"

Marti responded, "Sulphur fumes, morning fog and evening chill—the whole package."

"Just be sure you stay for the right reasons, Marti. Don't try to take Riba's place."

"I could never do that, Peter," Marti replied quietly.

Joe rested that afternoon while Marti unpacked. She awakened Heath from his nap and prepared them both for a light dinner to be shared at Joe's bedside. His color seemed slightly improved that evening and he cleaned his plate diligently, serving as a role model for his grandson.

While they ate, they talked. Joe detailed for Marti the offer from Moreland Enterprises. By the tone of his voice she knew how vehemently he opposed the idea of ever selling out. At the present time their offer was insultingly low, but even if they raised it to a fair price, she knew his answer would never change.

"What do you know about the men who run the corporation?" she asked, finishing off her poached salmon.

"Jake's dead. Used to know him in the old days. A mean sucker but one I could look in the eye and figure. Now these new whiz kids in three piece suits with their computers . . ." He shrugged angrily. "Moreland's son took over when the old man died, nearly four years ago. Him and Jake's brother-in-law Booth Allard make a nice pair of sharks. I thought the old man was good, but they've doubled their holdings up and down the Big Valley, even bought some prime vineyards in Alameda and Santa Clara. But up till now, they've been making junk."

"A good stable California jug wine isn't junk, Papa. I've tasted some of them and they're quite solid—for what they are," Marti argued.

"Let them cater to drugstore tastes," Joe replied disgustedly. "But if they get a foothold in Napa, soon they'll start squeezing the whole North Coast, Marti. We've fought too long and hard to make fine wines—wines to compete with the best French and German vintages. You want to see us lose what three generations of Beaumonts have worked for?"

She put down her napkin and reached over to let Heath down from his high chair. "No, Papa, I don't. No one's going to force us out. We can fight Moreland and Allard, but if you want my help, you may have to bend a little when it comes to some new technology." She arched a brow and looked over at him.

He sighed. "You talked to Boris, yet?"

"No."

"I can hardly wait to hear what the two of you plan," he said sourly.

When it came to facing the winemaster, Marti could definitely wait, but despite her personal trepidations, she knew what she had to do. That evening she called Boris at his home.

The coolness of his greeting to her over the phone was reflected in his face when he strode into the study the following morning. "It's good to see you, Marti. Four years and motherhood haven't changed you." A smile was in place, but his aloof, brooding demeanor said as much as his polite words.

Her sudden departure four years earlier had seemed to Boris a personal betrayal. She had rejected his courtship in favor of Adam Wade and then left her father and the winery when Adam drifted away. As she gazed into his fathomless dark eyes, Marti knew how his sense of duty, as well as his ego, had been offended by her behavior. She decided to go straight to the heart of the matter.

"Boris, I know you blame me for leaving Papa and my work here." *Perhaps for my supposed marriage and for Heath, too?* "But I had to find my own way and that was my year of decision. I'm a widow with a child now and I know what I want from life."

"Does that include taking an interest in the continued existence of Chateau Beaumont?" he interrupted with the merest hint of sarcasm in his voice.

"I wouldn't have returned home if I didn't care. And more important than the winery is my father's health. I know the vines are his life and I intend to fight for his sake." She ran her fingers through her hair unconsciously, tossing the tangled curls back over her shoulder.

"Even in jeans you look elegant now, like a European jet-setter, Marti. Eighty-three was a turning point in your life. In time I suppose I'll learn to accept that." Boris walked to the cluttered desk where she had been attempting to sort through Joe's papers.

Marti knew that was as near an apology for his curt words as she'd ever get from the dour winemaster. "What exactly have the Moreland people done to force this sale? Papa's told me their offer and it stinks."

Boris scowled openly now. "We can't prove it—at least I haven't caught them yet, but we've had the thermostats on two cooling tanks 'adjusted.' Your father found one in time to save five thousand gallons of Chardonnay. We lost another tank. A whole shipment of corks arrived from Benicia hermetically sealed—or so we thought. By sheer luck I decided to test one bag before bottling. The seal must've been broken because the moisture content not only was fifteen per cent, but that extra five per cent of water was contaminated with enough botrytis to turn every bottle so putrid we couldn't sell it as vinegar! The latest incident occurred last week. Half a dozen tractor engines were sprayed with aluminum paint. It'll take a week to clean them up so they don't stall out every time the engines are turned on."

Marti's face was ashen. "Has anyone been threatened or injured?"

"Not yet," Boris replied darkly.

"No clue to who's doing the actual sabotage? It

could be someone working here, Boris. Who was new on the payroll this past season?"

The Russian dismissed that with a wave of his hand. "Les and I've already identified all the new men and we have long-time, trusted employees watching them."

"What about posting security guards?"

He appeared to consider, then said, "If we do that, we'll just drive the saboteurs into hiding. We need to catch one of Moreland's hirelings and get the truth out of him. Besides, how long can we afford the expense of an armed, professional security force?"

Marti sighed. "Yes, I guess you're right. I need time to go over the books and check with our accountants about finances. Then you and I will have to plan some strategy."

At once Boris's eyes lit up. "You mean shift some of our markets to faster maturing wines—experiment with some of the newer fermentation techniques? I've tried to tell Joe he could still make fine wine and a greater profit, but he wouldn't listen to me. He'll listen to you, Marti."

Uncertainty flickered in her eyes, but she quashed her self doubts and replied, "Considering we have the wolf at our door, I guess it's time Papa made some hard choices."

Boris snorted. "It's time he came into the 1980's—if he wants to keep Chateau Beaumont for his grandson."

Marti fiddled with the papers on the desk now. This was Boris's first acknowledgment of Heath's existence. No one but Lese and Hilda Lee would ever know that the boy was Adam Wade's son, she vowed again, looking nervously at Boris. If he was angry at her sudden marriage to a fictional Frenchman, that was far better than his possessing any inkling about Heath's real paternity.

A few days after she returned home, Marti took Heath and drove into town to the gallery. Over the past years she and Alice had corresponded and talked on the phone frequently, but Marti had never burdened her friend with the secret about Adam Wade. *She encouraged my seeing him and if she knew how things turned out for me, she'd feel guilty,* Marti had reiterated to herself that morning as she pulled up in front of Alice's place.

Some things are immutable. The round smiling face and paint smeared smock of Alice Marchanti certainly were, thank God. Alice gave a whoop of delight and embraced her friend and the small boy held between them.

Heath's eyes widened as Alice pinched his cheek and planted a solid kiss on his forehead. "You are adorable, dollface. *Parlez-vous francais?*"

Marti laughed. "Alice he left France when he was a few months old. He's just now learning to speak English!"

"What do I know from kids? This is my first nephew. But Aunt Alice is a fast study, Heath," she said with a wink at the boy, who grinned back in spite of the strange lady's surprising antics. "I'll get the hang of having a little boy around real quick, you'll see."

Marti was amazed when the boy went into Alice's arms without protest. Heath was naturally quiet and shy around new people. Alice's smock, pungent with acrylics and varnish, fascinated the child, as did her large gold coin earrings that jingled with her every movement. After a couple of grabs at them, Alice laughingly sat Heath on a counter and removed the irresistible temptations.

The two women went into the sunny courtyard behind the gallery and sipped Columbian coffee that Alice had brewed. Heath explored the flowers and played with several plastic bowls and other harmless items, now converted to toys.

"He's really a good boy, Marti. He must look like his father. He isn't a Beaumont redhead or blond, that's for sure."

"Yes, he resembles his father a great deal, Alice," Marti replied quietly. *I am telling her the truth.*

"Hell, I'm sorry, honey. Even after years, you must

miss him like hell," Alice said contritely, squeezing Marti's hand.

"I think I always will miss him, but that doesn't mean I'm about to whither away with grief, Alice. I have a beautiful son, a solid career, and now, for a while, a winery to run. Life goes on," she said, smiling openly at her friend. "Now, tell me what's been happening in west coast art and I'll tell you about New Orleans."

They chatted for over an hour and then Alice sent a young girl who worked in the gallery for some wonderful delicatessen food.

"So how goes the wine biz? I've heard some nasty rumors about small outfits selling out to some big Frisco cartel," Alice said, licking a dab of mustard from her finger.

"And you've heard they've also made Papa an offer," Marti replied with a grim smile. "Let's just say they picked on the wrong family this time. We'll never sell, even if they offer twice what Chateau Beaumont is worth—and considering the last couple of offers, that's not likely."

"I hear these boys play rough, Marti. You be careful," Alice warned.

"Boris and Les are taking precautions against any more sabotage. And I'm a big girl now, so don't you fret."

"You and Boris getting along?" Alice asked with a speculative gleam in her eye. She had never liked the winemaster.

"Better than I expected, considering everything. Now and then I think he still harbors the delusion that I'll succumb and marry him."

Alice put down her mug and looked Marti in the eye. "Don't do anything stupid. I never met Eves, but I know he couldn't have been anything like that muscle-headed Russian. He's not for you, Marti."

"He's a hell of a better candidate than a handsome drifter who vanishes at summer's end," Marti shot back. It slipped out so unexpectedly! Marti reddened in mortification.

"I guess both of us have tiptoed around Adam Wade for four years now, haven't we, honey?" Alice had debated ever since Eve's death about whether or not to tell Marti that Adam had returned to Napa.

"He hurt me, Alice, but it *was* four years ago. I have a new life now. I've gotten over him. In a way he did me a big favor, giving me some breathing room away from my family and this valley."

"He came back for you." The words dropped like lead weights as Alice half whispered them.

Marti's eyes darted to where Heath sat playing on the grass, then back to Alice. "What do you mean, 'he came back?' "

"It was early December, a rainy raw day. You'd been gone since the end of August and married for over two months then. He'd been to the house and Riba told him about Eves. I bet she was pretty shitty about it. No wonder he asked me to verify her story."

Marti fought the pain welling up inside her like a tidal wave of agony. She scoffed, "I can imagine his wounded ego. What on earth possessed him to crawl back after all those months without so much as a word?"

"That's what I asked him, but once he found out you were married, he just stalked out of here without explaining. I wouldn't say he exactly crawled back either, honey." At Marti's disdainful look, Alice went on in a puzzled voice, "He was dressed like he had just won the lottery and he was driving a new Mercedes. Maybe he came into some kind of inheritance. You always said he must've come from money."

Marti felt catapulted back in time. Adams' face, stormy, then tender, flashed before her eyes. She could still smell the perfume of male musk and wine soaked wood that blended so beautifully the first time they made love. She could feel the heady warmth of the fire as he undressed her at the cabin.

Alice watched the emotions play across Marti's face, leaving her complexion ashen and her eyes haunted. "Shit, I have a real gift for saying the wrong thing at the wrong time, don't I?"

Pulling herself up from the whirlpool of memories, Marti forced a smile and said, "I always knew he was hiding something from his past. I doubt he won the lottery. But maybe he did mend his fences with a rich family somewhere. Don't go on a guilt trip over this, Alice. If he really cared about me, he would've told me the truth from the beginning, not vanished for months and then strutted in brandishing a bankroll to try and impress me."

"What if he came back tomorrow?" Alice asked on some unconscious impulse.

"I'd tell him to go straight to hell," Marti replied levelly.

"Bullshit," Alice said, staring into Marti's eyes. *She's more torn up over losing Adam Wade than over losing Eves Martin!*

"All right, I guess my reaction would depend on a great many things," Marti replied with a sigh. "But that was four years ago and so much has happened since then. The question's really moot, Alice. I'll never see Adam again and that's probably all for the better."

Chapter 17

The weeks flew by, budbreak passed and the vines leafed out; soon the grape flowers would appear. The spring was cool and dry, promising a bountiful crush. Joe's health was improving slowly and he once more walked the fields with Marti.

When she reviewed the state of the chateau's finances, she was appalled at how little care her father had shown to the business end of wine making over the past four years. It seemed as though he retreated among his beloved vines for peace, escaping the bewildering changes being wrought all around him, both in his family life and in the wine industry.

"If you want to keep Chateau Beaumont in our hands, Papa, you'll have to let Boris and me make some decisions that you're not going to like," Marti told Joe after being home only a few days. At first he balked, then changed his mind when Riba and her Hollywood husband came for a brief visit.

Oliver Bixley had been the boy wonder of the American film industry back in the 1970's, creating stars in epics that ranged from brutally realistic westerns to updated versions of Shakespeare. As he sat at the dinner table that evening, he looked to Marti like an aging hippie, a flower child gone to seed. His once broodingly handsome face had developed a perpetual sneer and his black hair was thinning. *He probably dyes it,* she thought in pique, then laughed to herself as she noted the paunch thickening his midsection, which was poorly disguised by an expensive Italian jacket. His body matched his hair. *He ought to see Burt Reynolds' rug man.*

Sobering, Marti realized that she had to give Oliver the benefit of the doubt in spite of what she already knew about him—or had read in the tabloids. Riba had convinced Joe that her husband was no longer doing drugs and that her marriage was a Hollywood fairy tale. Marti believed neither item, but prayed for a smooth, mercifully brief visit.

Over drinks earlier the four of them had exchanged nervous pleasantries about the weather and other impersonal topics. Oliver lived not only a different lifestyle than Joe, he hailed from an alternate universe. He had dismissed Joe's attempts to discuss the fall harvest. Marti had to bite her tongue to hold back a sharp retort when Oliver patronized her "swell little job running the family business." With scant lip service paid to the Napa Valley, he had launched into a tiring monologue about the film he was going to shoot in Yugoslavia and his hassles with customs officials in that provincial backwater. When Marti had asked innocently why he was forced to work in such an undesirable location, she saw a flash of pleasure in Riba's eyes and immediately dropped the topic. So much for the fairy tale marriage! Back to customs officers and cameramen.

Marti had been tied up in a meeting with several wine negotiants from San Francisco that afternoon and was unable to meet their plane. Max drove the Caddie to the airport and Joe and Heath were the welcoming committee. Heath had sensed in the uncanny way of children that his aunt Riba and uncle Ollie wanted him to become invisible. When she rushed home to dress for dinner, Marti had found him playing with his lego set in a corner of the kitchen beneath Hilda's watchful eye. Mrs. Lee had made several succinct comments about Riba and her new husband, all accurate and none repeatable.

Thinking of the shrewd old cook, Marti raised her glass and forced a smile for her sister and brother-in-law. "Here's to your visit and to another splendid meal from Hilda Lee."

"Yes, damn good. We never have time to eat dinner

at home, do we Riba?" Her husband regarded her with hooded black eyes.

"What Ollie means, Marti, is that he's never home," Riba replied with a cloyingly sweet bat of her lashes at Bixley. "He's always off on some shoot or other, galloping from Europe to South America. I prefer five star restaurants, anyway, and there are lots of them in southern California." As her green eyes narrowed on her husband, she added with thinly veiled spite, "And lots of escorts, too."

Joe exchanged a worried look with Marti, who quickly interjected, "Well, we have quite a few five star restaurants in San Francisco and some really outstanding places to dine right here in the valley. Of course, I realize Napa isn't Beverly Hills," she added as an aside to quell Riba before continuing. "This dill sauce for the tuna steaks is Hilda's own creation—I think she should have a five star rating." At Oliver's snort of tolerant derision, Marti let slip, "It's low calorie as well as low cholesterol," eyeing his obvious paunch and sagging facial muscles. This time when Riba laughed and drained her wineglass, Marti did bite her tongue.

Feeling bested in every encounter with his wife's acerbic sister, Oliver turned his attention to Joe. "No doubt this seafare is for your health. Riba always told me you were a steak and potatoes man," he said as he polished off the last bite of the huge slab of fresh tuna, broiled and sauced to perfection. He followed it with half a glass of their finest Chardonnay.

Joe toyed with his glass. "Yeah. I used to enjoy a plate full of juicy tournedos, blood rare, with a really full-bodied Cav. More people buying whites over reds now because of all the damned quack doctors pushing us to eat 'sensible,' " Joe said sourly as he studied the legs coating the sides of the glass, seeming to ignore his obnoxious guest.

"Fresh fish and veal are just as good as beef, Papa, if they're properly prepared," Marti soothed, watching Oliver refill his glass with the spider of the third bottle served with the meal.

"Pretty good wine, this white . . . er—"

"Chardonnay, Ollie," Riba interjected impatiently, holding out her own glass for a refill from bottle number four. His hand wavered a bit and she swore as he poured the wine down the side of the glass onto her fingers. "You're getting tiresomely drunk again, Ollie, my pet," she said silkily.

His face creased in a nasty parody of a smile. "You're a good one to talk, Princess." He used Joe's pet name like a maladiction.

When Marti had entered the living room for cocktails, she had sensed the tension in the air between husband and wife that seemed to grow with the passage of the evening and the consumption of alcohol. A conservative vintner and a Hollywood film producer would naturally have a difficult time making conversation, but it was not Joe and Oliver who were the problem. It was Riba and Oliver. Each time Marti had quashed Bixley, she had sensed her sister's pleasure. She forced herself to bear his rudeness in silence. They were through the main course and had only dessert to go. Just as Marti had hoped to finish the meal without a major catastrophe, the twist in the conversation got out of control. Her heart sank as she prayed, *Please, not here, not now, not in front of Papa!*

"So, sister, mine, what have you been doing besides toiling in the vineyards?" Oliver asked Marti, as if hearing a distorted version of her prayer.

His speech was slurred as he finished the wine, but Marti would be damned if she had Max open a fifth bottle! "I have lots of activities. I sketch and paint when there's time, mostly sketch since I've been home. And, of course, there's Heath to keep me busy."

The veil of boredom that lowered across his dark eyes was painfully obvious, but Marti was determined to keep him and Riba from each other's throats until she could get Joe to retire for the night. Before Oliver could make some disparaging comment about children in general or Heath in particular, she continued, "But, I know someone from your exciting background isn't interested in our mundane lives. Do tell us more about this new picture in Yugoslavia. When do you leave to start filming?"

"Yes, Ollie, dear. When *do* you leave?" Riba asked with a purr in her voice.

"Not nearly soon enough for you, I'm sure. Not that it matters." Oliver threw back his head and laughed raucously like the seasoned drunk he was. "You see," he said conversationally in a slurred voice, "my wife finds her own little amusements, whether I'm home or abroad." Now his hooded black eyes were fixed on Joe Beaumont's blanched face.

Before her father could react, Riba hissed, "Shut up, Oliver!" She was withdrawing from the ugly cat and mouse game they'd been drunkenly sparring at, warning her husband off with the brittle command.

He ignored it. Watching her fingers whiten impotently as she gripped the edge of the table, he suggested, "Why don't you tell your folks here how you spent your spare time with one of the script boys at the studio, got yourself knocked up and had to have an abortion?"

"That baby was yours, you dumb bastard!" Riba shrieked, leaping up from the table and overturning her chair in furious anger while Joe froze and Marti squeezed her eyes shut in helpless frustration. "I told you to stay in Hollywood and let me come home alone, but no, you had to do this—just to lie to my father and sister, didn't you?" Her face was splotched with rage. Tears trailed down her cheeks, running her mascara as she turned to Joe. "He's lying, Papa. He always does. Directors are just like actors—living in a fantasy world. They can't even tell a cheap script from real life. He's still snorting coke, too!"

Ignoring her tirade, Joe asked heavily, "Did you have an abortion, Riba?"

"Oh, shit!" Riba muttered, weaving unsteadily on her feet as she wiped at her eyes. "What was I supposed to do—have some deformed monster? Ollie does drugs, Chuck does drugs. I do, too! Everyone in L. A. does." She turned slowly and awkwardly from the table and walked from the room, sobbing drunkenly.

Oliver laughed and said in a braying voice, "Gotcha! You didn't think I'd tell, did you, Princess?" He turned back to his stricken in-laws and said conversationally, "I really don't give a fuck whose brat it was. Could've been half a dozen guys, even mine." He shrugged. "But she did get rid of it. I saw to that," he added with the venom suddenly returned to his voice.

"You son of a bitch!" Joe Beaumont lunged up and made a fist, but before he could reach Oliver Bixley, Marti was restraining him, pleading and crying.

"Papa, please! Don't. He's not worth it. Can't you see what he is?" *Can't you see what Riba is?* "Your heart, remember your heart. You owe it to Heath to take care of his one and only Grampa!" She played her final ace and it worked.

Joe crumpled against her and put down his balled up fists. Marti tried to lead him from the room, but he turned to the man sagging in the chair and offered Bixley one parting shot. "Be out of here when I get up in the morning, Ollie, boy. I'm a real early riser. Just thought I'd warn you. You never seen what a wine press can do to a man's arm . . ."

"Don't waste your breath, Papa. He'll be gone. He's done what he came here to do," Marti said with a look of scathing fury directed toward her brother-in-law.

They left the room and headed upstairs. "Maybe you better see to your sister, honey," Joe said hesitantly. He was very short of breath.

"Maybe I better see to you first," she replied as they walked toward his room.

"You think she'll leave with him? He's wrecking her life, Martha."

She sighed. "Don't you think by now Riba's done a pretty fair job of wrecking her own life?" She added softly, "We can't keep her here, Papa. She never wanted to live in the valley."

"I thought she was so like her mama. What went wrong, Martha?" Joe asked helplessly. "Bertrice loved the bright lights, sure. But she loved me even more—

me and her babies." He was near tears as he turned into his room, then paused at the door with his back to Marti. "I'll be OK, Martha. I still got you and Heath. You're right. We can't stop Riba from leaving if she wants."

Early the next morning Riba and Oliver took his specially chartered plane back to L.A. Neither Joe nor Marti talked to them before they left.

With Riba once more out of his life, Joe's only hope for the future of the family and the business became Marti and her child. Her father did no more than argue with her before letting her and Boris go ahead with their plans for T-budding white varietals onto red vines. The newly grafted, more saleable Chenin Blancs and Reislings would produce only a third to a half of the normal crop the next year but a full crop in the following one.

Joe's beloved Cabernets and claret-style Zinfandels took one and a half years of barrel aging, plus another six years of bottle aging. The light, fruitier whites they would be producing by next year could be sold the following year. The industry was shifting, and although Marti still agreed that Chateau Beaumont should make fine aged reds, they also needed the fast profits and marketing flexibility that their new products would allow.

Boris had a new enologist on the payroll who was studying the yeasts and malolactic cultures used at Chateau Beaumont. The winemaster and Marti presented a united front to Joe with their ideas for modernizing the winery.

Joe adored Heath and spent a good deal of time with the boy and Marti. But the business decisions about the winery he left to her. Boris and Les Reams were of invaluable help as Marti's frustration with her father grew. She feared being trapped again, duty bound to stay with Joe and act as his emotional crutch—the very thing Peter Kane had warned her not to do.

Marti was fearfully ambivalent about her life. She

realized she did not want to return to New Orleans. With every passing week, her sense of being home grew stronger. So did her pleasure in the little triumphs of successfully negotiating a deal with a cork wholesaler, or securing a good price from the company in Healdsburg that made white oak barrels. She lunched with her CPA, then returned from town to walk the fields with Les and Joe, and still found time to play with Heath before dinner. In a few months, she promised herself there would be time to sketch again, once the first crush had been completed under her supervision. It was a good and satisfying life.

What more do I want? she asked herself, still aware of a hollow ache that sometimes filled her soul in unguarded moments. *Gray offered me love and marriage—every conventional thing I once thought I'd leap at. But Gray is not Adam.* Adam, damn him! She had little time to think back to that bittersweet summer of love and betrayal, yet it never entirely left her mind. She refused to settle for a one-sided relationship with Graham Kley. He deserved better than that. But should she remain alone for the rest of her life?

"Such a brown study. Why the gloom, Marti? Everything's been going smoothly for weeks. No more sabotage, good weather. Smile for me." Boris's anger and hurt pride had quickly evaporated during the development of their working relationship. He smiled broadly at her and fell in step beside her as she headed toward the house from the plant.

"Just my usual fretting over Papa, Boris. Nothing to worry about," she replied with a shrug.

"He'll have to accept the changes sooner or later. If he wants to retire and play with his grandson, you'll just have to let him. Of course, I'm assuming you want to keep working with me and Les. Or do you still plan to fly south again and resume your art career?"

Marti looked into his face. "No, I've pretty much decided that while those years establishing my identity away from here were therapeutic, I don't want to return to New Orleans. That doesn't mean I don't want to pursue my art career, though."

"If you remarried the right man, you could have the winery and an art career," Boris said softly. He walked with his hands in his pants pockets, looking down at the ground.

Marti slowed her steps. "Boris, I know we've been working well together and I couldn't have accomplished alone what we've done, but . . ."

"I don't expect you to fall in my arms like I did four years ago. Pretty stupid of me, wasn't it?" He looked distinctly uncomfortable as he forced a smile.

Marti sighed and made no reply. She had grown to rely on Boris Staritz, but relying on him and being able to work well with him weren't enough to build a marriage on. She returned his smile. "I've been through a lot in the past four years. But I'm still sort of like a blind woman with suddenly restored sight. There's so much to see and consider. And I have Heath to think of, too."

"I won't rush you or put conditions on our working relationship, Marti. It only seems to make sense to me that we both think about the possibility of a future together. Heath needs a father. You need someone to share your life. Only think about it for now." He reached over and took her hand, holding it lightly in his. "Take all the time you need. We have the rest of our lives for decisions."

The rest of our lives. All that evening Boris's words hammered at her with their simple logic. She could continue the wine business and an art career with him to help her run Chateau Beaumont. He seemed genuinely fond of Heath and would be good for the boy. And perhaps most important of all, he was not desperately in love with her as Gray had been. Gray she would have wounded over the years because she could not return his love. Boris was practical. He wanted the winery and he respected her and liked working with her. Boris expected nothing more than similar commitment of convenience from her in return. If it was passionless, it was also safe. No one would get hurt.

But you're already hurt, some sadistic inner voice

chided. Marti knew she'd always carry scars from her past. But she had learned to accept her childhood and adolescent traumas, to survive Adam's betrayal, and to make her own way for herself and her son. She decided that Boris was right about one thing. There was plenty of time for whatever decisions she would make. He had been honest; now he would have to be patient.

Joe was not as patient as Boris. Once he became aware the winemaster still hoped to marry Marti, her father found a new interest in life. Matchmaking.

"There's going to be a big party at Meadowood this Friday. Seems some of those suits from the city are coming to town. You and Boris ought to go and nose around," Joe said casually one brilliant June morning. The fog had lifted early and the air smelled crisp.

Marti sat down at the patio table and poured herself a cup of steamy black coffee, then doused it liberally with cream, a vice she'd had even before moving to New Orleans. "Boris mentioned it last night. He thinks the offer from Moreland is a good one." She watched Joe scowl, then continued, "I only meant it's a lot higher than Allard was willing to go, not that we should take it."

"Well?" Joe said, squinting against the morning brightness.

"Well, what?" Marti sipped the rich coffee.

"Are you and Boris going to go to that party or not?"

Marti shrugged. "I suppose we might learn something. Know your enemy or whatever."

"It wouldn't hurt to see you dressed up in one of those fancy evening gowns, instead of spending day and night working around here, either."

As long as I dress up for Boris. "Why don't you come along, Papa?"

"No way. It's a night for young people. I'll just stay here with Heath and keep him out of mischief," Joe said fondly.

"More like he'll get you into mischief," Marti replied, happy with the bond between grandfather and grandson in spite of her own frustrations with Joe.

"How do you like having Riba back?" Boris asked as they walked up the front steps at Meadowood.

Marti's face creased in a frown. A scant few weeks after her disasterous visit with Oliver, Riba had returned, alone and contrite, pleading for Joe's forgiveness, blaming everything on her husband. Although far less gullible than before, Joe could deny his princess nothing. He forgave her. Looking at Boris, Marti replied simply, "I only thank God she left darling Oliver in Yugoslavia or wherever he's filming his latest epic. She'll be gone on Monday."

"Joe gets more upset every time she comes home, now. It all began while you were away, Marti. I guess her divorce and remarriage to that smarmy director really opened his eyes."

"Let's not discuss my sister, Boris," Marti said quietly. Riba was still the same willfully self-destructive, spoiled child she'd always been. Marti hated to see her disrupt their father's life again. One week with Riba home sent his blood pressure rising and his appetite plummeting.

Boris nodded in understanding and changed the subject. "I've talked over the phone with Moreland's agents again. Someone empowered to negotiate a final price will be in the valley this week. Art and Stan are all ready to sign the final papers for their places. I don't know what they got, but what we could get would be pretty favorable now, Marti."

"We aren't selling, Boris. We've been over and over this. I don't care if they offer us the moon." Marti's voice held an icy edge.

"I know how Joe feels, but dammit, if we can get the right price out of Moreland, Joe can retire. Hell, he isn't interested in the winery anymore. If he wants to, he could buy some land up in Mendocino and plant some good Cabernet and Zinfandel vines. That's all it is to him anymore, Marti—a hobby."

"That's not fair, Boris!" Marti replied heatedly.

"We've changed so many things, taken decisions away from him, he feels useless. If he lost the family lands in Napa, no where else would ever be home to him."

They entered the Starmont Restaurant and were seated at a table. The waiter took their drink orders and departed. Marti looked across her menu at Boris. He was preoccupied and obviously ill-at-ease about something.

"Boris, I get the impression you've been giving serious consideration to this buy out offer. Why?"

He put down his menu and took her hand. "Look, Marti, as long as they were using scare tactics and offering a lousy price, I was all for saying no. But now that's changed. We've had no 'accidents' in weeks and the new offer is a damn good one." His eyes left hers to scan the crowded room, as if he were deciding how to frame what he was going to say next.

She helped him. "Besides the money, what else has changed, Boris? There's more you're not telling me."

He smiled thinly. "You always were a good judge of people. All right," he plunged in. "I bought a tract of good land in Mendocino myself two years ago—several small wineries and some good blocks of Zinfandel and Chardonnay. I always wanted a place of my own, but I barely had the capital to float a loan, much less upgrade and consolidate the operations."

"Until now," Marti said in a deadly calm voice. "You want to marry me and use my share of the profits from selling Chateau Beaumont to start your own winery."

Boris made a placating gesture. "Marti, that sounds cold blooded and premeditated. It isn't like that at all. When I bought the land, I never dreamed that Joe would let Chateau Beaumont go downhill like he has. I never thought he'd sell and I sure as hell didn't ask you to marry me just to get my hands on your inheritance."

"But it would be eminently practical, wouldn't it, Boris?" She shoved the menu to the side of the table, the very thought of food repellent to her now.

His eyes darkened in anger. "You think I'm some

kind of gigolo like that pretty drifter you fell for four years ago? I never insulted your intelligence with flowery speeches, Marti. If you think I'm a fortune hunter—"

Stung bitterly by his reference to Adam Wade, Marti stood up abruptly. "I frankly don't know what to think. I appreciate your honesty in telling me about your plans in Mendocino, Boris, but I'll never sell Papa's land. Never!"

He, too, stood up, pulling his wallet out in a rough, furious motion. Tossing several bills on the table to cover their drinks, he said stiffly, "I'll drive you home. We both need time to think."

She turned and walked quickly toward the front door. "You go home, Boris. I can always get a ride with friends. I plan to stay for the grower's party and see some of these Moreland ogres. It seems everyone in town has met them but me."

"I'll wait for you in the bar, downstairs," he said quietly as he struggled with his fierce Russian temper, trying to be conciliatory.

"Don't bother. You're right. We both need time to think." With that she marched out the door leading to the front foyer. Angrily Boris turned and headed downstairs.

After gathering her composure, Marti walked to the Vintner Room where she knew the private party for area growers and San Francisco negotiants was being held. A waiter in a white jacket opened the door and smiled at her, remembering Joe Beaumont's older daughter from years ago when she had been the plain one. Now she was stunning, dressed in a shimmering metallic gown of gold and rust. Her long burnished mane of hair was pulled back from her face with jeweled golden combs that matched her dress. Nervously, she responded to the admiring glance of the man holding the door and walked inside.

Most of the people there were familiar and several old friends quickly engaged her in conversation.

"The Moreland people are here, Marti, and that

president who took Allard's place is really a hunk," Salee James whispered with a wink.

Her husband Steve only laughed tolerantly and added, "That's for the benefit of the unattached females in the room, like Marti here, not for you, my dear *wife.*"

Marti's sharp gaze swept the room as Steve and Salee bantered. "Just where is the fabled Mr. Moreland? He's made us an offer we're just dying to refuse."

Steve chuckled and said, "I knew Joe wouldn't do what Art did and I should've known you'd back him. But Art is getting close to retirement and his operation is a lot smaller than Chateau Beaumont."

"And a lot more vulnerable to coercion," Marti added darkly.

"I heard some rumors about a thermostat being sabotaged. Pretty ugly stuff," Salee said. "You think Moreland Enterprises was behind it?"

"I can't see some disinterested bystander spraying our tractor engines with silver paint, can you? Unless he was a frustrated artist with an Andy Warhol complex."

"What's this talk about pop art? I thought I was drowning in a sea of wine people," Peter Kane said as he joined their group. Marti turned and smiled a greeting.

"Hello, Peter. We were discussing wine people, or at least *some* wine people," she replied obliquely. "I understand we've had our valley graced by none other than the head of Moreland Enterprises."

"Want to meet him?" Peter shot back with a broad smile.

"You know him?" Marti asked in surprise. *Boy, do I want to meet him!*

"He's my cousin. Dragged me to this dreary wine affair. And I thought physician's parties were boring. How's your father? I was hoping Joe would be here tonight."

Marti sighed. "The outing would do him good, but he refused. Still, considering the presence of our illustrious wine magnate from the big city, I think his blood pressure's probably better served by his staying home. I'm keeping him on the diet and off the cigarettes, Peter."

"Good. I want him in my office first of the week." Peter took Marti's arm and excused them politely. "Now, I want you to meet Adam Moreland. You'll like him."

"Is that because he looks like a certain tall blond doctor I know?" she inquired archly.

"Not at all. He takes after his mother's side of the family, and Jake's mother, too, I think."

The barracuda strain, no doubt, with some jackal thrown in for good measure, Marti thought grimly as they approached a crowded circle of people near the bar. Suddenly, an eerie sensation washed over her as the crowd parted and she stared at the broad back of a dark-haired man. Something about the stance, the fall of his straight blueblack hair. No, it couldn't be! But Peter had said *Adam* Moreland. Marti struggled to breathe as Peter called his name and he turned.

Every face and sound in the room receded as Adam looked into Marti's stricken gray eyes. He expected to see old Joe, Staritz, or some new manager of Beaumont's—not her. Marti was supposed to be in New Orleans or off in the south of France, wherever the jet set spent its summers.

She was even more striking than he remembered. Her curly hair framed the strong, lovely facial planes that were stiff with icy disdain as she surveyed him. But Adam had become very adept at searching for small signs of weakness in people. The racing pulse at her throat gave away her carefully concealed agitation.

Marti stared at him as Peter made introductions. He was dressed in a custom tailored tuxedo, much as he had worn that night four years ago when he crashed the grower's party. Yet his handsome face was imperceptibly different now, just as his clothes were. A few threads of gray hair flecked his temples and faint lines were visible around his mouth. But those minor signs of aging were nothing compared to the coldness in his fathomless blue eyes.

Hard eyes set in a beautiful, cruel face, Marti thought as scant seconds rolled on like an eternity. "You've certainly come up in the world, Adam," she said in a stranger's voice.

"I picked the right parents, same as you, Marti," he replied evenly.

"You two know one another?" Peter asked, frankly baffled. Neither had ever mentioned the other to him.

Marti smiled glacially. "It was a long time ago, Peter. He was Adam *Wade* then."

"I'm not the only one with a different name, am I, Marti? What's your married name, Mouton? Marton?"

"Martin," she replied levelly, pronouncing the long "a" sound of the French name.

"Marti was widowed in an accident three years ago, Adam," Peter said with a hint of warning in his voice. The conversation made no sense to him, but the antagonism crackling between Adam and Marti was very apparent.

"A widow so young. How tragic." Adam's voice was flat.

"Yes, but she does have a beautiful young son named Heath—his grandfather's pride and joy," Peter said, hoping to defuse the hostile confrontation.

"You and your son visiting good old grandpa?" Adam asked, ignoring Pete, whom he devoutly wished would leave.

"I'm not visiting. I returned permanently this spring. Papa's in poor health. I run Chateau Beaumont now." The challenge in her voice was unmistakable.

"Really, Marti. I assume that means you aren't interested in my offer. I upped the ante quite a bit from Booth's original price." His voice sounded as if he was supremely indifferent about the sale.

"I don't care if you offer to throw in half of greater LA and all of Baron Rothchild's French estates! Chateau Beaumont is not on the block," Marti said with rising anger.

Adam turned to Peter and said smoothly, "Mrs. Martin and I have a lot to discuss."

Eyeing Adam and then Marti, Peter nodded uneasily. "All right. I'll catch up with you later."

"Where's your faithful Siberian husky? I expected to see him panting after you," Adam said, looking around the room for Staritz.

"Downstairs getting sloshed, no doubt. We had a slight disagreement about your offer," Marti said acidly, feeling doubly betrayed. *I'll never trust another man as long as I live!* "I take after my father—threats and sabotage only make me dig in deeper, not give up what's mine."

Adam's brows rose consideringly. Ignoring her reference to sabotage, he said, "So Boris likes our offer and you don't."

"Boris doesn't run Chateau Beaumont. I do."

"Does he still cherish the hope you'll succumb to his Slavic charms?" Adam asked.

"He's asked me to marry him, but somehow I doubt Boris's sincerity," she replied scathingly, with a glance at his face that left no doubt as to what she thought of *his* sincerity.

"Men seem to fill your life since the summer we shared, Marti. Maybe I should take some of the credit." Before he could stop himself, his fingertips brushed through the bright curls spilling over her shoulder.

"Take all the credit you want," she replied, pulling away from his touch angrily. Then lowering her voice she whispered fiercely, "You lied to me and then drifted out of my life like a summer breeze. Don't sashay back here and expect me to fall for your smoldering blue eyes a second time. Staritz doesn't get my winery. Neither do you, Moreland," she said through clenched teeth.

Unreasoning anger churned up in his gut, taking him totally by surprise. For years he had practised keeping an iron lid on his emotions, manipulating people and cooly assessing his moves. But this woman stripped every nerve bare, leaving him in mindless fury.

"Your father's thugs beat me half to death and threw me on a passing freight. I spent three months in a Fresno hospital courtesy of Joe Beaumont. I'd scarcely call that 'drifting off like a summer breeze,'" he lashed out, his hand unconsciously rubbing the scar on his brow.

"That's a monstrous lie! My father isn't capable of such a thing—he had no reason to do it. Someone from your past may have caught up with you—a past, I might add, that you refused to share with me." She began almost shouting and ended on a choked whisper of anguish.

"You were so heartbroken at my departure that you raced to France and married some jet-set dilettante two months later," he said scornfully. "Save the tears, Marti, and save your speeches about my past. I'm Jake Moreland's son. I may have wanted to be free from that years ago, but I don't anymore."

"Now you want the power, just like he did. You have quite a reputation, Adam. Small wonder you didn't trust me with the truth." She shivered at the ruthlessness she read in every gesture, every facial expression. *If he finds out about Heath* . . . Her mind shut down until his next words jarred her.

"You may be running the daily operation now, but the final say-so is still Joe's. I'll be out to see him Marti. One way or the other, we'll deal."

"I'll see you in hell first," she hissed.

He smiled coldly. "I think you already have your wish, lady. For both of us."

Adam stood and watched Marti walk away. The fury radiating from her slim body cleared a swatch through the crowded room like a bulldozer in a demolition derby. Her hair caught the light from the chandeliers and glowed. Even the metallic fabric of her elegant dress seemed to give off sparks. He was sure her silver eyes blazed like lasers at everyone in her path.

When she had vanished out the terrace door, Adam

turned, noticing Peter Kane standing beside him. "I'm too well bred to ask what's between the two of you, of course. But as the Beaumont family physician, I'll take the liberty of saying she's strung pretty tight, Adam. Joe's health is precarious and she's holding both him and the family business together. I've heard rumors about your reputation in the industry. As a personal favor, don't lean on her." He waited, as they exchanged looks, his probing blue eyes surprisingly like Adam's.

"Does she still muck around in the fields with Les Reams and the men like she used to?" Adam asked, neither refusing nor agreeing to Pete's request.

"Among other things, yes. She also works with their CPA's and marketing people. She and Staritz have begun a complete revamp of Joe's operation. Given time and new management, it should do well."

"If big bad Moreland Enterprises leaves them alone," Adam said with a sardonic grin.

"This is more than business, isn't it?"

"You're well bred, Pete, remember? It's personal. Very personal. If you'll excuse me, I feel the need for some solitary drinking. I recall there being a bar conveniently at hand." With that he walked briskly toward the same door Marti had used, without a backward glance at Peter Kane.

The bar was quiet, the bartender even quieter. It suited Adam's mood. His mind was in such turmoil that he didn't want to think, much less talk. Rubbing his temple, he downed a double scotch in a few swift, silent gulps, then ordered a second.

As he sat sipping it a good deal more slowly, he closed his eyes. Unbidden, Marti's face came into focus. After four years she still had a devastating hold on him. The pride and wounded fury of her words replayed in his mind.

As if she has a right to be hurt because I ran out on her! The injustice of that accusation rankled, but part of his conscience niggled that she surely could not have known what Joe had done. He had refused to tell her about his past and then had vanished without a trace for nearly a month before he sent that note. Of course, he argued with himself, by then she was already on her way to New Orleans and her rendezvous with her fancy Frenchman. If she really had been as betrayed and hurt as she would have him believe, why the lightening rebound marriage to a rich foreigner?

Adam slipped some bills from his money clip and tossed them onto the bar. God, his head ached. When he stood up, a smooth golden hand with long raspberry nails curled around his lapel and caressed his chest.

"Welcome back to Napa, Mr. Moreland," Riba purred.

Adam turned and looked at the slim blonde. In the light, Riba's face was harsh looking, with make up too liberally applied. Her speech was slightly slurred and her green eyes were dilated.

"You look like you've been snorting too many lines, Riba. That aristocratic little nose may just drop right off," Adam said without a hint of a smile as he unwound her hand from inside his jacket. His eyes swept down her legs, clad in a pair of skin tight silk pants. With spike heels on she appeared taller than he remembered, but her height only accentuated her thinness. *Christ, she'd make a Vogue model look overweight,* he thought with distaste.

"Aren't you the least bit curious how I found out you were here? Neither Marti nor Papa know."

"Marti knows now," Adam said with no interest in her question. "Your father will find out when I pay him a call in the morning. If you'll excuse me."

"An old pal from school days in god's country, Riba?" A nasal voice intruded. It belonged to a young man with a weight lifter's body and curly blond hair—the packaged look of a movie extra.

As he draped an arm with casual intimacy around Riba's waist, she said, "Chuck Rollins meet Adam Moreland. Chuckie works for Oliver—oh, I've kept up with you, but I suppose you didn't know I've remarried. His name is Oliver Bixly and he makes films."

"And blondes," Adam said in a bored voice, and started to move past Riba.

Chuckie grinned at that thrust, delighted with the hard looking stranger's obvious lack of interest in Riba. "Your old chum here isn't buying tonight, love. How about inviting him for breakfast with us at your daddy's place?"

Riba's eyes raked Adam's cool face with a disdainful look as she replied, "I'm not sure I'm free to see either of you tomorrow. I'll have to check my social calendar."

Adam replied, "If you're interested, Chuckie, it's written on the washroom wall in the men's bunkhouse."

Rollins gave a bellylaugh as Riba reached up to slap Adam. At the last second, she reconsidered. "You always were a prick, Adam, even when you grubbed in my father's fields. At least then you were an honest laborer. Working with Booth Allard I doubt you qualify now. Oh, did I mention I'd met your Uncle Booth at one of Oliver's parties a few months back?"

Adam's eyes flared for an instant, then the shuttered mask descended again. "He's not my uncle, Riba, only my employee." He turned to Rollins and said levelly, "Good night and good luck."

The blond raised his glass in a drunken salute as Adam walked from the bar.

At a dimly lit table on the adjoining deck, Boris Staritz sat nursing his fifth or sixth vodka martini; he'd lost count. He had watched the hostile exchange between Adam and Riba with grim satisfaction after his initial shock wore off. Imagine, the cheap drifter was none other than the head of Moreland Enterprises.

At least that bastard always had Riba's number, he thought bitterly, draining his glass and slamming it on the table as he rose.

Chapter 18

Adam drove toward Chateau Beaumont early the next morning, watching the fog evaporate as bright fingers of sunlight pulled it from the valley floor. He was reminded of an earlier ride down Highway 29 when he had been a hitch hiker looking for a job. He would face Joe Beaumont again, but this time their situations were dramatically reversed. No longer the supplicant, Adam Moreland would call the shots.

He tried to savor the long-awaited revenge when the arrogant old patriarch was forced to sell his beloved winery. But every time he focused on Joe's shrewd gray eyes, Marti's sparkling silver ones flashed before him. She had been so righteously furious with him last night, accusing him of leaving her! For the thousandth time he speculated whether or not she knew Joe hired those punks and set them after him.

The more he considered it, the more the same old answer came up. No. The old man would protect his precious daughter from a trashy drifter, but he'd never admit his methods to Marti. "That still doesn't excuse her taking off within a month for New Orleans and falling for that Frenchman," he muttered under his breath as he rounded the curve and turned onto Chateau Beaumont.

The fields looked good. All the groundwork was done, with clean, well turned earth between the rows. The vines had been carefully suckered and were spreading across the trellis wires in healthy formation, evenly admitting air and light. Adam fought the memories of how he'd enjoyed working these fields. Now he'd own them, he thought grimly, but satisfaction eluded him. Instead, he felt only a strange sense of unease and expectation.

He pulled his Mercedes up in front of the house and slid out the door. Standing with forearms resting on the car roof, he inspected the scene before him. It was still picture-postcard beautiful, with spacious galleries encircling the house like a lover's embrace. He swore and slammed the car door.

When Hilda Lee greeted him at the door, her smile of welcome erased his scowl. "I always knew you'd come back, Adam. Marti's—"

"Marti and I already had our reunion last night at Meadowood, Hilda. I need to see her father this morning," he interrupted gently as she ushered him inside. He didn't miss the look of worry clouding her dark eyes.

"He's upstairs. I'll tell him you're here. You can wait in the living room," she said, gesturing to the large open archway on the left.

When she turned toward the stairs, Adam's words stopped her abruptly. "Tell him Adam Moreland is here to talk a deal, Hilda." At her look of wide eyed amazement, he smiled. "Surely you didn't think a seasonal worker could afford a Mercedes."

"I didn't think a Moreland would work as a field hand, either," she replied with the beginnings of asperity in her voice. This cold-eyed stranger didn't seem like the Adam Wade she knew Marti still loved. "You want to buy Chateau Beaumont, don't you?"

Adam shrugged. "I want to talk to the owner first," he replied cautiously.

"He's got a bad heart, Mr. Moreland. Marti runs the winery now."

He could sense the animosity building as she addressed him so formally. "So Marti informed me last night, Hilda. But I still want to see Joe. Please." He stood in the hall, unmoving.

Hilda turned wordlessly and ascended the stairs. Only then did he walk into the living room. He wondered to himself if she'd warn the old fox about who he was. Probably so, if Joe really had a bad ticker.

Adam stood in profile gazing out the front window, engrossed in thought when Joe entered the room. The older man took a moment to survey his adversary. Hilda was right. Adam looked as hard as his father in his prime, *a goddamn cutthroat in a custom tailored suit,* he thought bitterly.

"What crazy game you playing, Moreland—Wade, whatever the hell your name is?"

Adam turned to face Joe slowly and deliberately while his right hand unconsciously stroked the scar over his eyebrow.

"You know I'm Jake's son now, don't you, Beaumont?" he said softly.

"Can't say you favor him, but your slippery-snake tactics sure do."

"I came to talk business, Joe, not throw insults," was Adam's cool reply.

"You and your pal Allard are real good at throwing insults—like you offer for my winery. Not to mention throwing a few little inducements to sell, destroying tanks of Chardonnay and burning up tractor engines! But that doesn't mean squat to me, Moreland. My father survived gangsters during Prohibition who'd make you boys in business suits look like runaways from a church picnic. Chateau Beaumont isn't for sale and never will be."

"So I've been told," Adam replied as he walked casually across the pale green carpet and stopped to touch the leaves on a Ficus tree by the front window. "I don't appreciate the accusations about sabotage, Beaumont, especially clumsy things like destroying equipment. If I decided to ruin you, I'd do it without anyone on my payroll even setting foot on Beaumont land. Do you know how much Moreland Enterprises can influence brokers and marketing companies? If I want to play hardball, I'll do it in wholesale and retail sales, not by hiring thugs. That's your specialty as I recall." His eyes were blue shards as they pierced the old man.

Joe knew his already gray complexion had turned more ashen and cursed himself for the frailty of age.

"Like I said, junior, I've faced a damn sight worse than you and come out on top. At fifty-nine I wasn't dumb enough to slug it out against a twenty-five year old gigolo with combat training. I heard how you beat Staritz. I only had them rough you up and get you out of the valley. After what you did to Riba, you're damn lucky I didn't empty a ten gauge into your guts!"

Adam's expression of cool control cracked. "Riba!" he echoed incredulously. "I never touched Riba, although God knows I'm probably the only man in California who hasn't!"

Joe felt his heart miss a beat as he held onto the back of a wing chair. The words seemed to come out of their own volition, with a dread certainty. "It was you and Martha."

"Yeah. It was me and Marti. And I bet that jealous bitch of a sister went to Papa with a beaut of a fairytale, didn't she?" His tone of voice was nasty now. He stared at the gullible old man before him, sick of what Joe Beaumont's blindness had cost Marti.

"You keep your filthy mouth off my girls! I was right to have you run off, regardless—Moreland's playboy kid masquerading as a field hand! What kind of a kick did you get out of deceiving a good girl like Martha? What kind of a sick degenerate bastard are you? You think I'll ever sell to a man who lies to me and my daughter, who worms his way onto my payroll under a false name? I'll see you dead first, Moreland!"

"You gave it a good shot four years ago. Come to think of it, maybe you or your Russian goon tried *more* than once," Adam said measuringly as he stared at Joe. If the old man thought he'd screwed the Princess Riba, Joe had as good a motive to kill him as Staritz, who knew he had a thing going with Marti. His consideration was interrupted by soft rapid footfalls coming through the front door.

Marti burst into the living room, flushed and breathless from her run to the house. "I heard your yelling all the way down the road!" She turned her flashing silvery eyes from her father's wan face to Adam.

"What the hell are you doing here? Trying to provoke my father into a heart attack so you can force me to sell?"

Adam noticed the way her fists clenched and unclenched at her sides. She was winded from her mad dash to the house and had obviously not heard the gist of their conversation. She looked painfully vulnerable in spite of her anger.

"I told you last night I was going to discuss buying the winery from your father. You *are* still the owner, aren't you, Joe?" Although he addressed the question to the old man, his eyes never left Marti's face.

"And I told you no sale, Moreland," Joe snapped furiously.

"Get out! Right now." Although she tried for a level tone, Marti knew her voice had a raw edge of panic to it. She could hear the back door open and small feet pattering up the hall. *Oh, please, God, don't let him get by Hilda!*

But Heath appeared at the door before his mother could finish her silent invocation. "Grandpa! Time for my story. You promised before my nap!" The boy was tall for a three-year-old and his high voice was strong and clear as he delightedly ran over to his grandfather, who quickly knelt and hugged the child, ruffling his shaggy blueblack hair.

"Heath, I want you to go to the kitchen and ask Hilda for milk and cookies, please. Grandpa will read to you later. The grownups have to talk first."

Just then Hilda rounded the corner as if in answer to Marti's prayer. "You were supposed to stay out back until I brought your snack, young man," she said sternly.

The boy turned from Joe's arms and looked guiltily up at the plump cook. *One Chinese can always tell another*, Hilda thought, although Lord knew, the blood was thin by this generation. Looking from Heath to Adam, she waited to see his reaction.

"I want Grandpa to read to me. Who's he?" the boy asked, turning from Hilda to the tall dark stranger standing next to his mother.

Some primordial instinct gripped Adam as he looked down at the boy. Keen blue eyes, fringed by an unruly shock of straight black hair, stared back at him. He had noted the surreptitious glance of Hilda Lee from Heath to him. Could it be? His voice lodged in his throat for a moment as he mustered every trick for covering emotions and gaining a psychological edge that he had learned in his years of corporate warfare.

Marti watched Adam consider Heath and quickly answered the boy's question. "This is Mr. Moreland, son. Now you go with Hilda for your snack." She was proud of her steady voice as she walked over and scooped the leggy child protectively into her arms, then handed him to Hilda.

Over the boy's protests the stout cook carried him from the room.

Joe looked at his daughter and sensed something was amiss. She had obviously met Moreland last night since she wasn't surprised at his deception. But something more was agitating her. Before he could consider the tense confrontation further, Adam's next words stunned him.

"Heath's my son, isn't he, Marti?" He asked the question in a tone of absolute certainty.

"No! I married Eves Martin in France. Heath is Eves' son," she replied with a sob in her voice.

Adam took a step toward her, closing in like a predator, but his gesture as he covered Marti's clenched fists with his hands was oddly gentle. "Marti, I'll go to France myself if I have to. I'll check on your dead Frenchman and his family . . . if they exist. I'll track down the birth certificate, Heath's medical records . . . whatever it takes."

Marti glanced at Joe's stricken face. She jerked her hands furiously away from Adam, hugging herself protectively as she replied in a choked voice, "All right, you win, Adam! I've always heard how ruthless the Morelands are. Yes, Heath is yours. You deserted me that summer. Aunt Lese helped me manufacture a father for my child. You can prove Eves Martin doesn't exist, but just try and prove paternity! No one in Napa would ever help you take my son away from me!"

She turned from Adam and looked at her father. "Oh, Papa, I tried to protect you . . . I'm sorry."

"Dammit, Marti! His stupidity's the reason for this whole mess—"

Joe Beaumont gasped and reached out for Marti, his breath coming in ragged, raspy little chokes as she steadied him.

"Papa, sit down! I'll call Peter! You," she whirled furiously on Adam after easing Joe into the wing chair by the doorway. "Get out! Haven't you done enough to us already?"

Without a word, Adam turned and walked down the hall into the study. He picked up the phone on the desk and quickly dialed his cousin's home. When Marti reached the doorway he was relating Joe's condition to Peter. Adam hung up the phone and said quietly, "He'll be here soon. Fortunately I caught him before he shoved off for his Saturday morning golf game."

Marti nodded, saying nothing and started back down the hall.

"Keep him in the chair and give him one of his nitro pills," Adam called after her.

"I already gave him a pill and he's resting in the chair." She kept walking with Adam behind her.

"Where's your darling sister hiding during all this commotion?" he asked. She stopped with a frightened glance toward the living room.

"I should've known you'd find her," she whispered contemptuously.

"She found me in the bar at Meadowood last night. She had some swell new date with her," he replied dryly.

"Funny thing how you and Riba seem to meet that way, isn't it? She didn't come home last night." She bit off each word. "You wouldn't happen to know anything about her disappearance, of course?"

He shrugged. "Of course not. By now you should've figured out she's not my type."

"Well neither am I, obviously. Now, will you please leave?" Her voice sounded on the verge of breaking.

"All right. But, Marti, I'll be back when things calm down."

By the time Peter Kane had departed, Joe was breathing easily and his face had lost its ashen pallor. He was sitting up in his bed with pillows propped behind his back.

"Quit fussing. I'm fine. In fact, I recall promising to read a story to Heath . . ." He paused and looked up at Marti, who was reading the labels on several pill bottles and arranging a water pitcher and glass beside his bed. He reached over and grasped her hand. "But first I think we need to talk, honey."

Taking a deep steadying breath, Marti forced herself to meet Joe's eyes. She sank slowly onto the edge of the bed, still holding tight to his hands. "Oh, Papa, I feel like I've betrayed your trust in me so abysmally," she said in a shaky voice.

Joe's eyes clouded, but he quickly covered up with a snort. "How? By giving me the most wonderful grandson any man ever had? Martha . . . I admit I was surprised as hell about you and Moreland, but whatever else he may be, he's got brains and guts—so do you and so does Heath. That's good. I'm only sorry you were hurt, honey, that's the bad part—that you were so afraid of telling me the truth you had to go to Lese and concoct a fake husband and live so far away these past years. I feel rotten about that."

"Papa, I know it's hard for you to understand, but I needed those years on my own—not just because of Heath, although that's why I left in the first place. I needed them for me, too. I had to prove myself." She hesitated, framing the words very carefully.

Surprising her, Joe supplied them. "You had to make your own way as an artist, be independent, not live in the shadow of Joe Beaumont and his winery."

Marti looked at him with wide eyes, relief and pain

oddly mixed in her expression. "That sounds so callous and selfish on my part—"

"No, honey. It isn't selfish at all." He scratched his thinning gray hair and his brow creased in concentration as he recalled his children from so many years ago. "I always kept this place for you, you know? That was selfish on my part because I needed your help and you were always such a willing worker. But you seemed to need the place, too. You belonged here. You loved the land like me. You made good grades and studied enology in college. I . . . I guess I convinced myself this place would be your security after I was gone. Now your sister . . ."

Joe could feel Marti tense but forced himself to go on. "Riba was like her mother, who I adored so much. But Martha, I never loved Riba more than you—only different. Riba didn't need this place or me. I always figured she'd find some nice rich young man from a good family and be a social lady, like her mama was . . . I turned a blind eye to her escapades. Always thought blood would tell in the end and she'd turn out all right. I was wrong. But then, you always knew that and tried to cover up for her."

Both pairs of gray eyes were shiny with tears now. "Papa, I know what it did to you, first Larry, then Oliver—"

"That wasn't your fault, Martha," Joe interrupted her sternly. "I always spoiled her and I guess she just never grew up. Everything came so easy to her—being pretty and having all the boys hanging around. She never learned to care about people or traditions the way you and I do. You . . . you always worked at everything so hard, took life so serious. You were never interested in boys."

Marti let out a sad little chuckle. "What you mean is I was a plain little wallflower."

"Some wallflower you turned out to be!" Joe scolded, holding her chin and inspecting her striking face. "That summer four years ago when you had your hair fixed and bought a new wardrobe . . . you changed and men started noticing you the same way they did your sister . . . it was Adam wasn't it?"

Marti swallowed. "He was the first man who ignored Riba and told me I could be attractive if I quit hiding behind glasses and frowsy clothes. He saw the real me beneath my disguise—or at least I thought so . . . for one wonderful summer."

"Oh, Martha, honey." Joe's voice choked as he enfolded Marti in his arms and they hugged fiercely.

"But I'm not sorry, Papa. Even though he deceived me and left me, he still taught me a valuable lesson," Marti said, straightening up and wiping the tears from her cheeks quickly. "I've learned to survive on my own and to believe in myself. And I have Heath. Adam Moreland will never take him away from me."

Joe watched her face harden into harsh lines and saw the leaden coldness in her eyes. Something inside him nearly snapped, but just as he was about to blurt out the truth regarding Adam's disappearance, Marti stood up and bent over to plant a kiss on his forehead. "You rest for a while. This morning has been full of shocks for you. Heath can have his story from Grandpa after lunch."

As she walked to the door, Joe's voice called to her and she turned.

"Marti . . . I love you, girl, and I'm proud of you."

She smiled and nodded. "I love you, too, Papa. Sleep now."

But sleep eluded Joe Beaumont as he stared at the ceiling, seeing images from the past replayed on it as if it were a movie screen. Adam Wade, the drifter sweating in the fields with Marti, and Adam Moreland, elegant and cold looking, challenging Marti in their living room. Then he pictured Heath. Heath with his dark blue eyes and inky straight hair, already showing signs off the tall angular man he'd one day be. Adam Moreland's very image. How blind he'd been!

"Oh, Martha, girl, what have I done?" he murmured softly as fear and guilt tore at him.

The silent walls had no answers for him.

Adam drove directly to San Francisco, using his car phone to call Pris Watson at home. She was used to working weekend hours. In ten minutes she called him back, saying, "Mr. Allard's having a luncheon delivered to your office. He'll be waiting for you." She could sense his scowl over the phone and added cheerfully, "Easy way to stay slim. Eat lunch with Booth Allard every day."

When Adam arrived on the thirtieth floor of their Embarcadero Center office suite, Booth had pulled two tan leather chairs directly behind his large walnut desk. Both seats overlooked the stunning view of the city from the wall length windows of the executive suite. A bottle of Chateau Beaumont Chardonnay stood on a small table, flanked by two crystal glasses, an assortment of fresh boiled shrimp, raw oysters on the half shell, cracked crab claws and a big loaf of crusty sourdough bread.

Booth looked up and gave Adam a greeting as cold as the Chardonnay he was pouring. He handed a glass to him, then held his up against the bright sunlight streaming in the window.

"Good color, nice body, not too flinty," he said downing a generous swallow. "To Chateau Beaumont, our next acquisition."

"Don't go counting your assets until they're signed and delivered, Booth," Adam said as he slipped into his chair. He broke off a heel of the crisp bread and popped it in his mouth. After cleansing his palate, he tasted the wine and nodded. "Joe always knew how to make a wine with backbone." He stared absently out the window, rubbing the bridge of his nose with his fingertips.

"Art Bridger and Stan Wollack are already signed and delivered. All that's between them is Chateau Beaumont . . . quite an impressive block of real estate for Moreland Enterprises to hold." Booth broke open a large crab claw and slid the iced meat into his mouth, washing it down with the wine, waiting for Adam's response.

"Those men are old, ready to retire, Booth. By the

way, you didn't offer them a little encouragement to sell, did you?" From the corner of his eye Adam watched Booth's hand freeze and drop a fat shrimp back onto the platter.

Allard smiled evilly then. "I suppose that's your oblique way of asking if I pressured them with threats about shipping their wine or having their migrants carded?"

"I was thinking a little more along the lines of sabotaged machinery and spoiled wine vats," Adam replied, looking levelly at Booth. His face was expressionless. "Using thugs is sloppy, Allard. They tend to get caught and point the finger back at the man who hired them. Even a 'suit' like you might go to jail," he added with a dark smile curving his lips.

"After all these years in the business, I'm beyond the crudities your father and his cronies practiced back in the forties. You and I both know how to squeeze a grower out, legally. Anyway, after you upped the offer to those small wineries, it's scarcely surprising they jumped in our hip pockets," Booth replied, with a sneer in his voice.

Adam split open a pink shrimp shell and deftly extracted the slab of meat from within. Dipping it in the blood red horseradish sauce, he bit into it, seemingly ignoring his associate. "I understand the winemaster at Chateau Beaumont wants to deal."

"Yeah. Staritz liked your latest offer well enough. Now if he can only convince that stupid old man."

"That 'stupid old man' and his father kept their business prospering in spite of my father and his cronies, and all the worst gangsters who ever hit the west coast. Don't underestimate him. You might make a deal with Staritz, but he isn't in charge of the winery. Joe and Marti Beaumont are."

Allard stood up after draining his glass. "Old Joe is bedridden and that girl would rather paint pictures than fight Moreland Enterprises."

Adam leaned back in his chair and watched Allard. "What about the other daughter . . . Riba? Does she want to sell?" The imperceptible tightening across Booth's shoulders caused Adam to narrow his eyes.

Allard shrugged and turned, "She's too busy bed-hopping from what I hear. I doubt she's given her father's winery a second thought. I've met her at a couple of parties here in town. We never discussed business."

Adam remained seated, his thick brows shading the penetrating blue of his eyes. "She ought to be just your type, Booth."

Allard flashed a cold, slow smile. "Used to be yours, too. But that was before you met your live-in lady. Someday that cop's going to arrest you, Adam, if you aren't careful."

"I'll be careful, Booth. Just see to it you are. I'd hate to have Moreland Enterprises dragged down with you if you try anything stupid. So much so, I'd cut the rope and let you drop." He stood up and looked out the thirty storey window to the pavement below.

Allard threw back his head and laughed. "Yes, you would, wouldn't you. The same as I'd pull the plug on you. We've always understood each other, Adam. But you know I get results. I want those prime vineyards in Napa and I'll have them—no muss, no fuss, no danger to our illustrious corporate image."

"Just remember, Joe and Marti won't cave in to threats. You send one goon on Chateau Beaumont land with a tool kit or a ball bat and they'll dig in deeper. They'd burn the place to the ground before they let you have it that way."

"Sounds like you know them pretty well," Allard said speculatively.

"The whole family," Adam replied with finality.

Chapter 19

Adam drove toward his penthouse late that afternoon, wondering if Linda would be there. He hadn't talked with her since leaving for Napa early Friday morning. That seemed years ago, not yesterday. As he parked his car in the basement garage, he nodded absently to the security guard, turning over in his mind all that had happened in less than two days. How was he going to handle it, and how would he tell Lin?

Their relationship had always been affectionate and honest, relaxing after the pressure-cooker days and nights they spent with their careers. When he walked into the living room he heard the fizz of the kitchen faucet and smelled the rich spicy fragrance of Lin's lasagne sauce simmering slowly on the stove.

Leaning casually against the door frame with his suit jacket tossed over one shoulder, he asked, "How'd you know I'd be back tonight?"

She grinned. "How do you know I'm fixing this for you?" At his touche shrug, she said, "I finally got a whole afternoon off and decided to treat myself to a decent meal. I swear if I ever see another microwave pot pie or bucket of fried chicken, I'll blast it with my .38."

He arched one brow. "Easy for you to say now. By Monday night you'll be sitting in an unmarked junker on some back street drinking silty coffee from a styrofoam cup and munching on a creme donut."

"I still keep my girlish figure, though," she sassed, throwing a dishtowel across her shoulder and sauntering over to press herself against him, wrapping her arms around his neck, and reaching up for a long slow kiss. When she pulled away, her soft brown eyes searched his face.

Adam reached up and stroked her cheek gently, saying nothing for a moment. "Maybe we should've gotten married. You can read me better than anyone I've ever met," he whispered in perplexity.

"All the more reason not to!" Linda turned and walked into the living room to the mirrored bar. She poured two generous scotches and handed one to him. "Now, while I finish the salad and layer the lasagne, you take a long, hot shower. Then we talk. Okay?"

"Sounds good." He kissed her nose and turned toward the bedroom. The hot needle spray stung his shoulders as he took long breaths of the steamy air, trying desperately to relax his body and clear his mind. Half an hour later he returned to the kitchen, dressed casually in an open collared shirt and jeans. His damp hair had been toweled almost dry and glistened blueblack in the bright light.

"Smells heavenly," he said. "You know, you're the first woman I ever knew who could cook."

She grinned. "That's because you always hung around rich girls before. Now, let's freshen our drinks and talk while the lasagne bakes. I have a feeling a lot's been going on."

Sinking onto the big sofa he leaned back and said without preamble. "I have a son, Lin. Three years old this spring."

Her eyes locked with his as she reached for her drink. "I take it you found out this weekend."

"Yeah. This morning to be exact. I went to have it out with old Joe Beaumont and make him a final offer for his winery."

"*He's* the grandfather? Adam, is there any connection between him and that beating you took in Napa four years ago?"

He sighed at her logic. "Always the cop, aren't you? Yes, Joe had me beaten and dumped on that freight, but not because of Marti. The old asshole thought I was messing around with his precious younger daughter." The look on his face amply illustrated to Lin how he felt about that prospect.

"And you saw her, this Marti . . . and your son?" she asked softly.

He looked measuringly at her. "Heath is mine, Lin. The resemblance is uncanny. I couldn't deny him if I wanted to."

"Which you don't," she supplied. "What about his mother?"

In the three years of their relationship she had never seen such vulnerability or confusion on Adam Moreland's face. The coldly beautiful mask had slipped, not in the passion or laughter they had shared so often, but in a way that revealed his innermost emotions.

He stared down into his drink and swirled the melting ice cubes in a circle. "What about her? She'd fight to the death to keep Heath from me. Marti thinks I ran out on her four years ago when her father arranged that 'long goodbye' for me."

"Did you tell her the truth?"

He shrugged helplessly. "She thinks her old man walks on water. She didn't believe me."

"But you want her to. Are you still in love with her, Adam?" The question hung between them for a moment as she watched him stare out the window at the gathering darkness.

Finally he replied. "I don't know. I was then, but it was a lifetime ago. When I saw her last night . . . shit!" He looked up at Lin, wanting desperately not to hurt her, yet feeling so confused and alone that he needed her comfort.

Intuiting that, she scooted across from her chair to the sofa and took his hand in hers. "Read my lips. You still love her. It's written all over your face. When I kissed you in the kitchen I could tell something had happened. For three years I knew you were holding back a part of your past. More than an unhappy childhood and that fracas with your stepmother." At his look of surprise, she grinned. "I always read the newspapers, even when I was studying for mid terms."

"I spent years drifting from vineyard to vineyard, calling myself Adam Wade. Then I drifted into Napa and got a job with Marti's father. I guess I was ready to quit running and settle down. When I saw her, I knew she was special. We spent the summer fighting, then making love. I planned to go to Jake and set things straight, then tell her who I was, ask her to marry me. The whole trite honorable bit . . ."

"But Joe threw in a couple of surprises to spoil your plans," she said softly.

"Three of them." He rubbed the scar on his eyebrow, remembering. "I sent a note to her after I woke up in the hospital, but that was over a month later, by the time my brain unfogged. Before then I guess Marti knew she was pregnant and had to leave."

"Nobody in 1983 runs away from home because she's pregnant, especially a rich kid with a doting father," Lin said in amazement.

"You don't know this family," Adam replied grimly. He went on to relate the background on Marti and Riba and their relationship with their father. After he finished telling her about the way he learned of Marti's supposed marriage, he grew silent.

Lin took the empty glass from his hand and pulled him up. "Dinner's ready, Adam. You talked and I listened. Now I'm going to talk and you're going to listen."

"Bossy cop. You'll be a great replacement for Blanchard when you make captain," he groused, following her into the kitchen.

Alice Marchanti finished wrapping the set of prints for Mrs. Velmer and handed them over the counter with a smile that froze on her face when Adam walked in the door. Bidding Mrs. Velmer a fast, friendly good day, she rounded the counter and walked to the far end of the gallery where he was browsing. Three of Marti's pastels were on display in that corner.

"It's a good thing you came on Monday morning. Always a slow time around here," she said as he turned. She quickly inspected the casually elegant polo shirt and slacks. Obviously, this wasn't a business trip. "Where'd you park your fancy wheels?"

He shrugged. "Across the street."

Her eyes traveled past his shoulder to the blue Mercedes sitting like a sleek Siamese cat in front of an exclusive boutique. "New. Last time it was a green one as I recall. You win the lottery or you dealin' drugs, Wade?"

He laughed mirthlessly. "Nothing so lucky or dramatic, I'm afraid. The name's Moreland, not Wade, Alice."

Her round eyes bugged out even more than usual. "Well, I'll be damned!" She whistled low, then narrowed her eyes and asked pointedly, "Why the alias, junker cars and ripped jeans? You sure as shit weren't slumming—working the vines is too damned hard for that. Your old man send you to spy on Joe?"

"My old man and I didn't speak for seven years, Alice," he replied quietly. "We'd had a . . . personal disagreement. I joined the navy and then worked the vines. I came to Joe's place because I heard he made damn fine wines."

"That why you're so eager to buy him out now?" Her shrewd hazel eyes missed nothing, including the ways he kept looking past her at Marti's sketches.

"My associate thinks there's money for Moreland Enterprises in Napa. He's been handling it. Until now."

"Of course you had no other reason to come to Napa but business," she said smugly.

"As a matter of fact, no. I thought Marti was off in France—or still in New Orleans—until I ran into her at Meadowood Friday night. I didn't know she'd come back to run Chateau Beaumont for Joe. Believe it or not, I didn't know about the sabotage either."

She studied him for a minute, then said, "Say I do believe you, what does that mean for Marti? You hurt her once and left her to rebuild her life. She hasn't done a half bad job either in spite of all the rotten luck with her husband being killed and her dad being sick. She's got a good career in art ahead of her and a beautiful little boy."

Adam now gave Alice a penetrating look. "You honestly don't know, do you?" At her blank expression, he glanced around the gallery to where a clerk was standing with a customer. "Is there somewhere we can talk privately?"

Alice's kitchen was a bizarre blend of kilns and cook pots, with racks of spices sitting across from bottles of turpentine. She always kept a large pot of strong Columbian coffee brewed on the stove. They drank the whole thing, sitting amid the clutter. In agonizing detail Adam told Alice why he had become a drifter, how he and Marti had fallen in love that magic summer and all the circumstances that had changed their lives in the past four years.

Alice clutched a chipped ceramic mug and stared into its silty contents. "So now you've just discovered you have a son and you want him. Like I said before, where does that leave Marti?"

"I didn't come here looking for Heath! I didn't even know about him." He ran his fingers through his hair in frustration. "I told myself I came for business, even finally admitted I wanted revenge against Joe, but once I saw her Friday night . . . everything changed. Then, when I found out why she left so quickly, I knew I had no reason to blame her for deserting me. But Alice, she has no reason to blame me, either."

Alice let out a long whistling breath. "No, I guess she doesn't, but we'll have one hell of a time convincing her of that."

He reached across the table and put his hand over hers. Looking into her eyes, he said simply, "Thank you for believing me, Alice. I take it I have a much-needed ally?"

She nodded. "Never did add up. Marti leaving here so sudden and then you coming back, rich, but walking kind of gimpy. When she came home this spring I told her you'd been here that December."

"Let me guess her reaction," he said darkly.

"You know how hurt and alone she was. It always

seemed to me she grieved more for losing you than for losing that French husband. Now I guess I know why!" Some of the old deviltry returned to her eyes. "Both of you are here and you want her back. I think we can figure out a way. Of course, there is her father to consider, Adam. He's a sick old man. Don't start out by attacking him. It'll only get her back up."

"Her loyalty to that old bastard is a double-edged sword," he said bitterly. "It holds her here, but keeps her from believing the truth about him."

"Sometimes the truth hurts. Go slow on that. All she needs to believe for now is that you ended up in that Fresno hospital and didn't desert her and Heath. Once she trusts you, the rest will take care of itself."

He grinned. "Anyone ever tell you for a street kid from Hoboken you're one hell of a cockeyed optimist?"

She winked. "Just call me Nellie Forbush!"

As they walked through the gallery to the front door, they made plans for Adam's first "accidental meeting" with Marti. Passing the pastels again, Adam stopped and examined them. "This all she's done since she came back?"

"Not much time what with running Chateau Beaumont for her dad, and trying to keep the place from being torpedoed. If you and Moreland Enterprises aren't hassling her, someone sure as hell is, Adam."

"I plan to find out who, believe me," he said as he pulled open the wide glass door and departed.

Adam hadn't told Alice about the attempts on his life when he was working at Chateau Beaumont. "It'll be interesting to see, now that I'm back, if they start up again," he muttered grimly as he drove up the twisting curves of the Knoxville Road toward Lake Berryessa.

Visions of Riba and Booth, then of Boris Staritz, all flashed through his mind. Then he recalled that before he had arrived at Chateau Beaumont, the winemaster had been rumored to have had a torrid affair with Riba. "Jesus, what a tangle of snakes," he swore. If Staritz wanted to take Booth's offer for Chateau

Beaumont, he might well be the saboteur. Adam knew that Boris had urged Marti to sell at the higher price he'd quoted. What would Riba have to gain from selling Chateau Beaumont? She could always find another rich sucker to marry. Of course, there was always Booth, who he knew was utterly ruthless.

He rubbed his eyebrow and swore, then turned his thoughts to pleasanter considerations—his afternoon outing with one very surprised Marti Beaumont. "Madame Martin, ha!" He laughed joyously as he turned into the marina at the lake.

Marti reached for the phone and recognized Peter Kane's warm, pleasant voice on the other end of the line. "Just a reminder about the party on my boat tonight. Bring a sweater. Heard the weather's supposed to turn cool."

"This is going to be a late bash, huh? I thought all cutters had to be in surgery at seven a.m. Sure you get enough sleep?" she teased.

"Oh, don't worry about me. I've never cut myself yet," Pete replied with a grin, thinking of how surprised she was going to be about the mystery guest on this outing. "Incidentally, my lab just phoned about the blood work on your dad. He's looking good, Marti."

"That's a big relief. He really gave me a scare Saturday!"

"Marti, you can't protect him from the world. He's lived over sixty years and fought his own battles. If he takes his medication and acts sensibly, he'll be fine." Sensing her imminent protest, he forestalled it. "See you this evening. Got to run."

Marti hung up the phone and looked around at the stacks of paperwork in her office. She really couldn't afford the time for this boating party. But Joe had been adamant, insisting she get out and have some fun. Since he wasn't pushing her to go with Boris, she had agreed. Alice was picking her up at five.

After the past tense and terrible weekend, lord knew she needed a break. The best thing would be a month alone on a desert island to sort out her feelings about Adam Moreland and draw up a better plan for protecting Heath from his rapacious father. *Who will protect you from Adam?* a nagging voice asked her. She pushed that thought aside and returned to the shipping invoices.

By five that afternoon Marti had showered, blown her hair into a welter of casual curls and selected a jaunty white broadcloth A-line skirt with chocolate piping and a matching blouse. As she fastened her white ankle strap sandals, she heard Alice pulling up the drive.

On the way to the lake, they chatted about inconsequential things. Marti deliberately did not bring up Adam's startling reappearance in her life. Somehow she knew Alice would ask questions she wasn't prepared to answer yet, if ever. When they pulled into the small marina, Marti hopped from Alice's Mazda and scanned the parking lot. A blue Mercedes caught her eye, but she dismissed it as a coincidence. There were lots of Mercedes in the Napa area. Any day of the week The Diner in Yountville had half a dozen in its parking lot.

Alice noticed the way Marti had quickly glanced away from Adam's car and smiled to herself as they strolled down the hill and around to where Pete's boat was docked. Lake Berryessa was a breathtaking man-made wonder, enjoyed by San Francisco yuppies and eastern tourists alike. It boasted 168 miles of jaggedly beautiful shoreline. Stands of Valley Oaks shaded grassy picnic grounds and vacation trailers, while the beaches beckoned sun bathers and water skiers. But the evenings belonged to the boat people—California style. The piers were lined with all kinds of crafts, bobbing gently on the clear rippling water. Plush cabin cruisers rode high and proud in the water next to sleek sail boats that seemed to recline in their berths.

Peter had an Avanti Sunbridge moored at the south inlet of the marina. Just as they neared the pier and she could see the boat, Alice snapped her fingers and swore. "Damn, I forgot! I promised Pete I'd bring him that print he had reframed. I left it in the trunk. You go on and tell him I'll be along in a few minutes."

She was gone in a shot before Marti could do more than nod. When she reached Peter's boat it appeared deserted. Marti wondered why no one was about. Stepping aboard she peered down the stairs and called out, "Peter?"

Over the rumble of an engine down the pier she heard a masculine voice invite her below deck. Carefully, she descended the narrow stairs, lowering her head to enter the cabin. When she straightened up, Marti felt her knees buckle. "What the hell are you doing on Pete's boat?" she accused.

Adam Moreland stood in the middle of the salon with a glass of sparkling wine in each hand. Foisting one into her trembling fingers, he grinned and answered, "Peter Kane's my cousin, remember? He lent me the boat for the evening."

When she turned to set the glass down and leave, he put a warm hand on her bare arm and said softly, "It'll be a long walk. Alice has gone back to Napa. I've taken the liberty of arranging a shoreline cruise." As she stared at him in open-mouthed disbelief, he climbed the steps to the bridge.

As the boat's powerful engines began to vibrate, Marti stood frozen in shock. Then, as she felt them moving slowly away from the pier, she followed him up to the helm. "This is kidnapping, Mr. Moreland! Turn this boat around this instant and let me off! I'll take a cab home!"

"You can't hide forever, Marti," he replied softly.

"I'll wring Alice Marchanti's neck! I'd wring Peter Kane's, too, if he weren't Papa's doctor! Maybe I'll wring it anyway."

Taking a deep breath, she looked at his casual clothes and relaxed pose as he guided the boat out of the inlet toward the open lake. Her heart did a queer little lurch that she attributed to the motion of the water. "What are you trying to do, Adam?"

"How about have a civil conversation without interruption? Over dinner. There's a basket below if you'd like to set the table while I find a good spot to anchor."

Marti retreated to the galley, more to get away from his unnerving presence than to comply with his suggestion. The "basket" offered up a gourmet feast of fresh artichoke salad, cold roast pheasant and luscious flaky pastries. She arranged the food on the table and sat down uneasily on a plush vinyl seat.

In what seemed to Marti to be a very short time, Adam had found an isolated cove and anchored the boat. As he joined her in the salon, she shrugged in nervous resignation and scooted over to allow him to slide behind the table, quickly shoving her shawl and handbag between them.

He grinned wolfishly as he dug into the pheasant, offering her a generous slab of snowy meat and a spicy mustard sauce to go with it. As he served the food, he talked.

"You accused me of deserting you that summer, and when I tried to tell you what happened, you didn't believe me." He could feel the angry retort springing to her lips and continued quickly. "I have photo copies of my medical records from Fresno and the release from a physical therapist in San Francisco a year later. Marti, regardless of who put me in that hospital, I was beaten, dumped on a freight and woke up a month later two hundred miles away. I sent a note as soon as I could, but you were gone by then." He paused and looked at her, willing her to believe him. "Now I understand why you left."

"Alice told me you returned in December," she said softly, shoving a leaf of endive around in her salad bowl.

"Your sister informed me you were honeymooning on the Riviera," he replied.

His voice sounded oddly rough and suddenly Marti realized how the situation could have appeared to him . . . if he was telling her the truth about why he vanished four years ago. Then she looked up at him and read it in his eyes.

"I . . . I suppose we've both been hurt by circumstances beyond our control, Adam," she began uncertainly, "but that still doesn't explain why you deceived me, pretending to be a drifter named Wade. You blame my father for what happened to you, but what about all the enemies Jake Moreland and his son must have made? We never had a relationship based on trust."

"There were things I had spent years trying to figure out, Marti. When I met you, the pieces had begun to fall in place. I was going to tell you—"

"When, Adam? You had all summer."

He knew she was recalling that last night at the cabin when she had wanted so desperately to hear words of love from him. "The morning I was attacked at the cabin I had decided to tell you everything."

She made a small strangled sob, and he slid instantly to her side, enfolding her in his arms. His embrace felt so warm, so safe, so right. She burrowed against his hard chest and wrapped her arms around his waist.

Gently, he stroked her hair and inhaled the lemon fresh fragrance of it. "We didn't get our chance to talk then because I was a mule-headed fool, still running from my past. But now, Marti, now we have time and I want to tell you everything . . ."

When she raised her head he could see the crystalline glisten of tears. Unable to stop himself, he kissed her softly, gently. She responded, hesitant and trembling as she had been those first treasured times that long ago summer. Slowly, he broke the closeness of their embrace and leaned back against the cushioned booth, pulling her with him. Then he began the story of Jake Moreland's son: rich, embittered, and lonely, and Jake Moreland's wife, young, beautiful and bored.

Marti sat very still as all the painful memories of his childhood spilled out. After his mother's death he had been isolated in a cold stone mansion, raised by servants, forgotten by his father. She could well imagine how a woman like Jolie Allard could manipulate the twenty-year old son after she had fooled the fifty-year old father.

When he had finished, Marti said uncertainly, "Riba used to do things when we were children . . . I guess she still does, uses people the same way your stepmother did. After all these years Papa's finally realized what she's like. I feel so sorry for them both, Adam."

Marti pulled away from him and stood up on shaky legs. She needed space to think, away from the mesmerizing warmth of this magnetic man who turned her world upside down each time they met. "Adam, we've talked about the past, our families, our childhoods . . . but I've built a new life now and so have you." She stopped, uncertain of how to go on.

"I quite running four years ago, Marti. It's hard to do from a hospital bed," he said ruefully. "The first thing I did in Fresno was to write you. When they released me I went to see Jake and made what peace I could between us before he died. I'm president of a wine conglomerate that symbolizes everything your father hates. But I didn't order the sabotage of your winery to force you to sell."

Again she knew in her bones that he was telling her the truth. "All right, Adam. But you still think my father is as unprincipled as yours was. You blame him for destroying our lives."

He was beside her in one pantherish stride. "Let's leave Joe Beaumont out of this for now. We have Heath to think of and he's a hell of a lot more important."

She pushed away from his arms angrily. "So that's it—you want your son—your heir for Moreland Enterprises, just like Jake wanted you."

"Marti, dammit woman, I love you! I love our son, too, but I won't—I couldn't take him away from you." He swore and turned away, combing his fingers roughly through his hair. She could see the tension quivering across his back muscles through the thin cottons shirt.

"Adam," she put a hand tentatively on his trembling shoulder.

"Shit! I can face down international financiers and never let them see me sweat. Why the hell am I botching this with you so badly?" He turned and reached out for her with the desperation of a drowning man.

As he embraced her, squeezing the breath from her, she whispered in his ear, "What I was trying to say is that I love you, too, fool that I probably am!"

He kissed her then, fiercely grinding his mouth down on hers, running his hands up and down her body as she melted against him.

"Every curve and line of your body, memorized," he murmured against her throat as his hot mouth trailed wet delicious licks and nips down toward the buttons on her blouse, which he quickly unfastened.

This was what she had wanted for so long. No other lover's touch could make her feel this way. "I'm dizzy, drowning . . ." her voice faded away to a shuddering gasp when his cunning fingers unhooked her bra and tantalized the aching fullness of her breasts. "Mmm, must be the boat ride," she whispered in a drugged voice.

"I love you, Marti, love you . . ." he murmured as he slid her unfastened skirt down her hips. In spite of the cool night air on the lake, Marti was warm. Stripped to sandals and briefs, she leaned against her lover, easing his shirt up between them and slipping it over his shoulders. He shrugged it off quickly and once more lowered his mouth to hers. She ran her palms in small, tight circles across his biceps and down the thick hair on his chest. When she reached his belt, he helped her, shedding his slacks as easily as he had rid her of the skirt.

For a moment they stood still, each studying the depths of the other's eyes, reading love and a desperate passion. Wordlessly, he took her hand and led her into the adjoining stateroom in the aft section of the boat. Smiling, he slid onto the soft double bed and pulled her with him. When he reached for one slim ankle and began to unfasten her sandal, he said, "Last time I did this you wanted me to stop."

"Please don't," she whispered hoarsely.

It took only a few movements to slip off her shoes

and briefs. Then he stood up and completed his strip as she watched through glazed silvery eyes.

"Witch, sea witch," he murmured as he lowered himself onto the bed beside her. The boat rocked gently in the lake. It was fully dark now and the only sound they could hear was the gentle lapping of the current against the hull. The rhythmic motion of the water lent an enticing, gentle nuance to their caressing, slowing their passion, letting every long-awaited touch and kiss blend liltingly into the next.

"I've dreamed of this for so long, so long," she sobbed, realizing how futile her attempts at other relationships had been.

If Marti had a fleeting, regretful thought for Gray, Adam had one for Lin, too. But then all memories were obliterated. This was so right, so necessary, so inevitable. He felt her legs open to him, felt her warm soft hand slide between their bodies and grasp him until he cried out her name. Rolling her on top of him, he impaled her, letting her ride him.

It was just like that glorious night at the cabin. He held her hips prisoner, slowing their frantic mating to the soft sensuous rhythm of the rocking boat. Through the dim filter of the moonlight, their bodies looked shiny with sweat, silvered and ethereal, but the passion that fused them together was as tangible as it was exquisite.

Marti lowered her head as he reached up to suckle her breasts. Her hair fell in silky curls over his shoulders as she pulled his face up to hers for a long, sealing kiss. They prolonged the magic, slowing and stopping, as if trying to hold back the dawn.

When he heard her moan unwillingly and tighten her knees against his thighs, he arched up into her in a last ecstatic thrust. She fell onto his chest, trembling and gasping with the unexpressible joy of what they had just shared.

Finally, they rolled apart and Adam reached over to stroke her cheek. "I love you, Marti," he whispered again. His finger came away with the wetness of tears.

"Don't cry, babe. You'll never have to cry again. I swear it."

"Don't make promises you can't keep, Adam," she said softly. "There's so much we haven't said. So many problems we haven't worked out . . ."

"We will," he assured her, reaching down for the blanket. When he pulled her back into his arms and covered them, she settled against him comfortably.

Chapter 20

When Marti opened her eyes, bright morning sunlight was filtering through the porthole of the cabin cruiser. The sounds of Adam in the galley had awakened her. Dreamily, she reached across the bed to stroke the indentation in the pillow where his head had lain. Then full consciousness hit her and she sat up abruptly.

"We spent all night here! Papa and everyone at Chateau Beaumont must be frantic," she whispered as she reached for her clothes, now neatly hanging in the open locker. How could she have done such a reckless, irresponsible thing? Adam had managed to return to her life and reduce it to shambles in a few days once again. Damn the man!

Just then the subject of her disturbing thoughts walked cat-quietly over to the bed from the galley. Clad only in a pair of chinos, he held a mug of steaming coffee in each hand. Self-consciously, she slid back and grasped for the blanket to cover herself.

"Drink this and you'll feel better," he said soothingly, ignoring her protective motions.

As she reached for the mug gratefully, the blanket slipped. He grinned and winked as he plopped casually beside her. Fortified with a gulp of steaming coffee, she turned accusatorily toward him.

"My father probably has the police searching for me by now, Adam! I never intended to fall asleep—"

"Pete called for you last night and told Joe you were spending the night aboard his boat. Calm down."

"You've arranged everything, haven't you?" she

snapped in mortification. "Now he'll think I'm going to marry Peter Kane, for heavens sake!"

"He been trying to marry you off?" Adam asked with a grin.

"Mainly to Boris since I returned from New Orleans." Marti was gratified to see him scowl. "It *would* be practical, Adam." She couldn't resist testing the water a bit.

"Very practical. He'd get Chateau Beaumont and you in the bargain and your father could retire in complete security, knowing you and his grandson would be there at his beck and call for the rest of his life."

Her eyes flashed with anger and he immediately regretted the attack. "Damn! I'm sorry, babe. I don't want Joe to stand between us. I'll try to make peace with him for your sake, Marti. I promise."

A cold feeling of dread washed over her as she looked into his dark blue eyes. What if Papa wouldn't accept Adam? What if she had to choose between her father and the father of her son? "Adam, let's take things slow for now. Papa's ill. Any confrontation can set him off, like Saturday. Let me talk to him . . . that is, when we decide what we're going to do."

He caressed her cheek. "It's only a matter of time, Marti. You and I both know what we're going to do—what we should have done four years ago. We're going to get married."

"Thanks for the proposal," she said drily, but something that had been coiled hurtfully inside her seemed to ease. Her spirit soared in relief.

"Do you need a proposal, *Miss* Beaumont?" He grinned and then took her cup and set it next to his own on the vanity. His face became very serious. "I love you, Marti. Will you marry me?"

"What can I say but yes," she replied simply. "But I want time, Adam—I need time. We have to give Papa a chance to know you and we have to settle the issue of selling Chateau Beaumont. He'll never do that, Adam." Her eyes locked with his, waiting for his response.

He shrugged. "Booth will just have to live with two

out of three vineyards in this area, I guess. I know it's important to you. But today I have plans that don't include business. You and I are going to take our son for an outing . . . but first . . . I think a proposal and an acceptance call for a little special celebration."

Marti felt the blanket being pulled down one delicious inch at a time as his mouth worked a blistering magic on the skin he bared. She found her hands drawing him nearer, pulling him down with her to recline on the bed. Then all thought ceased.

It was mid-morning when the Mercedes pulled up in front of the Beaumont house. The fields were full of men, busy with the endless chores of summer. Boris Staritz had just walked out of the plant door when he saw Adam and Marti drive past. He had watched her leave last night with Alice Marchanti and now she was returning with Moreland. Quickly, he cut across the hill heading toward the house. Marti was wearing the same clothes she had worn last night. When she stepped out of the car he could see her outfit was decidedly rumpled. Only a blind man would have failed to notice the way she and Moreland exchanged glances, touched each other and laughed together.

When Hilda came around the side porch with Heath in tow, the boy dashed toward his mother and flew into her waiting arms. Staritz watched from a distance as a few murmured words were exchanged and the boy went into Moreland's arms.

Pulled by some invisible current, the winemaster approached the laughing family. Seeing the black-haired child and the tall, dark man holding him, Boris felt the breath rush out of him. They *were* really a family, bound by blood!

"So, you've finally come back to claim what belongs to you, even if you can't buy the chateau," he said in accusing anger.

Marti gave him a stricken look. "Boris, please, this isn't the time or place."

"Seems to me it's the perfect time and place." He looked from father to son, unintimidated by Moreland's darkening scowl. "Now I understand a great many things."

"Hilda, take Heath inside, will you please?" When the cook reached for the boy, he protested but Adam quickly said, "Your mother and I are going to take you picnicing in a little while—if you're good now. Okay?" He turned to Marti and lightly kissed her nose. "You, too. Scoot and change. Mr. Staritz and I have a few things to discuss. I'll pick you up in an hour or so."

Hilda disappeared with the boy, but Marti refused to be dismissed. "Boris has a right to hear this from me, Adam," she said quietly. "Anyway, I've seen you two 'discuss' things before and I don't want a repeat in my front yard."

Boris looked at her with contempt etched on his face. "You just spent the night with this corporate raider. He deserted you four years ago. Any chance you're pregnant again, Marti?"

When Adam stepped toward the Russian with an oath, Marti placed her hand on his chest. "Please, Adam! Not here!"

"Get out of here, Staritz. What's between me and the woman I'm going to marry doesn't concern you."

"So, you finally plan to make an honest woman of her," he sneered at Moreland, then turned to Marti. "What do you suppose your father will have to say about that, Marti?"

"Papa already knows about Heath, Boris. I understand it's a shock for you, but I never led you to think I'd marry you. Now you know why," she finished simply.

"Nothing will be gained by a brawl, Staritz. Do like the lady asks and let it drop." Adam's voice was steely.

With an oath, the winemaster turned to storm off, but not before Adam's last words stopped him. "I'd hate to hear talk about Marti and Heath bandied around the plant or yards, Staritz. It could cost a man more than just his job."

Boris's mouth was a set slash in his gray-hued face

as he replied coldly, "I fight my battles with my fists or my brains, not with gossip, Moreland."

They drove along the Silverado Trail and took a familiar turn off. Without his telling her, Marti knew Adam was taking them back to Bill Dougherty's cabin, the place where the laughing delighted boy seated between them had probably been conceived. As they pulled up in front of the small building, Heath's parents exchanged a glance that spoke volumes, each remembering that summer, its exquisite joys and bitter sorrows.

As they climbed out of the car, Adam lifted Heath effortlessly on one arm while Marti reached for the lavish picnic basket in the back seat. The boy was becoming increasingly heavy for her to carry. He had grown rapidly this last year. Watching him squirm and giggle as his father tickled him and tossed him up in the air with ease brought a sudden tightening to her throat. They belonged together. Heath deserved to have a father.

But Joe's hurt, quiet demeanor when she had come inside to change that morning had dampened her spirits far more than Boris's accusatory remarks. Joe had seen Adam's car and knew she had spent the night with him. She had simply told her father Adam was taking Heath and her for a picnic. His nod of acceptance was better than an explosive argument, but she knew this situation must be painful for the old man.

"You going to let us starve, woman?" Adam's laughing question brought her out of her reverie. He had brought a hearty feast of fried chicken, potato salad and chocolate layer cake back with him from Meadowood. Quickly, she followed "her men" toward the open clearing by the lake, where she knelt down and opened the basket. Heath helped Adam spread a thick, brightly colored cloth while she unpacked the food and set it out.

"Guaranteed to please the most discriminating three-year-old palate, so the chef at the club assured me," Adam said with a wink at Marti as he handed the boy a drumstick.

"Mmm," was the only response.

"He's always had an appetite," Marti said with a laugh as she served them creamy potato salad and crisp pickles to accompany the chicken.

"So did I when I was a boy. It's why the Moreland men all get to be tall," he added with a wink.

They hadn't discussed how to tell Heath that Adam was his father yet. Since he'd known no other father, the boy was unlikely to be confused at such a tender age, but still it meant another irrevocable step toward confrontation with Joe Beaumont. Marti said nothing for a while, turning her attention to the food and attempting to keep Heath from knocking his juice over on the grassy ground.

"After lunch we'll try fishing. Can you fish, Heath?" Adam looked at the boy, busily tearing into his second drumstick.

"Never been," the boy replied.

"Don't talk with your mouth full, Heath," Marti remonstrated to no avail.

Good as his word, Adam produced a couple of simple cane poles from the trunk of the car while Marti was scraping gooey chocolate from Heath's face and hands.

Laying the poles down beside the minnow bucket, Adam laughed and grabbed the boy. "Let's wash off in the lake. You'll be sure to draw the fish with all that icing and chicken grease." With surprising skill for a man who had never cared for a child before, Adam managed to clean off most of the food adhering to his son.

"After we let lunch settle a bit, how about a swim before we take you home for your nap."

"Don't wanna go home," the boy replied reaching up to give Adam an unexpected and very wet hug. The startled man returned it fervently.

"Well, all guys your age need their sleep, but we'll worry about that later," he said with mock gruffness. It was an idyllic interlude with squeals of delight when the cork bobber on Heath's pole vanished beneath the surface of the water. Quickly, Adam was there, helping the boy yank up on the pole to set the hook. Heath swung the pole and its squiggly catch over the water and onto the bank, assisted by Adam's sure hands.

The boy watched in silent fascination while Adam removed the hook from the flopping bluegill and placed the fish on a stringer. Then he lowered his prize back into the lake for safe keeping.

"Can Hilda cook it when I get home?" he asked excitedly.

"She sure can," Adam replied.

"Aw. Just membered—fish taste yucky. Mommy, will you eat it?"

"I suppose so, but only if you promise to taste it, too," Marti said with a wink.

Later they changed into their swimsuits and splashed in the cool clear water. Heath had taken waterbabies swim classes at the local Y and was fairly good at staying afloat, but Adam never let the boy out of his reach as they splashed and wrestled.

By early afternoon Heath was droopy lidded and yawning. "Time for your nap, young man," Marti said finally, reaching for a towel to dry off the protesting boy as Adam hauled him piggyback from the water.

"Don't wanna," Heath said mulishly with a flash of temper when Marti began to take him from Adam.

"Do as your mother says, son." Adam put him down on the ground and knelt to hold onto him as Marti dried him.

"You can't make me," the boy said with tears welling in his eyes.

"Yes, I can, Heath," Adam said with a smile.

"You're not my mommy," Heath shot back as he squirmed away.

"No. I'm your father." The words slipped out so naturally Adam was surprised to hear himself say them.

Marti gasped in surprise as she enveloped Heath in

the towel and began to rub vigorously. Her mind was frozen as she worked frantically.

Heath looked from his silent mother to the tall man kneeling next to her. "I got a grandpa and a great grandma, but I don't got a father. Mommy said . . ." he hesitated and looked up at Marti for explanation about the dim memory of a man seldom mentioned.

Marti's eyes met Adams with anguish. *Not now! Not so soon*, they seemed to say, but the die was cast. Gently, Adam reached over and took her hand in his as he settled the towel-wrapped boy on his lap.

"Heath, your mother and I both love you and when you get a little older you'll understand about what happened when you were born. I'm sorry I couldn't be there, but now that I've found you, I'll never leave you again. I love you, son."

"Then . . . then you're my for real daddy?" the small voice hiccuped. He was very sleepy now and the flash of temper had long since passed.

Adam smiled and tousled the boy's wet hair as he squeezed Marti's hand in assurance. "I'm your 'for real daddy,' Heath."

Heath slept soundly in Marti's lap as they drove back to Chateau Beaumont that afternoon. "We have a lot to discuss, Adam," she said softly.

"I'll pick you up around six. We'll have dinner in Napa at La Boucane on Second Street. It's quiet and the food's good."

"All right." She smiled. "Let me put Heath down and take a good relaxing soak. I'll be ready."

When they arrived at the house, Marti took the sleeping boy and headed inside while Adam drove away. *Sooner or later I'll have to face my father and tell him I still love Adam*, she thought unhappily. Then she realized that Heath would awaken babbling the news about his newly discovered father. Sooner, not later.

Adam drove back to Meadowood, looking forward to a long hot shower himself. He could still see Heath's face, blue eyes alight with surprise and happiness at discovering that Adam was his father. A fleeting memory of Jake and Elizabeth when he had been a boy flashed into his mind. Had they ever been a real family? It seemed so long ago now. Elizabeth had died when he was scarcely ten. Jake threw himself into his work with renewed vengeance after that, leaving a heartbroken boy alone. He vowed that Heath would never experience that kind of desertion.

Preoccupied, Adam pulled into a parking space and slid from the Mercedes. Then a voice cut into his thoughts.

"Quite a cut above that old Chevy you used to borrow. You've come up in the world, *mano.*" Bob Vasquez's face split into a wide smile as he crossed the asphalt in fast strides, hand outstretched to grip Adam's in a hearty shake.

"I'd say you've moved up in the world, too, if that Caddie's any indication," Adam replied heartily. "You fulfill your parent's dream and become a shyster lawyer or what?"

Vasquez laughed. "No, I went east two years ago when I finished my business degree. Only came home for my youngest sister's wedding. I've been working in New York for Chateau and Estate Wines. Guess wine will always be in my blood."

"By the looks of it it's pretty rich blood," Adam replied. "But you're working for my competition in France and Spain. Maybe I could offer you a job," Adam said with a grin.

At Bob's look of confusion, Adam threw his arm around the other man's shoulder and said, "Let's have a drink and I'll fill you in on the last four years."

Vasquez let out a long low whistle and shook his head in amazement when Adam Moreland finished his story. They had been sitting in a quiet corner of the bar, nursing their drinks and talking for over an hour when Bob asked, "You think there's any connection between Joe's knee-breakers and the other attempts to kill you?"

Adam took a swallow of his scotch and narrowed his eyes consideringly. "No, Joe thought he was protecting Riba." At Bob's look of frank incredulity, he laughed bitterly. "Life's a bitch, isn't it? Here Marti and I lost all those years because of a gullible old man and a spoiled brat. No, whoever set me up with that crop plane and tried the other stunts wasn't working for Joe. I'm sure Nate Benteen was involved, but he hightailed it out of here just after I 'dropped out' in a Fresno freight yard."

Bob suddenly looked up and snapped his fingers. "Just before you disappeared, you'd asked me to check on that guy in the Wrangler Bar who was buying Ansel McGee drinks. My uncle found out his name was Riefe Luger, a real bad actor from Frisco. He used to be a free-lance strikebreaker. Worked for the conglomerates down in the Big Valley back in the seventies. Even heard rumors he was paid to hit Caesar Chavez."

"Lucky thing for the UFW and me the guy's a lousy shot," Adam said softly. "Frisco boy, you say?"

"I don't know for how long, but when my Uncle Hector checked on him, he hailed from there. You know him?" Bob asked dubiously.

"Let's just say we may have had a slight collision in a parking garage. Sorry to split so soon, Bob, but I have to call a cop and check something out. How long you going to be in Napa?"

As they stood up to leave, Bob smiled and replied, "My sister's wedding is Saturday. I came a few days early for a golf vacation—between relatives, that is. I'll be here all week. And, Adam, I just might be interested in that job with Moreland Enterprises. I always did prefer California wines to European!"

Adam mulled over the surprising news of the past hour as the steaming hot water beat down on him in the shower. He'd phoned Lin at the precinct and she was running a make on Riefe Luger. A gut instinct told him that Luger was going to be their shooter. But who had hired him?

"If only I didn't have so damn many enemies," he muttered as he wrapped a towel carelessly around his hips and walked from the bath into the bedroom. Just then the phone began to ring insistently in the sitting room of his suite. When he picked up the receiver, Marti's voice on the other end sounded tense and agitated.

"Adam, let me meet you at Meadowood."

"Why, babe? What's wrong?"

There was a pause on the line and then she said, "It's Papa. Heath came roaring downstairs for supper and announced to his Grandpa in front of a whole room full of people, including Les Reams and Boris, that you were his 'for real daddy.' "

"I gather that didn't exactly go over like a hot air balloon," he said dryly.

"You could have heard one passing over the house in the silence that followed his impromptu speech. Everyone at the meeting evaporated. Papa is furious with us for telling Heath."

"Don't you think he has a right to know, Marti, especially considering we're going to get married?" Adam countered.

"Things are moving so fast, Adam. Papa's blood pressure is already too high. I want to get him used to this gradually. Please, don't confront him tonight. He was embarrassed in front of his men and I could hardly blurt out our wedding plans then and there, especially considering we haven't made them yet," she added sweetly.

He sighed. "Okay. I'll be in the bar at six."

"Punctual as usual, I see," he said as she slid onto the chair beside him, dressed in a sexy concoction of clingy peach silk. One luscious tan shoulder was bare and the dress hugged every curve of her body like a lover's gentle hands.

Fleeting thoughts of taking her to his suite were instantly quashed when she looked at his considering gaze and smiled archly. "Dinner at La Boucane, remember, Moreland? We have to *talk.*"

Glumly he signaled the waiter for a check, signed it and they left. On the drive into Napa they discussed the situation with Joe.

"Marti, he's got to accept the fact that I'm back in

your life to stay." He bit back the urge to tell her it was Joe's own guilt over falling for Riba's lies and having him beaten that was responsible for the old man's depression.

"Adam, try to see it from his side. You came back after four years with a whole new identity—and your company has been trying to buy us out. He still believes Moreland Enterprises was responsible for the sabotage. And now you're threatening to take away his only grandchild."

He grinned at her. "We could always supply him with more grandchildren . . . as many as you like. I love the way you blush in that off-the-shoulder creation—all pink and peaches, babe," he said in a voice grown low and husky.

"Adam, will you be serious," she remonstrated, but the glow in her eyes belied her rebuke.

"Let's talk about getting married. *That's* serious," he replied. "You pick a date."

Marti shifted uneasily in her seat, then looked over at him and sighed. "Why am I fighting this? I guess my father will calm down once everything's in the family, so to speak." She chuckled.

"How about next week?" he shot back.

Her eyes widened. "Let's not get crazy. We do have some family and friends to notify. Of course, I guess we could make it a small private ceremony in Father Jameston's study.

Adam nodded. "Married by an Episcopal priest. Sounds binding enough."

They were in the downtown area and traffic was fairly heavy on Jefferson Street that warm summer evening. "It's been so long since I've driven in Napa. Second Street one way?"

"Yes. If you keep going south on Jefferson you can turn left onto Second at the restaurant as I recall," Marti replied.

Adam stopped at a red light on Jefferson. Just as he was about to pin Marti down about a wedding date, he saw the two men climbing out of the old Ford pickup across the street in front of a True Value Hardware Store. He'd never forget that truck . . . or the men.

The shock of recognition was replaced almost instantly by a red surge of rage. Gripping the wheel, he took a deep calming breath. He turned with forced casualness to Marti and asked, "Is Craig Williamson still in business?"

Marti blinked at the abrupt change in topic, then smiled and asked, "You plan to dash over now and order a tuxedo for the wedding?"

"Not exactly," he replied mysteriously. "It's back a couple off blocks south of Trancas on Jefferson, isn't it?"

"Your memory of Napa is pretty good," she replied as he took off suddenly when the light turned green. "What's the hurry? They're open till nine."

Out of the rearview mirror Adam saw the big, heavily muscled man gesturing angrily to the shorter thickset one as they walked into the hardware store. *Let them take their time, please*, he thought, teeth gritted.

Exceeding the speed limit perceptibly, he drove around the block and turned north on Jefferson. At the shopping plaza he made a right into the parking lot and screeched to a halt in front of the exclusive men's shop. Turning to Marti he said, "When I was here before there was something I wanted to buy and couldn't afford. Be just a minute."

Marti leaned back into the plush leather of the Mercedes seat, bewildered by his actions. Then a wistful smile played across her face. Craig Williamson was where Adam had purchased the evening clothes that he had worn to Meadowood that night so long ago. She warmed as she remembered her response when the tall, elegant figure strolled gracefully into the crowded room. The flush intensified as she recalled their exchange on the deck. *Oh, my God, why did things go so wrong? We've lost four years.*

Her reverie ended when Adam walked briskly out of the store and opened the car door. "What on earth did you buy?" she asked.

As he slid behind the wheel, Adam offered her his

purchase for inspection while he pulled out of the parking lot and headed rapidly south on Jefferson. For a moment Marti stared in amused disbelief. "Good Lord, Adam, a walking stick!"

Adam nodded. "Genuine black walnut."

She burst into laughter. "What next? A top hat and tails? No, darling, it's just not you."

Adam replied tightly, "Yeah, I know. The only time a Moreland wears tails is when they're accessorized with horns and cloven hooves."

Marti's laughter ceased. Something was wrong. They drove in tense silence for several blocks as she studied his harsh profile. He volunteered nothing and she was afraid to speak to this dangerous stranger.

A couple of minutes later, when he cut back onto First and pulled suddenly to the curb, she asked nervously, "Are we still going to La Boucane for dinner?" The coiled tension in his body transmitted itself to her. Something was very wrong!

Keeping his tone casual, he said, "I just spotted a couple of old acquaintances." Marti followed his glance to the two men who were climbing into an old truck that was parked several spaces in front of them. Both men were dressed in worn, faded clothing. They looked like they'd cut their grandmother's throat for a dime.

"You know them?" she asked, incredulously.

"Sure," he responded. "You ever seen them before?"

"No," she replied with a shiver of revulsion.

"I've owed those guys something for four years, and after all this time, I bet they never suspected they'd get it back. Well, today's payday." Adam moved the Mercedes out into traffic, keeping several cars between them and the pickup as it headed out of town.

With a sense of growing dread Marti settled back in her seat. *Could they be the ones . . . ?* Her mind shut down and she gripped the seat with whitened knuckles.

As they cruised over a winding country road, Adam maintained a discreet distance between his car and the

Ford truck up ahead. When the pickup turned off onto a gravel road, he slowed to allow the gap between the two to widen. In silence, he and Marti drove for several minutes, frequently losing sight of the old truck on the curving, twisting road. Rounding a bend, they saw it parked on the shoulder less than a quarter of a mile away.

Careful not to alter the speed of the Mercedes, Adam drove past it. The two men had left the truck and were walking toward an ancient tractor parked in a small swale farther off the road. The big man carried some sort of carton. Neither he nor his companion paid any attention to the passing automobile. Marti watched Adam covertly and her fear grew with the harshness she read in his face.

Around the next bend, he pulled the car into a farm lane and backed out onto the road, returning slowly to the pickup. When it came into view, Adam surveyed the scene carefully. The bigger man was on the far side of the tractor. He was lying on his back, his upper body wedged under it. His partner, on his hands and knees, was on the other side of the old John Deere, looking under it. Obviously, the two were trying to repair it.

Adam eased the Mercedes off the road, slipped the transmission into park and put on his sunglasses, although it was fast approaching dusk now. He reached over and grasped the heavy walking stick, then turned to Marti and said, "Drive the car back to town, wait fifteen minutes and then swing back. I'll be waiting by the side of the road, but keep the doors locked. If you don't see me, drive by fast as hell and call the cops. Don't stop for anyone. Got that?"

"No way, Adam Moreland! You're gong to risk your life with those goons. They're the ones, aren't they, the ones who beat you? Oh, Adam, don't! You'll be hurt—maybe killed!"

"No chance, babe," was his cold, level reply. "Get going."

"No chance, babe," she parroted. She slid behind the wheel as he got out of the car.

"At least lock the doors," he said, smiling like a black angel. When he heard the automatic locks click, he began to fondle the walking stick as he strolled down the road. The scar over his right eye began to itch furiously.

The short man looked up and saw a well-dressed stranger in dark glasses approaching. He scrubbed the back of one thick, dirt-encrusted hand across his beard-stubbed cheek, noted the expensive Mercedes, and smirked at the walking stick. Only half-attentively he speculated that the "dude" was some tourist, probably a dumb limey, looking for directions. Dismissing him, he turned his attention back to his partner. The clang of a wrench slipping off a nut was followed by a torrent of oaths.

Looking under the tractor, he chuckled maliciously, "What'd I tell ya, Bo? That wrench won't work neither. Shit, didn't I tell ya we'd have to haul ass over to the John Deere dealer?" He was aware that "the limey" was now standing alongside of him, but contemptuously, he did not bother to look up. *Screw the rich bastard. He can wait.*

But Adam didn't wait. With both hands gripping one end of the walnut stick, he raised it like a man working a posthole digger, preparing to plunge it into the earth. Then, he drove it downward against the right side of the stocky man's back, just over the kidney. "Hello. You still in a hurry like you were at the cabin?"

The short man gasped, paralyzed by searing pain. Adam drew the walnut shaft upward once more and thrust it downward at the man's other kidney. So intense was the thug's agony, that only a soft, sharp moan escaped his lips.

Adam left him, rooted to the spot on all fours, and walked around to the other side of the tractor. The large, heavily-muscled mechanic was clumsily sliding out from underneath the vehicle.

"Hey, what the fuck's going on?" He looked up at the smiling man in sunglasses. "Who the hell're you?" he asked belligerently as he pulled himself to his feet.

The slim stranger shook his head sadly. "How quickly they forget. You don't remember old friends?"

The brawny man was mute, but something akin to fear began to gnaw at him. "Eddie?" he called questioningly across the tractor.

Again Adam shook his head, his smile growing more wolflike. "Right now old Eddie's in greater need of repair than this tractor." He slipped off his glasses and slid them casually into a jacket pocket, then unconsciously touched the scar over his brow with one hand.

The big man studied the stranger who stood in front of him, caressing the length of a black, polished cane. "Who the hell . . ." Then his eyes began to widen in recognition and the fear came roaring down on him like an avalanche.

Adam understood. "Hello, Census Taker." The stick flashed upwards, one end gripped in both his hands, as a Samurai swordsman grips his weapon. Adam stepped forward and the Census Taker crouched slightly, throwing up his hands so that his forearms could ward off a blow directed at his head. The defensive move was exactly what Adam intended. Suddenly, he snapped the heavy cane diagonally downward in a slashing stroke aimed at the outside of the brawny man's unprotected left knee. It connected with a crack. The big man screamed. When he attempted to step back on the fractured leg, he crumpled into a sitting position. Gripping the shattered knee in both hands, Bo rocked back and forth moaning, "Jesus Christ, you broke it. You broke my fucking knee!"

Without a word, Adam stepped to the side, raised the walnut stick like an ax, and brought it wooshing down across the Census Taker's collarbone. There was a muffled sound like a green twig splintering and the big man screamed again, rolling onto his side, thrashing helplessly for a few seconds. Then he curled into a tight ball and lay still.

Moreland watched with detachment and then walked around the John Deere to where the one called Eddie whimpered softly, still frozen on his hands and knees. Adam stood silently for a moment. Then, in a voice tinged with resignation he muttered, "Like you said one time, my man, let's get it done. It's payback time." The cane connected with one of the short man's arms just at the elbow. Eddie pitched forward on his face without making a sound.

As Adam walked back toward the waiting Mercedes the rage that had driven him subsided, making room for another emotion. *Guilt? Why should I feel guilty? Those sons-of-bitchs almost killed me! They got off easy!* But when he slipped into the seat next to Marti, his countenance was frozen into a scowl that was not caused by anger.

Marti's face was the color of bleached bone and her voice was a strangled whisper. "In the name of God, how could you do something so . . . so cold blooded?"

Adam composed himself and turned to face her. "Those were two of the three 'travel agents' who arranged my departure from the valley. I told you, I owed them."

He dropped the car into gear, tromped on the accelerator, and sent the powerful machine down the road in a spray of gravel. Only then did he glance again at the beautiful young woman by his side. "And a Moreland always pays his debts."

Chapter 21

"You could have called the police, given them the license plate, lodged a complaint—anything but beat them insensate," she choked out as he drove back toward Napa.

"Marti, they cost us four years of our lives—over three years of Heath's life," he argued implacably.

"There are more facets to you than a brilliant cut diamond, aren't there, Adam?" she said in a hushed whisper. "I've never seen the Moreland in you until now."

"I did what I had to," he replied defensively.

When he pulled up in front of La Boucane she turned and said tightly, "I can't eat, Adam, not after that."

"Suit yourself. I'll take you back to Meadowood for a drink," he answered with a smoothness he was far from feeling. A tight, hard knot was forming around his heart, scarcely allowing him to breathe. The sweet taste of revenge had gone sour. *They weren't worth it, the dumb bastards*, he thought furiously.

"Look, Marti, I'm sorry, babe. I . . . I lost my head."

"You didn't lose your head, Adam. You calculated a termination like a bloody CIA agent," she whispered. "The police—"

"The police could've hauled in your old man, too, if those goons spilled their guts about who hired them," he interrupted in a gravelly voice.

Marti shook her head in vehement denial. "No, you're mistaken! When you overheard them—or *thought* you overheard them, you were beaten half to death. You couldn't have been thinking straight."

He reached across and took her in his arms, stroking her hair, stilling her trembling. "Oh, Marti, babe, I'm sorry, so sorry. It was a dumb, dangerous thing to involve you in."

Marti held onto him as if he were a life raft. She was dry-eyed but pale and drawn when the tremors finally stopped wracking her body. One soft hand reached up and touched the old scar on his brow. How many other hidden scars did he carry inside? "I'm okay now, Adam. I just need some time to think . . . time alone. All right?"

He nodded tightly and turned on the ignition, pulling out into the street. She whispered, "Could you . . . could you at least call an ambulance or something?" He nodded grimly.

They drove back to Meadowood in silence, each in a turmoil of emotions they were afraid to share.

Give her time, Adam thought, but said nothing. He considered the leads he'd given to Lin over the phone that afternoon. He had enough to think about while Marti sorted out her feelings. He despised himself for the rashness of dragging her into his vendetta. At the same time every instinct told him she still loved him, no matter how shocked she must be. Yet he had hurt her, just as her father had, something he had sworn never again to do. And worse, if the cops questioned them, that pair might panic and implicate Joe. No matter how much he hated the old man, Joe Beaumont was Marti's father and Heath's grandfather. He had to bury the hatred and get on with their lives. As he pulled into the parking lot at Meadowood next to Marti's Cadillac, he looked over at her pale but composed face.

"You going to be all right driving home? Sure you don't want a drink to calm your nerves first?"

She looked at his handsome face, so calm and strong. What really went on behind those restless blue eyes? Did nothing ever make him lose control? "I'm okay, Adam. I don't need a drink. Just a good night's sleep."

She reached for the door handle, but before she

could open it he leaned across the seat and pulled her into his arms. Adam buried his face against the curve where her neck and shoulder met, smelling the faint wildflower scent of her hair and feeling its silky curls. Taking a deep breath, he murmured softly, "Let's just take it one day at a time. I'll call you in the morning. Okay?"

He seemed to be absorbing her very essence. His touch, his very nearness had always done that to her. Once more, this was the familiar Adam she loved. The brutal stranger was gone. Marti gave in to her instincts and raised his head with both hands framing his face. The fathomless eyes were filled with love. But what other mysteries did they hold? She kissed him softly, then pulled away. "Good night, Adam," she said quickly, daring to reveal no more.

He did not press her when she slid from the Mercedes and fished for the keys to her Caddie, but walked around to stand by the car. As she pulled away, he watched with arms casually crossed, leaning against his Mercedes like an elegant model on a GQ cover.

Looking in the rear view mirror, Marti remembered Riba's description of Adam four years ago: *From sweaty brazero to GQ model.* She began to shake again. She loved a man she did not know. Last night he was the tender lover from her past; this morning a laughing, spontaneous father with Heath. But he was also a "suit," as her father contemptuously referred to corporation men, and tonight he'd become a ruthlessly brutal street fighter.

"Who are you, Adam Wade . . . Moreland?" she asked herself fearfully as she turned off the Silverado Trail onto a deserted stretch of gravel road, a shortcut between the club and Chateau Beaumont. Deep in reverie about Adam, Heath and their relationship, Marti struggled to suppress her response to Adam's disturbing belief in her father's guilt.

She did not notice the car behind her for several minutes. A plain sedan of some neutral color, it was being driven with only fog lights, seeming to follow the twists and turns of the road by keeping in bare sight of her taillights.

Finally, when the car put on its beams and speeded up, closing the distance between them, Marti realized something was wrong. Only growers and other locals knew about this road. Somehow, the rapidly approaching sedan didn't strike her as being headed for a winery. She hit the gas and gravel flew up behind her, spraying the windshield of the other car. The Caddie was powerful and Marti had driven the cutoff dozens of times, but she still wished fervently for her Jeep instead of the luxury car as the sedan pulled alongside, trying to force her off the narrow road.

She tromped the accelerator again, turning the wheel sharply against the lighter car, and was rewarded by the sickening crunch of metal as she crushed the sedan's fender. Then a dull thunk was instantly followed by the shattering splinter of flying glass. They'd shot out her rear window!

Shaking her head to clear the shards of glass from her hair, Marti went into a curve by a stand of eucalyptus. She was driving far too fast for safety, but she knew her life depended on negotiating it. When she felt her left wheels bounce on the edge of the grassy, tree-rooted ground, she straightened the car just seconds before it hit one of the trees. That cost her speed and time. The sedan again pulled abreast of her and another shot hit the fender with a solid thud, followed by yet a third, aimed at her left front tire. She could feel the jarring explosion of air as the slashed rubber collapsed. The Caddie was riding on the rim, going wildly out of control. When the left rear tire blew, too, she knew it was only seconds until it would be all over.

Things were happening in a blur. Her big car lurched off the road into a block of grape vines, uprooting canes and popping trellis wires. The heavy Caddie spun out, whirling in a complete revolution to stop facing the road. Marti's hand poised on the door, as she prepared to jump clear and dash into the leafy embrace of the vines. Suddenly the sedan roared down the road and vanished into the night.

Another car appeared, stopping in a spray of gravel. The driver opened his door and ran toward her. Marti debated making a run for it, then decided the intruder was unlikely to be another assassin. She recognized the Mercedes at the same time she heard Adam's frantic voice calling her name.

In seconds he was at her side, pulling her from the broken glass and ripped metal of the Cadillac. Gently, but thoroughly he ran his hands over her, picking away the glass and examining her for cuts. "Are you hit?" His voice was low and tight, as economical as his movements.

Marti felt her arms and moved her legs experimentally. "No . . . no, I don't think so," she whispered, feeling the breathless fear capture her now that the crisis was past. She threw herself into Adam's arms and held onto him fiercely, absorbing his quiet strength through every pore in her body.

"How did you—"

"I decided to follow you home. You were so uptight after what happened tonight, I was worried about your driving." He smiled and held her face up for inspection as he dabbed at a small scratch on her cheek. "You're one hell of a driver, lady. Ever consider Indy or Daytona?"

"I'm just grateful your protective male instinct wasn't misplaced this time," she said, taking a deep, calming breath.

Adam could see she wasn't hysterical or seriously injured. "Cool Hand Lady," he said softly and stroked her cheek. Then he propelled her toward the Mercedes. "We need to call the cops and get you to a doctor. There's a phone in my car."

"Who was it, Adam? Why on earth would anyone want to shoot me, for God's sake!"

"Not any*one*—there were two of them in that sedan. I got a partial on the plates, but I couldn't see enough to identify either the driver or the shooter."

He helped her in the passenger side of the Mercedes

and reclined the seat so she could lie back. Then he walked around to his side and punched the operator on the car phone. It took only a moment to put a call through to the county sheriff. Leaning inside the car, he touched her hand and asked, "You okay for a moment?"

"Yes, but what . . ."

"I'll be right back," he said. Marti watched him stride back to her car, examine it for a minute, then open the back door and do something inside. He returned, pocketing a small article carefully wrapped in his handkerchief.

"What were you doing? What is that?" she asked, starting to sit up.

Gently, he pushed her back against the seat. "You've been pretty badly shaken up. Lucky you only have a few superficial cuts, but I'm still going to take you to Pete's place as soon as the Sheriff's car arrives."

"Don't try to change the subject, Adam. I'm fine now and getting madder by the minute at those . . . assassins! Now what did you do and what's in your pocket?"

He knelt alongside the open car door and took her hand. "There are at least three slugs in the car for the sheriff to dig out, Marti. I just removed the easiest one from the upholstery for my own comparison."

"Comparison to what?" she asked in dawning horror.

He sighed in resignation, not wanting to frighten her, but knowing he must have her cooperation for her own safety. "When I first moved to San Francisco someone took a shot at me. The cops there have a ballistic record that I want to match against this one."

She blanched and squeezed his hand. "Someone tried to kill you, too! Oh, Adam—"

"Heath, I know," he interrupted. "Marti, for better or worse, you and Heath are Morelands now and I'm afraid you may have inherited my enemies . . . or I made a new one for you," he added darkly.

"What do you mean?"

"Someone could be trying to get to me by hurting my family, or they could want to hurt you because they found out about us." He waited a beat as recognition dawned on her.

"Boris?" she asked incredulously. "I can't believe it. I know he has a terrible temper and he was jealous of you, but murder, Adam? No! He just isn't capable of hiring killers."

Adam bit back the urge to tell her that if her own father was capable, his winemaster sure as hell was! Instead, he quickly detailed the earlier attempts on his life at Chateau Beaumont. "Back then, Staritz could've hoped with me out of the way, you'd turn to him. When you left and supposedly married, he gave up. Then . . ."

"Then I came back a widow and he resumed his courtship," she supplied reluctantly.

"And *then* he found out who Heath's father was. Kind of puts a different complexion on things, doesn't it?" He paused while she digested that and then said, "There's another possibility, too. Booth."

"Your associate? The one who was your father's surrogate? Yes, I've heard Papa say he's shrewd and unethical, but you've worked with him . . ." Her voice trailed off as she recalled her scathing accusations about Moreland Enterprises and the sabotage.

Adam smiled grimly at her flushed cheeks. "Yes, Booth's been my leashed pit bull, turned loose when I could use him and reined in before he got out of hand."

"Only now you think he may be tired of having you rein him in?" she asked quietly. This part of Adam Moreland, the ruthless tycoon, frightened her almost as much as the gunmen. Perhaps more.

His face was bleak as he replied, "Worse than that, Booth may have learned about you and me and Heath and wants you out of the way so when he goes after me, no one's left to inherit."

"Oh, Adam, tell the police everything! Let them handle this. Quit being a vigilante." She leaned from the seat and embraced him.

He held her fast and stroked her hair, but then took her firmly by the shoulders and said, "I have a friend on the San Francisco force who can check this out faster if I take the bullet now. No vigilante stuff, just saving time. I don't want you to tell the sheriff anything about the attempts on my life. Stick to what happened here tonight and don't speculate about Staritz or Allard. All we'll do is drive whoever it is underground if the local law starts sniffing around. Okay?"

"You promise your city cop will handle it?"

"Promise," he said quietly as the sheriff's cruiser pulled up with lights flashing.

After a careful but mercifully brief interrogation, the deputy let them go, saying he'd be in touch for a follow up in a day or so after they'd had the Cadillac checked out for bullets, paint samples from the sedan and any other evidence they could uncover.

"You positive you don't want me to take you to Pete's place for an exam?" he asked as they drove down the dark gravel road. The winking red lights of the cruiser and yellow ones from the tow truck looked faintly surrealistic to Marti as she gazed dazedly at the bouncing reflections in the rear view mirror.

"I don't need a doctor, Adam. Just . . . just take me to your room and let me clean up first so I don't frighten anyone when I get home."

He turned north at the intersection and drove quickly back to Meadowood. Once in his suite, he filled the tub with hot water, and, as an afterthought, added some fragrant bath oil from the guest packet on the vanity. While he did that, Marti called Chateau Beaumont and told Hilda what had happened, assuring her she was fine and would be home later, and instructing the level-headed old cook not to tell Joe anything until she talked to him herself.

When he returned to the sitting room, Marti had hung up the phone and was stretched out with her stockinged feet on the coffee table.

"Your bath awaits, madame," he said with a flourish, pulling her from the sofa and handing her one of his silk robes.

"Thank you, you're a lifesaver in more ways than one," she said with a smile.

Adam listened to the sounds of her splashing as he called room service for a vintage bottle of Cabernet, two rare strip steaks, a Caesar salad and a loaf of crusty French bread. It was delivered just as she opened the bathroom door.

"Smells heavenly," she said, inhaling the fragrance of the beef as she watched him check the wine cork and then pour the ruby liquid into two crystal glasses.

Offering her one he said, "A brush with death always sharpens the appetite. Anyway, I owed you dinner."

"And a Moreland always pays his debts," she parroted with troubled eyes as she accepted the glass. His robe swallowed her slim figure and was belted tightly around her waist, holding the gaping folds together over her breasts.

When he stood in front of her and rolled up the voluminous sleeves, he could see she wore nothing under it. "Now I'm the one who needs the tub—for a cold shower," he murmured. He pulled up a chair for her at the small oval table in the sitting room.

Taking the proffered seat, she looked at the softly flickering candlelight and the single yellow rose in the bud vase. "You think of everything," she said quietly.

He lifted his glass and chimed it against hers in a toast. "To our health."

"To being alive," she added and took a fulsome swallow of the rich mellow wine.

They devoured the salad and beef while they discussed the incident on the road, the attempts on his life and the possible motives various suspects might have.

"Never did a steak taste so good," she said, wiping a fleck of bread crumb from her mouth with a snowy napkin.

"It's the adrenaline rush and aftermath. Works up one hell of an appetite every time," he said with a smile.

"More than one kind, I think," she replied softly,

rising from her chair and crossing the floor to stand in front of him.

Adam reached up and took her reed slim waist in his hands, then ran his fingers lightly over the thin silk to graze the flair of her hips, moving down her thighs. His hands pressed into her buttocks as he drew her closer to him. Marti held his head firmly against her breasts and ran her fingers through his straight, silky black hair.

"Adam, hold me, make love to me," she pleaded as his hands caressed her. Her own hands worked their way inside the open collar of his shirt and felt the hard, sleek muscles of his back and shoulders. He stood up and embraced her, unfastening the robe as she unfastened the buttons on his shirt.

On the way to the bed, they left a trail of his clothes. By the bedside he finally peeled the silk robe off her and let it whisper to the floor.

Hefting a breast in each hand, he played with the hardened nipples and whispered, "You are so perfectly beautiful." She moaned and thrust them against his hands, arching her back and grasping his head to bring it down to hers for a fierce kiss. He could feel the desperate, life-seeking hunger in her as she pulled him with her onto the bed where they rolled in a welter of entwined arms and legs, feverishly caressing.

Once, when Lin had come home after shooting an armed robbery suspect, she'd reacted with this desperate fervor. In the midst of death, making love was an affirmation of life, primitive . . . elemental . . . essential. Understanding Marti's need and feeling such gratitude that she was unharmed, he returned her passion with rough, reckless abandon.

Adam pulled her up onto her hands and knees as he stroked her breasts from behind her. He ran his hands around her ribs and down the curve of her hips, onto her rounded buttocks. When he pulled her toward him, she arched back and sheathed him as his large hands imprisoned her hips and thrust them against his pelvis in a swift penetrating stroke. Marti moaned and tossed her head in a frenzy of ecstasy as they mated in this most primal way, grinding back and forth in hard, long strokes.

She felt his hand glide around her hips and over her silky belly, then move lower to touch the swollen wet core of her passion. It took but a few deft circular strokes of his fingertips in sinc with his long thrusts to send her crashing over the brink into spasms of climax so intense her arms buckled. Her head fell against the pillows as she felt him swell and spill himself deeply inside her, collapsing over her back and rolling them to lie like two spoons, on their sides, panting in the soft welter of covers.

Slowly, he nipped and kissed her neck and shoulder as his arms held her fast. He murmured soft, indistinct love words against her tangled mane of damp hair. As her breathing returned to normal, Marti turned in his arms and buried her face against his chest.

"Hold me, just . . . hold me . . . forever," she whispered.

He smiled into her hair. "I'll never let you go, darling, never again." He paused a moment, then said very gravely, "Babe, you have to promise me you'll stay indoors at the house and keep Heath with you for the next few days."

She tensed in his arms. "Surely we'll be all right in broad daylight!"

"Like I was, coming back from Healdsburg, or flying Ansel's plane? No, you and Heath stick like glue to the house, please."

"What are you going to do?" she asked in a worry-tight voice.

"Take you home first, then head to San Francisco with the bullet I took out of your car. Before I met you last night, I ran into an old friend—Bob Vasquez."

Marti looked puzzled. "He graduated from San Francisco State over two years ago and took a job back east. What's he doing in Napa?"

"Family wedding." He went on to tell her about Bob's information regarding Ansel's benefactor.

"And you think the San Francisco police can find a

connection somewhere in all this tangle?" She shivered. "Adam, I don't like this. Let's go home to Heath."

He rubbed her back affectionately. "I've had a deputy at the house watching things since we left that shot up Caddie. You'll both be all right."

"It's you I'm worried about now."

Adam Moreland rode the elevator to his penthouse, deep in thought. He glanced at his wristwatch as he stepped out. Two a.m.

Lin should be asleep, but he'd have to awaken her. When he walked through the door, he knew she wasn't there. She wasn't just working late, although that was often the case. She had already moved out. With a wistful smile he picked up the note tacked to the leather ice bucket on the bar.

> *Dear Adam:*
> *We had three good years together and we're still friends. That's more than I can say for either of my husbands! Maybe I'm onto something—just live with a man, don't marry him! Next time I'll do my detective work and pick one who's not in love with another woman. Happiness to you and your lady.*
>
> *Lin*

He swore fondly and folded the note, inserting it in his jacket pocket as he reached for the phone.

The voice that answered, "San Francisco Police Department" sounded as beat as he felt. Sprawled across the sofa, he propped the phone under his chin and asked if Sergeant Drake was on duty.

In a moment Lin's calm husky voice came on the line. "Sergeant Drake. May I help you?"

"I thought you'd sworn off night desk," he said easily.

"Shit, Moreland, what can I do with my partner and two other detectives down with some Asiatic bug? Are you in town?"

"Yeah. Got your message. There was no rush moving out, you know."

"I know. It just seemed tidier to pack up and get it over with. Besides, I read about this swell vacancy near Telegraph Hill—in the obits."

He chuckled. "Okay. I understand, Lin. You hear anything about that shooter yet?"

"Luger, right? Yeah. Seems your informant was right on the money. He's been a Frisco boy for the last five or six years. Used to work for a few of the Big Valley growers, strictly on the QT. Never could pin anything on him down south."

"I wonder who he's working for now," Adam speculated aloud. "Got a present for your ballistics guy."

"Someone using you for skeet practice again? Damn," Lin swore.

"Not me. Marti," he said quietly.

Lin let out a few honest Anglo Saxon expletives and said, "Bring it down, right now. I'll pull the reports on the one they dug out of the garage wall four years ago."

They sat in Lin's "office," which consisted of a large, battered oak desk, out of the traffic pattern in the big squad room. She had appropriated an ancient Naugahyde sofa that sat across from the desk, against the wall. Over it her bulletin board was overflowing with everything from dog-earred FBI flyers to very obscene graffiti, some of it illustrated, all of it cheerfully contributed by male colleagues.

Adam lay draped over the sofa, poked by several springs but too tired to care. Lin sat behind her desk, one elbow slumped over a pile of computer report forms that were liberally stained with an assortment of delicatessen food. They both sipped what the desk officer swore was freshly brewed coffee.

"Fresh when they put Tut in his tomb," Lin had interjected with a wink. It was inkier than the bottom of a gallon jug of cheap mountain red.

"I think if they boiled the grave wrappings from Tut's tomb, the juice might taste better than this,"

Adam said with a grimace, setting the scummy mug on her desk.

Just then the phone rang and Lin picked it up. She made a few quick notes and thanked the technician. "Bingo," she said, hanging up the receiver. Adam leaned forward and Lin continued, "Your shooter and the guy taking potshots at that Caddie are using the same piece, a Model 59 Smith and Wesson, .9mm. Now, if I can just get a line on Luger. I've got a good snitch who's been asking around for me since you gave me the name yesterday. Point of interest—Luger's been known to pack a .9mm Smith and Wesson."

Adam looked at her. "Lin, if you get a call on him, I'm going with you."

She shook her head. "Against policy, doll."

"Your partner's got the flu. Deputize me. Isn't that what they used to do?"

"Only in B-movies," she shot back as she dialed a number from a grimy black book.

"You love B-movies, remember?" She ignored him.

While Lin checked with her street people, Adam put in a call to the Napa County Sheriff's office. It was five a.m., but the desk officer assured Adam they were watching the Beaumonts around the clock. He went back to Lin's desk and began to massage her shoulder blades as she slumped forward. "You're beat, Sergeant. How long since you had some sleep?"

"Less time than the longest time I've gone. I'm fine, Adam, really." She looked up into his concerned face. "Hey, lighten up. We'll break this case and your family will be fine."

"How about you?" he asked softly.

She gave him a cheeky grin. "Don't sweat it. I was always afraid of staining the furniture in your fancy digs, anyway!"

Chapter 22

The phone awakened Marti, but stopped on the second ring. Hilda or Max must have answered it, she thought sleepily, then rolled over and looked at the clock. It was eight a.m., normally a scandalously late hour for her to be in bed, if not for last night's harrowing events. Marti stared at the ceiling, unable to keep all the terrible things that had occurred yesterday from running through her head.

She could see Adam relentlessly beating those two men like a professional executioner, then calmly driving her away for dinner as if nothing was amiss. Uneasily, she recalled his defensive accusations about her father. Adam was so positive Joe had sent those men. But why? Her father didn't even know about her summer fling with Adam.

Remembering some of the men whom Joe Beaumont had hired when union organizers had come into the valley years ago, Marti was forced to admit her gentle Papa had been ruthless back then. But her relationship with Adam was a different matter. If Joe had found out, he would have summoned her and Adam before him. It wasn't as if his winery, his very livelihood were threatened by one lone drifter!

Of course that lone drifter had become a virtual stranger to Marti over the past four years. She loved Adam Wade, but she was not certain about Adam Moreland—at least she sometimes felt she wasn't certain. His hypnotic attraction still drew her and now she knew he had not deserted her. She believed he loved her and Heath and wanted a family. But the dark side of his personality that she had sensed Friday at Meadowood had been brutally revealed to her last night. "And still I went back to his room and seduced him," she whispered aloud with a rueful sob. She sat up on the edge of the bed and rubbed her aching temples.

Just then a soft knock sounded. Max's unperturbable voice carried through the door, martyred, but punctilious. "Miss Marti, it's your sister. I explained you were asleep but she was most . . . insistent." That roles should be so reversed as to have Marti asleep at eight a.m., and Riba awake, obviously had not escaped his notice.

"I'll take it, Max. Thank you—oh, Max, I *was* awake, just not stirring yet," some imp made her call through the door.

As she reached for the phone, Marti, too, wondered about Riba's uncharacteristic call.

"Oh, Marti," Riba's voice broke into wracking sobs on the other end of the line.

"Calm down, Riba." Marti interrupted the crying jag, eerily reminded of the last time Riba had carried on like this. She had been fourteen and pregnant. A premonition of disaster washed over Marti as she asked, "Where are you? What's wrong?"

"Oliver . . . Oliver's left me. I'm at my house on Lake Tahoe," came the muffled reply.

"It would seem to me if you're in Nevada, you left him," Marti reasoned drily.

"No, no, you don't understand. I'm . . . pregnant again and he wants me to have another abortion, Marti. He doesn't want children. Oh, Marti, after I saw you and Heath, I can't . . . I just can't!"

Marti's hand whitened on the receiver as a sudden rush of bile choked her. *That coke-snorting bastard!* "Riba, you haven't told Papa this have you?" *Please God, no!*

"No, I know how upset he was with Oliver and me about the other abortion . . ."

"Good," she said with a sigh of relief. "His blood pressure can't take much more. You stay at your place. I'll fly up this morning and we can talk this out."

"Marti? Could you bring Heath with you? I . . . I'd like to see him," Riba said awkwardly.

"I suppose I could pry him away from his Grandpa for a few days," Marti replied with the first real smile she'd felt in years for her sister.

As she dressed for breakfast, Marti mulled over her plans. In spite of the undeniable physical passion they shared, she and Adam Moreland were still strangers. Someone had tried to kill her because of Adam's past. Even Heath might be in jeopardy. The best thing to do was get away for a few days. She must take Heath with her for his own protection. She would gain some breathing space, time to think things out before Adam made any more marriage plans.

Her promise for a wedding next week seemed rash in the hard light of day; even rasher had been the wantonly abandoned way she had seduced him last night! Marti admitted unblushingly to herself that she had been the aggressor that time, terrified by her brush with death, wanting oblivion. Adam Moreland offered all-to-easy a recipe for oblivion.

"A couple of days with Riba will give me a chance to think, Papa," she explained to Joe across the breakfast table on the sunlit patio. "She's lonely and upset over her fight with Oliver."

Joe snorted and slammed down his cup. "She'd be damn well rid of that Hollywood coconut."

"I tend to agree, but it's her decision. I'll only give a little moral support." She hesitated as Joe's shrewd gray eyes watched her.

"What about you and Moreland?" he said finally.

"What about us, Papa?" She shrugged in pained perplexity.

"Heath talks about nothing but his newly discovered father. I don't want my grandson hurt, Marti. You going to marry him?"

"I . . . I don't know. He wants to—next week in fact, but . . . there are some things I need to sort out first. I'm still not sure I can trust him," she finished lamely, unable to explain her ambivalence over the violent side of his nature. She could not tell Joe about that! Nor about the attempt on her life last night.

"Are you still in love with him, Martha?" He held his breath as she fidgeted with her coffee spoon.

"Yes. Oh, God, yes," she blurted out suddenly, surprising herself. "I've never stopped loving him . . . only . . ."

Joe sighed and braced himself. "Marti, girl, there's something I have to tell you, should've told you the day I found out Heath was his son."

Marti's heart skipped a beat. Suddenly she wanted to be anywhere else, hear anything else, but what she knew Joe Beaumont was going to tell her.

"Marti, Adam Wade, the drifter, didn't just walk out on you."

Marti stood up, unable to bear anymore. "Oh, Papa, he tried to tell me, but I refused to believe him! You hired those horrible men to beat him and put him on that fright, didn't you?"

Joe looked at her, his face gray and drawn. But he was relieved to have it out in the open at last. "Yes, Marti, I hired them," he confessed raggedly.

"Adam almost died! He spent three months in a hospital. He still has permanent injuries and scars," she accused, tears choking her voice. "You're all alike—you and Jake Moreland, Boris, Adam—all of you macho bastards. You think a balled-up fist or a fistful of dollars will solve any problems!" She whirled away from the table and ran toward the house.

"Marti, wait! Where are you going?" Joe called after her.

"To Tahoe! I really do need time to think. Just let me alone for a while, Papa. You *and* Adam!" With that she vanished indoors.

"I'm sorry, honey, so damn sorry," Joe whispered brokenly, sinking into the wicker patio chair, staring out at the vineyards spread across the shimmering valley floor like rows of green lace ribbon. For the first time in memory they didn't matter to him. Not a damn.

* * *

As Adam drove from the city toward Napa, he digested the information he and Lin had unearthed since last night. Damn little, really, except that the illusive Mr. Luger was known to pack a Model 59 Smith and Wesson and that the .9mm slug Lin dug from his garage wall four years ago matched the one he'd dug from Marti's car last night. His well-honed survival instincts all whispered to him that both slugs had been fired by Riefe Luger. But Lin's street people had come up dry. Luger had vanished like north coast fog on a sunny morning.

Figuring that there was every chance Luger and his driver might still be cruising the highways of the valley, Adam decided he'd best head back to Marti and Heath and let Lin handle the cop thing. She was good at details, he realized with a smile. Yes, a damn first-rate police officer.

His thoughts drifted from Lin to Marti and Heath. "His family." It had a nice sound, yeah, a real nice sound. He speeded up, feeling the exhaustion that had plagued him for the past twelve hours dissipate.

By the time he arrived at Chateau Beaumont it was nearly noon, an overcast gray day. He scanned the drive, searching for the sheriff's car. Maybe they were using an unmarked one so as not to frighten dear old Joe. He swore. The problem with her father would have to be solved as surely as the attempted murders—if he could keep from killing Joe Beaumont himself, he thought grimly.

The last person he wanted to see that dreary morning was the old man, but there he was, with Les Reams, standing on the front porch. For a man supposedly at death's door, to hear Marti talk, he looked tough as a squirrel to Adam. Both men turned to watch him stride up the steps, noting, he was sure, his rumpled clothes and unshaven face. Well, dammit, five o'clock shadows were in now, so they could jam it.

Les nodded with embarrassment at the man he'd known as Wade and now knew was Heath's father.

Quickly, he excused himself to let Joe and Adam talk in private.

Deciding it was as good a time as any to get a few things settled, Adam asked, "Did Marti tell you what happened last night?"

At Joe's blank look, Adam swore.

"What are you talking about, Moreland?"

"I might have known she'd still try to protect you. Someone took a potshot at her on a back country road. Her Caddie's been impounded by the Napa County Sheriff's office." He watched Joe's face turn gray as the rain-laden skies overhead.

"I don't suppose you know who? Was she with you when it happened?" Joe accused.

"Luckily for her I was following her home. The gunmen took off. The sheriff sent a car out here to watch the house. Have you seen it?"

"What's going on, Moreland? This has something to do with you and your power plays, doesn't it?"

Adam shook his head tiredly. "Hell, Joe, I don't know. Maybe. Probably. But it could be something more personal, too," he added obliquely, thinking of Joe's volatile winemaster.

"You say a sheriff's car was supposed to be watching here. That mean you think those men might try again?"

"Yeah, they just might." Adam was getting tired and surly. "Let me talk to Marti and I'll explain," he said, starting for the front door.

"Marti left about a half hour ago, with Heath."

"She what! Talk man! Jesus Christ, where did they go?"

Joe shook his head. "Riba called early this morning. Wanted Marti and Heath to come up to her lake place for a visit."

"She left here to drive across state, alone with my son!" Adam ground out in horror.

"No. They were flying out of Oakland. I didn't know about the sheriff's car, Moreland. Max helped her load her bags." Already rushing past the shaken old man, Adam called for the butler and was gratified when he appeared immediately inside the door.

Marti had apparently talked the deputy into driving her and Heath to Oakland Airport. A quick call to the sheriff's office confirmed this. Adam hung up the phone in disgust.

"She's on her way to Tahoe, dammit. Why the hell did she leave after I told her to stay put?"

"I guess she wanted to get away from both of us," Joe said softly. When Adam looked up, Max had unobtrusively vanished down the hall, and Joe stood, looking somber and chastened. "I told her the truth, Adam," he said simply.

Immediately Adam knew what the old man meant. Great timing! *First I beat two men stupid in front of her, then her father tells her he hired those same two goons to put me in the hospital! No wonder she grabbed Heath and bolted.* "Give me Riba's address. I'm going after them."

Bob Vasquez had mentioned flying into the Napa Airport from Las Vegas on one of his company's private planes. If that plane was still there and he could use it, Vasquez could name his salary with Moreland Enterprises!

A couple of quick calls settled the transportation issue, if not Vasquez's salary. On the way to pick up the plane Adam imagined how much Heath would enjoy the ride back with his "for real daddy" flying him. Somehow he figured Marti might not be so pleased.

The subject of his musing sat in the Oakland Airport, stepped in misery, trying her best to hide it from the babbling, delighted child by her side. To add to her mountain of frustrations, a sudden summer rain squall had delayed all flights, even her brief hop to Nevada. The deputy who had driven them to the airport hovered nearby like a pudgy sentinel, trying to remain inconspicuous yet watchful until his charges were safely tucked on the plane.

Marti had a throbbing headache and Heath's incessant questions about how soon he'd see his father again were making it worse. Finally, she grabbed the boy by one wrist and thrust him at Deputy Sims.

"Heath, Mr. Sims is going to tell you all about being a policeman while I check on our flight." She looked up at the plump, balding man with a plea in her eyes.

"Got four kids myself, Mrs. Martin. Sure thing." He knelt down and began to spin the boy a tall tale about bank robbers while Marti rushed off to the ladies room for a wet, cool towel to soothe her aching head.

The perfidy of her father had shaken her to the core. When she forced herself to examine the facts, they all fit. He must have found out about her and her worthless drifter having an affair. Exercising the boundless omniscience of the male species, he simply decided to eliminate an unworthy suitor.

"Just like Adam, damn him! The two men I love most in the world betrayed me," she whispered brokenly. Why couldn't she have loved a gentle, honest soul like Graham Kley? He'd given her peace, let her be herself, and never made demands on her.

She shook her head and reapplied the compress. Then, seeing a stewardess who had just entered the ladies room look at her as if she were about to be airsick, Marti straightened up from the basin, patted her face dry and departed without a backward glance.

Before she returned from Riba's place, she knew she had to make a decision about Adam and Joe, if not for herself, then certainly for Heath's sake.

Adam pulled up in front of Riba's lake front house. Some layout, he thought to himself, vaguely remembering the Philadelphia lawyer who financed it, the poor slob. He paid the cabbie and walked briskly toward the low cedar and glass structure.

When he received no response to his knocking, Adam headed around the side of the house toward the back patio. Despite the hellaceous weather he'd flown through to get here, the Nevada skies were azure and cloudless. Funny she wouldn't have at least a few servants underfoot, he thought idly as he unlatched the high cedar gate.

As expected, Riba lay on a chaise lounge sunning herself by the pool. Her body glistened with oil. "You look like an overly groomed Siamese cat," he said, latching the gate behind him.

Riba rolled over and sat up with an audible gasp, taking in his beard, rumpled clothes and harsh, exhausted face. "And you, darling, look like a pit bull who just tangled with a crocodile . . . and lost," she replied.

He shrugged. "So, I'm not Paul Hogan. Where are Marti and Heath?"

Riba's cold green eyes glowed as her mouth widened into a smile. "She called from Oakland. Her flight's been delayed. Something about a storm. She won't be here for over an hour," she said with a sudden surge of forbidden delight.

Adam swore, then looked at the blonde unfolding herself from the chaise with feline grace. She looked better than last time he'd seen her. Less make-up and more sun. "You scarcely appear to be grief-stricken, Riba. Recovered from your producer's desertion even before your sister arrives to hold your hand?" A prickle of unease ran along the base of his spine.

"I just wanted to mend some fences. With Ollie gone, it seemed like a good time," she replied carelessly. "You look like you haven't slept in a week," she purred.

He ran his fingers through his hair and along his bearded cheek. "Seems like it. I came to take Marti and Heath back to Napa."

"So I gathered. But they won't land until two. You might as well get . . . comfortable."

"You never give up, do you?" he muttered incredulously. "I'll be at the airport."

"No, wait," she replied too quickly as she clutched his arm. "You might as well wait here. I promise to behave. Take a hot shower and shave. You could sure use it," she added, wrinkling her nose in distaste.

He threw back his head and laughed. "Shit! Why

the hell not? The way I look I'll scare my son to death."

Riba's eyes narrowed. "Then the gossip *was* true. You are his father. And to think my poor sister went to such lengths to cover up all these years."

Adam's face hardened into grim lines. "If you hadn't given Joe the performance of your life, your sister could have been spared that. Ollie missed a bet. He should've put you in his films, not his bed. You would've made a million."

Riba shrugged. "There's a bathroom off the first floor bedroom. Help yourself to the razor and towels." She turned and dove into the pool in a clean slice. After Adam disappeared inside, she swam slowly to the pool's edge and climbed out, then walked back to the chaise and picked up the portable phone.

Adam felt almost human after a hot shower and a shave with a disposable razor. There was even a cellophane packaged toothbrush. She must have more male visitors than the YMCA," he thought with a grin as he wrapped a towel around his hips and considered what to do about his rain-soaked, slept-in shirt and pants. He picked them up and took a whiff. Essence of squad room, one part day old coffee, one part wino and two parts stale cigarette smoke. No wonder Riba made a fuss. The Wife of Bath would be repelled!

On impulse he opened a closet. It was overflowing with silk dresses and slinky peignoirs. Obviously this bedroom was hers. He wondered if dear old Ollie had left any clothes around and if so, what size he might be. He strolled into the next room and opened the closet. Luck. A row of brightly colored sport shirts materialized like a psychedelic dream. He checked sizes. Ollie was a 16, but in a short sleeved shirt with the collar open it would serve. He chose the least offensive of the shirts and quickly decided there was no chance Ollie's slacks would work, unless he wanted a very baggy fit.

He padded silently over the hot pink shag into Riba's room with his prize and started to slip the towel off. Then he saw her standing in her string bikini, dripping silently on the rug.

"Don't let me stop you," Riba cooed, gliding over to take the shirt from his hand and toss it over his pants laying on the chair. One long, lacquered nail traced the arrow descent of black hair down his chest to his navel. She tugged at the towel, but he held onto it tenaciously.

He shook his head in disbelief. "Was there ever anything you wanted that you didn't get? Until now, that is." He walked past her and dropped the towel unabashedly as he slid his slacks on and belted them. "You will forgive me for borrowing one of Ollie's shirts? After all, we're almost family . . . if only briefly. I enter, he exits," he said conversationally as he slid the shirt on and buttoned it.

"You fucking bastard! Just wait until . . ."

He looked up, eyes narrowed. "Wait until what, Riba? Marti and Heath are arriving at the airport at two, aren't they?"

"Yes, yes, of course," she replied quickly, controlling her anger.

"Then that's where I'll meet them. Thanks for your hospitality, future sister-in-law," he said with a jaunty smile as he began to walk past her. "Oh," he picked up his soiled shirt from the chair and tossed it at her, "you might launder this and keep it. Always pays to have a better range of sizes for your visitors."

"You should've died in that freight car, damn you!" she hissed venomously, throwing the shirt back at him.

"But, alas for us both, he didn't," a cold masculine voice replied from the door. "I suspected the method you'd employ to keep him here . . . and that you'd fail, my pet." Booth Allard stood in the doorway, shaking his head reprovingly.

Adam didn't ask what Booth was doing in Tahoe. He was already figuring the answers and he didn't like them. Two men stood in the hall with drawn guns as Allard walked into the bedroom. One was a skinny, squint-eyed man who looked as if he belonged on Sunset Boulevard selling obscene postcards—or ten-year-old kids. Next to him stood a large, beefy gunsel with chewed up ears. The man had a wicked-looking grin and an even more wicked looking Smith and Wesson, Model 59. Moreland knew he was Riefe Luger.

"Shall we all go into the den and make ourselves comfortable while we wait for our other guests?" Booth invited.

Adam measured his chances with a few quick sweeps of the room. Riba was the closest to him, but as if reading his mind, Allard pulled her away, leaving Adam directly in Luger's line of fire.

"It would be stupid to try heroics, Adam," Booth said softly, "and whatever your excesses of youth, for the past four years you have *not* been stupid."

"Oh, I don't know. I kept you on the payroll," Adam replied darkly.

"That you did, even had me watched after that unfortunate mishap in the parking garage." Allard looked at Moreland's flicker of surprise. "Yes, I suspected your mistrust as well as dislike. Only your paranoia's kept you alive until now."

"Don't be stupid, yourself, Booth. If you want Moreland Enterprises, have your goons finish me now and be done with it."

"But darling Adam, we've already worked out a whole plan and we need my sister and your little bastard for that," Riba said with cloying venom.

Adam looked at her as if she was a particularly repellent species of cockroach, with about as many brains. "Don't be a fool, Riba. He's using you."

"Oh, he's using me, all right," Riba replied with a silky laugh, rubbing Allard's cheek and draping her bikini clad body around his immaculately attired figure. "Booth and I will be married after my divorce. Of course, poor bereft Papa, with no grandson and no Marti to run the winery, will be so grief stricken, he'll sell to Booth and do whatever I say with the money."

"You stupid . . ." He choked with rage and frustration. "Chateau Beaumont is petty cash to Booth Allard! He's using you to get rid of me so he can control

Moreland Enterprises!" Adam fought down the urge to rush the lethal guns.

"You know quite well, dear nephew," Booth watched Adam bristle at the old reminder, "that killing you and leaving your heirs alive would avail me nothing." Booth motioned curtly for Adam to walk out the door. The two gunmen escorted him into the sunken den. Allard crossed to the well-stocked bar and poured a drink for Riba and one for himself. He continued conversationally, "I'm afraid Riba and I have common cause, even if she is a sluttish cunt who still wants to lay you before she has me dispose of you."

Riba clenched her drink in white-knuckled fury, obviously fighting to control her urge to fling it in Allard's cold, sneering face. Looking from Riba to Booth, Adam said stiffly, "I always was reminded of the resemblance between Riba and Jolie, Booth."

Allard's ice-blue eyes glowed like frozen flames as he reacted to the younger man's insolent manner. "What is it about you, Moreland? Jolie married old Jake for his money, to give me an entre into the business, but after that I gave her everything! Everything! I slaved for her, pampered her." His voice cracked as he whispered in anguish. "I *loved* her!"

I know some things about her you couldn't even imagine. Jake's words flashed through Adam's mind. He felt a sudden twist in his guts, followed by building nausea. "You fucked her, too, didn't you, Booth? Such a devoted brother!" He turned to Riba, who stood speechless. "Did you know you were just a convenient stand-in? Any greedy, green-eyed blonde would do. You just happened to tie in with me and Marti. He's using you to get Moreland Enterprises, Riba. Once he's got my business and your winery, do you really think he'll keep you alive, knowing all you know?"

Riba turned to Booth with a numb look on her face. Before she could voice her question, the front door opened and Marti's voice carried down the hall. "Riba, we're here. They let us take off early. The storm was—" She stopped and scooped Heath into her arms protectively.

Adam stood in the far corner of the den with a big bull of a man holding a gun next to his head. Another smaller, evil-looking punk, also armed, was standing across from him while her sister faced a tall blond man in a custom tailored business suit.

Turning the sleepy child's head so he couldn't see the guns and become frightened, she said, "Riba, who are these men? How did Adam—"

"Your darling Adam is the reason they're here, sweet sister." Riba's voice was calm now, her fright over Adam's insinuations forgotten as she focused on the woman she'd hated for so long.

"I don't understand." Marti looked at Adam and clutched Heath tighter.

"You're the Phi Beta Kappa! You figure it out. The brilliant one, always little miss prissy. A real lady. Sooo polite, sooo hard working. 'Be like your sister, Rebecca,' " she parroted in a sing-song voice as she advanced on her stricken sister.

"But I helped you, I covered up for you—I even took you to that abortionist and lied to Papa so he'd never find out what you'd done," Marti blurted out in bewilderment.

"You'll never know what it cost me to come crawling to you . . . to have you see me all bloody and begging in that car, a scared kid at the mercy of her omniscient, perfect Big Sis!"

Marti's eyes flashed in fury at the injustice of the insane accusation. "Papa loved you! He lavished everything on you! You were the one who was blonde and beautiful like Mother!"

"Yes, our dear dead mother. I don't even remember her, you know. All I ever heard was that I looked like her. Do you have any idea how often I had that thrown up to me? 'Be beautiful, Rebecca. Smile! Dance! Curtsy!' I was a stupid marionette, a doll. Papa always favored you—he talked to you about his business, about serious things. He sent me off, with servants to buy me things. He spent his *time* with you . . . you, the smart one. Well, you're not so smart now!"

Marti blanched and backed away from Riba's schizoid onslaught. Heath had started to cry and she crooned to him as childhood memories flashed through her mind. She recalled Joe's words to her when he found out about Adam and Heath last week. He'd said he wanted her to have the winery, that she loved it like he did. Despite all his lavish gifts and indulgences to Riba, had he favored *her*?

"What are you going to do?" Marti asked Booth levelly, fighting down panic. The eerily mad light in her sister's eyes left her bereft of hope.

Allard smiled and it made his cold face as handsome as a German movie star's. "Allow me to introduce myself. I am your lover's . . . er . . . step uncle, Booth Allard."

Marti's heart sank. Allard, the ruthless associate Adam had never trusted, whose sister he had been involved with. "You sent those men to kill me last night," she said faintly.

He shrugged. "A regrettably foolish gesture, picking you off one at a time. Especially considering what bad shots my employees can be," he said with a scathing glance at Luger. "Your dear sister here gave me a far better idea when they reported their failure last night."

"Lure us all to Nevada and arrange a little accident?" Adam supplied, edging slowly nearer Riba.

Booth shook his head, divining Adam's desperate gambit. "Don't be rash, Moreland. Take your boy from his mother. She's going to run a little errand for us." The small man, Leo Scali, nudged Adam in the ribs and then guided him across the room toward Marti.

As they exchanged the bewildered, frightened child, his parents touched hands. "Don't worry, babe. Do what he says. Okay?"

"Very smart, Adam. I said you weren't a stupid man." Allard turned to Marti as Leo directed Adam and Heath across the room and motioned them to sit on the sofa. "You, my dear, are going to the nearest car rental agency." He produced a business card from his pocket and handed it to Marti. "Mr. Luger here will drive you there and watch you pick up the car. Do not indicate any distress to the rental agent or ask him to call the police. I can assure you Mr. Luger will be observing you through the glass window of their office. You won't like what he does if you fail to follow orders." His eyes traveled to where Adam held Heath, comforting the boy.

Marti nodded woodenly. "I wouldn't dream of it, Mr. Allard."

"Let's hit it, lady," the big man said with a grunt.

As they walked down the hall, Adam's mind flashed frantically through one scenario after another, rejecting each in turn. Having to hold a frightened child completely thwarted any move he might try. Not even when Joe's three thugs had closed in on him at the cabin had he felt the paralyzing sense of dread he did now as his son clung to him in complete trust.

Chapter 23

Boris Staritz was not having a good day. Early that morning Les Reams reported to him that the last spray Ansel McGee had applied to the Zinfandel block had been mixed improperly. The vines were clogged and suffocating. Ansel swore he was not at fault and had checked the equipment before taking off. Les backed him up. Someone had begun tampering again. Their saboteur was back!

Mid morning, after checking on the damage, Boris headed to the house to confer with Marti, only to see her and Moreland's boy driving away with a stranger. The suitcase she carried indicated she was taking a trip. Of course, she had told him nothing of her plans. "Perfect timing," he muttered under his breath as he looked at the threatening skies. It was too late in the season for a rain squall.

Boris also needed to talk to Marti about the new yeast strains they had developed, and a thousand other details. But she was too busy reigniting her tawdry affair with Moreland. Why not just give him Chateau Beaumont and have done with it?

For now, Boris decided against discussing the sabotage with Joe. If he could only catch the saboteur red-handed and link him to Moreland, that would write *finis* to Marti's lover for good! "The best thing I could do would be to apply for a bank loan to develop my Mendocino property and forget the goddamn Beaumonts," he swore savagely as he headed towards his car. But there was still a chance that the off-again, on-again romance between Marti and Moreland would turn sour once more. Lord knew the man stood for everything her father despised, which should carry some weight with her.

The winemaster was not adverse to accepting Moreland's latest offer for Chateau Beaumont. But if Joe would sell—a big if—he would still have to interest the old man and Marti in investing in the Mendocino property. *If she would marry me, it would work out,* Boris thought. But that likelihood seemed exceedingly remote now. He cursed the fickle nature of women in general and Beaumont women in particular.

By late afternoon Startitz felt like getting good and drunk. He was dog-tired as he shifted his vintage MG into reverse and headed down the lane toward his house.

The unseasonable rain that afternoon had left the fields a quagmire. At least the rain had washed away some of the damage from the improper spraying, he mused wryly. "Moreland, you and your agro cartel haven't won yet."

Boris drove slowly over the bumpy back road, taking in the peaceful summer scenery. The sudden storm was over and the twilight sky promised more warm, clear weather tomorrow. Taking a deep breath of the fecund air, the winemaster settled back, enjoying the fall of evening. He was ultimately a man of habit, of earthy tastes and pleasures, bound to the cycles of the soil, to the living thing symbolized by the wine he made. He dreamed of his own place on the Mendocino coast and how good life would be one day.

On impulse, Boris decided to stop and check a new field of bud grafts that had been set out that spring. He drove up the steep winding hillside behind the big house. Random images of his trysts with Riba on the back road flashed through his mind, but he quickly pushed them aside. "Bitch. At least I'm well rid of her. Even Joe's finally got her number," he muttered as the MG coasted to a stop.

The light was fading as he walked between the row of vines, stooping now and then to check on a graft that had not taken, marking them with the bright yellow plastic strips all the field workers used for this purpose. This block was one of his first experiments in rapid transition to whites, and he wanted everything to go perfectly.

A sudden flash of light caught Boris's eye as he knelt in the field. He looked across the steep falling slope of the land and saw it glimmer again down on the valley floor, near the furthest outlying tractor shed. A small hiss of breath caught between his lips. He froze, then broke into a malicious grin.

Could he be this lucky? Boris ran back to the car and took the .44 magnum from the glove compartment. He'd been carrying the gun since the first sabotage had occurred early in the spring. He checked the cylinder and stuck it in his belt, then walked quickly toward the shed, taking an oblique route.

A large mechanized harvester, one of their newest acquisitions, was housed in that shed. The rail-shaker had been a damnably expensive purchase made over Joe's protests. This fall would be the first real test of his and Marti's plans using automated harvesting machinery to do a field crush. She and Boris had a great deal riding on convincing Joe and Les of the superior results gained from the pricey equipment.

Staritz approached the shed stealthily. The lock on the door was not forced, but the door stood slightly ajar. He pulled the gun from his belt when he heard soft rustling sounds inside.

Peering into the gloom, Staritz gave his eyes a moment to adjust. A Coleman lantern glowed dully in one corner of the shed next to a slight figure bent in concentration over the harvester engine.

"Wouldn't happen to have a can of spray paint in your hip pocket again, would you, Nate?" Boris said in a sibilant whisper.

The small mechanic whirled, then paled at the huge gun in the Russian's hand. "Mr.—Mr. Staritz . . . what are you—"

"A better question, Benteen, is what are *you* doing here? But we already know the answer to that, don't we," Boris said in a menacing voice.

Nate Benteen looked like a cornered weasel as he

backed away from the stocky bulk of the big winemaster. "I was only hired to do a job," he began on a whine. Then seeing the flash of fire in those fierce black eyes, his mouth tightened in a grim line and he raised the wrench in his right hand, making a desperate swing at Staritz's gun. He connected and the weapon went flying. But Boris's big hand caught Benteen's thin, wiry wrist, forcing him to drop the wrench. He picked the little man up and shook him like a terrier worrying a rat, then threw him back against the sharp metal edge of the conveyor. The machine rumbled in protest and Benteen let out a whooshing sound as the air was forced from his lungs.

"Now, Benteen, you and I are going to have a little talk about who hired you and how you got in here without breaking the lock," Boris said smoothly, relishing the pasty-faced terror of the saboteur. *Now I have you, Moreland, you son-of-a-bitch!*

Boris was certain Adam could've taken a key from Marti's purse on any number of occasions. He slammed Benteen against the machinery again, harder. "Talk. First, the key. How'd you get in here?"

A look of half-relief, half-disgust crossed the crafty face. "No key. I'm a mechanic, a locksmith. I can pick any lock you wanna put in my way."

"I'll remember that," Boris replied grimly, with a trace of disappointment. "Who hired you?"

"I dunno the big honcho. A guy from Frisco named Luger's been paying me," he gasped out quickly, just before Boris's fist sunk deeply into his midsection.

Benteen doubled up, but the Russian yanked him upright and repeated the question. "You've been working for someone since you left Chateau Beaumont—or maybe you were working for them even when you hired on," he considered abruptly. "How long have you been spying on us?"

Benteen coughed and wheezed out, "Luger hired me to go to work for you four years ago as a mechanic."

Staritz's eyes gleamed with an unholy light now. "So, you've been in their hip pocket from day one.

Those fancy references you brought me were from an agro cartel in the Big Valley, as I recall. Who, Benteen? Who? "He punctuated the requests with whumping shakes and slams of Benteen's body.

"It was Moreland Enterprises," Benteen finally gasped out.

Boris grinned wolfishly. "I figured as much. That's what that son-of-a-bitch Adam Moreland was doing here, masquerading as a field laborer named Wade. You ever take orders from him back then?"

Benteen's eyes clouded over in fright and confusion. He didn't know what answer to give now. "Wade? You mean that fellow who crashed in the pickup? The young pilot?"

"That one," Boris answered.

"But . . . he isn't Moreland—at least, he's not the one who hired me."

"What do you mean?" Boris tightened his grip on Benteen's frayed, greasy collar until the threads loosened and the mechanic's face grew red.

"Luger had me try to kill him! I rigged the brakes on the truck and doctored the Steerman's tail assembly with turpentine before he flew it."

Boris suddenly loosened his hold. "You saying you were hired to kill Adam Moreland?" he asked with obvious disbelief written on his face.

"I didn't know who the hell he was! Luger just told me he was a drifter named Wade," Nate choked out.

Boris released Benteen for a moment and considered out loud, "If Moreland Enterprises hired you and sent you to kill Adam Moreland . . . Who else besides this Luger have you met? Anyone else from San Francisco?"

Benteen's eyes narrowed. "Once, a couple of months ago when Luger paid me for the tractor job . . ." He hesitated as Staritz's face darkened, then went on quickly with his story, "I met Luger in the city outside the Embarcadero Center, on Drumm Street. I was sorta curious about who was bankrolling the operation, you know. Anyways, I watched him walk back to this big limo and talk to a man inside."

"Go on," Staritz said levelly.

"Well, the car took off and left Luger standing there but it only went about a half block, over to the center tower. I cut across through the mall and saw this big blond guy get out in front of one of the office buildings—the one where Moreland Enterprises has its headquarters. That's why I figured he was Moreland."

"Blond you say? Describe him some more." Nate Benteen sketched a perfect description of Booth Allard. Boris had met him only once, last spring when Allard had made the initial insulting offer for Chateau Beaumont. But the winemaster would never forget those glacial Nordic features.

"So, it seems our friends in Moreland Enterprises are at one another's throats and we're caught in the squeeze play." Dragging the battered little man with him, Boris scooped up his gun and headed toward the big house.

Since Marti and Heath were gone, Joe was having a simple meal at the kitchen table. When Staritz burst into the room with Benteen in tow, Hilda Lee was standing at the sink and Joe was caught with his fork poised in midair.

He dropped the fork with a clatter as Perkins appeared behind the winemaster, wringing his hands. "I tried to find out what's going on, Mr. Beaumont," the butler began.

"What's going on is that I've caught one of our saboteur's here. This little weasel," Boris shook Benteen, "was about to do a number on the new harvester."

Hilda eyed the gun in Staritz's hand and backed off with a startled gasp.

"Isn't this the mechanic—what's your name . . . Benteen?" Joe asked, as he scooted his chair back and sized up the small nervous man who was obviously the worse for his encounter with one irate winemaster.

"Yeah, he was our mechanic, but someone else was paying him even then. Call the sheriff, Hilda," Boris said as an aside to the shaken cook, who gladly quit the room to do his bidding.

Joe's face was pale and he could feel a faint sweat breaking out on his forehead. Things were happening too fast for him. "The sheriff was here last night, too. Of course, no one saw fit to tell me then," he added sourly.

Boris looked up. "The sheriff was here? Why?"

"Someone took a shot at Martha on her way home," Joe replied distractedly, turning his attention back to the trembling mechanic. His flint gray eyes hardened like the old Joe Beaumont Boris remembered from years past, as he asked, "Who hired you, Benteen?"

"Some big honcho who works for Moreland Enterprises," Benteen replied in a surly voice.

"Booth Allard—and get this, Joe, Allard tried to have Moreland killed while he was here playacting as Wade the drifter," Boris added ironically.

Joe's brow rose in consternation. "So, there's trouble between the suits, huh? Damn! Martha and my grandson are being dragged into this now."

"You say someone shot at Marti?" Now Boris picked up on Joe's earlier remarks with growing alarm. "Why isn't the sheriff protecting her then?"

Joe shrugged. "Same thing Moreland asked me. Seems the pair of them decided not to tell me what happened last night. Only Martha took off for Tahoe with Heath this morning. Then Adam came, looking like he'd been prowling back alleys all night, and raised hell with me for letting her go! As if I could stop her."

Boris felt his guts twisting. "You say she went to Riba's place on Lake Tahoe?"

"Took a plane from Oakland. She had the sheriff's deputy take them to the airport. Adam called the Napa airfield and practically commandeered a King Air from one of his friends to fly after her during that damn storm. I wish to hell we could untangle this, Boris. I don't like having my family in the middle."

"I'll untangle it, Joe," Boris said quietly. "Think you can keep this little weasel here until the sheriff comes for him?" he asked, looking around the kitchen for some cording to tie up his captive.

"I imagine I can handle that. Where are you going?" the old man asked warily.

"To Tahoe. I have a few questions for Moreland myself. Not to mention a few for Booth Allard and Riba," he added under his breath as he quickly bound Benteen with several lengths of Hilda's best poultry twine, lashing him securely to a kitchen chair.

Several attempts to phone Riba proved futile. The phone rang and rang with no answer. With each ring Boris's face became grimmer. Finally, he instructed Joe not to try and call her again after he left. Although he refused to elaborate, he knew the old man suspected something was amiss between Riba and Marti. He headed toward his MG, still parked up on the hillside. If he left right now he could make it to her lake place in a little over three hours.

Marti sat in the car rental office, nervously looking out the window at the innocuous sedan parked across the street. The young clerk processing the paperwork for the rental was new on the job and slow. Marti prayed Luger wouldn't report unfavorably to Booth. She closed her eyes and prayed for Adam and Heath.

"Something wrong, Mrs. Martin?" the pretty saleswoman asked solicitously.

"No . . . no, just a slight headache. Please, is my car ready yet?" Marti asked with a smile and a shake of her head.

"That ought to be it now, pulling up out front . . . the blue Buick. If you'll just sign one more time for me . . ." The clerk rustled through the paper morass until Marti's nerves were frayed raw. Finally, she came up with the right sheet.

Marti signed it without even glancing at the terms of the lease. Practically grabbing the carbon from the girl, she made her escape for the car. It was all she could do to turn the key in the ignition and pull away. The sedan across the street followed. Fighting down panic, she tried to think, but nothing occurred to her except to return as instructed with the car.

Adam would know what to do. He knew Allard! But then, she had thought she knew her sister, too! What a tragic and costly mistake. Her guts wrenched again as Riba's twisted hate replayed itself in her mind. "I have to think of something else or I'll go crazy," she said aloud and reached for the radio dial.

When she finally pulled into the driveway, Luger's sedan followed at a discreet distance. Like a marionette on a string, she walked woodenly to the house. As if on command the front door opened when she approached it. The small, nasty looking gunman Allard called Leo let her in and looked out, signalling to the big man in the car across the street. The wooded drive of Riba's lake front property was winding and isolated. Not a witness to question their fate, Marti thought with a sudden stab of panic as the door slammed behind her and Leo motioned for her to return to the den.

Adam reclined on the sofa with Heath sleeping in his arms. Allard paced near the bar and Riba sat perched on a stool, observing the scene nervously. Marti wondered what had occurred in her absence.

As if reading her mind, Allard smiled and said, "You were a bit tardy. Your sister here thought it, er, uncharacteristic of you, but I assured her maternal love would win out. Of course," he added, turning to Riba, "you wouldn't have the faintest inkling about that, would you, pet?"

Marti stared at Riba, looking behind the fixed, harsh expression into her cold, green eyes. Was this the kid sister she had grown up with? Attended schools and parties with? Vied for Papa's attention with? *Papa.* The seeds of this destructive scene all began with their father, she thought with a pang. They had always been rivals, just competing in different ways. But until now, only Riba had perceived it as a bitter rivalry in which she always came out second.

"How tragically ironic, Riba," Marti said softly, calling her sister's attention from contemplation of the drink in her hand.

"What's ironic? I'll just bet it's tragic for you now," Riba said spitefully and tossed off a quick gulp of gin.

"You thought Papa favored me all these years, when I thought—"

"He didn't *favor* you," Riba interrupted furiously, "he *bought* me with favors. He *loved* you!" She said the word "love" with such contempt it made Marti's blood run cold. With quaking knees she sank onto the sofa next to Adam.

Booth finished his drink and checked his watch. "Well, I think we can proceed pretty soon. We've had plenty of time for our little family reunion. Now, onto the next phase."

"You have everything figured, don't you, Booth," Adam said conversationally, easing the sleeping boy onto Marti's lap. His eyes never left Riba's nervously twisting fingers even though he addressed Allard. "You improvised this little scenario too fast. It's as full of holes as a paper dummy on a police target range."

Allard smiled glacially. "No. I'm good with details. You always said so yourself, Adam. Mr. Luger here has located a night's lodging for you and your family while Riba and I arrange to be otherwise occupied."

"Your alibis," Adam interjected scornfully.

"Just so. You came up to collect your true love and your son and were persuaded to spend an extra day, sightseeing in the mountains."

"I'll just bet Leo here knows some dandy nature trails," Adam said sarcastically.

The ugly little thug gave him a snort of derision as he stood in the doorway, poised to move.

"Tomorrow morning, early, you three will go on a junket up a high and winding road. One I've selected with great care."

"And not come down," Marti whispered brokenly, her eyes again straying to her sister's in a silent plea of disbelief. Riba continued twisting the stem of her glass, never even looking at Marti.

"Oh, you'll come down, girlie," Leo said with a

nasty laugh. "Boom!" He made a smashing gesture with his fist crashing against the door frame. Adam reached over and squeezed Marti's fingers in reassurance.

Just then the patio door whooshed open and the big gunman called Luger entered. Allard spoke to him. "Car in the drive?" At the affirmative nod, Booth continued. "All right friends. I know it won't be what you're accustomed to, but your night's accommodations await. Riba and I have other matters to attend."

Adam's eyes narrowed as he studied Riba. "You'll barely outlive us by hours, Riba. Count on it," he added with level intensity.

Booth tsked at him in mock reproval as he sauntered over to Riba and ran one large well manicured hand up and down her back in a soothing, hypnotic caress. He eased her from the stool and whispered. "You know what you have to do, right, love?"

"Yes, Booth. I know *exactly* what I have to do," she replied with a defiant glare at Adam. With that she walked toward her bedroom without a backward glance. "I have to dress for a very heavy date with a man on a yacht."

"Let me guess. She establishes an alibi here and you have one in San Francisco," Adam said smoothly to Allard.

"You used to figure all the right moves, Moreland. Pity you didn't anticipate this one. Ciao." With that he nodded to the two men, tossed down the last of his drink and set the glass on the bar with finality. "I'll meet you gentlemen at our usual spot the first of the week," he said to Leo. Both men nodded as he left.

"Okay, Slick," Scali said in his nasal insinuating voice, pointing his Beretta at Adam. "Take the kid again. Then you and her follow Luger outside to the cars."

Marti drove the rented Buick with Leo sitting beside her as guard and guide. Heath slept on the back seat of the gunman's sedan while Adam drove it.

Luger positioned himself next to the sleeping boy, behind Adam. Any attempts at stunt driving, the thug had warned him, would result in immediate reprisal against the child.

It took them over an hour to reach the deserted airstrip. From the wire fencing and rusted over signs, Adam suspected it had been some kind of military base, probably closed after Viet Nam. They passed the fallen down gate and headed across a crumbled asphalt strip toward a deserted building at the far corner.

The two car cavalcade pulled up in front of the building and stopped. Made of corrugated steel set in concrete, the shed must once have been a hanger for small planes. The area around it was shabby and weed infested. Dry brush had blown against the door. There were no windows.

"Not the Ritz, but it'll do for one night," Leo said with a grin as he slid out of the Buick.

Riba soaked in a scented tub to calm her jittery nerves, then began her elaborate toilette for the party on Jimmy's yacht that evening. She would mention conversationally that her sister and nephew and her sister's fiance were visiting her, planning to get an early start in the morning for a day of sightseeing in the mountains. Since she had the excuse of a late night party, Riba would not accompany them the next day. She would go home and sleep in, only to be awakened with the tragic news of their fatal crash.

Recalling Adam's admonition about Booth not needing her after she had helped him, Riba shivered and dismissed it as a desperate man's last ditch attempt to foil a perfect plan. She smiled slowly, thinking of Adam Moreland locked in that dingy, filthy shed all night, contemplating his own death . . . his death and the death of his mistress and his bastard! Ever since that night when she'd watched Adam and Marti make love at the cabin with such pagan abandon, Riba had thought of her prim, chaste sister as the drifter's cheap whore. All her own sins since adolescence were transferred onto Marti's shoulders. Finding out that the boy was Moreland's brat only confirmed in her warped mind what a fall from their father's grace his elder daughter had taken.

The evening went exactly as planned. Riba laughed, drank and let drop bits of information about her sister's family outing with the heir to the Moreland millions. *Millions Booth and I will enjoy, not Adam and Marti,* she thought to herself with a gratifying surge of spleen as Jimmy Rivera, a Vegas playboy she'd been dating, pulled up in front of her house around three A.M.

"I know you'd like a nightcap, honey, but you know how it is," she whispered conspiratorially, "with my little nephew in the house, you just can't . . ." She let her words trail off suggestively and leaned over to give him a quick good night kiss. The young man in the Jag grabbed her for a torridly thorough embrace.

By the time Riba fished out her key and walked up to the side entrance behind the big gate, she was thoroughly out of sorts. She could hear Jimmy's Jag purr its way down the deserted winding road as she rubbed her beard-abraded cheek and neck. The pig! He'd torn the rhinestone strap on her Calvin Klein gown! She jammed the key in the lock and entered the darkened house.

Kicking off her spike-heeled slippers, she padded across the thick carpet, illuminated by bright moonlight filtering in through the sliding glass doors. The bar had a dim light over it. Enough not to give her eyestrain while she poured another gin and tonic. Just as she reached for the switch by the sink a large meaty fist covered her hand and crushed down on the delicate bones.

"Need some light, Riba?" Boris Staritz's voice was low and menacing.

With a sharp oath of surprise, she yanked free of his grasp as he flicked on the switch. "You bastard!" she hissed, rubbing her hand and backing away from him at the same time.

His broad, flat face creased in a grim smile. "Is that

any way to greet a former lover? You were lots more accommodating to the punk out front, but you always did like the gigolo type, didn't you?"

"How the hell did you get in here?" she asked, looking nervously around the room.

Boris glanced at the patio door and shrugged eloquently. "You always were careless about locking up, Riba. But then I guess it must be all those years of habit, sneaking out to meet your lovers."

"What do you want, Boris?" she asked warily, reaching past him for the gin bottle.

He intercepted her slim arm and held it between both his big hands. "Where are Marti and Adam?" He could feel the pulse in her wrist accelerate. He squeezed and repeated the question.

"Why, I don't know. I guess they've left already. They rented a car—"

"Cut the crap, Riba," Boris said as she hissed in pain. The pressure on her arm increased. "I'll cheerfully break every bone in your filthy little body to find out what you and Allard have done with Marti."

Riba thrashed and swore inventively, struggling to reach a bottle of Galliano on the bar. She grabbed it and swung at his head, but he easily blocked the blow, knocking the long heavy bottle from her hand. It shattered across the sink in a golden explosion and small rivulets of the sticky sweet liquor trickled down the cabinet. The smell of overripe bananas filled the air.

Riba looked into Boris's face and saw the leashed fury in his implacable black eyes. She knew he wasn't lying. He'd beat her bloody!

"Now, let's go over it again," he said, grabbing her quickly and twisting her arm brutally behind her back. "We're gonna play mess-the-make-up. You always did like that one, remember?" His big hand came up and framed her delicate jaw, the blunt fingertips digging in painfully. "But this time I'll add a new wrinkle. I'll use some of that broken glass in the sink . . ."

She moaned and collapsed against him in defeat.

Chapter 24

"Mommy, I'm scared." Heath's voice quavered in the darkness.

Adam flicked on his cigarette lighter, and the flame illuminated the child's face with its puckered cheeks. He was clutching his mother's skirt, obviously on the verge of tears. The man was amazed at his reaction to the sight. *Jesus,* he thought, *I'm about to start crying myself!* He kept his voice steady as he asked in mock astonishment, "Heath, you're not afraid of the dark?"

"Am, too," the child responded with stubborn vehemence.

Adam forced a chuckle. "Okay, I was only joking. All kids are afraid of the dark. I was, too."

In spite of his fear, Heath was intrigued by this confession. "You were scared?" Adam shook his head, "yes." The boy continued, "But not now?" Adam shook his head "no." The small interrogator became suspicious. "Just 'cause you're a grownup?" This last was more of an accusation than a question.

Moreland shook his head again. "Nope, I got over being scared when I was just about your age. And I had fun doing it, too. Come on, I'll tell you about it." He extended his hand, and Heath seized two of the long fingers in his small fist, eager to hear of a "fun" escape from the terrors of the dark.

As Marti watched the scene, she felt her throat constrict and her eyes grow dangerously moist. She blinked and looked away quickly. *No,* she thought, *please not now!* When she had gained control, she turned to face father and son and was startled to discover Adam staring at her.

"Marti, maybe we can find something in all this junk to get us out of here." The voice was soft and the tone reassuring, but the glow from the lighter's flame transformed the smile on his handsome face into a disturbing grimace. She nodded and, using the faint light, began to pick her way slowly through the accumulated debris scattered across the concrete floor of the shack.

For a moment, Adam turned his attention back to Heath. "Okay, the way I got over my fear was by going on overnight camp-outs."

The boy interrupted. "What's that?"

"Well," explained the man, "you go out into the woods and put up a tent."

Heath interjected with excitement, "Like a Indian house!"

"That's right," Adam nodded. "And when it gets dark, you build a campfire and sit around it and roast hot dogs. Then—"

The boy interrupted again, "Gotta go by yourself?" The fear was back in his voice.

"Nope," the tall man scoffed gently. "You go with a big brother, or an uncle . . . or your father." He paused ever so slightly. "When we get out of here, I could take you. Would you like that?"

Mercifully, the response was quick in coming. "Yeah!"

Moreland looked down into the shining face of his son and snapped off the lighter, only partially because it had grown uncomfortably warm in his hand.

Marti hissed in surprise, "What's the matter?"

When Adam finally responded, his voice sounded oddly husky, "Just cooling down the lighter." He held tightly to Heath's small hand in the dark.

When the flame flicked to life again, she continued her methodical rummaging, and he surveyed the interior of the shack with greater care. Obviously, the large shed had served as a catch-all for discarded equipment and junk long before the small airstrip had been abandoned. The floor was covered with parts of broken tools, shards of rotting lumber, oily rags, and empty cans.

Adam moved slowly along the back wall of the structure and Heath followed, two of his father's fingers still clutched tightly in his tenacious fist. As the man searched for some means of escaping their prison, he kept the boy occupied with answers to a flurry of camp-out questions. In a nearby corner, Adam noticed a stack of empty five-gallon pails, likely some sort of asphalt patch that had been used on the runways.

Marti's excited whisper distracted him. "Adam, I think I've found something!" As he moved toward her across the shack, she whispered, "Stay back! I'll come to you."

Quickly, she emerged from a dark corner. "Here, let me hold the lighter and Heath. You go take a look." Moreland picked his way carefully through the dimness until he caught the faint odor. He stepped to the side so that the light could more fully penetrate the darkness. "Gasoline," he breathed softly. He stepped forward and hefted the squat container. It was over half-full. He twisted off the rusty cap that Marti had been unable to loosen. "Gasoline," he assured himself, "and maybe our ticket out of here."

Adam put down the can and replaced the cap. Then, he made his way back to Marti and his son. "Babe," he whispered, "let the lighter cool down a bit." He stood in the darkness, his mind racing. He felt her hand on his arm.

"Don't worry, darling," Marti's soft voice caressed him. "We'll think of a way out."

An idea seized him. "You can bet on it, but right now I think it's time for Heath to get some camp-out practice." Adam took the lighter from her and snapped on its flame. Then, he began to search for rags and wood, piling them in a small pyramid in the middle of the shed directly opposite the door. He lit the small mound and it appeared to be a reasonable facsimile of a campfire. "What do you think, son?" As the boy opened his mouth to shout his approval, the man warned, "Quiet now."

"Awesome!" the child squeaked in a loud whisper.

Adam placed a finger across Heath's lips to silence the eruption of excited chatter that was building.

Marti watched as Moreland pulled a small crate into position and motioned for his son to sit near the campfire. The tall figure bent over the tiny one, for a whispered conference. Then Adam came back to her side, having left their son with careful instructions on how to feed a fire with one small sliver of wood at a time.

"We can't burn our way out of here, can we?" The walls were corrugated metal, so she knew there was no chance of that despite the flammable materials inside the building.

"Try this idea. We dump this gas into one of those plastic pails over there, make a torch with some gas-soaked rags tied to a piece of this green lumber. You take the torch and sit across from Heath. Keep it hidden behind the crate. When our 'chauffeurs' come in to take us on our last drive, I'll be over here in the darkness. While their attention is on you and Heath, I'll dowse them. When they turn toward me, you just touch the torch in the fire and shove it in their noses. They'll freeze," he finished on a note of certainty.

Marti lowered her head and stared thoughtfully at the floor that she could barely see in the dimness. Adam misunderstood her silence. "Look, babe, sure they might get off a round or two at me, but they'll be partially blinded from looking at you over the fire. Besides, as soon as I pitch the gas, I plan on kissing the floor, real quick."

With head still lowered, Marti spoke very carefully. "Adam, the plan might work, but it has one serious flaw." She raised her head and stared directly into his tight face. "If those men don't see you in plain sight as soon as they open the door, they won't come into the shed . . . I'll have to pitch the gasoline." She watched his face harden.

"No," he snapped too loudly and threw a glance over his shoulder at their child. The boy was curled up on the crate, drowsing in the warmth of the small fire.

Marti continued in the same inexorable fashion.

"Adam, if this is our only chance and we blow it, we're all dead. Think, Adam. If you make a mistake, you'll be responsible for our son's death."

As soon as she spoke the words, Marti was afraid that she had gone too far. His face seemed to crumple, and suddenly, he looked for all the world exactly as Heath had looked a few moments earlier when he had been clinging to her skirt. Shocked, she realized that the enigmatic man she loved was filled with even greater fear than she was. The arrogant drifter who had survived a near-fatal beating from three thugs, the brutal avenger who had mercilessly repaid two of those men, the ruthless wine baron who had shrugged off a half-dozen attempts on his life was struggling to fight back panic!

Adam Moreland had never before had to worry about anyone but himself. Marti knew with absolute certainty that if he were alone facing this danger his fatalistic courage would sustain him. But now he was terrified for her and Heath. She knew the thought that one or both the gunmen might get off a shot at her as she threw the gasoline filled him with horror. Women were conditioned to deal with fears for themselves, as well as fear for loved ones; men were not. She suddenly realized that a man, even a strong man, might not be able to handle that double burden. Marti lowered her head and said quietly, calmly, "Please, Adam, think, think!" The seconds dragged.

"Your logic is impeccable. Somehow, that seems a bit unfair for so beautiful a woman."

Caught completely off guard, Marti snapped up her head. Adam was managing a wobbly grin. "Chauvinist," she replied tenderly. "Would my logic be any easier to accept if I looked like this?" She crossed her eyes and ballooned out her cheeks.

Adam threw back his head, but managed to stifle his laughter. He admonished her in a strangled whisper, "For Christ's sake, Marti, don't do that. You look like a constipated Jerry Lewis."

Marti wasn't sure whether he had reached for her or she for him, but the two wound up hugging each other fiercely until the suppressed convulsions of tension-purging laughter subsided. He tilted her face upward and looked into her clear gray eyes. "Marti, I love you. I've always loved you—ever since you threw yourself at me, missed, and landed in that mud puddle." His smile was wistful as he ran his fingers through her tangled hair.

Soberly, Marti returned his searching look. "And I love you, Adam Moreland. I guess I loved you even when I hated you." Then she grinned impishly. "After all, I even had to kill off a 'husband' because of you."

She pulled his head down for a gentle kiss, and for a moment, there were no killers, no Booth Allard, no danger. But the moment was brief. Adam broke the kiss, and with a jauntiness he did not feel, proclaimed, "Time to get to work. Tonight, sweetness, you get to play duck in the shooting gallery. Just remember, as soon as you heave the gas, get that beautiful ass down. Hit the deck."

She nodded, "Yes, sir, I intend to protect my ass—at least from our 'chauffeurs'."

Quickly and quietly, they made their preparation and refined their plan. When the work was completed, they faced each other in awkward silence. Adam quirked a smile. "Remember?"

Marti nodded, "Watch out for my . . ." she patted her rump. "You can count on it. I've grown attached to it." As Adam opened his mouth to speak, she quickly added with a smirk, "Yes, Mr. Moreland, I am well aware of your own attachment."

Hefting his unlit torch with a chuckle, Adam moved over to the sleeping child. He added a few more sticks to the dying fire as Marti, obscured in the darkness, sat down on the plywood square they had placed over the open mouth of the gas pail to keep its stench from filling the shed. Now the wait would begin.

Adam was dozing, but the sound of crunching gravel awakened him as quickly as if it had been a splash of icy water. He heard Marti's soft warning voice from the darkness and acknowledged it. He checked the fire. It had to be just right—enough light to impair the killers' vision in the shed, but not enough to reveal Marti's exact location. He added another stick just as he heard the rasp of metal and saw the door jerked open.

Framed in the doorway against the gray light of the dawn were two silhouettes. The big, burly Luger moved into the gloom of the shed, followed cautiously by the short, scrawny Scali. Luger giggled in his bizarre high-pitched voice. "Well, what the hell we got here, a goddamned cook-out?" he asked Adam with inane good humor.

"Shit, Slick, you ain't got enough time left to help that kid earn his merit badge." Scali's voice chimed in with a nasty, vicious edge."

Moreland had to keep their attention focused on him as long as possible. He swallowed the taste of vomit and forced a provocative sneer to cross his handsome face. "Twiggy," he addressed Leo, "anyone ever tell you your mouth's as foul as a skunk's ass?"

Scali's small face hardened into a venomous mask and his gun hand twitched as he stepped past Riefe Luger. Luger's vacuous grin froze at the insult. In the light from the fire, he looked like a ventriloquist's dummy.

With a hiss of fury, Leo commanded, "Cut the shit. It stinks in here. Say, where's the broad?" The question was answered as both men were drenched, head and shoulders, by a cascade of gasoline arcing out of the darkness.

Marti had been ready, standing in the shadows, bucket cocked. True to her word, when she had heaved the gas, she tossed the bucket aside and dropped immediately to the concrete floor, pressing her body so firmly against it that she thought she would surely stamp an impression on the hard surface. But no shots came, only a choked cry from a voice she thought belonged to the smaller killer. "Wait, don't shoot!"

Another long moment passed and Marti looked up. Both Riefe Luger and Leo Scali were facing in her direction, frozen in a crouch with gun-arms extended. They resembled greasy wax statues in a cheap amusement park.

Adam was standing to the side, his flaming torch not three feet from them. "Holding your fire was a good decision, Leo," he complimented sardonically. "I bet the muzzle blast would have set off you two bastards like Roman candles."

Leo was mute, but Luger's giggle, now bordering on hysteria, filled the shed. "Shit, Moreland, watch that torch. Jesus!"

Adam inched closer. "I am watching it, you vicious son-of-a-bitch, and I want you to watch it—real close!"

Still sprawled in the darkness, Marti saw Adam's contorted face and heard the rage pulsing in his voice. Her own voice was soft but firm, "Don't do it, Adam." She remembered witnessing his savage reprisal against the two muggers. "Please, for Heath's sake. Don't do it . . . *unless we have to.*"

Marti's voice had an impact on all three men. Adam halted his slow advance and Leo gave a quiet order to Luger. "Drop your piece." The big man complied immediately. Unaccountably, the woman's voice from out of the darkness was almost as terrifying as the nearby torch. Slowly, Leo dropped his own weapon. He had caught the steely emphasis, *unless we have to,* and knew that he was scant inches away from a horrible death.

Adam's voice was calm now, "Okay, boys, link arms and back out of the shed very slowly. You better hold tight to each other because if either of you tries to break the link, I'll weld you together permanently." He brandished the flame menacingly.

As the tense procession got underway, Adam called to Marti, his attention never once shifting from the two in front of him, "Babe, pick up the guns."

Crossing behind him, she complied, handing the big revolver to Adam and keeping the smaller automatic for herself. With a surge of guilt, Marti suddenly realized that she had not paid any attention to her sleeping son for the past several minutes. A quick glance toward the crate quelled her rush of panic before it could fully develop. She almost laughed in relief. "Darling, would you believe our little engine of wrath hasn't even twitched!"

As Riba drove through the dim morning light her attention kept wandering from the road to the man at her side in the careening car. Her face was marred by bruises, her eyes red rimmed and puffy from tears and lack of sleep.

Staritz didn't look much better, exhausted and frightened by Riba's garbled, hysterical tale of hate and vengeance. "Just keep the car on the road. If Marti and her son are hurt, I'll see you fry for it," he snarled as she narrowly missed the gravel shoulder. "You sure this is the way? We've made two false turns already. Playing for time won't work for you. If they're dead . . ."

"How the hell do you expect me to find this godawful place, especially in the dark! I only heard Booth and his men discuss it. I've never been here!" Riba swore at him as she turned the car recklessly, spraying gravel from the rear tires once more.

Suddenly the fallen fences and signposts of the airstrip materialized in the morning haze as they crested a rise. "That it?" Boris grunted.

"I think so," she replied uncertainly.

"Pull in slowly and cut the engine when I tell you," he instructed her carefully, gun held openly in his right hand.

Just then two men in dark suits emerged from the doorway of the big metal hulk at the end of the runway, hands raised. Boris watched Adam Moreland walk after them with a gun aimed at the pair. Marti and Heath were nowhere in sight. Then, in a blur of motion, the taller man lurched against Moreland and the two men went down, rolling and punching in the dirt while the smaller man attempted desperately to reach between them and grab the fallen weapon.

"Hit the gas!" Staritz yelled, waving his own gun

under Riba's nose. Chunks of dried tarmac sprayed as she gunned the motor and headed toward the melee. The car hadn't even stopped when he jumped clear and raced into the fray.

Just as Leo grasped the big Model 59 revolver, the cold metal of Boris's .44 magnum rammed into his temple. "I wouldn't pick it up," the Russian said, enunciating distinctly.

Adam and the big burly thug separated and scrambled for footing, then both regained their balance and resumed the fight. Staritz remembered those lethal hands and feet well from his bout with Moreland. A quick snap to Luger's kneecap, followed by a well placed knee in the solar plexus, and a lightening chop to the back of the neck collapsed Luger's body. He fell against the hangar wall and it reverberated with a dull thud as he slid into an unconscious heap on the brushy ground.

Marti, with Heath crying in her arms, rushed from the building. "Oh, Adam, Adam," she choked out. He turned and enfolded her in his arms. The boy, too, reached out and fastened his small wiry body monkey fashion onto his father.

Soothing them both, Adam looked over at Staritz and Leo. Leo didn't look happy. The Russian didn't either, but his gun was definitely pointed the right direction.

The sound of a car careening off in the distance suddenly intruded and Staritz swore, glancing at the vanishing Continental. "That bitch'll warn Allard," he grated out furiously.

Adam smiled. "Only if she can reach him before we get to her." He paused and said earnestly, "I owe you a big one, Staritz."

Noting the protective way Moreland held Marti and Heath, the Russian nodded tersely. "I found Nate Benteen doing some of his 'specialty work' on one of our harvesters last night."

Adam grinned. "And you 'convinced' him to tell you about Booth?"

As the two men quickly exchanged information

about what had transpired in Napa and at Riba's place, Adam securely trussed up Scali and Luger with some rope from the shed and then locked them in the dank prison.

"We need to call the San Francisco police, Adam," Marti said as he slipped the bolt on the door.

Adam shook his head. "We'll only muddy the water and let Booth get away if we alert him. Let him think his boys have succeeded for now. The thing is to get to Riba. She's his weak link. The only way to keep her alive is to get her to talk." Even as he said it he could feel the lash of agony spearing through Marti.

Tears blurred her eyes but she held firmly to Heath and said quietly, "Yes, you're right. We have to get to her before she contacts Booth."

"She's got maybe five minutes on us," Boris said, moving toward the rented Buick Marti had driven last night.

Adam had taken the keys for the sedan from Luger. "Marti, give me about an hour. Then you take Heath and go with Boris to the local sheriff. Tell him about these gunsels and where to find them. But leave me out of the story. I'll handle Riba."

"No way." Her clipped words stopped both men abruptly. "She tried to kill my child. She's insane and dangerous, but she's still my sister and my responsibility." Without even looking at Adam she turned to Boris with a wry smile. "Please, you've done so much already, but could you take Heath home? I have to go with Adam."

Looking between the man and woman, Staritz grunted in acquiescence and reached out for the exhausted boy who was dozing on her shoulder. "I'll drive back to Chateau Beaumont with him and then place an anonymous call to the local sheriff's office about our friends in there."

"This is crazy! You've never fired a gun in your life, have you?" Adam quietly asked the determined woman who sat beside him as he sped madly over the gravel road toward Riba's house.

"I'll do what I have to do, Adam. I don't plan to

shoot Riba, if that's what's worrying you." Without skipping a beat, she asked, "You're going to lure Booth back here, aren't you?"

His mouth was a grim slash. "Riba's the key. If she can get him here to face me, we can have this thing finished, once and for all."

"It's dangerous, Adam. We've seen what they're both capable of."

He smiled harshly and the lines around his mouth eased a bit. "Without their gun-packing friends, I have a significant advantage."

"But you need me to deal with Riba, Adam." It wasn't an argument, just a simple statement of fact.

While the Buick sped toward the lake house, Riba's Continental screeched into the driveway. Leaping out in her satin cocktail dress and the incongruously mismatched beach sandals she had grabbed last night, she raced to the door and entered.

"Think! Think, dammit!" She swore a long colorful string of oaths as she searched her handbag for any stray cash it might yield. Two bank cards, half a dozen department store charges and fifty dollars in bills were all she could find.

Pulling off the cocktail dress, she rummaged wildly through her bedroom closet and yanked out a comfortable sun dress. Should she run? Where to go? Booth was in the city but she was afraid to call his office. His home line, where she customarily left discreet messages, would take too long. She worried her lip for a few moments as her mind darted from one erratic plan to another.

She'd go home to Chateau Beaumont and throw herself on her father's mercy. If nothing else, he'd have to protect her to avoid a scandal on the precious Beaumont name. She could plead insanity. Yes, that was it—too many pills and drugs from Oliver and his friends! She massaged her head, a very real ache blurring her vision as she searched the dresser drawer for one of those wonderfully calming capsules Oliver always supplied. Finding the bottle, she headed to the bar in the den.

As she swallowed several pills and stuffed the pill bottle in her handbag, Riba heard a car pull in the driveway and footsteps rush toward the front entrance. With an oath she grabbed her car keys and headed for the patio door, only to collide with Adam, who had yanked it open. He stepped inside. Wrenching from his grasp, she turned back to the hall, but her sister stood poised in the doorway.

Like a desperate wild thing, Riba froze between the two hostile figures. "Don't let him hurt me," she whispered to Marti, her voice breaking dramatically at just the right place. "I . . . I didn't mean to do it," she continued in a child's far away voice, beseeching her sister. "I had to tell Papa about him. I couldn't let you and Adam go away together. Papa did it! He sent those men after Adam." She put a hand on Marti's shoulder limply. Her large green eyes were almost black with a bizarre, numbed look in them.

Marti felt the bile rise in her throat. "Oh, my God!—it wasn't even *me* Papa thought he was protecting, was it?" She looked at Adam who nodded grimly as he pulled Riba onto the sofa next to the phone.

Marti walked over and sat on the opposite side of her sister. "You accused me of having Papa's love, his favor. But all the while he wrecked my life and my child's life he did it out of love for you! You set him up and now you have the warped, insane nerve to blame everything on him. It's over, Riba. The day you put my son's life on the line, you lost any claim to my loyalty. Papa will do just as I will. We'll see you in prison, right along with Booth Allard."

"Or, Booth will see you dead. Take your choice," Adam interjected.

Marti's silvery eyes glistened with tears, but Riba was too wrapped up in self pity to notice. She hadn't slept in two days and the effects of pills and alcohol were fast undermining her ability to think.

"No! Don't let Booth hurt me. I can tell you things about him—lots of things. I don't want to go to prison." Her hands clutched Adam's arm like claws as she leaned instinctively away from Marti.

Adam held the phone up to her and said slowly, as if talking to a child, "I'm going to dial Booth's private line. Here's what you're going to say to him, Riba . . ."

Chapter 25

Booth Allard swore savagely as he slammed the receiver down in his private office. Damned valium-fried little tart, coming unraveled on him at the crucial minute. *Just like Jolie*, a voice taunted him, *unreliable, unstable.* He forced the thought aside and concentrated, making his mind go blank, become a cold, calculating machine, separate from the emotional part of him that still threatened to erupt ever since childhood.

Childhood. That was a joke. He'd never had one. By the time he was twelve and Jolie seven their father had run through the last of their family's money, leaving them in the unwilling care of a destitute spinster aunt. The removal from a Chicago Northshore brownstone to a tacky south side tract house had been shattering. Booth Allard swore not to remain poor, and he had succeeded beyond even his own adolescent expectations. Now everything, everything was within inches of his grasp—if Riba didn't ruin it, just as Jolie had.

Damn, why did his sister's memory keep rising? Her blonde hair and green eyes kept blurring over Riba's. It was Riba now who was spoiling things, he reminded himself. Jolie had nearly destroyed his alliance with Jake Moreland when her disgusting affair with the boy had been exposed. Now Riba was going to undermine his final triumph, his chance to destroy old Jake's son, who had taken Jolie from him. He would see Riba dead in the same grave as Adam and Jake—all of them dead, and himself in control of Moreland Enterprises.

Riba's hysterical call, babbling about her guilt over

the deaths of her sister and nephew only meant a temporary setback, he assured himself. The icy calm he'd developed through the years spread over him in soothing waves. It would have been better to attend the board meeting this afternoon when the news about Adam's death came, but that could be addressed later.

The immediate problem was his unstable mistress. He knew when he'd first plied her that Riba's hatred of Adam and bizarre jealousy of her sister would be useful. He'd also planned to get rid of her after he had control of the cartel. But he hadn't expected her long-held, seething hate to turn to maudlin guilt just because a child was involved. Under the duress of liquor and pills, lord only knew if she'd crack up and decide to confide everything to her old man or, God help him even to the Nevada police!

Flicking on the intercom, he leaned forward and said, "Kate, have my private car brought around front. I've been called away on a vital matter. Make my excuses to the board this afternoon." He reached down and pressed a tiny key into the walnut panel of the bottom desk drawer. When its metal-lined interior opened, a .45 caliber Detonics gleamed dully.

Adam watched Booth's sleek Lincoln pull into Riba's driveway. It was almost noon. "Good time," he muttered to himself, then looked over to where Riba sat, clutching a cup of tea in a white knuckled death grip. "Remember . . ." he said softly to her, then slipped into the hallway to conceal himself.

Riba's mind was still jumbled and panicky, but Adam's words rang clearly in her brain: *He'll try to kill you. Your only chance is to expose him, Riba. We'll protect you if you cooperate. Just wait and see what he does. Then you'll know.*

Then you'll know. The words had an ominous ring. What if he just walked in and shot her in cold blood? Riba took a steadying sip of the tea Marti had been pouring down her all morning.

Booth let himself quietly in the patio door and walked over to Riba. "You look like hell," he said quietly, holding up her chin to inspect the bruises on it. "Who worked you over?" he asked with a sudden cold click in his voice.

She jerked herself free of his imprisoning grip. "Rivera," she replied in a whisper.

He snorted in disgust. "And in reprisal, you came home and drowned your sorrows with gin and pills. I don't have time for your hysteria, Riba. I need to be in the city, not here. In fact, this is precisely the last place I should be."

He paused and she looked expectantly at him. "I made a couple of phone calls before I arrived. I've arranged a place for us to stay until you get over your guilt trip. Pack a bag," he added with a casual gesture she instinctively mistrusted. "Now." His tone became ice cold and demanding when she failed to move.

Frozen in terror, she heard her clogged voice reply, "I don't want to go anywhere with you, Booth."

His pale blue eyes glowed an eerie white as he snarled, "You get your bags packed, darling. You are going with me, make no mistake about it."

"So I can have a convenient accident like Adam and Marti?" She knew her lines pretty well, although she spoke them like a somnambulist.

He threw back his head and gave a sharp laugh. "That would be a bit too much of a coincidence, wouldn't it? No. You'll just disappear for a few weeks. Then when all the furor over Moreland's death dies down, I'll have Scali and Luger arrange something . . . You always did like taking chances, sleeping around with unsavory men, here lately even doing some very exotic designer drugs with your estranged spouse's friends." He pulled the Detonics from his jacket and said levelly, "Pack."

If there had been some small part of her that still hoped for a reprieve from two equally unthinkable alternatives, Riba now abandoned that pipe dream. "I need a drink, Booth. This tea's giving me the jitters," she said, moving with fast, jerky strides toward the bar as she heard his snickering laugh at her back. *Bastard! I'll fix you and them!*

"Take your false courage, my dear. Who knows, perhaps you'll be able to convince me of an alternative plan once this crisis is past," Booth said in a deceptively soft voice. He slid the gun into his coat pocket, his anger evaporated now that he had her under control.

Riba poured a very generous slug of gin and raised the glass to her lips. She was shaking so badly she had to steady the glass with both hands as she swallowed convulsively. Then she turned to Booth with a slow, calculating smile. "I can think of all sorts of ways to 'convince' you, darling." She finished the drink and set the glass on the bar, giving him a sultry look that was a blatant invitation.

For an instant Booth felt his vision blur and Riba's green eyes and blonde hair seemed to fade into another's . . . she was destructive, manipulating, beautiful *Jolie!* He wasn't sure if he said the name aloud or not, but a strange expression crossed Riba's face.

She waited for him to come to her, leaning against the bar provocatively. He hated himself after the first step. But by the time he had crossed the room, he could sense her fear, see the ravages of too many pills and too much booze coupled with too little sleep. Her eyes were bloodshot and the pupils were dilated. Anger quickly replaced the self-loathing and lust of a moment before as he reached for her.

In the bedroom across the hall, Adam motioned for Marti to stay back as he eased toward the door for a better look. Damn! Riba was supposed to draw Booth out and get him to talk. Had she panicked and forgotten her lines? They'd coached her all morning and set up an exact scenario. She began well enough, then suddenly stopped milking him about his plans and started in with the booze instead. She had to realize now that Booth meant all long to kill her once he had Moreland Enterprises in his hands!

"You stupid little cunt!" Allard's sharp curses were abruptly followed by the dull crack of a small caliber pistol. In a blur Adam raced around the corner and into the large den where Riba and Booth struggled over a Walther PPK clutched in her whitened fingers. She had apparently had it hidden somewhere in the bar and pulled it on him, but missed her shot. As the man and woman fought, locked closely together, Adam froze for an instant. He could not shoot Booth without endangering Marti's sister. Just as he moved cat-quick to come up behind Allard, a loud shot rang out and Riba crumpled, her small automatic uselessly clutched in her right hand.

Before Booth could squeeze his .45 again, Adam was on him, knocking the Detonics across the floor. Both men went down and rolled toward the steps. Unlike Boris Staritz and the hapless thugs Adam had dealt with earlier, Booth Allard was a very methodical student of the martial arts who worked out in an exclusive gym. Linda Drake had investigated that for Adam.

Slowly the two men arose, each guardedly watching the other for the slightest telltale move. "I knew something was wrong. But I couldn't put my finger on it until now . . . I never gave Riba my private number." He shrugged. "Ah, well, I always wanted to spar with you, Adam." Allard's gun lay near the patio door where it had been flung when Adam hit him from behind, but his eyes never left Adam to search for it. Not yet. Moreland's gun, too, had been knocked out of reach, landing behind the bar. They circled one another.

Marti watched from the door. Hearing Riba's moans she was painfully torn. Her first instinct was to rush to her injured sister, whose blood was rapidly reddening the pale plush carpet. But she realized that any sudden move could distract Adam and cost all of them their lives.

She held Leo's Beretta in her palm, concealed in her skirt pocket. The safety was off and Adam had showed her how to fire it, but in such close quarters, she had just seen a horrible demonstration of what could go awry when someone unused to firearms attempted to use one. As the men circled, Marti waited and measured her chance. *Only if Booth gets near his gun, or he gets Adam down,* she thought to herself as she eyed the dully evil gleam of the .45 in the corner. Then she would have to get as close to him as possible before she shot. Slowly, she edged toward the patio door, staying well clear of the antagonists as she stalked Booth's weapon. How lethal was he bare handed?

As she watched, the two men suddenly crashed heavily to the carpeted floor. Allard rolled free, his eyes searching for his lost gun. *Goddamn,* he thought, *all the way across the room.* He gave up any idea of retrieving the weapon. Regaining his feet, he spun to face his opponent. He was slightly taken aback to find Adam already up and poised on the balls of his feet. The older man studied the arrogant face, searching for any signs of weakness. "Afraid, Adam? No matter. You will be." He relaxed and casually assumed a favorite fighting stance.

Adam watched the heavier man drop into a position that he recognized as the "horse stance." *Well, Linda's information was right on the money,* he thought. *Booth is a karate-ka.* He pondered, wondering why karate-ka called it the "horse stance." Left foot forward, right foot back, it looked more like a fencer's posture. Allard held his left arm ready to block, his right fist at hip level ready to strike. He returned his opponent's scrutiny.

Adam began to circle, keeping just out of range. For the past three years at Linda's urging, he had been working out in judo with her and some of her detective friends. At first the other judo-ka had designed his workouts as mild physical rehabilitation for the lingering effects of the beating commissioned by Joe. But as the recuperation process had accelerated, the sparring sessions had become more and more vigorous. Adam was quite confident of his fighting ability, despite having to compensate for the weak left knee. Now, he knew he must be very careful with this heavier, stronger enemy.

As Adam circled slowly, Booth shifted his stance to keep the slimmer man directly in front of him, but

Adam noted, while the shifting foot movements were practised, they were slightly slow. In the gym, Adam had observed many karate students at their workouts. Most seemed to specialize either in kicking or in punching. *Well, Booth,* he thought, *it's time to see what you are—a puncher or a kicker.* He hoped Allard wasn't versatile. Adam moved deliberately within range of the deadly hands and feet.

Allard snapped his right foot forward, directly at Moreland's belly. Instead of trying to block the kick, Adam simply pivoted his body away from the attacking foot while deflecting it with an open palm. Booth's sharp triumphant yell pinched off into a surprised gurgle. Meeting no resistance, the momentum of his own attack unbalanced him, almost sending him sprawling to the floor. Quickly, he resumed his defensive stance, expecting his opponent to counter attack.

However, Adam had resumed his circling, now with a slight grin on his face. *Well, Booth, that answers that question. You're a kicker and a shade slow at that.* Now, he knew how he would attack. The two men circled in silence for a few moments. Then, Adam suddenly straightened fully erect. "Okay, you son-of-a-bitch," he growled. "I'm tired of your Bruce Lee shit. I'm going to beat your goddamned face in." Rolling his shoulders and raising his fists like a boxer, he moved in on the surprised Allard.

The bigger man gloated to himself and swallowed the bait. He launched a kick, designed to get in under those upraised fists and smash Adam's testicles. This time, however, instead of pivoting away from the kick, Adam lunged forward in a crouch. Twisting his body to avoid the attack, he grabbed the extended leg at the back of the knee, thrust the heel of his hand under his attacker's chin in stiff-arm fashion, and clipped the man's supporting leg out from underneath him with a leg-hooking judo technique.

Booth was thrown flat on his back with Adam's weight coming down heavily on top of him. Adam's stiff arm drove the back of his head against the floor. Had the surface not been so plushly carpeted, the back of Allard's skull would have been crushed. As it was, the only thing that kept the big man from passing out was sheer panic. He lashed out with a clumsy back-fisted karate strike that, by pure luck, caught Moreland's jaw a glancing blow. Vaguely attempting to capitalize on a momentary advantage, Allard rolled groggily onto his hands and knees, but before he could clear the fog from his brain, Adam was on him again.

As he straddled Booth's back, he encircled his neck from behind with his right arm. Clutching the left lapel of Allard's jacket, Adam used this grip as a fulcrum to lever his forearm against his foe's carotid artery, clamping off the blood and oxygen supply to his victim's already jumbled brain. Scissoring Allard's lower body between his legs, Moreland toppled them both onto their sides. At the same time Adam intensified the pressure on Booth's neck by pushing his head forward against his clamping forearm.

Across the room, Marti watched as Booth's complexion turned from pink to red to purplish crimson. His face seemed to swell. Suddenly, his eyes, already bulged open, rolled up until she could see only the whites. His hands, which had been pawing feebly at the arm that encircled his neck, suddenly dropped limply. His entire body seemed to collapse inwardly, but Adam did not relinquish his grip. As she stood frozen, Marti remembered a tabloid she had seen in a wildlife film: a lion with its jaws clamped on the throat of a water buffalo, slowly suffocating the larger beast.

Adam broke the spell. "He'll be out cold for quite a while," he grunted, releasing his hold and rolling away from the unconscious man. He stood up and turned toward Marti.

With a wounded cry she ran over to Riba and knelt unsteadily by her side. "Oh, Adam, call an ambulance," she whispered. As she heard him dialing the phone, she reached up for a towel from the bar and pressed it against Riba's chest. It was immediately soaked with blood. Marti squeezed back her tears. *Be calm. Going to pieces won't help.* Even as she heard

Adam talking to the emergency operator, Marti knew it was already too late. Riba had been dead within a minute or two of the shot, which must have severed an artery. Her skin was waxen from blood loss and the carpet was covered with blackish red gore.

Marti felt for a pulse, knowing there was none, but searching desperately anyway. Nothing. She crumpled into a small, tight ball close beside her dead sister and began to cry silently in tight, wracking sobs, covering her face with her blood smeared hands. Then she dug her fists into her eyes, trying to shut out the gory scene that surrounded her. She felt Adam's arms around her as he held her, crooning soft words of comfort.

Images from childhood ran through her mind in blurred, random flashes. She saw the birthday party when Riba turned three and she was five. They each had a fancy new dress and there was a big cake. Riba's little blonde head lowered as she blew out the candles and made her wish. *What did you wish for? Not this, God know. What did I wish for?*

"She wore a pink lace dress and got chocolate ice cream on it," Marti said aloud before she realized it. She turned into his arms, now unable to hold back the loud choking cries. "She was so beautiful and innocent then. Oh, Adam, now she's dead . . . and I'm alive! It's all my fault. I should've told Papa about the men. I should've—"

"No!" Adam interrupted, pulling her hands from her eyes and forcing her to look at him, away from Riba. "No, you're not to blame! No one could've saved her, not even Joe. She was always doomed. Trying to shoot Booth was just another insane attempt to destroy herself. From what you've told me and what I've seen over the years, she's wanted to kill herself since she was a kid. This time she finally succeeded," he added grimly.

"Why? Oh, Adam, why? She was so bright and beautiful. She had everything. Maybe she had too much. Maybe Papa and I *were* to blame . . ." Marti's voice trailed away as she felt Adam pulling her up, away from the unanswerable riddles of Riba's wasted life.

He held her trembling body in his arms and stroked her hair. "You aren't guilty of any of the crazy things she accused you of. Neither, God help him, was your father. You both tried to over protect her, but think, Marti, think! The problem was in her, not you." He shrugged helplessly then. "Who knows why a kid starts to self-destruct? You hear it on the news every day—grade school kids taking drugs, rich kids stealing . . . all sorts of crazy stuff. She went sour when she was a kid. But, Marti, you grew up in the same house and it didn't happen to you. She had just as good a chance."

Marti nodded. Her rational mind knew that Adam was right, even if her emotions couldn't accept it yet. The shockingly violent way Riba had died would take a long time to forget. Perhaps she never would get over it. "Adam, I still *feel* guilty, even if I know I'm not. Did Papa favor me? Why was I too blind to see where Riba's life was taking her?"

"You couldn't have stopped her, Marti. Now you have your son's life to think of . . . and your father. He'll be devastated by this," Adam said earnestly, holding her firmly by her shoulders as his words sunk in. He could feel her shudder in realization.

"Yesterday when I left he told me . . ."

Adam knew what she meant. "Riba set him up, Marti, just like she did you, Boris, Larry, even Booth, although that's where it finally backfired."

She looked into his eyes and swallowed resolutely. "Yes, I think maybe I always knew you were telling the truth about Papa. I just couldn't face thinking he had hurt me that way, taking you from me when I needed you so. But he was as much a victim as anyone, I guess."

"You'll have to forgive him, babe. For Heath's sake, and for your own, too. You've already forgiven your sister. Now don't look back on guilt or grudges."

She held onto him tightly. "For such an implacable

foe of Joe Beaumont's, you've suddenly become the devil's advocate," she said uncertainly.

Marti could feel a low, grudging snort of laughter. "I guess I'm stuck. We're family now and he is my son's doting grandpa." He tipped her chin up and looked into her red-rimmed eyes. "I'll make my peace with Joe and I think he'll manage to do the same with me. But it's you he needs now."

Marti could hear the police and ambulance sirens as they roared up the deserted road to the house. Booth stirred and let out a cough as he began to regain consciousness. Adam turned his attention to the man on the floor while she huddled on the sofa to await the inevitable interrogation. She did not look at Riba's body.

After a couple of expeditious calls to Sargeant Drake in San Francisco and Deputy Simms in Napa, Adam and Marti were free to go. Scali and Luger were in the Douglas County Jail, both demanding a lawyer, but more than willing to discuss their employment history with Booth Allard once their rights were protected.

Adam held Marti's hand while the ambulance drivers wrapped Riba's body and loaded it on a gurney. There would have to be an autopsy and a full investigation, but until Booth's top-drawer San Francisco attorney was by his side, he refused to speak a word to anyone.

As a deputy loaded Allard into a police car, Adam and Marti walked outdoors. The forensics people from the coroner's office were busy inside. Adam turned to Marti and said, "Let's get out of here. We'll find a hotel in Zephyr Cove and get a room for the night. We both could use some sleep."

She nodded dejectedly, then turned back to him and said with quiet resolution. "As soon as we get there, I have to phone Papa."

Adam nodded in understanding.

Dawn was relentless and golden on the high Nevada desert. The brilliant reflection on the lake arced through the curtains of their hotel window, bathing the room in warm soft light. Marti stirred and opened her eyes. Instinctively, she felt herself reach out for Adam's reassuring presence in the bed. The space next to her was cool and empty. Disorientedly, she sat up and tried to clear her head. They had eaten a light meal and then dropped off to sleep last night, too emotionally and physically exhausted for conversation.

After her long painful talk with Joe, telling him of Riba's death, Marti had been drained. Adam, who had not slept in several days, was out as soon as his head hit the pillow. Taking the sedative he had secured for her from the medical examiner at Riba's place, Marti had quickly drifted into oblivion, too. Now she sat massaging her sleep-drugged head when a soft tap sounded at the door.

Adam silently emerged from the bathroom and opened it to admit a waiter with a breakfast tray. Quickly he paid the boy and then turned to her with a lopsided smile. "I let you sleep until the coffee arrived."

Standing at the table, clad only in his slacks, bare footed and bare chested, Adam poured two cups of black coffee and stirred heavy cream into the one he handed her. She was struck by a feeling that they should have been a married couple, having a comfortable weekend outing away from kids and jobs. She smiled sleepily back at him as she took the cup. "Thanks. I can use this," she mumbled as she swallowed a steaming mellow gulp of the golden liquid.

Adam sat at the foot of the bed, cross-legged with elbows perched lightly on his knees, cup clasped in both hands. "I recall you went heavy on the cream."

His soft words caused a heady flush to steal up her neck. Again a sense of comfort and familiarity filled her. "You always did have a good memory. You look rested." She peered over at the clock. "Only eight hours after going so long without any sleep. I'm not sure I can keep up with you, Mr. Moreland."

Adam's heart warmed at her smile. Suddenly he knew everything was going to be all right. The guilt and the terror could be put behind them, all the ugliness and violence of the past. "You can keep up with me. You've kept up with Heath and he wears me out," he said with a grin. "I miss him already," he added soberly.

"So do I. I know how frightening the past day and night must've been for him. We need to get back, Adam. For Heath . . . for Papa, too."

He swung his legs over the bedside with effortless ease and sat the cup on the table, then turned back to her. "There's something I'd like to do first, before we pick up Bob's plane at the Douglas airport . . ." He hesitated for a moment.

Marti read the uncertainty in his voice. "What?"

"Get married. We're in Nevada. It wouldn't take long." He stood very still, watching her as she combed her fingers through her tawny mane of hair. He suddenly realized he was holding his breath.

She returned his steady gaze. His face was unshuttered now, the blue eyes vulnerable and trusting as he said, "When we get back, there'll be a hundred arrangements to make, the funeral, the police, the mess with Booth. I just thought it would be simpler if we faced it as a family."

Marti's mind shut down at the import of his request. Then slowly, as she looked at him, she began to think. Yesterday, he had been her rock, her solace in the maelstrom of guilt over Riba. He had phoned the authorities and handled everything, had held her and talked about Riba, set things in perspective for her, and allowed her the privacy to call her father while he arranged their accommodations. He even ordered a meal brought to their room. Now he was asking for her trust, her solace before the chaotic weeks ahead consumed them.

"I guess we need to be together to survive this, don't we, darling," she answered, raising her arms to welcome him into a warm embrace. "Oh, Adam, yes, let's do get married, right now! We'll never be separated again!"

And so they were married in a small chapel overlooking the sun-washed glory of the lake. No glamorous clothing, popping flashbulbs or even familiar witnesses, but there was a long overdue rightness to the simple ceremony. They were at last united on that warm, clear morning. A morning reminiscent of the ones four years earlier when they first spent the summer discovering their love. Now there would be endless summers to come, each as full of promise as this bright new day.

Chapter 26

Heath's squeals of delighted laughter blended with the admonitions of his Grandpa and Grandma Lese, who were assisting him in the assembly of a lethal looking space port, complete with robots, ray guns and a starship cruiser.

Marti stood by the large cut crystal punch bowl, filling two cups with frothy eggnog while Adam poked at the logs in the fireplace, then walked across the big living room to join her in watching their son's antics.

"I think we were right to come here for the holiday," he said quietly as he looked around the elegantly furnished Victorian room, now warm and cheery, bathed in firelight and the reflected glitter of a huge spruce Christmas tree. Odd, growing up in the old mausoleum, he'd always thought it a cold place, especially after his mother died. But now, echoing with his son's laughter, it seemed like home.

"I was right about the need to exorcize your ghosts?" she asked with a smile.

He kissed her cheek and put his arm around her. "Something like that. You and Joe faced yours in Napa. I faced mine here. You know, now that I see us gathered here, a real family, I don't feel so . . ." he searched for a word, "disembodied from my past, from the good memories of my father. There were some, back when I was Heath's age. My mother always made this place a home."

"It's a lovely old house, Adam. It deserves to be lived in. Your cousins and their families were so pleased to have you gather everyone here," she said, recalling the dinner earlier. Morton Yung and all the remaining side of Elizabeth's family had fairly beamed in delight to see the old place reopened. Even Peter Kane had come, not he informed Joe Beaumont to check on how his patient followed his diet, but to show off his new fiancee, a sparkling girl named Lacy. The day had rung with laughter and camaraderie. Now as it neared its end, Marti could feel the peace emanating from her husband.

She raised her cup and clinked it against his. "This should be Chardonnay, not eggnog," she said with a grin.

"Cheeky broad. Just because your fall harvest was the best ever. Chateau Beaumont's going to take a chest full of gold medals in the coming years. I hate to admit it to Staritz." Adam laughed.

"You can admit it to me instead. Anyway, now that you've made him that loan to develop his Mendocino property, I expect Papa'll be looking for a new winemaster come spring."

"And you'll be right there helping him interview prospects. Just don't neglect your painting. Alice told me this afternoon she expects that show to be ready by February first."

"It will be, not to worry. I wonder if Aunt Lese'll stay to see it?" Marti replied with a glance across the room.

Overhearing, the white-haired matriarch swiveled in her chair, two intricate pieces of the inner hub of the space station clutched in her elegant hands. "I was thinking only this afternoon, Marti, about how very salubrious this dry, warm climate is compared to the damp gulf air. And such an art colony! I could retire to the Napa Valley." She cocked her head toward her nephew who was sitting on the floor with his grandson.

Joe Beaumont looked aghast. "Now just a damn minute, Celestine Kidder! If you think you and those artsy craftsy Creoles are taking over my vineyards to set up their easels, I'll run them over with my John Deere!"

She made a grand gesture of dismissal with one beringed hand and laughed tolerantly. "I thought that would get your goat, you stodgy old rascal. You need me to keep you young."

Joe snorted. "I have a grandson and a winery to keep me young. Of course, if you're bored back there in that polluted big city, I guess you *could* move here," he conceded magnanimously, "but no New Orleans artists! That Marchanti woman's sent enough local coconuts out to sketch the 'romance of the vineyards' already!" He drew out the first syllable of the word romance and rolled his eyes for effect.

As if on a prearranged signal, Adam raised his punch cup at Lese, who winked in return. Observing her aunt engage both Joe and Heath in putting the final touches to the space station, Marti was suddenly sure something had been orchestrated between Lese and Adam. She looked questioningly up at him as he whispered conspiratorially, "Come with me, Mrs. Moreland."

Silently they filed out of the room, leaving the sounds of young and old voices raised in ebullient laughter. Adam led the way up the winding staircase to the bedroom at the far end of the hall, opposite the tower room that his father had favored. The room they had been sleeping in was not quite as large as Jake's circular one, but it exuded a quiet warmth that Marti much preferred. Let Jake's ghost preside over his domain, she had jokingly said to Adam when he informed her that he'd never spend a night in the master suite.

When she walked into their room a cheery fire had been set in the small stone fireplace and the covers turned down on the massive walnut bed. It looked inviting. She cocked her head at Adam, who smiled and took her hand, leading her to the small loveseat in front of the fireplace.

"Why do I have the feeling you planned all this?" she asked with gleaming eyes. "I assume Lese and Papa are in charge of Heath's bedtime tonight."

"And I'm in charge of his mother's," Adam replied with a lecherous grin. "But first there's something I have to give you."

He walked over to the landscape painting on the wall, an unremarkable oil rendering of an apple orchard that Marti had already decided to replace with one of her own works. She was taken aback when he clicked a small switch and swung the picture open like a door to reveal a wall safe. He turned to her with a dramatic flourish. "Jake was obsessed with secrecy. There must be at least a half dozen of these hidden in this house. I think Randolph may know the locations of several I've never even found yet."

"But what if there are important papers in them—something you should know about, stock certificates . . . ?"

Adam shrugged in indifference. "Mort and I have managed to figure out all of my father's business affairs, even Booth's tangled web. No, all that's here are a few personal things—letters, some jewelry. It'll all sort out in time. Right now, though . . ." He turned to the safe and began to turn its combination with obvious practice. "This one was always my personal domain, ever since Jake died and I came back to take over Moreland Enterprises for him. Four years ago, I put something very valuable in here . . . for safe keeping. I didn't know then if I'd ever take it out again."

When the safe clicked open, he pulled a small velvet box from its dark interior. "Then again . . . maybe I always knew I would," he added mysteriously.

By this time Marti was thoroughly baffled at her husband's cryptic remarks. She had some important news herself that she'd been saving for their time alone that night. Now she was not sure if this was the best opportunity to share it. She waited expectantly as he walked over to her and sat down on the loveseat, the small box hidden in his large hand.

"When I got out of the hospital in Fresno, I came here. As soon as I could get free of Jake's business problems . . ." he began slowly, then stopped. His hands fidgeted rather nervously with the box, like a boy with a gift he was suddenly too shy to present.

"You told me about coming to Chateau Beaumont at Christmas when Riba was home," she said softly, her hand gently stroking his knuckles. She knew how painful the news of her supposed marriage had been to him.

"You never received the note I'd sent from the hospital either," he said in perplexity.

"Riba was home after I left for New Orleans. I'd be more inclined to blame her than the U.S. mails for its going astray. But Adam, all that's behind us now."

He smiled in a dazzling white slash that always made her heart stop. "So it is. But in my insecure and unseemly haste to legally bind you to me last summer, I never did give you this. You deserved a real wedding with all the trimmings, Marti. I forced you into that fast ceremony at the lake—"

"Because it was the only sensible thing to do under the circumstances," she interrupted, placing her fingertips on his lips to silence him. "I don't know what I'd have done without you beside me, Adam. It was such a nightmare—all the guilt and grief, not to mention the press with their ugly headlines. Papa and I both leaned on you. You were right, we needed to be a family then, not wait for some storybook wedding. I never needed that. Besides," she hesitated and gave him a lopsided smile, "I already had that in France, remember? Lese even has pictures to prove it."

"She's a fraud, but I adore her anyway," he said with a grin. He opened the box and let the dazzling, silver-white fire of the two carat diamond in its simple platinum setting cast its brilliance around the room.

Marti gasped in surprise. "Adam, its magnificent . . ." Suddenly she realized how long the ring had been waiting in that safe, waiting for her.

"I couldn't give you the wedding you deserved, but this was part of the plan. Do you like it?"

Marti's hands trembled as he slid it on her finger next to the white gold wedding ring she wore. "It's breath-taking. You brought this with you four years ago, that day you came to the house, didn't you?" Her eyes glowed with empathy as she imagined the pain and betrayal he must have felt that day.

"The diamond belonged to my mother's family, although it wasn't her engagement ring. I had it remounted for you in a simpler setting," he said quietly. "I guess I wanted it to be a link of sorts between her and you."

She held out her slim, long-fingered hand and admired the fiery sparkle of the stone. "I'll treasure it especially because it was Elizabeth's and because of all you had to go through to give it to me."

Adam drew her up, into a long, slow kiss that she returned with fervor. All memories of pain and separation from the past evaporated like fog at sunrise as they continued to deepen the embrace. Their bodies melded together, his shirt studs pressing sharply against the soft velvet of her royal blue gown. The dress was a simple creation that molded with elegance to her slim body, from the mandarin collared neckline to the hemline at her ankles. Now, as Adam ran questing fingers up and down her back, he searched out the devilishly concealed zipper, with no success.

Since he had shed his tie and opened his collar after their guests departed, Marti was having considerably more success unfastening the starched shirt and snuggling her face against his chest. She placed her left hand against the accelerating thud of his heartbeat and admired the silver blue winking fire of the ring nestled in the thick black pelt of his chest hair.

Hearing the growl of frustration from deep in his throat as he continued his feckless quest for the illusive zipper, she giggled like a schoolgirl on her first back seat excursion into the delights of sex. With Adam, making love was always new, always unexpected. Her hand guided his over to her side, beneath her arm.

He felt the ingenuously concealed placket and expertly glided the zipper open. One warm, incredibly deft hand reached inside to cup a breast and tease it to a hard point through the filmy bra she wore, then quickly moved back to unhook the bra and do maddening things to her spinal column, memorizing each delicate vertebrae along the sensitive path until he came to rest at the swell of one silky buttock. Here the dress, tightly fitted at the hips, thwarted his journey.

He withdrew his hand and leaned away from her softly seeking mouth, saying raggedly, "How in the hell do I get you out of this creation?"

She chuckled wickedly, stepping away from him. "I thought you loved the way it fit me when I modeled it for you this morning." With a deft slither of her hips the velvet glided up, revealing her long sleek legs and frothy bikini briefs. She pulled the dress over her head and tossed it in a soft pile across the loveseat. Shaking her hair back from her face, she shrugged the unfastened bra off and then advanced toward him, intent on peeling the open shirt from his shoulders.

"No, wait. Let me look at you," he whispered. He reached up to take a full upthrust breast in each hand. Gently he cupped them and watched the pale rose nipples contract and harden to tight points as his thumbs worked slow circles around them. His eyes devoured her, running from her slim waist to her sleek hips, then down her long, nylon-clad legs to the elegant blue suede pumps on her feet. He reached down and stroked the frilly white garterbelt holding up the stockings. "Delectable," was his only comment.

"I know how you hate pantyhose," she said teasingly. "So, you'll just have to get me out of this male-chauvinistic regalia."

In answer he swept her into his arms and carried her to the bed, but before he could toss her onto the sheets, she held fast to his neck and wriggled her lower body free to plant her spike heels firmly on the floor.

"First I get to finish what I started." She slipped the shirt from his shoulders and tossed it onto the floor as she ran her hands up and down the lean muscles of his arms, lingering to plant a kiss on the scars on his arm and neck. Then she reached down to his belt and unfastened it slowly. By the time he stepped from his hastily discarded slacks he was too impatient for more languor. Adam took her in his arms and rained kisses over her face and neck while his hands seized great masses of tawny curls and massaged her scalp roughly.

Marti moaned as her tongue twined with his and her teeth bit and nipped at his demanding lips. She ran her hands down and slid his shorts past his narrow hips, then pressed her lacy, bikini-clad pelvis against his rigid shaft, slipping it inside her silk undergarment. "Umm, nice fit," she murmured, squeezing her thighs together.

"Not as good as it's going to be," he ground out as he tumbled them backward onto the bed, still held prisoner in the silk cocoon of her panties. They rolled back and forth, kissing and laughing with passion roughened voices as their hands and mouths devoured each other. Finally, he rolled to the side of the bed to free himself of his shorts, caught most cumbersomely around his ankles. He quirked one brow scowlingly at her chuckle while he slipped off his loafers and sox as well. So much for practiced seduction!

"Now, lady, it's your turn," he said as he knelt over her, running his hands down the length of one garter, softly snapping it against her silky thigh. She arched and lay back to let him enjoy the frothy concoction. Reverently he unfastened both garters on her right leg and slowly peeled down the sheer stocking, kissing and nuzzling her thigh, knee and calf. When he reached the slim ankle, he slipped the spike-heeled pump off and tossed the stocking after it. By the time he'd repeated the process on her left leg, she had impatiently pulled the garter belt from around her hips and tossed it onto the floor. When she reached back to slip the bikinis down, he stopped her.

"Let's examine this ingenuous device again," he murmured, laying over her and sliding his pulsing shaft inside to press deliciously between her legs. Experimentally, he slid back and forth, letting the rough lace rub against him. "Very erotic," he whispered hoarsely.

Marti, feeling the slick hard penis gliding beneath her aching need, quickly reached down and guided it home, deep inside her. "Now," she gasped in pleasure, "finish undressing me."

Adam moaned as she arched up against him, wriggling her thighs free of the bikinis. Slowly, careful not to break their joining, he worked the soft, stretchy briefs down her legs until she was able to kick them off. Then she spread her legs and wrapped them eagerly around his hips as he thrust deeply into her.

After a few fierce strokes, they calmed and slowed to a delicious, languorous pace, matching their gentle kisses to the pops emitting from the low fire on the hearth. Its rosy glow cast flickering shadows over the pair as they made love with exquisite thoroughness. Time. Now they had all the time in the world. The rest of their lives for this bliss, this complete harmony of oneness.

Finally, unable to bear the haze of ecstasy drowning her, Marti stiffened and expelled a small involuntary cry. Responding to her need, Adam raised up to gaze deeply into her eyes as he thrust with long, fast strokes, at once sending her over the brink to a series of spasms that simultaneously broke his own control. He followed her to mindless, blissful oblivion, spilling himself deeply inside her.

Afterward, as they lay side by side, he traced the soft rosy patterns across her breasts and throat with his lips. As the splotches slowly faded, she finally regained her breath and focused her eyes on him. Her fingertips caressed the scar over his eyebrow tenderly, realizing how close she had come to losing him. That fearful memory was quickly lost in the warm assuring satiety that his long, hard body always gave her. He held her so tenderly yet possessively. The look of pure love in those dark blue eyes softened every angular line in his face, turning its harshness to dazzling handsomeness, the same dazzling good looks she had first been so arrested by in the tasting room of Chateau Beaumont four summers ago. No longer mysterious or menacing, now he was life and love, her very future.

"I adore you, Adam Moreland," she whispered, knowing that now was the moment she had been waiting for.

Taking her left hand in both of his hands, he inspected the lovely ring and kissed her fingertips. "I waited so long to give you this, babe. We could still have a real wedding, if you want—big fancy church, long dress, the works," he said earnestly. "Heath would love being my best man."

Marti grinned and shook her head as she snuggled into his embrace. "Doing that would be unconventional enough without the added scandal of an obviously pregnant bride!"

Adam looked into her sparkling silver eyes. She nodded at him. "I was saving a last special Christmas surprise for you, too, my darling. Are you pleased?"

"Oh, Marti, yes, yes. When?" He hugged her so fiercely she had a hard time catching her breath to reply.

"Another fruit of summer—July, if I've calculated right. I have an appointment with Peter next week, but these new test kits are pretty conclusive. Won't Heath be pleased?"

"He wants a little brother," Adam said with a chuckle, "but I had a girl in mind. One with tawny hair and gray eyes—like her mother. I always thought that ring picked up the silver fire in your eyes," he murmured, inhaling the sweet bouquet of her breath, then once more claiming her lips.